A Difficult Trade

The Baseball Mystery

by

Sam Leonard

Robert D. Reed Publishers

San Francisco

Robert D. Reed Publishers

750 LaPlaya, Suite 647
San Francisco, CA 94121
Phone: 650-994-6570 • Fax: -6579
E-mail: 4bobreed@msn.com
http://www.rdrpublishers.com

Typesetter: **Barbara Kruger**
Cover design: **Irene Taylor, it grafx**

ISBN 1-885003-63-3

Library of Congress Catalog Card Number 00-102834

Manufactured, typeset and printed in the United States of America

1

"How about Chicago?"

"Only straight up for Beltran and he's more money."

"Colorado?"

"They'll only part with their mistakes. Again, no net savings."

"The Yankees?"

"Would you believe it? They said they couldn't afford him."

"Toronto?"

"They said they're going in a different direction. The only offer on the table is Boston and we assume 80% of his salary... and we're not sure he'd waive his no trade."

With that assessment a noisy silence fell over the conference room. Coffee cups clattered. Drinks were poured and smoke was exhaled but no dialogue was exchanged.

After a long pause, a well dressed suit spoke for the first time.

"We could kill him."

Louis Redmond glanced at Paddy McGraw, who raised his eyebrow at Frank Roy, who smiled at Dave Grabowsky, who tried to stifle a laugh which now snowballed into outright laughter throughout the room.

"People have been killed for less."

"Much less," Harry Hvide said to himself.

Instead of further protest, Greg Barrett laughed along with the assembled group at his solution to the Dick "Don't call me Richie" Johnson problem. He noticed that team owner Harry Hvide was not smiling, his deep blue eyes turning an angry purple. Harry Hvide had called this meeting, not only for his baseball braintrust, but also for his top executives of Capital Industries. Their specific mission was to rid the defending World Series Champion Florida Manatees of Richard "Big Dick" Johnson and his six-year, sixty-six million dollar contract.

Just twelve weeks after winning the World Series, Harry Hvide wanted out of baseball and the thirty-five million dollar a year losses he was incurring. Since no one was lining up to give him his asking price of one-hundred fifty million dollars, Harry decided to cut his losses and thirty million dollars of his fifty-five million dollar payroll. His baseball people had put together a viable business plan which allowed them to field a competitive team that was predicated on dumping "Big Dick." The only problem was revealed in the meeting—no takers.

The meeting lingered on another forty-five minutes without any resolution before breaking up with baseball and Capital Industries Group going their separate ways. Clearly, Harry Hvide was not happy. And when Harry Hvide was unhappy, no one sensed it more than Gregory Barrett. Known throughout Capital as "Gung Ho Greg," Gregory Barrett had risen to the very apex of the conglomerate world through very, very hard work plus an incredible ability to anticipate Harry Hvide's every mood, thought, and idea. What Greg Barrett thought Harry Hvide was now thinking sent a chill down his spine.

At home over dinner Greg Barrett was preoccupied, his concentration tuning in and out like a weak radio signal. This was not characteristic of him. He prided himself on his devotion to family time. No matter what the job pressures or travel schedule, he tried mightily to block off the two hours from 7:00 p.m. to 9:00 p.m. for his wife and two children. He wanted to hear everything going on at school, all details of soccer games and ballet classes. He listened attentively to piano practice and would assist with homework and spelling words. If he really, really focused, he could appear interested during his wife Allison's recap of her tennis match and which bitch gave the most bad calls, and which of her friends' marriages were on the rocks, and which new bistro of the moment they had lunched at and what charity function was upcoming and how all afternoon she couldn't find a suitable dress in Fort Lauderdale's finest stores and how she needed to fly to New York for the day and so on and so on.

"Daddy."

"Daddy," repeated his seven-year-old daughter Kristin. "You're not even looking at me." He stared at his daughter dressed adorably as a Cherry Blossom.

"I'm sorry, sweetheart, Daddy's not feeling well. You look fantastic. I'll bet you're the cutest Cherry Blossom in the entire play."

"You haven't touched Consuela's Veal Oscar and that's your favorite. You must be coming down with something," said Allison. "Kristin, Harley, no hugs or kisses for Daddy tonight."

"If it's all right, I'm going to lie down." Greg got up from the table, assuring Consuela that there was nothing wrong with dinner. He went out to the veranda, then up the spiral staircase to his upstairs office, saying goodnight to Lucy the maid and Inga the child-care specialist along the way. He shook his head. With gardeners, pool men, decorators, carpenters, plus Lucy, Inga, and Consuela, Greg often felt like a stranger in his own house. Allison had stopped cooking five million dollars ago. He never in his wildest dreams envisioned a lifestyle like this. It was certainly a long, long way from Bridgeport, Connecticut.

Born in that working-class Southern New England city, Greg's parents were the proprietors of a small neighborhood hardware store. From age eight he worked with his parents after school and on Saturdays. While other kids in the neighborhood had Scouts and Little League, Greg could mix paint and duplicate keys. He had a loyal following—customers astonished that such a young boy was so proficient at his work. The neighborhood itself was an ethnic mix of Italians, Irish, Jews, and Hungarians, all, like the Barretts, working hard to get by. The Barretts were a one-car family sharing a dilapidated Buick Electra. There was no extra money for stylish clothes or restaurants. Their only extravagances were summer Sundays at Seaside Park Beach and a savings account for Greg's college education.

Alvin and Ruth Barrett were thoroughly devoted to their only son. Both in their late thirties when Greg was conceived, they stressed and stressed how important an education was. To them, it was a way up, a key that unlocked everything a free enterprise system had to offer. They envisioned their son a professional man who could profit off his brain and initiative, not penny nails on a shelf.

Greg was a good student. He was organized and thorough, spending slow times in the store reading and studying. His dream was to be an architect. By far his favorite birthday present was an erector set. He would duplicate the models in the instruction guide, then alter and modify them into original creations. He understood the concept of a solid foundation and how to build upon it.

Circumstances changed for the Barretts while Greg was attending junior high school. Slowly and steadily, their city was decaying. Blacks and Puerto Ricans who once lived only in housing projects or specific areas were branching out into all neighborhoods. At first, there were subtle changes like graffiti and an increase in minority composition in the schools. Business dropped off a bit. Before long the minority was a majority and life as the Barretts knew it would never be the same.

It started with crime. Minor stuff like shoplifting and stolen hubcaps blossomed into stolen cars and burglaries. Barrett's Hardware was twice victimized. Greg seethed with anger as he helped his parents clean up the aftermath of each incident. He hated with every fiber of his being the anonymous perpetrators who wreaked such havoc on their tidy establishment. Couldn't they just take what they wanted without destroying the place? Didn't they know his mom and dad put their heart and soul into their little business, that neither had ever taken a sick day in fifteen years, that they were slaves to it? He wanted to get a gun and sleep in the store. While touched by his son's dedication, Alvin Barrett would hear none of it. Under no condition would he put his only child at risk. He told Greg to have faith. Things would work out. They always did. Alvin Barrett was wrong.

After the second break-in, the insurance premiums skyrocketed. The Barretts couldn't afford the plate glass surcharge and the next week a rock was thrown through the storefront window. Their regular customers were moving out to the suburban towns of Fairfield, Stratford, and Trumbull, taking their business with them. Others patronized the huge discount outlet, Caldor's, taking advantage of their lower prices. They tried offering credit but had only bad debts to show for it. In their own neighborhood, over half the houses were for sale. By the time the Barretts had enough, they were caught in a downward spiral of falling real estate prices. Mr. Katz, who owned the dry cleaners next to the hardware store and lived on the same block, was despairingly philosophical. "Not even Moses could bring a plague more destructive than Schvartzas."

The next year, Barrett's Hardware closed for good. There wasn't enough income to cover the rent, the phone, the lights and other expenses. A "Going Out of Business" sale didn't even raise enough to pay off the suppliers. They sold their home for peanuts and moved to an Italian neighborhood in Stratford, living upstairs in a two-family home. Twenty years in business and Alvin and Ruth Barrett had nothing to show for it. They were living in a smaller house and after spending two generations being their own boss were now forced to work for others. Ruth worked as a cashier, taking the bus each way. Alvin got a job at the Shelton Lumber Company. Even Greg's college fund was gone, used for past due bills and needed to cover closing costs on their new residence.

Alvin Barrett put up a brave front. He lectured his son on the intrinsic value of work. It didn't matter what job you had as long as you were working and giving an honest effort for your paycheck. There was dignity derived just by the act of working on its own. The sins were idleness and accepting welfare. As hard as he tried, he could not hide the fact from his wife and son that he was a broken man. It was evident in the blankness of his eyes and a dramatic loss of weight. Never a heavy man, Alvin Barrett was withering away right before their eyes. He was the incredible shrinking man incarnate. His spirit had been bleached from his body and within months he just passed away.

Greg took the loss of his father very hard. In his sixteen years, he couldn't recall a cross word exchanged between them nor a moment that his dad was not his best friend.

To Greg, Alvin Barrett, the hardware store proprietor, was his only hero. His grades in school dropped as his motivation shriveled. The bitterness of watching his father age twenty years in one year since the closing of Barrett's Hardware clung to him like a sweaty tee-shirt.

Despite his grief, his mom now needed him more than ever. Greg persevered as his father would have wanted. He found work after school and during the summer helping his mother barely meet expenses. He started as a busboy at the Ocean Sea Grill, Bridgeport's finest seafood restaurant. The Sea Grill was famous for its oversized lobsters and shrimp scampi, cultivating a loyal clientele that seemed to insulate it from the eroding city surrounding it. His salary and tips were a big help to his mother and came with an added benefit. Since he was working nights and weekends, his after-school afternoons were free for interscholastic football. He had never participated in any extracurricular activity before, but high school football served as a perfect outlet for all the pent-up hostility festering inside him. By age seventeen, Greg had grown into a man's body. He was already much taller than his father was with sinewy muscles and a pleasant face his female classmates took notice of. While he didn't fully understand the game or possess any natural instincts for it, he played with such unabated fury that it far overshadowed his shortcomings. A guard on offense and a linebacker on defense, he played with so much intensity, his teammates hated to practice against him. His coach was constantly complaining to the referees about the unnecessary roughness penalties he would incur for clean but vicious tackles.

As graduation neared, Greg and his mom decided that the best course for his future would be enlisting in the army. Upon separation the G.I. Bill would give him the opportunity to pursue his dream of a college education. Army life was a big adjustment. It marked the first time in his life Greg had ever spent a night away from home. He persisted through basic training in Fort Dix, New Jersey, gradually adapting. He was growing an affinity for the military. He enjoyed the discipline and the precision inherent in it though his enthusiasm and exuberance put him at odds with his fellow soldiers. Growing up as an only child who spent so much time with his parents, Greg never had many nor made friends easily. He wasn't a crowd-follower and abstained from the usual G.I. pursuits of drinking, strip clubs, and whoring. He was the target of many practical jokes, the cruelest occurring when a grenade tumbled out at assembly. As shouts of "Live! Live!" ignited a frenzied dispersal, Greg Barrett instinctively dove on the grenade fully expecting to be blown to bits. Only uproarious laughter revived him from a trance-like state. He had risked his life covering a dud. Fed up living with these assholes, Greg decided to police them. He finished his stint in the army as an M.P. with tours in Korea and West Germany.

While her son was in the service, Ruth Barrett relocated from Connecticut to sunny tropical South Florida. She moved near some friends from the old neighborhood to a mostly French Canadian enclave in Hollywood, Florida. Though wages in that service economy state were below those in the Northeast, the living expenses were commensurately low as well. Ruth worked in sales for Burdines, the Florida Department Store. She enjoyed her new lifestyle. Her small apartment was within walking distance from a beautiful public beach. In the evening she would stroll with her friends along the boardwalk amidst the warm breezes with the ocean waves washing over the sand. She was ecstatic when her only son was released from the army, and joined her in her new home. Though it took adjustments on both their parts to cohabit in such a small apartment, their special bond overcame the inconveniences.

Greg didn't waste any time. He took advantage of his G.I. benefits, enrolling at Nova University of Fort Lauderdale. After classes, he studied and worked nights as a waiter. Life improved dramatically after Greg answered a classified ad and started working for Seacoast Waste Service. The salary was three times what he was making and the hours fit his schedule perfectly. Once he worked up to driver he could pretty much set his own hours. Starting at 3:00 A.M., he could do his whole route unobstructed by morning traffic. He would drop off at the dump, go home and shower, and still make his 10:00 A.M. class. After school, he had plenty of time to study. He was in a good situation. He was fully matriculating as a student and taking home a healthy full-time paycheck. He was able to afford his own efficiency apartment and still supplement his mother's income. He wasn't sure though where his college education would take him. Becoming an architect would take many years, so he hedged a little by also taking courses in business, accounting and police science.

At his job, the conditions were in a state of flux. Since he didn't view being a garbage man as his life's work, Greg isolated himself from the usual shoptalk and complaints intrinsic with any workplace situation. All he cared about was doing his job properly and efficiently and picking up his paycheck. His supervisor was pleasant and so was the office secretary. While he had never been introduced, the owner of Seacoast Waste Service, Harry Hvide, would always smile and ask how he was doing whenever their paths crossed. That was the extent of his involvement. But an undercurrent of tension and unrest was seeping into the Seacoast environment. The International Brotherhood of Transportation Workers had singled out Seacoast Waste Service and was putting on a big push to organize its workers and drivers. Harry Hvide was the ideal target. His company was by far the fastest growing in the business, it was family-owned with no underworld connections, and Harry himself was known to be so anti-union that a victory over him would send a loud and clear message industrywide in this right-to-work state. Drivers whispered to each other about the anonymous phone calls they received at home that could not guarantee their safety if they continued driving. Leaflets to the same effect were plastered on their windshields, sometimes through their windshields, in the parking lot. The union set Wednesday, April 5th, as the target day to shut down Seacoast Waste Service. More anonymous phone calls to Seacoast's customers advised them to look for a new crater as their usual service would likely be interrupted. They even had a county health inspector on standby to cite all of Seacoast's restaurant customers as their unprocured trash would be a health hazard. Both the union and Harry Hvide had so much at stake. Harry Hvide had incredible ideas for mega-expansion and unionized workers were not part of the plan. For the International Brotherhood of Transportation Workers, beating Harry Hvide would have a domino effect with all the other haulers falling into line. As April 5th dawned, Greg reported to work at his usual time. He was surprised to find he was the only one in the parking lot and that a large, angry crowd was milling outside. He slipped unnoticed through the fence to report to work. As he approached the main trailer, he was spotted by someone in the mob.

"Hey, where do you think you're goin'? No trucks roll today." Another shouted, "It's that college faggot! Hey, boy, no work today, no work tomorrow unless it's on your knees!"

Greg ignored the derisive taunts. The only people present at the trailer were the supervisors, Harry Hvide himself, some family members and a couple of family friends. They had all spent the night there parking their cars safely inside the barbed wire fence. They were shocked to see anyone else show up.

"What are you doing here, son?" Harry Hvide asked incredulously.

"I'm reporting to work, sir. It looks like you could use a driver."

Harry Hvide smiled. He had the deepest blue eyes Greg had ever seen. "It could be a little dangerous today."

"That's all right, sir," Greg replied. "I need the money and it's your name on the bottom of my paycheck, not the union's."

"What's your name?"

"Greg Barrett, sir."

"Today we'll double up. How about riding with me?" Without another word Harry Hvide climbed into the passenger seat of the lead truck. Greg took the driver side and ignited the engine. Harry Hvide gave a nod and the electric wire fence gate slowly slid open. The noise and smell of the diesel motor energized the outside mob, begetting curses, shouts, and a very ominous thwacking sound of baseball bats pounding asphalt. Greg put the truck in gear, inching it forward. A giant, menacing, very dark black man with bodybuilder arms and eyes as wide as credit cards emerged from the crowd and yelled, "No trucks movin' today, Boss."

Greg put one hand to his ear and held out an open palm apparently confused about what had been said.

"I said 'No fuckin' trucks leave this yard,'" as he took a few steps closer.

Greg put his hand to his lips and mouthed silently "I didn't hear what you said."

In a rage now, the black man jumped up on the running board and screamed into the open driver side window at the top of his lungs "Lissen, motherfucker... no trucks work tod..."

Before he could finish his sentence, Greg Barrett put his shoulder to the door and with his entire weight behind it slammed it open, splattering the black man to the pavement like a carton of eggs dropping out of a shopping bag. Instantaneously Greg flew out of the truck and with all his might gave the downed man a vicious kick to his groin. As the man's eyes rolled to the back of his head and the color drained from his body, Greg jumped back in the truck, floored the accelerator and sped through the gate, scattering the mob in his wake. As the other Seacoast trucks convoyed behind, a union organizer looked at the hurting man on the ground and said aloud to no one, "Man, Lavelle got albinoed by that White Boy."

Harry Hvide sat in absolute silence as Greg went about his normal route. After the fifth pickup, he turned to Greg looking him directly in the eye and said, "What did you say your name was?"

That day ended without further incident. Seacoast Waste Service remained staunchly non-union; nor was there ever again any attempt to unionize any other Harry Hvide-related business or enterprise. The only casualty was Greg's 10-year-old Chevy Nova which was found smashed to pieces where he had left it in the parking lot.

"Don't worry about it, son. You can borrow my car," Harry Hvide told him.

"I couldn't do that, sir."

"Please, I insist." Harry Hvide reached into his pocket and handed him the keys to a beautiful navy blue Oldsmobile 98 with thick leather seats and power everything. Greg had never driven a car that new or nice.

"Can I at least drop you somewhere?"

"No, I'll be fine. See you tomorrow... and thanks."

When Greg finished work the next day, he was told to report to the office trailer. He was met cordially by Harry Hvide who gave him keys to a year-old Cutlass Supreme in near mint condition.

"From now on you drive a company car. Someone else will take your route tomorrow. Let's meet for breakfast. I'd like to talk to you about the waste disposal business."

That breakfast meeting was Greg Barrett's first glimpse of the amazing energy, foresight and genius of Harry Hvide. In a detailed account, Harry Hvide gave Greg a synopsis of the waste removal business, his future plans, and how Greg could be part of it. The commercial trash hauling business in South Florida had many idiosyncrasies in that there was no soliciting of other companies' customers, nor was there any underbidding a competitor. Italians from New York were the first organized haulers in South Florida and they brought down with them the system they knew and were successful with. Each pickup or stop was granted inalienable "land rights." If a hauler was serving a business at a certain location that closed, that hauler would automatically inherit any new business that took over that location as its customer. The new business had no choice who would pick up their garbage. If they were unhappy with the price or service and called other trash hauling companies for a price quote, it would always be two or three times more than what they were now paying, making their present situation seem like a good deal. If a new hauler decided to service the new business, he would "owe" the original hauler a stop of equal value or the cash equivalent. If one hauler did underbid another or "steal" a stop without compensation, the other haulers would combine together and underbid every stop on the offender's route. While this system had the benefits of establishing equity in the customer base and controlling prices and expenses it also made it difficult to solicit new business. You could increase revenues by giving your customers regular price increases but you could only grow the business by finding businesses with no established land rights, trading stops with your competitors, or purchasing them at multiples of the monthly rate. The only exceptions were construction sites which were attained on a "finders-keepers" basis, and municipalities, which were awarded to the lowest bid.

"To be honest," Harry told him, "I'd prefer a more competitive system and we'd see who'd come out on top but this is what was in place when I got into the business and this is what we have to live with."

In reality, Broward County was growing at such a phenomenal rate there was plenty of business for everybody. The companies that would most prosper would be the ones positioned to meet the rising demand and could expand efficiently. This would necessitate a large reservoir of capital for the trucks, rolloffs, dumpsters, and manpower needed to meet this demand. A line of credit from a bank would not be enough. It would require, explained Harry, a public offering!

Greg had never seen anyone so animated or enthusiastic. He was like an author or artist describing his masterpiece for the first time. His blue eyes were afire and Greg could almost feel the energy from Harry's brain as he pressed on.

"We'll issue stock and use the money from its sale for equipment, capital improvements and to buy up smaller companies. While there might be initial resistance to buying into a garbage business, the stock will be a good value because our business is so profitable we'll be able to offer it at a very favorable earning multiple ratio. As we grow and competition lessens, we'll be even more profitable. As we become more profitable the stock will have more and more value."

Greg was spellbound. This very unpretentious man who rarely wore a jacket and tie, who would drive a garbage truck to the dump himself if someone were out sick, who would get under a truck to fix a broken axle, was laying out to him his own blueprint for a multimillion dollar company that would be listed on one of the major stock exchanges.

Harry Hvide continued. "We're going to need the most productive work force in the industry. I have a plan to offer every employee—driver, secretary, yardman, executive, whatever, interest-free loans to purchase stock. This way we'll have motivated PARTNERS with a personal stake in the growth and well-being of the company instead of employees watching the time clock." He stopped, caught his breath, then stared Greg Barrett right in the eye and said, "We're also going to need a very productive and dedicated management team. I want to have the least top-heavy, smallest number of executives of any company of a similar size. I'd like you to be a part of that team. Bottom line, there's a lot of money cleaning up after people."

Greg was overwhelmed, so caught up in what he'd just heard, he struggled to find the right response.

"You don't have to give me an answer right away. Think about it. I understand you're attending college. If you decide to come aboard we'll be happy to cover your tuition."

Greg thanked him for his generosity, then explained about his G.I. benefits.

"No problem. When you get your business degree we'll give you the tuition equivalent as a bonus."

"Mr. Hvide, I... don't know what... I can't thank... "

"Call me Harry."

2

Harry Hvide's pitch to Greg Barrett proved prophetic. Within months Seacoast Waste Service was incorporated into International Crating, listed ICX on the New York Stock Exchange. Harry Hvide began the task of growing the business. At first Greg concentrated on the core business in Broward County. His first successful project was reorganizing the drivers' routes. Because new business was so coveted, companies would take it wherever they could get it. This led to hodge-podge routes crisscrossing the county. Greg simply restructured each route so that it would make the maximum pickups per shift. If another hauler had pickups along that route ICX would trade for those stops with others even if they were of lesser value. Every driver was making twenty-five percent more pickups in the same amount of time. Productivity soared as did profitability. Greg's next major undertaking was acquisitions. ICX was expanding very rapidly, buying up market share and branching out into new markets. Some companies were purchased with cash, others with ICX stock. Greg would study every prospective company thoroughly. If one was asset rich (trucks, heavy equipment, buildings, property) with relatively little debt, ICX would pay cash by borrowing from its bank against those assets. Harry called it "buying the cow with its own milk." If a company was desirable but had considerable debt service on its balance sheet, ICX would buy it with shares of its stock. Greg learned at Harry Hvide's side sitting in on negotiations before handling deals and purchases on his own.

Learning deal-making from Harry Hvide was similar to learning the art of hitting from Ted Williams and getting tackling lessons from Dick Butkus. There were times to wait for your pitch, to have the patience of Job. But when you got your pitch, when the deal was right, don't foul it off. There were other times when you needed to close with such swiftness and ferocity the other guy never knew what hit him.

Fairness and persistence best characterized Harry Hvide's negotiating style. Fairness, however, was a relative term as it was always defined as what Harry Hvide deemed fair. He would establish a market value for a business in his head, then negotiate with a range of that price. He never paid for potential, advocating that if the business thrived, its success would reflect in the stock price. Harry tutored Greg on learning as much as possible about the principles, the decision makers on a deal. Often there was something important and personal that wasn't as important as the purchase price. It might be a salaried management position to stay on with the company. This was often the case with original owners who couldn't part with their creations, who had worked their whole lives and just needed a place to show up, to give structure to their life. Deep down they knew intuitively they couldn't handle retirement and would quickly die or go crazy spending so much time with their wives. With others, it might be as trivial as a company car or health care coverage or a deal structured for the maximum tax benefits. Whatever the case, if you could find that key it would make the difference in "doing the deal" on your terms.

Persistence was simply sitting down and not leaving until a deal was struck. This involved showing the sellers the benefits of the offer and how good it really was. Harry would say, "We're not buying companies, we're selling our stock. The key to closing these deals is how good a salesman you are." Greg was very good. In great detail he would extol the vision of Harry Hvide and how that vision manifested in the growth of ICX and the value of its stock. Left unsaid were the consequences of not sharing that vision and competing against ICX. Greg genuinely liked most of the people he met in the disposal business. They appreciated his earnest, enthusiastic, well-prepared approach. He talked to them entrepreneur to entrepreneur and would close the vast majority of transactions within Harry Hvide's parameters and without lawyers. Publicly, Harry Hvide was never satisfied, implying Greg left too much money on the table or overpaid. Privately, he knew Greg was invaluable, almost an extension of himself, allowing him to be two places simultaneously.

On complicated negotiations, Greg would consult with Harry by phone. Greg became adept at detecting Harry's mood by the tone of his voice, the pauses and coughs. On megadeals which required Harry Hvide's presence, Greg was equally adept at deciphering his body language. They made a formidable team. Often Greg would decode a tug at his sleeve or a glance at his watch as a signal to go hardline. This gave Harry negotiating room, an opportunity to smooth things over and come off as the magnanimous good guy and deal saver.

By and large Greg Barrett had gained the reputation as a straight shooter, a man enjoyable to do business with. Only one fabled incident deviated from the norm. Greg was working out the final details involving the purchase of a medium-sized Atlanta Company with ICX stock. The final meeting should have been a formality as Greg and the company founder, Bert Levin, had reached an accord on all the major issues. A brusque, hard-working man, Bert Levin had moved to the South from Elizabeth, New Jersey, and carved out a substantial niche of the Atlanta market. He was a physically imposing man whose word was as sure as his steely handshake. Greg had developed a good rapport with him and had a handshake agreement. At the closing, however, Bert Levin was represented by his son-in-law, Seth Feinberg, who personified the term "smarmy lawyer." The son-in-law contested every single point of the contract. The price was too low, the payoff too long, the assets not given enough value, and the debts overstated. When Greg politely tried to demonstrate the benefits of the deal, the son-in-law angrily retorted, "We're not going to be pushed around by Harry Hvide who didn't have the decency to show up and we're surely not rolling over for his errand boy."

Greg tried mightily to resurrect the deal but his efforts were going nowhere. The atmosphere was getting heated and all sides agreed to a recess. Exasperated, Greg left the conference room to phone Harry Hvide and relay what had occurred. Harry Hvide insisted on hearing bad news right away. Just before making the call, Greg stopped in the men's room to relieve himself. At the next urinal was Seth Feinberg. Greg looked at him and, without hesitation, turned and urinated all over his $900.00 Italian suit and $300.00 loafers.

"Wh… what are you doing?"

"You've been pissing over this deal all day. I just thought I'd get a little balance."

Amid the commotion, Bert Levin emerged from a stall laughing uproariously. Addressing Greg, he blurted, "I could never figure what my daughter sees in him anyway. Let's do business."

Bert Levin and Greg Barrett completed their business on the original terms with the one caveat that Harry Hvide buy Bert Levin a new pair of pants to replace the one he'd soiled in the men's room.

ICX was thriving and so was Greg Barrett. It seemed like one day he showed up for work to drive a garbage truck and the next he was a top, upper echelon executive of a highly profitable, multimillion dollar company. He owed Harry Hvide a lot. He had even met his wife through him. At a lush private affair at the Hvide home, Greg was introduced to a Miss Allison Lodge, a Federal Judge's daughter, attending the party with her parents. The former doubles partner of Chris Evert's youngest sister Clare at Cardinal Gibbons High School, Allison Lodge

and Greg Barrett were similar in that they were both shy, good-look-
ing and relatively inexperienced with the opposite sex. Greg had never
had a serious relationship. From the army, he went straight to being a
full-time student with a full-time job to the frenzied workaholic pace of
ICX. While he dated occasionally, he was always too busy for them to
develop more intimately. His mother worried about him, pointing out
that success was fine but far more cherished when shared.

Allison Lodge was a rarity, a born and bred Florida native. She
attended an all-girl middle school, and all-girl high school, an all-girl
college, and a predominantly female graduate school. She had been to
proms and debutante balls and college mixers but had never connected with Mr. Right. Allison's passions were tennis, art history, and an
affinity for saltwater fishing which she inherited from her father and
was cultivating in Greg. She would take him out in the Judge's twenty-
eight foot Bertram, showing him how to select the proper bait and tackle. They would bottom fish the wrecks for amberjack and grouper, or
in the Spring, troll the weedline for dolphin and wahoo. On exceedingly calm days they would make the two-and-a-half hour crossing to
Bimini, stalking billfish and picnicking on Honeymoon Harbor Bay. She
liked him a lot. He was considerate and handsome. He didn't come on,
didn't get seasick and seemed to lack any pretension. He had no problem catching and releasing an occasional marlin or sailfish. All the guys
she knew would insist on a mount, a silly plastic mold a taxidermist
could make anyway without the fish itself. She had some reservations
about his job description, but her father vehemently advocated Harry
Hvide was no ordinary garbage man and anyone Harry trusted and valued so deeply was someone special.

They had a reserved, tasteful wedding attended by Fort
Lauderdale's most eminent business, political and judicial luminaries.
Harry Hvide beamed throughout the ceremony and reception. He
exuded genuine happiness toward Greg and his bride. Both were
shocked at his generosity when the envelope he bestowed on them as
a wedding gift contained a check for twenty-five thousand dollars.
Greg was somewhat perturbed that his mother was pretty much left out
of the planning and proceedings, a precedent that would continue
throughout his marriage. But Ruth Barrett would not make a fuss and
didn't say a word. She was thrilled her only child had entered into marriage and would start a family. Besides, she had a gut feeling her son's
bride would not be that easy to live with and didn't need any mother-
in-law complications. Greg and Allison Lodge Barrett honeymooned in
St. Croix, one-third of the U.S. Virgin Islands. They enjoyed the beaches, fishing, snorkeling on coral reefs and each other. Each day Allison

would play tennis, either hitting with the pro or finding a doubles game with the better players available. Tennis was not his game and when Greg tired of watching his wife he would meander the quaint streets of Christianstad, window shopping and absorbing the local culture. He observed there were no dumpsters and no trucks to service them. Despite the boom in condominium and time-share construction there were no rolloffs to handle the debris. All waste was handled in cans and cardboard boxes, and removed by pickup trucks. He talked to the local merchants, who complained bitterly about the system in place. Not only were they paying a small fortune, the service was spotty and irregular. Upon his return to work he brought with him signed commitments from every store owner, condo association, and construction site on the island for ICX service. Harry Hvide chuckled to himself. He had done exactly the same thing a few years before when on a Bahamas vacation.

Greg and Allison had just moved into their first home, a four-bedroom, three bath with a pool and circular driveway in the new development of Emerald Hills in Broward County when ICX was sold. GT Ltd., a British-based concern, first obtained a substantial position, then eventually a controlling interest in ICX stock, making it the largest waste management company in the world. Greg had heard rumblings of the transaction but for the most part was kept out of the loop. Like the deals with municipalities, this was strictly a Harry Hvide transaction. While technically a merger with the combined companies keeping the ICX moniker, International Crating was clearly a subservient partner. Harry Hvide had many titles, CEO, co-chairman of the board, but he answered to Charles Thatcher III, head of GT Ltd.

He could only play second fiddle for three months before exercising all his stock options and severing his relations with ICX. There were no golden parachutes, no sweetheart walkaways, just the fruits of his hard work and foresight. He was entirely consistent with himself as he was to the many businesses he acquired. Success would reflect in the stock price and Harry Hvide would try retirement living on the forty-five million dollars in cash and stock options he departed with. Before leaving, he made sure Greg was secure, installed as Southeast Regional Manager and Vice President in charge of acquisitions. He also gave Gregory Barrett a solid gold Rolex Presidential with the inscription on back: "See, there is a lot of money cleaning up after people. H.H."

Greg adjusted to executive corporate life. The hours were less. The pace less frenzied. He had a two hundred thousand dollar house, two new cars and a personal portfolio of stock, CDs and bank accounts worth over seven hundred thousand dollars. He discovered large corporate entities survived on their own momentum. The new ICX was profitable, its earning ratio acceptable. It was a growing, viable, billion-dollar-a-year Fortune Five Hundred company, preeminent in its field. What was missing was the energy and vision of Harry Hvide. Prior to the merger, Greg Barrett had a front row seat to his genius. He had a taste of the "Big Deal" and deep in his soul, he hungered for more. More so than the financial rewards he missed the exhilaration of staking out a company and the process of closing on it. He yearned for that feeling when all his senses were ablaze and his brain working on overdrive. Just one year after the merger, with his wife expecting their first child, Greg was ecstatic to get a call from Harry Hvide.

"Can we meet for breakfast? I've got something for you to look at."

Fifteen minutes after breakfast Greg Barrett gave ICX his thirty-day notice. His face couldn't disguise the initial disappointment and skepticism when Harry's something turned out to be a proposal for a chain of video rental stores. Harry Hvide laughed. He had anticipated just that reaction. General consensus was that video stores were sleazy, darkly-lit outlets for porno movies. That wasn't exactly what he had in mind. Just as he had done with ICX, Harry Hvide laid out for Greg his blueprint for a national chain of movie rental superstores that would expand across the country at a bullet train pace. As with ICX they would issue a public stock offering and use the proceeds to build and acquire, then build more and acquire more. Harry had already invested in a four-store operation in Texas and was using it as a model. With pictures, schematics, and profit and loss statements, he demonstrated his plan for his latest venture—VIDEO NATION. He explained why it would succeed.

In the early eighties, the price of a VCR had fallen so dramatically they were found in virtually every home that had a television. Newer model television sets were coming out with the VCR already built in. Home entertainment studios were becoming a bona fide fad and a staple of new model homes, replacing dens and family rooms. People simply preferred viewing movies in the privacy and comfort of their own homes. They could watch with invited friends. They didn't have to put up with waiting in line or the crying babies and general rudeness found in the theater complexes. They could make use of the movie rental as a babysitter. This was a major key because one aspect that would differentiate Video Nation from any other movie rental chain was that it would be family-oriented. Harry Hvide had nothing personal against x-rated films, you would just have to go elsewhere to rent them. Each store would have a large section devoted exclusively to kids—the Video Nation Kids Club. Within those sections were specially displayed Disney Boutiques and Warner Bros. Boutiques and areas for Nintendo and Sega game rentals as well. Video Nation stores would be brightly lit with over five thousand square feet of inventory. They would have far more titles in far more categories than any of their competitors. You could also take the tape you wanted right off the shelf, contrary to the standard practice of bringing only the cover to the cashier who would then search for the video. Membership cards could be accessed by electronic scanners which would instantly total up the current rental plus add any late fees or rewind charges. The rental cost to the consumer would be cheap—"Three Nights, Three Dollars" would become a nationwide marketing campaign. Another key difference was that Video Nation would have no membership fee. Harry Hvide wanted no barriers between the stores and potential customers. You could walk in, fill out a membership and walk out with rented product in less than twenty minutes. Greg could obviously see there was nothing close to Harry's model in size, scope, capacity and marketing potential. In fact, that premise would become the corporate motto—"Video Nation...There's Nothing Like It."

Best of all, the video stores were wildly profitable. Perusing the ledger sheets, Greg had to look twice as he couldn't believe his eyes. These stores were netting forty percent, an unheard of profit margin that would improve as the concept expanded. Harry could see Greg was impressed. "If our numbers are off by half, we've still got a slam dunk. These stores will be the greatest cash cows of the decade."

He paused a moment and with his piercing blue eyes lasered directly into Greg's, continued, "We're not just building a company, we're starting an entire industry."

Starting an industry from scratch took more hard work, initiative, and resolve than Greg had anticipated... even more than Harry Hvide thought possible. Sixteen-hour days seven days a week were the norm. Meetings that started at midnight and resumed at six o'clock A.M. were weekly occurrences. The travel schedule was insane, crisscrossing the country with sudden, unplanned stops and inflight changes of course. More than once Greg would end up in Chicago or Boston in February with nothing but short sleeves as itineraries changed on the fly. This workload took a toll on the Barrett family and the families of other Video Nation executives too. Harry Hvide wasn't oblivious to this but things were moving so fast and circumstances changing so rapidly they simply couldn't afford to slow down. Harry would comment about the workload, "This is our tennis, this is our golf for the next couple years. Let's keep it up a while longer and the financial payoff will justify our efforts."

Regardless, Greg could never justify to Allison missing the birth of their first son, an event also missed by Ruth Barrett, who passed away in her sleep two months prior. The death of his mother had a profound effect on him. For many days he couldn't sleep and had haunting memories of his mother and father toiling away in the Bridgeport hardware store. His sole respite was work. Only by concentrating even more on his job could he thwart off the tormenting images of his parents. It was ironic that, if a boy, he wanted to name his son Alvin. Allison was adamant about naming him after her father, so maybe it was a blessing that his mom was spared that small indignity. Their son was christened Harlan Chase Barrett in his absence.

With Video Nation on a meteoric rise, Greg poured himself into his work with a demonic obsession. Sustaining that growth rate required such an effort. What made movie rental stores an attractive investment to Harry Hvide—the low startup costs and high profit returns—made it equally desirable to others. Already Mom and Pop stores were proliferating and he was wary of potential competition from the super discount stores and possibly from grocery stores as well. If they were going to hit the bases-loaded home run Harry projected they needed to create and duplicate a category-killer—an outlet store with such a staggering inventory in so many different categories available at such a low price in an atmosphere so pleasant to shop at there would be no reason to go anywhere else. Equally important was location, location, location. It had to be convenient to patronize Video Nation and that required prime nationwide store sites. Like the waste disposal business, the secret to any successful growth was expansion; expansion at any cost. They needed to open new stores at a feverish pace, absorb competition, consolidate expenses, establish a brand name ingrained into the national psyche, and build a faithful core of card-carrying members. One way to achieve this was through franchising. Harry was opposed.

"If the numbers are so good, why settle for a franchise fee and a small percentage of the gross? Let's keep it all in house."

To attract some necessary investors, territories were granted and franchises awarded but kept to a minimum. The main thrust was acquisition and new store expansion.

They bought out existing, competing chains and opened new stores at a dizzying rate, sometimes three a week. In a year, the four stores were four hundred. In two years the four hundred were one thousand and in five years the one thousand were three thousand with an international posture too. With every new store, Video Nation became more and more profitable. Accounting and legal fees were spread over the entire chain. Advertising and marketing campaigns were amortized on a per store basis. The more stores sharing expenses the less they were per store. While a neophyte at advertising, Harry found the right agency and soon "There's Nothing Like It" was embedded into the national consciousness almost as deeply as "Coke Is It" or "Have It Your Way." The company sponsored a New Year's Day Bowl Game and initiated an Academy Awards-like ceremony attracting major personalities from Hollywood and the music industry. Harry Hvide himself was getting into the high profile world of sports ownership. The stock price was a rocket ship through the stratosphere. Seemingly it split every other week, and a ten-thousand dollar investment on the initial offering, if left untouched, was over eight hundred thousand dollars in less than seven years. In that same time span more people would carry the Video Nation membership card than Discover and Diners Club combined.

Greg Barrett's initial role concentrated dually on acquisition and startups. Buying up the competition was old hat to Greg, just what he did at ICX. He was now a world-class negotiator and deal maker, seldom needing Harry's assistance. The only difference was that garbage companies had defined territories. Greg was making so many deals so fast, some of the chains he amassed infringed on some of the existing franchisees' territories. It took a staff of ten just to keep the deals straight.

Startups were different, requiring Greg to learn about site selections, traffic counts, construction and lease negotiations. The importance of site selection was essential. High volume stores needed prime locations. Its difficulty was overrated. Fast food chains had already done the legwork and it was very common to find strip centers with a Toys R Us, a Burger King and a Video Nation Outlet all as neighbors. Greg told Harry, "If it's good enough for McDonald's, it's good enough for us."

Greg enjoyed the construction end of the business. He was in his element and dealing with his kind of people. Employing exclusively non-union labor, Greg cut the cost of a new Video Nation store from four hundred twenty thousand dollars to just over three hundred thousand, a figure a high-grossing store would pay off in only two years.

Lease negotiations were less tasteful, requiring lawyers, a four-letter word around Harry Hvide. Bottom line, however, landlords and shopping center developers were dying to have Video Nation either as a tenant or buyer of outparcels and take advantage of its brand name and the traffic it generated. Terms were usually signed favorably to Harry Hvide as landlords and developers were willing to take a hit on Video Nation and make it up in higher rents from other tenants anxious to piggyback on its success.

During this time Greg's personal fortune mirrored Video Nation's. By exercising all his stock options, cashing warrants and reinvesting the proceeds, he amassed a personal net worth close to fifteen million dollars. He considered himself the luckiest man in the world. If he hadn't met Harry Hvide, where would he be? A cop on a beat? A struggling architect? Because of Harry Hvide, Greg Barrett's grandchildren would be able to live like royalty off the interest of his legacy without ever touching the principal. Harry had even included him on some personal side deals; limited partnerships in real estate ventures and luxury hotel properties that proved to be exceedingly lucrative. There was no adequate way to express his gratitude but he was secure that Harry Hvide knew he could be counted on. There was nothing he wouldn't do for him. Greg only wished his parents were alive to witness and share in his success. He dreamed of the houses he could have bought them or the vacations he could have sent them on.

He didn't have to dream how his family would spend his money. Allison Barrett had definite ideas. As a respected Federal Judge's daughter, Allison was welcome into the elite of Fort Lauderdale society, but her father's income limited her participation. As it was, the Lodges lived above their means and though money was never discussed, she knew that private schools, summer camps, and private colleges for her and her siblings were a burden on her parents. Now there were no more restraints and she spent with a vengeance. A waterfront mansion in Fort Lauderdale's most exclusive address was purchased, remodeled and redecorated, and redecorated, and redecorated... and remodeled. She had a new Mercedes every other year and a luxury sports utility too. There were jewelry and designer clothes and country clubs and lots of paid help. There was a forty-eight foot Hatteras docked behind the compound they hardly ever used. Greg denied her nothing. Who should enjoy the fruits of his labor if not his family? Besides, he felt eternally guilty about his work and travel and all the time away. He had missed the births of both his children and hoped in some way the money would compensate for his absences and that, in time, his workload would lessen.

Greg Barrett wasn't the only one doing well. Video Nation had amassed a mountainous cash surplus and was looking to divest. Personally, Harry Hvide ventured into sports. He started with a piece of the privately owned football stadium with options for the rest and a right of first refusal on the team. He became a local hero by bringing Major League Baseball to South Florida, converting the stadium to house both sports. He had his eye on a National Hockey League franchise and before long exercised his options and owned the entire stadium and the football team. Harry's vision was to evolve Video Nation into a sports and entertainment conglomerate. The word revolving in his brain was "synergy"—businesses creating businesses and all under one umbrella. He sought a Hollywood production company and a cable TV channel. He envisioned housing them all in a megaplex that would rival Disneyworld in scope and size. They would produce the movie, rent the video, then show the reruns on the TV channel. People would stream in for baseball and hockey, eat in the restaurants, shop in the stores, patronize the IMAX and virtual reality theaters, then stay after the game or movie at theme clubs and bars. The sports teams would also provide hours of valuable programming on cable.

The video stores evolved from the original format, branching out into retail. To take advantage of the traffic generated by the movie rentals, CDs and tapes were now available, and Video Nation became a force in the music industry.

Harry was as energized as Greg had ever seen him. His enthusiasm was contagious and the new corporate mantra was to make Harry's dream a reality. Greg didn't even object when he was appointed CEO of Phoenix Pictures, a Hollywood film and television production company. He was clearly out of his element and he knew it. He told his secretary that if he ever gave the "thumbs up" or "down" on any movie project she had his permission to shoot him.

She never got the chance. The massive cash reserves and growing profitability of Video Nation made it the supreme takeover target. After a fierce bidding which sent Video Nation's stock price through the roof, Harry Hvide announced a merger with Galaxy Entertainment. Aside from putting up the most money, Harry thought it was the perfect fit. Galaxy had Hollywood's most successful studio, producing one blockbuster after another. It owned four cable networks, including a music channel. It was huge in publishing, controlling one of the most venerable New York publishing houses. Its news weekly and sports magazine enjoyed large circulations. The successful Platinum Recording Company was also a subsidiary. Now the combined companies could publish the book, make the movie, cut the soundtrack, rent the video, sell the compact disc, and show the rerun on cable. But like the situation with the ICX-GT Limited merger, Harry Hvide couldn't exist in a subservient role and walked away a few months later. Again, with no golden parachute, Harry simply benefited from the success of the company reflected in its stock price. He parted with over seven hundred fifty million dollars.

Greg stayed on in charge of the video stores and the cable network divisions. The new Galaxy Entertainment Group didn't share Harry Hvide's enthusiasm and desire for a theme park and within a year quashed all plans for Entertainment Nation. Shortly after that, Harry called. "Can we meet? I've got something new to show you."

Harry Hvide's third NYSE-listed billion-dollar corporation in fifteen years was a conglomerate of super-sized used car stores, signature hotel properties and a host of varied service businesses. Greg was thrilled to be a part of it, juiced at the excitement and allure of starting up another new venture. He enthusiastically joined on with the proviso that one-hundred hour work weeks were a thing of the past. He could no longer afford to neglect his family.

"That's not a problem," Harry said. "This time we're not starting an industry from scratch. We're just refining an existing one."

At last Greg Barrett had attained his Nirvana. He was working with Harry Hvide on an exciting and challenging new project with quality time available for his wife and kids.

As usual, Harry's projections were dead on. Third time around they had the drill down pat and Capital Industries was formed and up and operating with a minimum of glitches. Greg had the spare time he needed for his family. He was no longer an absentee father and husband. Investors by the thousands flocked to Capital Industries, desperate to be on board another Harry Hvide enterprise. Harry was the holy water of Wall Street and lines formed to immerse and get well. But blind loyalty went only so far. Capital Industries would have to produce results sooner than later. The businesses didn't run by themselves. The used car superstores required vast amounts of product to flourish, necessitating the purchase of new car dealerships and rental car agencies across the United States. An elite management company was needed to operate and maintain the four-star hotels. They were making inroads into alarm and security companies, bottled water and lawn service. There were complex real estate deals on the table. They were even getting back into the ever-lucrative waste disposal business. What they really needed was Harry Hvide at his best. They needed his clarity of thought, his business creativity and genius. Only Harry could keep all the plates spinning without a drop. Only he could forge a clear corporate direction. Yet lately Harry seemed distracted, spending a disproportionate amount of time on the baseball franchise... Sports!!!... Greg never fully understood Harry's involvement. The investment was high, the returns negligible and the losses could be staggering. The players were absurdly overpaid, and for the most part, a group of flaming assholes. Of course, there were exceptions. Most of the hockey players were decent guys and so were some of the football players. But down the line, the baseball players were a bunch of arrogant, ungrateful turds; and Richie Johnson was the biggest turd of all. He remembered last year when Harry invited the team to his own private club for a gala black tie event to kick off the season. The Governor and both United States Senators attended. Richie Johnson would appear only if he was provided with a chauffeur-driven limo.

What was Harry thinking when he gave him that contract? That had to be the worst deal he ever signed off on. Greg wasn't surprised, as the conference revealed, that no one else wanted him... The conference!... Harry insisted he attend knowing Greg had zero knowledge of baseball. He tossed and turned on the large brown leather sofa in his study. His head throbbed. He desperately tried to fight through the pain and think. What did Harry say to him on the way out? He struggled to remember.

"Maybe this needs a completely different approach—someone from the outside looking in. Please take a look at it. See what you can do." Yes, those were Harry's words but what could he do? When he subconsciously blurted out the only thing to come to mind, he was rightfully laughed out of the room. Only Harry Hvide didn't laugh. Greg spent the entire night in his study thinking the unthinkable. He tried to sleep, realizing nothing would be resolved this evening. Maybe in the morning the whole thing would look different. Who knows? Maybe, just maybe, circumstances would change.

3

The next morning, a limousine pulled into the Capital Industries building garage at exactly 6:15 AM. Harry Hvide exited the limo, entered the executive elevator and got off at the twenty-fourth floor office suite. Already some of his people were busy reviewing numbers, fine-tuning proposals or setting up the day's agenda. Harry helped himself to a cup of coffee and a plain doughnut. He looked around at the activity and smiled. He remembered in the heyday of Video Nation, there was a subliminal competition between himself and his top execs as to who would get to the office first. Once Roberts and Barrett busted their butts to arrive at 5:20 AM, only to find Harry making coffee. Without acknowledging their presence, he uttered one questioning word, "Oversleep?" The memory of the looks on their faces still brought a chuckle.

It was his lifelong habit to start his day early. Even on vacation he rarely slept past 5:30 AM. Today, for instance, he had to go over a counterproposal for a midwest car dealership chain, review and sign off on the luxury hotel property deal in Scottsdale, and put the finishing touches on an offer for a Pebble Beach golf club and resort. There was contention between a Japanese auto manufacturer and the amount of market share his dealerships were amassing. That had to be sorted out. In the afternoon, CNBC was coming to the office to tape a short piece on Capital Industries' future direction and his response to some stupid analyst's lukewarm projections. He had a late afternoon meeting with his services division and had to coordinate a time he and his waste disposal people could discuss some issues with TransGeneral, the insurance company. He had to leave himself enough time to get ready for the evening's big charity event benefiting the Miami Project. And he had to remind himself to call Redmond and Roy, the president and general manager of the baseball team to clear complete access for Greg Barrett. The damned baseball team! Lately it was taking up too much of his time and was causing far more trouble than it was worth. At least he held a small degree of comfort that Barrett was taking shot at it. He could think. He was tenacious. He had always come through before and he had been there. Almost from the beginning.

The very beginning was St. Paul, Minnesota. Of German and Norwegian lineage, the Hvide family was in the businesses of waste disposal and construction. As a boy, he worked for his uncle in the garbage business. After a family falling out, the Hvides moved to Fort Lauderdale and struggled to get a piece of the booming construction business. Harry made it through high school and was laboring away in his first year of college when he was overcome by his entrepreneurial instincts. Observing Fort Lauderdale's flourishing economy, he wanted to take advantage now, not wait for graduation. Besides, he was an ordinary student. He didn't want to be a doctor or engineer, trades that required specific training. There was nothing he'd learn in Ancient Greek history or calculus that would prepare him to earn a better living that he could start on now. While studying he was so easily distracted. His thoughts would drift, then a fragment of an idea would start to form in his head. It would turn and spin, gaining momentum, spinning faster and faster until, like a seed, it germinated, spreading throughout his brain. Then a blinding light would fill his head and immediately everything would be so clear. Sometimes he would get these flashes while sleeping and awaken in a cold sweat. Lately he was preoccupied with the garbage business. He had an affinity for it from his days in Minnesota and could just sense its potential in booming South Florida, and how much money could be made. After his latest flash, he had a new perspective on waste disposal. It wasn't about picking up garbage. When broken down to its basis it was really a rental and service business. The dumpsters were rented out on a monthly basis and you provided service by clearing them a certain number of times per week. As long as you were diligent, your customers had no reason to go anywhere else. The assets could be rented again and again and again. Within twenty years, Harry Hvide would be the first person in history to establish three different billion-dollar-a-year companies. All would be rental-service oriented. A longtime business rival once begrudgingly remarked, "If prostitution was legal, Harry Hvide would be the world's biggest pimp. He'd positively love all those reusable assets."

Harry talked his family into giving him college funds for investment. He befriended Ray Jenkins, a veteran Fort Lauderdale hauler, and begged him to sell one of his trucks and a small piece of his route. Initially Ray Jenkins resisted, but Harry Hvide was so persistent he finally relented and Seacoast Waste Service was born. Its entire assets were a beat-up red truck, a mish-mash twenty-five stop route, and the vision and genius of Harry Hvide.

Harry started out working sixteen-hour days Monday through Saturday. Starting at 4:00 AM. He would make his stops and drop off at the dump. The afternoons were used to solicit new business. After an hour break for dinner he would spend his evenings maintaining his books and preparing the billing. Friday afternoons were needed for banking and negotiating acquisition of new equipment. He spent all day Saturday working on his truck. It was very simple. If his truck didn't run he didn't eat, and Harry's meal ticket required a full day of maintenance. Sunday was only an eight-hour day reserved for painting dumpsters and delivering them to new customers. His diligence was paying off and business was thriving. He poured every penny back into the business. To keep up with his new customers, Harry needed capital. He needed more and more dumpsters and new trucks to service them. He recruited cousins from Minnesota to join him. He wasn't only looking for drivers and yard men. Harry was one of the first in the industry to employ full-time salesmen to solicit new business. He borrowed from banks, relatives, and friends. He put his heart and soul into his work and Seacoast Waste Service profited.

Another way to garner new business was through service contracts with municipalities. Under the system in place, one disposal business couldn't undercut another. The only aspect of the business put up for competitive bids were contracts with city and county governments. It was disdained by many in the industry. The bidding was so competitive it was hard to make money on the contracts. Dealing with government was a pain with so many bureaucratic regulations and stipulations that, if not anticipated, were actually hidden costs lessening the profitability. Many in the industry were just plain hard-working guys and deeply resented dealing with greedy politicians always with their hands out. It was hard enough to get ahead on a government contract without paying off. Harry Hvide had a different take. Yes, it was difficult to break even, but there were fringe benefits making them worthwhile. Business resulting from new construction was up for grabs. If handled correctly, you could gain an inside track into the building and zoning department and to whom and where permits were issued. Seacoast Waste Service was very often the first at construction sites delivering and servicing their rolloffs. And when new strip shopping centers started popping up on every corner, each store owner would find a Seacoast dumpster already in place.

Harry also had a different perspective on politicians. In Florida, the vast majority of local governments were operated under a strong manager system. The city or county manager was in charge of the everyday workings of government. He answered to an elected commission or board of councilmen who had the power to hire and fire him. The Mayor, for the most part, was merely a glorified commissioner whose duties included chairing town meetings but whose vote on public issues was equal to the other commissioners. The manager whose job security depended on the commissioner's goodwill took to heart any and all of their suggestions and recommendations. Despite the time required and responsibilities of a full-time job, the position of commissioner paid around five thousand dollars a year. Nobody could live on five thousand dollars a year, much less raise a family on it. Harry realized some people went to medical school and became doctors. Others became nurses, cops, tradesmen and so on. The point was, you had to file, raise exorbitant amounts of money and campaign to be a politician knowing it paid five thousand dollars a year. You had to make a conscious decision to run. Politics was the business they chose and Harry Hvide treated them as businessmen. Consequently, he also realized the big money was in zoning. Zoning codes were deliberately restrictive, necessitating variances to circumvent them. Commissioners voted on variances. Variances were very expensive. It miffed him that lawyers who specialized in zoning were often held in high regard, the pillars of their communities, when actually they were nothing more than a developer's glorified bagman.

Harry Hvide's businesslike approach was successful and Seacoast Waste Service operated in municipalities throughout the state. The only exceptions were Miami Dade County and the City of Miami. There, corruption was so widespread, with so many handouts, it was practically impossible to do business. Corruption was so much a part of the local fabric that, to voters, a federal indictment was worth a Congressional citation and a conviction the equivalent of an endorsement from Mother Teresa.

Seacoast was expanding so fast it was running out of traditional means to finance the equipment and infrastructure necessary to maintain and accelerate that growth. Pouring every dime of profit back into the business wasn't enough. Their credit lines with their lenders were maxed out. Harry had already borrowed all he could from family and friends. Somehow, Harry had to locate a new source of capital. The pursuit of new capital consumed him. He couldn't sleep, often getting up in the middle of the night, pacing back and forth. His mind was in overdrive, turning and spinning, making it impossible to think about anything else. Slowly an idea started to form, sprouting throughout his brain. A blinding light eradicated all thought... and then... everything was so clear! He would take Seacoast Waste Service public and issue stock. Harry Hvide was never so sure of himself as he was at that moment. He had traveled through a puzzling maze and found the solution.

Not everyone shared his enthusiasm. At the time there was no such entity as a garbage company listed on any major exchange. There was a general perception that the industry was run by the mob, or, at least, mob influenced. The whole concept was different and Wall Street was much more receptive to known quantities. None of this deterred him. He would welcome the most thorough investigation to prove there were no ties to organized crime. And just because his idea was new and different didn't diminish the fact that his company was a money-making machine. He was confident an underwriter existed on the street who would see its potential. Harry was right, starting an amazing string of Wall Street successes.

Shunned by the traditional investment houses, Harry hired First Securities of Boston to be its underwriter. A relative newcomer in the financial world, First Securities was anxious to be a major player. Spurred on by a lucrative option deal, it proffered the Initial Public Offering of International Crating, Inc., listed ICX on the New York Stock Exchange. At first investors greeted the new issue with resounding apathy. Managers of mutual funds completely ignored its existence. But ICX, as Harry Hvide foresaw, performed too well not to gain attention and what started as an insider's secret soon was on the "hot buy" list of every major brokerage. The single bump in the road was the occasional class action antitrust suit challenging the waste industry on the issue of "Land Rights." Represented by a former United States Attorney General, ICX was able to fight them off in court. When they lost, the ruling would be overturned by the U.S. Court of Appeals of the Eleventh Circuit. Only after Harry Hvide had sold out and left the industry did the United States Supreme Court rule the practice of "Land Rights" to be in violation of Anti-trust laws. By that time, the ruling was in the best interest of the powerful newly-merged ICX anyway. After the sale to G.T. Limited, ICX's annual revenues exceeded one billion dollars; all started by one man with one truck.

By any calculation, Greg Barrett played an essential role. There was no way to minimize his importance. Harry remembered way back to the days of labor unrest and how Barrett showed up out of the blue, unafraid and ready to work. And to him it was just a part-time job! Harry's instincts told him he had found a keeper who would fit right in with his plans for the future. As usual, Harry was right on the money and Greg Barrett developed into the hard working executive and expert deal maker/negotiator he envisioned. He was at his best when things were complicated. He was most creative when deals unraveled. He also seemed to possess a sixth sense that could predict Harry's thoughts and actions.

When Harry Hvide started Video Nation, Greg Barrett was his first hire. Barrett could have stayed on at ICX and been wealthy and secure for the rest of his life. Instead, he chucked it all to join Harry in a new enterprise. Hell, it wasn't even an enterprise. It was something totally new, a radically different concept. They were venturing into unexplored territory and Greg didn't flinch, even with his wife expecting.

Harry Hvide wasn't cut out for retirement. He tried golf. He collected antique cars. He traveled the world. He developed an affinity for water sports and deep sea fishing. None could sustain him full-time. His mind kept spinning and turning and he couldn't shut it down. After six months of retirement, he was anxious to conquer new worlds and this time there was no shortage of capital. He looked at deal after deal. One of his old friends, Arthur Birnman, told him he had a proposition he must look at. When Harry learned it was movie rentals, he told Arthur not to bother. Thank God his friend persisted. If ICX was the Wimbledon of investments, Video Nation was the World Series, Stanley Cup and Super Bowl combined! It was all so clear. They had the right product at the right time. It was a rental-service business and, best of all, it was wildly profitable. So profitable that breakneck speed expansion was a necessity. More stores meant more dollars and less expenses per store. It created a brand name and froze out competition. It also created a mind-boggling workload. Starting an industry from scratch took its toll on Video Nation's workforce. Its main headquarters was nicknamed "Hotel Heart Attack." Employees joked that the only thing going up faster than the stock price was the number of double bypass operations. Or the divorce rate. The hectic schedule was murderous on family life and many of the marriages didn't survive. Main topic around the water cooler was how many stock splits it would take to cover alimony. Video Nation stock didn't disappoint and no one missed a payment. Some CEOs liked to brag how many people they employed. Harry liked to point out how many millionaires they made. Stockholder meetings were coronations with all exalting Harry Hvide. Kingly status, however, was not a universally held opinion. There was a persistent minority in the financial world wary of Video Nation's unprecedented success. They held to the old notion of something too good to be true and were buoyed by a Wall Street Journal article questioning Video Nation's long term health. The writer referred to the video rental business as a modern dinosaur soon to be wiped out by new technology.

Why go out to a video store, the article opined, when you choose from a menu off a satellite channel or order the movie of your choice over the phone on a pay-per-view basis. More investors took a short position, betting the stock would go south faster on Video Nation than any other issue on the Exchange. This infuriated Harry Hvide. The technology mentioned in the article was years away, and would take years more before it gained enough widespread acceptance to be a threat. In the time it took to implement Video Nation would rack up billions of dollars in profits. Also by the time the new technology was ready for the mass market, Harry had no doubt Video Nation would be a major player.

Harry detested short sellers. He hated the fact that they rooted against success and profited by a company's failure. Harry knew the market and money could be made, but it was against his nature to sell short. He loved to burn them. After the Wall Street Journal article the stock took a short term hit. But savvy investors couldn't ignore the bottom line and flocked back in droves, sending Video Nation stock back up through the stratosphere. Many of the new buyers were the short sellers themselves, forced to cover their position or get wiped out.

Video Nation was so profitable it had what every business dreamed of—a surplus of cash. It was important for its future growth and well-being the surplus was invested wisely. Harry's instincts told him to diversify, not just in any business even if it was rental-service. Harry wanted related businesses. Businesses that fed into each other creating a bigger market for all. He wanted businesses he could cross-promote. Their business was renting movies. Movies were entertainment. Their new investment would be in entertainment; entertainment and sports.

Their first foray into the entertainment biz was in music retail. Video Nation stores already generated traffic for movie rentals and had an existing section for music videos. It was easy to dedicate a portion of each store for the sale of CDs and related items. It became a store within a store titled "Music Nation."

Next were ventures into cable TV and a Hollywood studio. Real money could be made in cable. Ted Turner went from a falling-down drunk yachtsman to a multibillionaire environmental spokesman starting with one crummy UHF station in Atlanta. The key to a successful cable channel was distinctive programming. For forty years, Phoenix Pictures had been a player among Hollywood studios, turning out a string of quality movies, some of them award-winning classics. For the last twenty-five years, they had done well in TV production and owned the rights to some of the medium's most beloved sitcoms and dramatic series. A New York investment bank convinced Phoenix's management to go public. Television and movie production is a risky, mercurial business and the stock was languishing. By itself, Phoenix's stock price was right where it should have been. In context with a cable channel, its library of films and old TV shows made it grossly undervalued. This was exactly the programming Harry had in mind. Phoenix's management was receptive to selling a small piece to Video Nation. After all, their largest profit center came from Video Royalties and Video Nation was the largest video rental chain. Within months the small piece became a majority interest and Phoenix Pictures a subsidiary of Video Nation. Harry was sure Hollywood viewed him and his guys as the Beverly Hillbillies riding into town and ripe for every scam. Barrett wanted no part of it and was reluctant to be the temporary CEO. Harry reassured him. It was only for a short time. Don't interfere in the creative end, just monitor the costs and keep projects close to budget. It may be glamorous, but it was still a business. Treat it as one and they'd be fine.

Harry's other source of programming was sports. Personally he was already involved in South Florida's new stadium. Tired of fighting with the City of Miami for a new facility, the local NFL owner told the politicians to screw themselves. He'd build it himself. Sam Miller was a man of his word and constructed a beautiful state-of-the-art stadium on the county line between Dade and Broward. The problem was he really couldn't afford to do it. Compared to the other NFL owners, he was a relative pauper and didn't have the financial wherewithal of the other owners. Originally he bought the team for a pittance and ran it on a shoestring. With prudent management and great hires, the team was a big winner on the field with a loyal fan base, Harry Hvide among them. He was an original season ticket holder, and over the years, developed a friendship with Sam Miller. To privately finance his new stadium, Sam Miller had to pledge the team itself as collateral. To pay off the construction loan, he had to dedicate the entire revenue from sky boxes and club seats. It was a tough decision. Building a new stadium without public funds was a great accomplishment, but without the sky box and club seat revenues, the team was always strapped for cash. The money from sky boxes and club seats was precious. By league agreement it was the one revenue source not divided equally among the teams. Sam Miller needed help and Harry Hvide provided it. He purchased fifty percent of the stadium and ten percent of the team and gave Sam Miller the breathing room he needed. To make the deal more palatable, Harry retained "right of first refusal" options on both the stadium and the team. If Sam Miller wanted to sell out and found a buyer for either the stadium or the club, Harry Hvide could claim ownership by matching the offer. It all happened much faster than Harry had anticipated. Sam Miller died, leaving a tremendous estate tax liability on his large family. With the family squabbling over the estate and in dire need of funds, the balance of the stadium was sold to Harry Hvide. Not long after, he exercised his option on the club.

While he was sole owner of the stadium, he was approached by his longtime friend Arthur Birnman.

"How would you like eighty-one dates for your stadium?"

Harry listened.

Arthur Birnman had been friends with Harry Hvide for many years. They were also business partners involved in many different deals. In fact, it was Arthur Birnman who brought Video Nation to Harry's attention and was an original investor. He was now in baseball, president of the team in Montreal. Major League baseball was expanding and awarding two new franchises. South Florida would make an excellent choice. The demographics were good and it was the largest television market without a team. The stadium was built with baseball in mind and could be easily converted. Baseball was popular with Latinos and the area had the country's largest Hispanic population. All it needed was a "deep pockets" owner.

Harry Hvide was intrigued. He was already in business with Major League Baseball. Video Nation had a licensing agreement to market their bloopers and highlight videos. Working on a major project side by side with Arthur would fulfill a lifelong dream and present a formidable challenge. Other aspects appealed to him as well. South Florida was the cultural and economic gateway to the Caribbean and South America. His mind was buzzing with all the possible marketing tie-ins in baseball-mad hotbeds like Venezuela, Puerto Rico and the Dominican Republic. Plus, it provided a hundred-fifty or so nights of programming for his planned cable network.

Harry Hvide gave the baseball project serious thought. As he researched, he found aspects he didn't like. Some were minor but he had three major areas of concern that had to be addressed. First, he wasn't sure the stadium could support a franchise long-term. During the summer it rained in South Florida every night right around game time. It might not rain right over the stadium but assuredly it was raining somewhere. People were unlikely to trek out to a ballgame if it were pouring where they lived. Harry dreaded the possibility of rain delays. He was a bottom line, punctual guy and baseball didn't abide by any timeline. It was the only major spectator sport without a time clock. Theoretically each game could last forever. Lovers of the game romanced about its timeless quality. Harry wasn't immune to the game's charm, but worried the slow pace, coupled with long rain delays, would make going to a game an all-night affair. Working people had to get up early and parents would hesitate to bring their kids on school nights. Ideally, his team would play in a facility on natural grass with a retractable roof. A retractable roof took the weather out of the equation. But putting a roof on his stadium was more costly than building a new ballpark from scratch. Also, in the long run, they would need the skybox and club facilities built with public funds and still keeping all the skybox and club seat money, his team would be at a competitive disadvantage. All their skybox money went to the stadium debt, not the team.

Secondly, he was hardly enamored with baseball's financial structure. More than any other sport, baseball was divided into haves and have-nots. The only revenues shared equally among the teams were the national TV contracts and apparel licensing agreements. Everything else was "each man get as much as you can," leading to enormous discrepancies between major market and small market teams. Local television and radio broadcasting rights could exceed fifty million dollars a year in New York and be less than four million dollars in Kansas City. The Chicago owner rationalized, "When we bought our franchise, we didn't buy Pittsburgh's market." That parochial thinking was pervasive among the big market clubs and, in Harry's opinion, stunted baseball's long-term stability. Buying a franchise meant more than just the local market, you were buying a part of Major League Baseball. The present system insured perpetual competitive imbalance. The teams with the most money would always have the best players. If a small market team had the foresight and skill to develop a young player into a star they would surely be outbid once the player was eligible for free agency. This robbed a team's fans of its most valuable asset—hope. The whole allure of fan support was the dream of improving, winning and competing for a championship. With a pay differential of fifty million dollars, what realistic shot did a small market team have? Their hope of improvement down the road was stripped because their developing players would surely desert them. Harry knew the novelty of a new team wouldn't last forever. Before too long they would have to give their fans a promising team on the field. Even from the start they would need a team that gave its fans hope and promise of a better day. Their new franchise was a middle market team and he had no intention of making it a personal subsidy.

Also, player development costs were out of whack. Unlike football and basketball, baseball didn't have a free minor league system via the colleges. When a pro football team made someone a first round draft choice, that player was virtually a shoo-in to make the team. In base-ball first round draft picks were mostly teenagers, not even in college, and years away from the major leagues. Multimillion dollar bonuses were no guarantee a highly touted prospect would ever make it to the big leagues. If he busted out he surely didn't return any of his bonus money. It was crazy and made the ninety-five million dollar franchise fee misleadingly low. Adding in the player costs and the money need-ed to set up a minor league system and scouting network, the real fig-ure was closer to one-hundred-forty million dollars.

Third, and by far his greatest concern, was the strength of the play-ers' union. Philosophically, he was opposed to unions in general, main-ly because of their arrogant disregard for their employer's well-being. As long as they got theirs, everything was fine; no matter the financial consequences to management. Someone who once showed up for work during a labor dispute told him he came because it was the boss's signature on the bottom of the paycheck, not the union's. He was cer-tain few, if any, ballplayers shared that sentiment. For more than two decades the players' union had beaten management at every turn. They were more unified and outsmarted and outlasted the owners on every issue. If there was a stalemate, they would outlawyer them too.

What emerged was a system so tilted in the players' favor it was the laughingstock of every other professional sport. All the contracts were guaranteed. If a player signed a multiyear, megabuck deal and under-performed, you were stuck with him. If he had a good year and out-performed his contract, he would hold out for more money while whining to the media how he was so mistreated. When management wanted to hold a young player for a set time period to compensate for development costs, the union negotiated an arbitration system that inflated salaries faster than free agency. Players loved it. When they had their arbitration hearing, to a man they would say, "Today I'll be rich or richer." After three years in the big leagues a player became arbitra-tion eligible. The player would submit a figure for what he thought he was worth and management would counter. The arbitrator picked one or the other. No middle ground. It was in the player's interest to sub-mit an artificially high figure. Management would be forced to offer a more than fair contract just to cover the possibility the arbitrator would side with the player. Any management mistake boomeranged back, hit-ting them right between the eyes. If a player with a five million dollar a year contract had an off year and hit fifteen home runs and drove in sixty runs, another would make the case in arbitration he deserved two million five hundred thousand dollars because he had eight homers and thirty RBIs. If another had better numbers he'd want more.

Mediocre statistics were then the benchmark for five million dollars per year. It was crazy. Salaries were spiraling upward and upward with no end in sight.

Arthur Birnman shared Harry's concerns but believed they were manageable. The stadium wasn't perfect. Their dedicated revenue stream could be better and it had too many seats. Too many seats meant there was no immediacy to purchase tickets in advance. With so many seats available, anyone could wait until game time and buy right at the ticket window. Less seats made for more demand and it was always preferable to get the money in advance. But the stadium also had much in its favor. The location was convenient and had good access. There was plenty of parking. The facility itself was state-of-the-art and converted easily into a damn adequate ballpark. There was room for picnic areas and special sections for corporate groups and families. They could cover up unused sections in the outfield and limit seating capacity. There was nothing they could do about the weather. Maybe they'd get lucky. All in all, the stadium would be fine. Harry agreed it would serve well in the short term and he was starting to formulate some ideas for the future.

Baseball's financial structure and labor problems were another matter. Arthur Birnman didn't try and sugarcoat them. Only a fool would make a one-hundred-forty million dollar investment in baseball under these conditions. Harry Hvide was no fool. The kicker was the current collective bargaining agreement between players and owners would expire after the team's first season. This time baseball's ownership was united. This time they wouldn't roll over for the union. This time they would hold out until they had an agreement addressing their needs. This time the owners had a backup plan if the players went out on strike.

To demonstrate their resolve the owners took the precaution of firing the Commissioner of Baseball. They appointed one of their own to fill the vacancy and deleted the "in the best interest of baseball" clause. For years the Commissioner had used that proviso to end statements and issue arbitrary, enforceable rulings. This time there would be no imposed settlement. Arthur Birnman had Harry canvass other owners and gauge their determination. Harry was impressed. To a man they pledged to stay the course and put the business of baseball back on a stable financial footing. Harry Hvide gave the go-ahead and the Florida Manatees were born.

The inaugural season could not have been better. Attendance was sensational, way above their predictions. They averaged forty thousand per game and over three million for the season. Their radio and television ratings were high. Manatee apparel and paraphernalia were everywhere. On the field the team showed promise. They seemed to strike a hidden nerve and it was no overstatement to say South Florida had Manatee Fever. Even the weather cooperated and the team had less rainouts than any other National League team.

Harry had never seen anything like it. He personally was treated as a local hero, receiving standing ovations at the ballpark, restaurants, public functions, wherever he went. Building two different billion dollar companies didn't give him a tenth of the publicity and notoriety he got from owning a ball club. He was so well known he didn't even need a last name. In the newspapers or talk radio, he was never Mr. Hvide. Mention the name "Harry" and everyone knew who you meant. Astonishing! In South Florida he attained equal status with Pele, Madonna, and Fidel. The only negative was the premature death of Arthur Birnman who never got to see the Manatees take the field.

The team was doing so well it could afford to trade for Richie Johnson. Stuck on a small Market team who couldn't afford him, Richie Johnson made it plain he wanted out.. Tired of his nonstop complaining and sour attitude, his team was happy to dump him for a few prospects and to anyone willing to assume his six-million dollar a year salary. The Manatees were willing and the trade was made. His baseball people explained there was a downside to Richie Johnson. He was moody, surly to the media, and never signed autographs for fans. He had an upside as well. He was, potentially, as good a hitter as there was in baseball. He had almost won the triple crown the previous year and possessed the fastest bat speed in the game. He was Florida-bred and his disposition might improve playing in his home state. He was still young with the bulk of his career ahead of him. Moreover, he would give the Manatees their first marketable star, a marquee name usable for wide ranging promotions. He was expensive but his contract had a few years left and he probably would cost more on the open market. Harry approved and Dick "Don't call me Richie" Johnson became a Florida Manatee.

4

Buoyed by the team's first year success, Harry Hvide accelerated the timetable for his latest brainstorm, Entertainment Nation. He started by purchasing a National Hockey League expansion team. It was a little impetuous and not researched as well as his baseball decision. The cost, however, was relatively low compared to other pro sports and it fit right in with his master plan. Also, Disney was buying the other NHL expansion team and their track record was pretty good. The game itself was superfast and exciting. They had a built-in base core of fans among all the relocated northerners living in South Florida. Harry was certain new fans would gravitate to the game once exposed to it.

Harry's master plan made its debut at the Video Nation Annual stockholders meeting. With slides, architect's drawings, scale models and videotapes, he made his presentation. It was quite an exhibition... awesome in its scope and imagination. There were plans for a sparkling new hockey arena at one end. At the other end was a magnificent retro ballpark, complete with a retractable roof. A retro park was a facility with an old-time classic feild plus every modern convenience. Phoenix Pictures was represented with a fully-working sound stage where TV shows could air in front of live audiences. Special IMAX and virtual reality theaters abounded. A megamall, theme restaurants and entertainment centers were all a part of it.

Before the audience could catch their breath, Harry informed them it was only Stage One. Stage Two was a completely new and different theme park. No robots, no mechanical rides. Entertainment Nation's park was totally interactive. There were ski lifts and toboggan runs. There was a giant saltwater aquarium for snorkeling and diving. There was an actual track for race cars. There were beautiful resorts and spas with tennis courts and championship golf courses. Plans included other hotels priced for the family. Harry explained how every aspect of the park was intertwined, each feeding into another. He predicted to his audience that in five years Entertainment Nation would surpass all but

Disney World in attendance and be the second largest tourist attraction in the world. They wouldn't even need to borrow money! They could finance it themselves, out of Video Nation's cash flow, and carry no debt on the books. He went over the details, how both he and Video Nation either owned or had options on the necessary land sites. He explained how they had successfully lobbied the Florida Legislature for a special taxing district and why it was so essential. Disney was granted a special taxing district in Orlando allowing it to basically form its own government and control its own destiny. This was so crucial, Entertainment Nation could not exist without it. Harry remembered his past experiences and there was no way he'd let a project of this magnitude get bogged down in local politics. He didn't have to remember back that far. Just recently the City of Miami tried to renege on a signed lease with the hockey club and hold him up for more money. His lawyers advised him it was such a clear violation he could temporarily move the club to another city and win a summary judgment. The damages would be so astronomical he would literally own the City of Miami. Harry dismissed the idea, countering, "Who'd want it and what would I do with it?" They won in court and simply had the terms of the lease enforced. The special taxing district insulated Entertainment Nation from similar situations. The stockholders were enamored with the whole concept. Their response was gratifying to Harry Hvide and validated his leadership of the corporation and the new direction he was taking it.

Regrettably, Entertainment Nation never got off the ground. Video Nation's cash flow was too big a plum and the company was fetching many suitors. Among them was the entertainment conglomerate Galaxy, Inc. Harry preferred a friendly merger to a hostile takeover and Galaxy was the ideal partner. It had the most successful studio in Hollywood. It had four cable networks, a publishing house, and a recording studio. Galaxy was everything now Harry envisioned Video Nation would be. It had everything except his enthusiasm for Entertainment Nation. Soon after the merger, it died on the drawing board. Harry Hvide parted company with Galaxy, left only with his sports teams and nine-hundred million dollars in stock.

During the off season the owners and players' union could not agree on a new collective bargaining agreement and the second season started under a cloud of labor unrest. The novelty of the first year was wearing a little thin but attendance was still good, averaging about thirty-two thousand a game. Richie Johnson was everything he was cracked up to be. For weeks at a time he could carry the club, hitting vicious line drives to all fields. Off the field he wasted no time in alienating fans, the media, his teammates and management. He hissed at autograph seekers and feuded with the beat writers, finally refusing to say anything. He blamed management for not surrounding him with better players and had no problem publicly labeling them cheap and incompetent. Every nick and scrape kept him out of the lineup and he showed up his teammates every chance he could. He was hated in the clubhouse.

On the labor front everything was at a standstill. The owners' proposal was exactly what Harry had been promised and directly addressed their needs. The owners offered the players a partnership where all revenues were split down the middle. They guaranteed the union a minimum of a billion dollars. The owners' proposal called for a hard salary cap which no team could exceed. It eliminated arbitration. It eliminated the designated hitter rule in the American League. It called for the teams to share revenues and set a minimum salary level to go along with the maximum cap. This minimized the huge payroll discrepancies and evened the playing field.

The players scoffed at the proposal, rejecting it point by point. They were happy with the present system and wanted to keep it. They adamantly vowed never to accept a salary cap. Their counter offer cut the arbitration period from three years to two. With no movement on either side, the players' union set August 13th as a strike deadline. The mid-August date was purposely chosen to inflict maximum damage on the owners.

The players were paid in equal increments. By the strike date they would have three-quarters of their salaries in the bank. The majority of the owners' money from the broadcasting rights was geared to the post season and would be forfeited if the League Championship Series and World Series were canceled. This confirmed Harry's worst suspicions about unions. They were out for themselves with no regard for their employers' welfare.

The union went out on strike as planned. They countered at the last minute with a proposal for a luxury tax. It kicked in only when a team's payroll exceeded sixty million dollars. The owners dismissed this out of hand and the sides remained deadlocked. For the first time in ninety years, the World Series was canceled. Scandals and World Wars couldn't accomplish what a work stoppage did. The timeline of the country's oldest professional sport was broken. Lucifer had fallen out of Paradise and any innocence baseball had left was forever gone.

Both sides underestimated the backlash from fans and the media. A sacred trust was broken. To many, cancellation of the World Series was the last straw. Some blamed the money-hungry players. Some blamed the stingy owners. Most called for a pox on both houses. Fans everywhere swore they'd never attend another game. Reporters swore they'd never cover another game. Congressmen called for hearings and introduced bills on the floor to strip Major League Baseball of its Anti-Trust Exemption. Pressure was building to settle. Even the President got involved. But the owners hung tough. They all had a lot to lose, no one more than Harry Hvide. He was establishing a brand new market and couldn't afford to alienate his new customers. In the long run, though, it was more important to install an economic system they could sustain for the long haul. As Harry said, they needed to get it right. The owners now implemented their backup plan.

First they rejected binding arbitration and petitioned the National Labor Relations Board to declare an impasse in negotiations. Once granted, the owners were free to implement their system. They opened spring training camps on time and held tryouts for new players. Owners referred to them as replacement players. The union called them scabs. Whatever their names, they were an essential part of the owners' master plan. Purists cried foul. The owners had no conscience and were further desecrating a hallowed game. Minor leaguers, has-beens from Japan and guys out of retirement were now taking the same fields as Koufax, DiMaggio, and Mays. To the purists, it was abundantly clear; the owners had no shame.

Harry Hvide respected their passion. He and the other owners just couldn't let it interfere with their game plan. He remembered back to the video rental business. Whenever a Star Trek movie was released, its devotees would dress in costume and try to rent the video by speaking Klingon to the cashier... dedicated to be sure. Harry was also quite certain Alan Greenspan didn't consult them on the trade deficit. They could not allow themselves to be swayed by a vocal minority. Replacement players were vitally important because it allowed Major League Baseball to keep its doors open. By playing the season all their revenue streams would start to flow again. There would be plenty of complaints about paying to see second-rate baseball but they could lower ticket prices to compensate. The owners could also give discounts to their radio and television rights holders and keep them mollified. It was essential to restart a positive cash flow. This put the financial onus of the strike squarely on the players. In previous work stoppages, both sides got nothing. Now only the players were cut off. Also, by playing out the schedule it gave the players a game to come back to. Many of the players were millionaires and, in private life, politically conservative. Harry laughed at the thought of UPS drivers and union carpenters joining the players on the picket line. Ninety-nine percent of the players wouldn't look back to see who they ran over if strikers ever inconvenienced their personal lifestyle one iota. Some of them would look past the union rhetoric and see the owners' offer guaranteed a billion dollars for salaries. Even with inflation that's a lot to go around. Some would start to worry about keeping three kids in private school. Some would feel the pinch of alimony and child support payments. Others had wives and girlfriends to support. Some had both. For the first time, the players were under greater pressure to settle than the owners.

It would only take a few. Just one player tired of the union "spin," another who needed a paycheck, and a trickle of strikebreakers would soon be a flood. If not a flood, a steady stream would do. It happened in football. In the meantime, some fans would take the new players to heart. Many could watch the game on any level. They appreciated its pace, the geometry of the diamond, the battle between hitter and pitcher. Modern players were seen as lazy and selfish. The replacement player could be portrayed as a hustler who ran out every ground ball. This and other endearing qualities might find an audience.

As the season was about to start the players went to their fallback position. If they couldn't break the owners, they'd take them to court. The players' union was granted an injunction prohibiting the owners from imposing new work rules and using replacement players. The owners didn't relish alienating more fans or losing another season. A majority voted to play the season with the regular players under the terms of the old Collective Bargaining Agreement and continue to negotiate a new agreement. Harry couldn't believe it. He pleaded with the other owners to challenge the injunction, fight it all the way to the Supreme Court if necessary. He was stupefied that the other owners would let the union outlawyer them, just when they had the upper hand. Playing under the old agreement was like dying a painful, slow death. The majority prevailed, however, and a slightly shorter season started in late April. Harry gave each of his replacement players a check for twenty-five thousand dollars. Most of the other owners gave their replacement players busfare.

As Harry predicted, the season was disastrous. The fans were angry at both the players and the owners and attendance suffered. The players were surlier than ever and the media got in its shots about the decaying state of baseball. The owners had canceled the World Series, estranged their customers, and suffered severe financial losses with nothing to show for it. They were still stuck with the same untenable system, complete with arbitration and free agency.

The Manatees finished that year and the next under the terms of the old Collective Bargaining Agreement. Before the next season the owners and players reached agreement on a new one. Instead of a salary cap, a luxury tax was implemented. Under the new agreement the teams with the four highest payrolls would pay a tax over a set amount. The taxed money would be divided among the smaller market teams. The majority of owners wanted extended labor peace and the new Collective Bargaining Agreement lasted six years. They felt any deal was better than no deal. Harry Hvide was in the minority. The new agreement did nothing to alleviate the owners' problems. It did nothing about runaway salaries and nothing about arbitration. It didn't address the problem between big and small market teams. If anything it widened the chasm. Baseball was stuck with a do-nothing deal for six years and Harry Hvide was pissed off about it. To compound his anger, the Chicago owner who professed to be among the hard-line owners signed Alfonso Beltran to a seventy-two million dollar contract. This nightmare never ended. Now the entire salary structure of Major League Baseball was skewed, affecting every free agent signing and every arbitration hearing.

With his baseball franchise at a crossroad, Harry Hvide had a hard decision. Either they continue in their present direction of developing young talent in-house and adding a few free agents, or they go all out to win now. Harry gave the go-ahead to his baseball people and told them, "Do what it takes."

His decision may have been clouded by anger toward the union and the other owners but it had a sound business basis too. Harry wanted to know exactly what he had and what the possibilities were for the future. Could South Florida support expensive baseball? Would they turn out in sufficient numbers to meet a high payroll? Would success on the field translate into public support for the retractable roof, baseball-only facility necessary to stay competitive? He wanted the answers right away. Delaying was the same as slowly bleeding to death. By the time their farm system had produced enough young players to challenge, the losses would have piled up to an unconscionable number. Without a salary cap, their plan would take too long.

His baseball people went straight at it. Their first new hire was Patrick Timothy McGraw, widely considered the best manager in baseball. Stuck on a small market club with the League's lowest payroll, Paddy McGraw wanted the opportunity to challenge for the World Series. He was pursued by many teams but chose Florida for several reasons. He preferred the National League. The style of play in the

National League fit his managerial style and philosophy of how to win. He hated the American League's designated hitter rule and how it limited the manager's options during a game. In all other team sports, the top man was the head coach. In baseball, he was called the manager for a reason. His primary purpose was not to instruct the players. There were pitching coaches and hitting coaches for that. His main role was to plan strategy, to manage the game. The designated hitter rule compromised that role. Paddy McGraw was at his best when all his senses peaked and he was planning two, three, four innings ahead. He loved juggling his bullpen, giving him the matchup he wanted for just the right situation He loved the double switch. He loved saving the right pinch hitter for exactly the right moment when the game was on the line. He loved all the intricacies of baseball and, as a manager, the control he had in determining a game's outcome.

He had known Harry Hvide for many years, meeting him through Arthur Birnman. Harry Hvide impressed him as a self-made straight shooter, a billionaire with little pretension. If Harry Hvide said he was committing for a championship now, then Florida was his best opportunity.

The hiring of Paddy McGraw paid several dividends. It sent a message to the fans that the Manatees were serious about winning. It sent the same message to prospective free agents. Paddy McGraw enjoyed the reputation as a players' manager. He was popular among superstars, rookies, and journeymen. He had a knack of keeping the whole team involved in the game and making each player feel he played an important part in the team's success. He was approachable in the clubhouse. He never showed up his players and stood by them when they were criticized in the media. He gave a stolid appearance in public and chose his few words very carefully. Off the field, he was a chain smoker with a fine tenor voice and a fondness for a good off-color joke and a touch of Irish whiskey. He was surprisingly well read with an appreciation for classic literature, and he was also a keen student of history.

His hiring had its desired effect. Major League Baseball was on notice that the Florida Manatees were serious contenders. With the allure of Paddy McGraw, no state income tax, and Harry Hvide's open checkbook, baseball's best and most expensive free agents flocked to the team. They filled in every weak spot, adding an all-star left fielder and power-hitting third baseman. They added costly reserves for the field and beefed up the bullpen. They signed Rodrigo Hernandez to a tremendous contract, over seven million dollars a year. The Manatees hoped Hernandez, who was Cuban-born and Miami raised, would appeal to the Latin market and fill out the pitching staff as well. The payroll almost tripled and to show for it they had assembled one of the finest teams in baseball. They were solid throughout the lineup, not one easy out in the batting order. Defensively they were good everywhere and exceptional up the middle—catcher, shortstop, centerfield—where it mattered most. Their bench was the envy of every other manager. Most important, they had the pitching staff Paddy McGraw wanted. Pitching was the crux of baseball. Without it you didn't stand a chance. There were many different ways to score runs; only good pitching prevented them. When he looked over his staff, Paddy McGraw had to pinch himself. Any of his top three starters would be premiere stoppers on almost any other club. Their other starters were potential stars. The bullpen had the ideal mix—an equal number of lefties and righties, crafty set-up men, and a dominating closer. This was the pitching staff he'd always craved. At the very least, they would provide quality innings and keep the Manatees in most every ballgame.

Off the field the Manatees promoted with equal vigor. Television, radio and newspaper advertising were budgeted with large increases. They opened a ticket office in Miami's Little Havana district. They lowered ticket prices on many seats and introduced some innovative promotions, including a "four-for-thirty-four" where for thirty-four dollars you got four tickets, four hot dogs, four Cokes, four bags of peanuts, and a program. The last little matter to clean up was Richie Johnson's contract. His current deal was in its last year before he was eligible for free agency. Both Redmond and Roy felt it was best to work out a new contract now rather than letting it drag out into the season. Johnson was coming off a career year and was on the verge of fulfilling his vast potential. Possibly he would perform even better without the pressure of a new contract hanging over his head. Without one, he'd probably sulk and moan all year long and his attitude could poison the clubhouse atmosphere. Besides, what was exorbitant today might seem a bargain in the future. They had already spent so much, committing in excess of ninety million dollars. They weren't going to let one last deal spoil their planning. Richie Johnson got his six-year, sixty-six million dollar extension. To Harry, they now met the criterion of doing everything they could. They had only to await the fans' response.

On the field the team lived up to its expectations. The Manatees posted their best season by far. They easily qualified for post season play for the first time in their history, making the League Championship Series as a wild card. The free agents performed well as did their existing players. Everyone except Richie Johnson, who as soon as he inked his new contract, promptly went straight into the tank.

Off the field, the results were mixed at best. Attendance increased.

In fact, the Manatees had the biggest percentage increase in the National League. It wasn't nearly enough, however, and the losses were piling up . Even with the increase, they were averaging less than thirty thousand a game, below what they did the first two seasons. Their overtures to attract more Hispanics were fruitless. Attendance was actually below their per-game average when Rodrigo Hernandez pitched at home. To make matters worse, the weather was horrible. Like all the naysayers said from the beginning, "It rains every summer night in South Florida right around game time." Almost every game was delayed by rain, some by several hours. When they floated trial balloons for a publicly-funded new stadium, the politicians' reaction ranged from indifference to hostility.

Harry Hvide was bitterly disappointed. They had lowered prices and fielded an exciting, winning team. All the so-called experts had purported, Miami only supports a winner. He provided them a winner, but where was the support? He knew going in that even if they sold every seat they would lose money. He could live with that. It took money to build a brand. In the future, they could cut some salary, raise some ticket prices and still be competitive. But the Manatees were drawing ten thousand less fans per game than projected and a river of red ink was now the Pacific Ocean.

His disillusionment with the business of baseball was absolute. They were stuck in an inadequate facility with a ridiculous payroll under a horrible labor agreement before an apathetic audience. Harry Hvide felt trapped with no foreseeable way out. The final straw for Harry came in late June when the storied New York Yankees made their first visit to South Florida. This was the inaugural season of interleague play and the American League Yankees and National League Manatees were playing each other for the first time. The three-game series was sold out months before the season started. It was the lead story of the newspapers and television stations and the only topic on Sports Talk radio. There was a huge contingent of Yankee fans living in South Florida and their zeal for their team made for a lightning-charged atmosphere. For the first time, South Florida felt like a real baseball town. Rivalries were great and team officials were hoping "Yankees-Manatees" would approach "Giants-Dodgers" or "Yankees-Red Sox" status at least for a weekend. They were hoping all the enthusiasm and passion would carry over for the rest of the season. All the plans were made and everything set in place for a showcase event. Everything was perfect... except for the weather. It rained. It really, really rained. The skies opened up and torrents of rain flooded everything in sight. Friday night's game took over seven hours to complete with several different long interruptions. Saturday's game was totally washed out and rescheduled for a Sunday double header. It rained more on Sunday, delaying the first game over two hours. To minimize the fans' inconvenience and take advantage of the window of clement weather, management asked the players to play again after a short delay. According to the Labor Agreement, the players were granted ninety minutes between games. Under these special circumstances, the Manatee organization asked the players to waive the ninety minutes and play right away. The players said no. They had buffets to eat and card games to play. The ninety minutes was in their contract and the fans were management's problem. For Harry Hvide that was it. He made up his mind on the spot this was his last season in baseball.

His decision had no impact on the club's on-field success and they opened the league playoffs at home before a less than sold out crowd. If his decision to get out of baseball needed affirmation, the non-sell-out gate in the post season was it. Florida swept the first round and moved on to play for the National League Pennant. Finally South Florida got behind the team. The front runners were leading the parade and the bandwagon jumpers were all on board. Fan support was at a new level and every player was a local hero. Publicly, Harry Hvide put on a good show. He was courteous to the media and was always seen with a wide smile. Among his tightest inner circle, he let it be known his opinion of baseball hadn't changed. While watching a game from his skybox, he muttered, "Let me know when I'm having thirty-five million dollars worth of fun."

Florida won the pennant in six games and now represented the National League in the World Series. Fan enthusiasm and passion for the team increased a hundred-fold. More press credentials were issued for this World Series than any other. It was truly a World Series, too, gaining attention throughout the Caribbean Island Nations and across Central and South America. Even in the Super Bowl years, the Miami football team couldn't approach this level of adoration. Every home game was completely sold out. For the World Series, the entire stadium was used as they removed the covering from the sections unused during the regular season. People were paying hundreds of dollars for seats with obstructed views. Fans showed up in the parking lot and watched on nine-inch portable TVs just to soak up the atmosphere and be a part of something very special.

The Manatees prevailed, coming from behind and winning the seventh game in extra innings. It was a pulsating, heart-stopping game and showcased everything wonderful about baseball. Emotions swung on every pitch and each play was monumentally important. Like a symphony, the movements went faster and faster, culminating in a magnificent crescendo. There was no describing South Florida's euphoria. The celebration lasted days with a procession through the streets of Miami and a boat parade up Fort Lauderdale's Intercoastal Waterway. A final tribute in the stadium filled every seat with thousands more turned away.

It was a team of firsts. They were the first wild card team to win the World Series and the expansion team to do it in the least amount of time. They didn't have a single player who led the league in any statistical category. They were truly a team and that was a credit to Paddy McGraw.

Harry did nothing to spoil the party. Not yet. He graciously accepted the trophy from the acting commissioner and gave all the credit to the players, manager, coaching staff and front office. He invoked the memory of Arthur Birnman. He bided his time. He waited a couple of weeks to see if his lobbyists could garner any support for a new stadium. Not even the euphoria of the World Series could shake loose any change from public coffers. A new stadium had no groundswell of support. Harry Hvide then announced the World Champion Florida Manatees were for sale. If a sale could not be consummated before the next season, the team would drastically cut its payroll, lopping off twenty-five to thirty million dollars. Harry Hvide would no longer write his personal check to cover thirty-five million dollar losses. He would set a firm budget and that was that.

As great as the joy and elation was after the Series, the backlash to Harry's announcement was its equal. He was portrayed as the billionaire grinch and a greedy robber baron. Those were the printable characterizations. He was the topic of every radio talk show, all of them negative. The newspapers took personal shots, parodying his baldness in their editorial cartoons. The fans were smart enough to realize a twenty-five million dollar reduction in salary would gut the team, leaving it with no chance to defend its title.

The firestorm of hatred did not dissuade Harry Hvide. One of his most coveted principles was never fall in love with a business. The business of baseball was easy not to love. Deep down he wasn't even that enthusiastic for a new stadium. With crime rampant and the public school system a disaster, he could see where South Florida politicians had other priorities. He certainly didn't want to pay the bribes... he meant... make the campaign contributions necessary to change their minds. Even if the new stadium was built, the majority of the revenue would go to the players. It would simply allow them to keep their heads above water while millionaires became multi-millionaires. It would serve to perpetuate a system needing change. Without a cap, salaries would continue going through the roof. Without revenue sharing, the same teams would dominate year after year. The National Football League conducted its player draft two months after the season ended and six months before the new one began. ESPN covered it live for two full days. No pass was thrown, no tackle made. Just a group of talking heads and reporters spread out in different venues opining on the prospects of college kids who had never played a single down professionally. Yet, year after year, it was one of the highest rated shows on cable. When the draft was over, every newspaper in the country would issue report cards on how the teams fared. Some devoted their entire lives to the NFL draft, taking the whole year to write books and send out newsletters. To Harry, the draft was such a major event because it gave fans the promise of a better future. It raised their expectations and gave them new players to cheer and a reason to get excited about the new season, even if it was six months away. Baseball's economic system stripped that from its fans. Any change surely wasn't around the corner. It was time to move on.

Getting out wasn't quite so simple. People with a loose hundred fifty million dollars weren't on every street corner. Finding a buyer was taking more time than anticipated. With no offers on the table, Harry called for Plan B. Harry ordered the front office to cut salaries. Lou Redmond, Frank Roy and Dave Grabowsky were disappointed. Faster than any other expansion team, they put together a world champion. They developed players in their own system and spent wisely in free agency. Now they had to break it up. They asked Paddy McGraw for his input. Surprisingly, he lifted their spirits, telling them, "It won't be that bad if we can hold on to the pitching."

Paddy was adamant they could still field a representative team and good pitching was the key. Truth be told, Paddy McGraw was sensitive to backbiters who inferred the Manatees bought the World Series. With the payroll cut in half that inference lost all basis.

Paddy disdained the style of play where teams waited around for a three-run homer. He much preferred aggressive baseball. Bunting in the first inning to take an early lead, stretching a base at every opportunity, delayed steals, hit and run—those were the tactics he favored. His model team was the Dodgers, especially the Dodger teams of the sixties. They invented the term "manufactured run." Maury Wills would walk, steal second, go to third on a sacrifice bunt, and score on an infield out. One run with no hits and not a ball hit out of the infield. It worked as long as Koufax and Drysdale were your pitchers. You could fill out the staff with a Claude Osteen here, a Larry Sherry there. The star position players came and went. One year it was Tommy Davis, the next Wes Parker or Jimmy "the Toy Cannon" Wynn. Pitching was the constant. That philosophy continued to win three National League pennants in the seventies and a World Series in 1988 when the fearsome Oakland As with Bash Brothers Jose Canseco and Mark McGuire couldn't hold up to Orel Hersheiser and Tim Leary. Who was the clutch hitter all Series long? Journeyman Mickey Hatcher. The aggressive style of play kept everybody in the game and on their toes. If pitching could keep a ballgame close, Paddy McGraw would take his chances. He'd find a way to get his share of wins.

With Paddy's input, Redmond, Roy, Grabowski, and Barone drew up several different rosters meeting Harry's budget. Not one included Richie Johnson and his eleven million dollar salary. The problem was there wasn't a single team in either league they could pawn him off on. Their only offers were from Chicago, who would trade back Beltran, and Boston, who wanted the Manatees to assume 80% of his salary plus take their over-the-hill, overpaid right fielder. Both offers left them worse off. Beltran was just as big a jerk as Richie Johnson off the field and even more expensive on it. Boston's offer wasn't worthy of discussion. Anxiety filled the front office because, to a man, no one thought Harry Hvide was bluffing. They had less than three weeks left on Harry's deadline to move Richie Johnson or the pitching, the heart of the team, would be decimated.

"George, could you please step on it? This time I'm afraid Mrs. Hvide is going to divorce me."

"I'll have you home in fifteen minutes, Mr. Harry. You sit back and relax."

Harry Hvide slouched down in the backseat of his limo and closed his eyes. The day had not gone well and he was running very late. He couldn't reach an accord with Honda and would have to prepare for a deposition. Just what he needed, spending more time with lawyers. He found it difficult to even say the word. There must be something he held in lower esteem than lawyers, but he just couldn't think of it. To Harry, lawyers were... shortsellers! Like the investors who took positions betting against Video Nation's success, lawyers sucked the vitality out of the economy, adding layer upon layer of extra costs. In the waste service business, the workman's comp rate was 50% of salary, largely because of lawyers. Also, there were snags in the Scottsdale negotiations. The CNBC interview ran over, causing him to reschedule with TransGeneral. He absolutely needed more time to prepare the numbers and make that his top priority. When he started Capital Industries, skeptics abounded. Sure, the initial offering went great. Harry Hvide inspired great loyalty among the many investors he made wealthy. They were anxious to follow him wherever he went and hand over their money. This time, the analysts cautioned, was different. They questioned Capital Industries' direction. They understood his invest-ment in the auto industry. A national used car mega dealership was a novel idea with much potential. They understood his buying up the largest new car dealerships in every region of the county. They saw the logic in Capital Industries' purchase of the third biggest car rental agency. These businesses were all related and Harry had shown with Video Nation, he liked business with synergy. He was asked in the CNBC interview if he wanted control of the entire seven hundred bil-lion dollar a year car industry.

"No," replied Harry. "I'd be happy with fifty percent."

Cars were fine with the analysts. What they questioned was their connection to luxury resort properties, extended stay hotel chains, security companies, waste service companies, and bottled water com-panies. Harry would simply answer cryptically, "They're all good busi-nesses."

The smart guy analysts were too myopic to foresee his master plan. And it was all so simple. Waste service, security monitoring, and water delivery were all rental-service businesses; his kind of busi-nesses. A luxury hotel was a glorified rental-service business. You provided impeccable service for guests staying in elegant rooms you rented again and again starting at three-hundred dollars a night. These businesses were all profitable with positive cash flows. The hotels themselves could be depreciated while the properties appreci-ated in value. They would boost Capital Industries stock which, in turn, would be used to buy up car dealerships. Buy with paper, save the cash was a Harry Hvide staple going back to the days of ICX. Now that the auto division was big enough to stand on its own, the time was right to split it off from the rental service businesses. The rental-service businesses would be under one banner and named Capital Services Industries. Everything auto-related would remain under Capital Industries. Not only was Harry Hvide the first person to estab-lish three different publicly-traded billion-dollar companies, before the year was out he would be the first with four! First Securities would again do the underwriting. They needed tons of accounting records, tax receipts, depreciation schedules, everything they had. And they needed it yesterday. Harry grimaced. Here he was working multibillion-dollar deals affecting thousands of investors and employees, and his day was constantly interrupted by baseball. Baseball didn't work out for him. He could live with that. What he couldn't get out of his system was Richie Johnson. Everything about Richie Johnson was like a smell you picked up at the garbage dump and couldn't wash away. Everything about him made Harry want to puke. He wasn't with the team three weeks before he denigrated the whole organization. He openly berated the general manager, whining about how he couldn't possibly put up big numbers surrounded by minor leaguers. This past season when he was surrounded by a championship team, one of the best money could buy, he barely hit his weight. He shrugged it off, offering up excuse after excuse. Habitually referring to himself in the third person, he said, "Dick Johnson is all about winning. He don't care about statistics."

Harry's defining Richie Johnson moment came two seasons ago. Rounding second base, Johnson tripped trying to get back. Instead of making an effort to get back to the bag, he stayed on the ground holding his thumb. The base was two feet away and rather than scramble back, he stayed where he was, crying like a baby. Harry had a nineteen-year-old hockey player who took a high stick to the face, lost four teeth and suffered a cut requiring sixteen stitches. He was back on the ice the next period.

Harry Hvide preferred making a graceful exit from baseball. He felt a certain loyalty to Paddy McGraw. Paddy had other offers and could have gone elsewhere. He chose the Manatees and did an outstanding job. In fact, the whole front office performed superbly. He gave them a budget and they produced a World Series Champion. They all deserved better. They just needed to dispose of one albatross and his ridiculously inflated contract. Somebody had to get rid of Richie Johnson.

The limousine went through the gate and stopped in the circular driveway. "Thanks, George. We'll be down in about twenty minutes. Can I get you something? Would you like to come in?"

"No, thanks, Mr. Harry. You'll have to face this music on your own."

Harry laughed, got out and opened the front door. He was met by his wife, Betty. Her arms were folded and a stern look highlighted her face.

"I know, I know. I'll be ready in ten minutes."

Her mock frown vanished, instantly replaced by a sympathetic smile. They embraced for a good thirty seconds, then went up the stairs holding hands.

"Rough day?" she asked.

"Usual. Just ran late. How was your day?"

"Fine. I picked out patterns for the lobby with the designer. When we're finished, the Boca Raton Hotel and Resort will be a jewel, among the finest in the world."

He looked deep into her eyes. "Of that I have no doubt."

He leaned toward her and they kissed passionately. He affectionately patted her on the rear and whispered, "I have to get dressed. By the way, you look radiant."

She smiled. "I took out everything you need. It's on the bed."

He went over to the bed and started to change. She, already dressed, went to her salle-de-bain, took out her jewelry box and looked for her sapphire and diamond necklace. Through the mirror she could see her husband of thirty-eight years struggling with the studs on his shirt. She laughed to herself. After a thousand or more black tie events, he was still uncomfortable in a tuxedo. She sighed. If only the public could know him like she did. Right now their treatment of him was unbearable. She was afraid to turn on the radio or read the papers. The hatred and vitriol that spewed forth made her blush. It was so distasteful. They made Harry Hvide the source of every wrong. She was somewhat surprised that no one blamed him for Hurricane Andrew or El Nino. There were even parodies on the radio comparing him to Hitler. If only they could see a different side of him.

Tonight he was giving the Miami Project a check for one million dollars to aid its search in the cure for paralysis. It was a personal donation and did not come out of a corporate account. There were similar unreported donations to many other charities. When a retired football player injured himself in a skiing accident, her husband sent his private jet to bring him to Miami where he could obtain specialized care. When his insurance lapsed, her Harry picked up the tab. The player had retired before her husband even bought the team and to the best of her knowledge, they had never met.

As she searched for her necklace she came across an old gnarled red toothbrush, its bristles worn to the nub. She held it in her hand and remembered back to when they first started dating. It wasn't easy being a single mother in the fifties. Divorcee carried a negative stigma. Harry never let it get in the way. She liked him from the start. He was always on time, impeccably neat, and had the cleanest, sweetest smelling hands she had ever seen. Harry Hvide was not a handsome man. He was prematurely bald and had a pockmarked complexion. He was self-conscious of his appearance and his vocation. The garbage business required dirty, smelly, sweaty work. It didn't matter to her. He was ambitious, had a great sense of humor, and those eyes were so blue. Later on she discovered he meticulously scrubbed each fingernail and soaked his hands in lemon juice before each date. Betty Hvide's jewelry collection rivaled any in value. Single pieces were worth several hundred thousand dollars. Of her entire collection, that worn red toothbrush was her most precious possession.

5

"I'm leaving now, Martha. What do I have for tomorrow?"

"Mr. Redmond confirmed he'll be back in town tonight and will contact you at 8:00 AM tomorrow morning. At 11:00 AM, you're representing Capital Industries at a press conference announcing the restoration of the Boca Raton Hotel and Resort. Luncheon to follow. At 3:00 PM, Mr. Hvide wants to go over details of the Capital Services Initial Public Offering in his office."

"Thanks. Anything urgent, you can reach me on the cell phone. Good night, Martha."

"Good night, Mr. Barrett."

Greg Barrett got out of the elevator into his car and drove straight to his son's Jr. Soccer League game. Leaving work while there was still some daylight was a new perk he much enjoyed. On the way he left a message for his wife.

"Hi, it's me. I'm on my way to the game. I'll bring Harley home with me. See you around 6:00 to 6:30. Bye."

Traffic to the park was horrendous. He impatiently drummed on the steering wheel as a drive that should have taken fifteen minutes dragged past thirty. He turned off the radio and reflected on the day. Most of it was spent in organizational conferences.

They needed to set up the structure for Capital Services Industries and revamp the one at Capital Industries. For the time being, he would concentrate on CSI and Dave Roberts would head up Capital Industries. Harry would chair both boards of directors. This was fine with him. He shared Harry Hvide's affinity for rental-service businesses. The waste disposal business was blossoming, more profitable than ever, with new opportunities abounding in landfills and recycling. They were at the forefront in the new technology, converting garbage into a marketable energy source. As Harry liked to say, "There was a lot of money cleaning up after people."

In two and a half years the waste management division was already the nation's fifth largest and fastest growing. There were even rumblings on Wall Street that his old employer ICX had its eye on it. Extricating the service businesses from the car business would fuel the speculation. Greg chuckled to himself. That indeed would be a Harry Hvide special... selling the same business to the same people. After twenty years, he was in awe of Harry's genius. In less than four years he had built a new conglomerate rivaling Video Nation in gross revenues replacing what he had. If the new IPO went as planned, Harry would make another killing, at least three hundred million dollars. Greg would do okay too. Exercising his options and warrants should net him between ten to twelve million dollars. Not a bad payday. No doubt about it, Harry Hvide was one money-making machine!

Except in baseball. There was that word again. Every time it crossed his mind, it was preceded by "goddamned." And every time he thought of goddamned baseball, he associated it with Richie Johnson. Harry asked about him again today. After he talked with Lou Redmond in the morning he would have to get on it. He needed to come up with something for Harry. He couldn't put him off any longer.

Greg finally reached the park and drove to the athletic fields. He parked and walked quickly to the far field where his son's game was being played. On the way he loosened his tie. It was very windy with a chill in the air; unseasonably cool, especially for early March. As he approached the field, he saw Harley in his red uniform with the name Fort Lauderdale P.A.L. inscribed above the number ten on his jersey. He was running back and forth, part of a red herd intermingling with a blue herd. Every now and then a white ball would emerge and the red and blue herds would surge in its direction. He proceeded to the bleachers occupied primarily by very well-coiffed women dressed in expensive ski parkas and exercise tights. All wore designer sunglasses. A smaller group of darker-skinned women sat apart speaking Spanish. They uniformly wore the same outfits of grey button-down dresses with white collars. Men were slowly starting to filter in. Like Greg, they arrived alone, coming after work dressed in business suits. Apart from the soccer moms and maids and working dads was a woman sitting by herself. She had on green hospital scrubs with a pink buttoned sweater draped over her shoulders. Her light brown hair was put up in a neat bun. Focusing her attention totally on the game, she wasn't embarrassed to cheer loudly.

"Go, Bobby, go! Move, move! All right, Red Team!"

Greg sat down next to her and said, "Hi."

She smiled back. "Hi."

His eyes were on his son. "How are we doing?"

"Pretty even." She replied. Two bruised shins aside. We had three leave crying, they had two."

Greg Barrett laughed. He was at ease enjoying himself. No work pressures, fresh air, watching his son; he could be doing worse. As the sun set, the temperature dropped quickly. He blew on his hands and uttered aloud, "I can't remember a dry season this wet or this cold."

"Neither can I. Must be El Nino."

They continued watching, occasionally exchanging small talk. Sitting next to and talking with Jody Sellers had become a weekly ritual. He had met her before. Their sons were best friends and attended the same school. He knew she was a single mother and wondered how she could possibly afford the ten-thousand-five-hundred dollar yearly tuition at Hillcrest Academy on a nurse's salary. Greg Barrett was ashamed by the way his wife treated her. Her son, Bobby, often played at their house, sleeping over on occasion. When his Mom picked him up, Alison acted so condescendingly it embarrassed him. He had to admit Alison treated her no differently than the other mothers. At school functions, she was always by herself. To her credit, Jody Sellers always kept her head up and pretended not to notice. Greg admired her for that. She was also raising a great kid. Bobby was smart and well-mannered. Greg couldn't think of any other boy his son's age that wasn't spoiled to death. Deep down he looked forward to their little chats.

She enjoyed his company as well. He seemed to be so well grounded. Around the school she would overhear the other mothers point him out as Harry's Hvide's righthand man. At Hillcrest, where a neurosurgeon's child would be considered underprivileged, great wealth was taken for granted. It was rare for anyone to be singled out from the other rich parents. The first time she dropped Bobby off at the Barrett residence, she couldn't believe her eyes. The fountain in the foreground was as big as her house. The backyard pool was twice the size. Inside, the décor was right out of "Lifestyles of the Rich and Famous" and the waterfront view was breathtaking. Harley's mother was pretty but very haughty. His father was exactly the opposite.

The game ended and the parents and maids filed out of the stands to claim their children. Bobby Sellers and Harley Barrett ran to meet their respective parents.

"Hey, Mom. Hi, Mr. Barrett. How'd you like the game?"

"Very exciting, Bobby."

"Dad, can we stop at McDonalds? Please?"

"Can we go too, Mom? Please, please, please?"

Both parents looked at their kids, then each other and shrugged.

"Fine," she answered.

"Sure," said Greg. "It's okay with me."

"Mom, can I ride with Harley?"

"If it's okay with Mr. Barrett."

"I'll tell you what... let's all go in my car."

"You sure it's no bother?" she asked.

"No problem. McDonalds is only five minutes from here and we have to come back in this direction anyway. Let's go."

The two boys rambled into the back seat and Jody Sellers sat in the front passenger seat of Greg Barrett's Lexus 400.

"Nice car."

"Company car," he replied. "One of the perks of the auto business."

He left the park and drove to McDonalds. The boys ordered Happy Meals and sat at their own table. Jody and Greg took a separate booth nearby. She started eating her McChicken sandwich. He added two creams to his coffee.

"How are things at the hospital?"

"I'd complain but who'd listen?"

Greg smiled. He glanced across and for the first time noticed how green her eyes were. He also realized she had a keen sense of humor and found himself often smiling and laughing in her company.

"Actually I'm transferring to a new department." She continued, "I'm leaving the OR and going to Recovery."

"Is that better?"

"It is when the patients wake up."

Greg laughed again. She went on.

"The schedule is better for me. It's more flexible and I can take more overtime calls."

"Overtime? Don't you work hard enough?"

"Tell that to my bill collectors. I need all the overtime I can get... unless Hillcrest will accept needlepoint for tuition, but I have my doubts. What's new with Harry Hvide? Did he buy the universe today?"

"Yes, he did. But he's leasing it back at very favorable terms."

They shared another laugh. She was enjoying herself. Rarely did she ever get the opportunity any more for regular, normal, adult conversation. At work, it was limited to shop talk and gossip among the nurses; or ignoring the passes and sexual innuendoes from the married doctors. Her exchanges with her mother, sister, and other relatives revolved around family. She really didn't have any close friends. None of the other mothers at Hillcrest would give her the time of day. And if they did, what would they talk about? They lived in different worlds. Her day started at 5:00 AM and ended past 10:00 PM. Raising her son, keeping up a house plus her work schedule occupied all of her time. She hadn't been on a date in over a year, ever since that plastic surgeon went back to his wife. That was it for married men, separated men, and men on the rebound. In her circles, that pretty much covered all bases.

It didn't matter. As long as she could make a life for her son and provide him a promising future, it didn't matter. Besides, to keep Bobby out of the hellhole they now called public school and in Hillcrest, she would gladly take all the overtime she could. If her social life suffered, so be it. Bobby was all that counted. It was the one positive she took from her failed marriage. Her son was such a delight it counterbalanced the bruised lips and bad debts courtesy of her ex-husband. Married at twenty, pregnant at twenty-one, she gave birth before her twenty-second birthday. Her ex split soon after but not before running up her credit cards. She hadn't heard a word from him in a couple of years. Just as well. The last time she had to put up her house to bond him out on a D.U.I.

She knew there were many times a boy needed a father. It just wasn't to be. Doing the best she could would have to be good enough.

The boys finished their meals. While they were eating, it had started to drizzle. As they stepped into the parking lot, the drizzle escalated into a hard rain, forcing them to scurry quickly to the car. On the way back to the park the skies opened up, raining so hard Greg had to put on the emergency flashers. By the time they reached the park, the parking lot was flooded, the water halfway up the wheelbase of Jody's 1988 Chevy Cavalier. They stayed in the Lexus waiting for the rain to subside. Greg looked out the window and commented, "It's rained more this winter than the last ten combined."

"I know," she answered. "I read where they had so much rain in Fort Pierce they had to open up the canals and run the overflow back into the ocean. Must be El Nino."

Oblivious to the weather, Bobby spoke to Harley. "Are you coming to my party on Sunday?"

"I guess. Am I, Dad?"

"I don't know. I can't say for sure. This is the first I heard about it."

"We didn't get an RSVP yet." Jody turned away, gazing at the pulsating raindrops on the windshield. Before turning her face, Greg detected a hurt, sad look in her eyes. He could picture Alison opening the invitation and throwing it away without even telling Harley about it. He turned to his son in the back seat and said, "Of course you're going. We wouldn't miss it for the world."

The boys high-fived each other. A smile returned to Jody's face. She didn't speak but Greg was certain her sparkling green eyes said "thank you"!

The rain let up and Jody and Bobby made a dash for her car. Greg waited for her car to start... and waited. The engine sputtered and sputtered trying to turn over... then died completely. Greg got out in the rain and walked to her car.

"What's the matter?"

"It won't start. It's nothing new. I hate to be such a bother."

"Don't worry about it. You want to try jumping it?"

"Thanks, but it won't do any good. I put a new battery in last week."

"Well, if it's not the battery, we better call Triple A. Would you like to wait in my car?"

"Thanks. But we're soaking wet. We don't want to mess up your car. Besides, you've done more than enough. If you would just call we'll be fine here."

"Don't be silly. I insist you wait in my car. The boys will entertain each other."

Greg opened her door and they all hustled back to the Lexus. He dialed Triple A on his cell phone pleading for them to hurry. He knew Triple A would be busy on a stormy night. They'd be lucky if they showed within an hour. Amazingly, the tow truck arrived twenty minutes later. The driver looked under the hood, then came back with the bad news. "The distributor cap is cracked. No way will it start. Where would you like me to tow it?"

Jody had a disgusted look on her face. She paused for a few seconds before responding, "Oh, I don't know. You better tow it to my house. I don't know where else."

Greg looked at her and said, "I have an idea. Tow it to Auto World off I-595. I'll make sure they take care of you."

"Thanks. I appreciate what you're trying to do but I can't afford a new car right now."

"They only sell used cars. If they can't help you at least they'll get it running or tow it again wherever you want. It can't hurt. You might be pleasantly surprised."

She shrugged her shoulders. He turned back to the tow truck driver, gave him directions and handed him three folded fifty-dollar bills. "Thanks for coming out so fast in this weather."

The driver looked at the bills and replied enthusiastically, "My pleasure. Don't you worry about the car. I'll have it there and tell them what you said."

Greg turned to the back seat. "Where to, Bobby?"

"245 Wiley Street, Mr. Barrett."

His mother added, "It's east off US 1 in Hollywood. I'll give you directions."

"It's okay. I used to live in Hollywood."

By the time they arrived, the rain was back to a drizzle. Her house was tiny, more like a cottage. Bobby and his mother exited the Lexus. Before closing the door she squeezed his hand and said, "I can't thank you enough."

"No problem. Here, take this. When you get to Auto World give this to Tony Lampone. He'll be expecting you." Greg reached into his jacket, took out one of his business cards and wrote the letters FOGB on the back and handed it to her.

"Thanks again," she replied. "Good night, Harley. See you Sunday." She looked up at Greg and asked, "Do you know where West Lake Park is?"

"Sure, I used to live in Hollywood."

"Right. One P.M. at the canoe docks."

"See you there. Good night."

Greg backed out of the driveway and began driving home. He glanced at this watch. He was over an hour late and at least fifteen minutes away. At the next red light he picked up the cell phone and called home.

"Hi. We got caught in the storm. We're on our way. We should be there in about ten minutes."

"You said you'd be home an hour ago. Consuela's dinner is ruined."

"It's okay. Harley ate and I'm in the mood for peanut butter and jelly."

"Suit yourself."

"See you soon." Greg put down his phone and continued to drive, secretly wishing he had ordered a quarter pounder and fries for dinner.

Greg Barrett was in his office at 7:00 AM. He started by reviewing a counter-offer on a new landfill site. He wrote a little note in the margin: MAKE SURE the attorneys clear paragraphs four and five with the EPA standards. G. B.

At 8:00 he saw the light flashing on his V.I.C. line and picked up.

"Yes, Martha."

"Mr. Redmond is on the "Important Call" line. You instructed me to put him through."

"Thank you, Martha."

Greg pressed the button to Line 4. "Hello, Lou, Greg Barrett. Thanks for getting back to me."

"No problem," answered the President of the Florida Manatees. "Harry briefed me. I've got Richie Johnson's contract, his bio, our scouting report, scouting reports from other teams, and his medical. Do you want the insurance policy on his contract and the security reports?"

"Better give me everything. I haven't a clue how I can help. It's really a courtesy for Harry."

"I hear you. But maybe he's right. We've pretty much exhausted all avenues from the baseball end. Maybe somebody from the outside looking in will have a fresh approach. I'll have everything to your office within the hour."

Greg spent the next two hours returning phone calls and working at his desk. As he was about to leave for his conference/luncheon in Boca Raton he remembered he hadn't done anything about Jody Sellers' car.

"Martha."

"Yes, Mr. Barrett."

"Could you please get Tony Lampone at Plantation Auto World for me?"

"Certainly, Mr. Barrett."

Tony Lampone was the general manager of the first Auto World, the nation's largest used car dealership. A nationwide chain of super-sized dealerships specializing in quality late model used cars was another Harry Hvide brainstorm. The Plantation store was a prototype of many to follow. It was essential it produce good numbers and run smoothly. Tony Lampone was the right man for the job He spent his life in the car business. Starting as a mechanic, he worked as a used car salesman, new car salesman and credit manager. When Capital Industries hired him he was the General Manager of the country's second largest Toyota Dealership located in South Miami near the Dadeland Mall. Greg met him at the grand opening and was impressed. Tony was smooth, salesman-slick, and very knowledge-able. He was also something of a local celebrity, gaining notoriety from some "so bad they were funny" TV commercials. He talked in a Brooklynese car lingo rap Greg found amusing. He was sharp and ambitious, poised to move up the management ladder rapidly. Splitting the car businesses from the rental-service businesses would hasten his rise.

"Tony. It's Greg Barrett."

"Gung-Ho Gregory! How ya doin'? What can I do for ya?"

"Last night I had a car towed over. I think it's a Chevy. It belongs to the mother of my son's friend from school. She's probably going to need a lot of help."

"Tell me it's not the '88 beige Cavalier?"

"Okay. I won't tell you."

"Man, what a disaster! It's gonna be a tough one."

"If it were easy, I'd call someone else."

Tony laughed. "Okay, okay. I'll take care of it. We got a couple of other dogs. We'll fleet them down to 27th Avenue, Miami. Should be a sensation with the Haitians."

"Thanks, I owe you one."

"Hey, before you go. I've been hearing some things about a reorganization within Capital. Anything you can tell me?"

Greg smiled. Tony was on the ball. He was given stock options to come over to Auto World. The planned IPO would make him a very wealthy man. "You know I can't discuss that... but between you and me, your wife and daughters can shop for their Easter bonnets at Saks."

"Both families?"

"And your next two."

"Thank you, Mr. Barrett. I will personally guarantee your friend will be VERY satisfied."

"I know. Her name is Jody Sellers."

"Is she a looker?"

"Tony, please."

"Okay, Mr. Straight Arrow. One day you and me. Pure Platinum at Happy Hour. They have a new redhead who will friction-dance you through the floor. You'll wake up in China."

"I can't wait. Remember, Jody Sellers. She has my card."

The card was Tony's idea. Everybody and their sister claimed to be a friend of Harry Hvide or some other CI bigwig. To help, in Tony's words, separate the pretenders from the contenders, he suggested giving legitimate special friends and relatives their business cards with a special code on the back. "ROHH" was "relative of Harry Hvide."

"FODR" was "friend of Dave Roberts." While he kibitzed with the cardholder his secretary would make a confirmation call and flash him a thumbs up or down. Greg had never given out a card before. He called Tony Lampone as a courtesy and had every confidence Tony would work it out.

Greg came out of his three o'clock meeting a little worried about Harry Hvide. Harry seemed quiet and reserved, lacking his usual energy and dynamic spirit. The Capital Services Industries initial public offering was a major, major step and Harry appeared distracted. Greg worked very had coordinating a rough draft of the prospectus for the First Securities. Normally Harry would be all over it, breaking it down point by point, item by item. Today he gave it a perfunctory reading and approved it as is. Greg knew the prospectus was accurate; he double and triple-checked every figure. It just wasn't Harry's style to sign off without comment. Even if he loved it he would never let you know. Greg sensed the problems with the baseball team were affecting him. The press conference today was a prime example. They were putting a fortune into renovating the Boca Raton Hotel. When they finished it would be a five-star property among the finest in the world. It was Harry's kind of project and his wife was also involved. The press conference was an ideal forum. His brilliance and passion would add excitement and heighten expectations. Greg wasn't nearly as good at it. He wasn't afraid to acknowledge he was no Harry Hvide when it came to public speaking. Did Harry send him because he was afraid if he was there the press conference would degenerate into a debate about the Manatees? He had to admit it was possible. Harry would want the whole focus on the project and might stay away it he thought his presence would be a distraction. Greg went back to his office cursing goddamned baseball under his breath. Somehow they needed a quick resolution. On his desk was a file box Lou Redmond had delivered. Greg pulled out the bio. It was time to get acquainted with Richie Johnson.

Richie Johnson was a major leaguer by the time he was nineteen. Growing up he was a legend in the Tampa-St. Petersburg area and led his high school to back to back state championships. He set state records in home runs and batting average that still stand. He was the third person chosen in the amateur draft, picked by the Detroit Tigers. He spent one year in the minor leagues before being brought up to the big club. His tenure in Detroit was checkered at best. Richie Johnson was a manager's nightmare. He complained about the cold weather in spring. Richie Johnson had a compact, densely muscled physique, prone to ligament pulls and muscle tears. To Richie the cold weather exacerbated the condition so he lobbied to play in games only when the temperature was above 65 degrees Fahrenheit. To Richie, the fact that he never bothered to stretch before games had no impact. Even as the weather warmed he missed games due to sinus infections, sprained pinkies, root canals, allergies, strained elbows, ingrown toenails and bee stings. He never ran out ground balls. When the fans booed Richie felt disrespected and responded by making errors on purpose and throwing the ball at fans in the bleachers. He was an easy target of the press and reacted by pouring a bucket of water over one beat writer's head and tried stuffing another into a locker. A Detroit Free Press poll listed him below George "The Animal" Steele and just above a posthumous Woody Hayes as least favorite sports figure.

He also flashed signs of remarkable talent, hitting tape measure home runs and exhibiting phenomenal bat speed. Before long he wore out his welcome in Detroit and was traded to San Diego just before becoming eligible for arbitration. The Padres were willing to take a chance. He was still very young and immature with a lot of growing up to do. His career reached a new level in San Diego. While still fighting with the press, still injury prone, and still not running out ground balls, he became a feared hitter and was developing into one of the best young players in the game. Potentially he was a superstar. As a hitter he became more disciplined, nearly leading the league in walks. He hit for average and his home run and RBI totals increased each year. San Diego gambled, signing him to a lucrative five-year twenty-five million dollar contract. Despite his good numbers many experts felt he hadn't scratched his potential.

Off the field he was an All Start caliber complainer and Hall of Fame delinquent. He picked fights with teammates and whined about everything. With the ink barely dry on his new contract he threatened a holdout if the team didn't renegotiate a better deal. Off the field Richie Johnson wasn't exactly a boy scout. He had thirty-one moving violations in a two-year period. One clocked at 131 mph in his 961 Porsche required a team of lawyers to get his driver's license reinstated. Two disorderly conduct misdemeanors from early morning bar altercations were dismissed. A resisting arrest charge evolving out of one of the traffic violations just vanished into thin air. Two civil suits, one involving domestic violence, the other signing exclusive endorsement deals with three different athletic shoe manufacturers, were settled out of court. He was also the father of five different children with five different mothers, three of whom were named Richard Johnson, Jr. It went on and on.

Greg read enough. His wife's plan for the evening would be torturous enough. He certainly didn't need Richie Johnson as added company. He decided to take the file box home and look at it over the weekend. On the drive home he tried shutting off his mind as his thoughts drifted from one sore subject to another. He worried about Harry. His mood darkened when his thoughts drifted to Richie Johnson. And tonight Alison had in store the perfect evening to worsen a horrible day—dinner on South Beach.

Greg Barrett hated Miami-Dade County. He considered it the end product of years of poorly planned development, mass illegal immigration, and rampant government corruption. It resembled a foreign country and he was surprised when a passport wasn't required when crossing the county line. Miami International Airport was a nightmare. Greg dreaded the occasions it was his only option. MIA was noisy and confusing. The gates seemed miles away. Less English was spoken there than any foreign airport and you could never find a cart. Forget about international flights. On a Lynx or Bahamas Air flight into Fort Lauderdale clearing customs, immigration and claiming your bags took ten minutes. If you arrived in Miami around the same time as the flight from Bogota, the lines for customs were so long War and Peace might not be adequate reading material. Greg's only traffic violation occurred in downtown Miami. He exited a three-dollar per half hour parking lot near the courthouse when a car ran a red light, causing a minor fender bender. With the other driver, his passengers, the witnesses, and the mounted police officer all speaking Spanish, he was written up for failure to yield the right of way. He had a better chance pleading his case to the horse. Greg tried limiting his trips to Dade County to the one football game per year he attended and four or five hockey games at the downtown Miami Arena. At least the football stadium was just south of the county line and next season the hockey team moved out of Miami and into a fabulous new complex in West Broward County. With countless great restaurants all over Fort Lauderdale, Alison had to pick one on South Beach.

Since Greg moved to South Florida the southernmost end of Miami Beach had gone through three distinct incarnations. When he first arrived and lived with his mother in Hollywood, South Beach was a refuge for the predominantly Jewish elderly, euphemistically referred to as "Heaven's waiting room." Most were seasonal residents living in the New York area until Thanksgiving and returning back for the Passover holiday. From December to April they occupied the small kosher resident hotels along Collins Avenue. Days were spent combing the beach. The more active played golf at Normandy Isles or tennis at Flamingo Park. At night they played cards or, for some curious reason, sat on the porch in front of their hotels and watched the passing pedestrian and vehicular traffic. Another major activity was eating dinner. The term "early bird" originated on Miami Beach as local restaurants such as Wolfie's and the Famous offered specials to those eating between four o'clock and six o'clock PM. As the Seventies progressed the Jewish population on South Miami Beach dwindled. New, more affluent transplants preferred the tall, beachfront condominiums in Hallandale or bought into the new country-club-style senior communities like

Century Village. The neighborhood started to decay. A steady decline turned into a precipitous freefall in 1980 when Castro opened his jails and mental institutions, instigating the Mariel boatlift. Within a month's time one hundred thousand Cuban refugees jammed into the Miami area, many of them desperate, hardened criminals. All of them destitute and needing social services. Housing was so limited a sprawling tent city was created. The government tried relocating the refugees in different states but within months nearly all found their way back to Miami. With housing scarce everywhere in Dade County the only area with a sizable number of vacancies was South Beach. The old hotels and garden apartments abandoned by the Jewish elderly were basically converted into low cost housing. In short order one of the planet's most valuable tracts of oceanfront property became a teeming, high crime, low rent, drug infested slum. It remained underdeveloped for several years. The location was simply too good and the land too valuable to remain a slum any longer. The lure of beachfront property was too big a prize and savvy speculators and developers began buying up South Beach. With a booming Reaganomic economy and Miami banks flush with cartel drug money loans were easy to come by. The developers could afford to evict tenants and not renew leases. They could afford to sit on the property. In an area where planned housing communities popped up overnight the turnaround of South Beach was amazing, even by South Florida standards. The old buildings and hotels distinguished by rounded corners and cantilevered window shades resembling eyebrows were suddenly in vogue. The area was designated the "Art Deco District." It was officially listed in the National Registry of Historic Places. The architecture was considered a national treasure. Developers took advantage, adding bold colors to the tropical pastels. Among the white buildings with aqua and yellow trim were additions adding hot pink and blueberry blue. All had cool neon accents. South Beach possessed "The Look" and high fashion models and photographers from the haute couture capitals of the world flew in for photo shoots. Groups from London, Paris and New York used the ocean and Deco buildings as backdrops for their magazines and catalogs. Cutting edge night clubs became the places to see and be seen. Madonna and Sylvester Stallone built homes nearby. Rock bands used South Beach as the setting for their music videos. There were even sightings of Leonardo DiCaprio. It was the kind of environment Greg Barrett would pay serious money to avoid.

Compounding his discomfort were his dinner companions, Stephen and Kim Bennett and Barry and Robin Lewis. Kim and Robin were tennis friends of Alison and they all had children attending Hillcrest

Academy. Besides tennis, the girls often shopped and lunched together. Greg could tolerate the women. Their husbands were another matter. Both were lawyers. Steve Bennett was the managing partner of Green-Tauber-Quinn, Florida's largest law firm. His specialty was real estate law and zoning. He represented most of the biggest developers and realty companies. He was extremely well connected and a fixture at political fundraisers for the Republican party. Behind the scene whispers intimated he might be the state's next Lieutenant Governor. A graduate of Yale Law School, he exuded class. He enjoyed an impeccable reputation for honesty throughout the community. Greg Barrett had direct knowledge to the contrary.

Barry Lewis was a high profile divorce attorney. Many local movers and shakers and nationally known celebrities were among his clients. He was most proud of his claim that a pre-nup didn't exist he couldn't circumvent. Somehow he wormed his way in on the cable TV lawyer shows and became a talking head expert on the O.J. Simpson trial, the Donald and Marla, Jon-Benet, Bill and Monica, and others. He was seen on Hardball with Chris Matthews, Larry King, and Geraldo, with Geraldo being his personal favorite.

It promised to be a long evening. As he was getting ready Alison knocked on his bathroom door.

"Come in, I'm washing my face."

"I bought you a new shirt It's hanging on your closet door."

Greg bit his lip. He hadn't planned on changing. His wife obviously felt his wardrobe was inadequate for South Beach. He decided against making an issue of it, responding meekly, "Thanks."

"Wear it with your khaki pants."

Hanging from his closet was a beautiful deep royal blue shirt. It was exquisitely soft, probably made of silk. Greg took the shirt off the hanger and stared at it with a puzzled look.

"There's something wrong with the shirt."

"What are you talking about?"

"It's defective. The collar's missing."

"It's supposed to. It's a banded collar by Armani. I spent an entire afternoon shopping for that shirt."

Greg detected a tinge of disgust in Alison's voice. The evening was off to an inauspicious start. After some thought, he decided looking like an idiot was a lesser evil than arguing over the shirt. "I'm sorry," he said. "I didn't know. It's really very elegant."

Alison sounded somewhat appeased. "I'll wait for you downstairs. Barry and Robin and the Bennetts should be here any minute."

Another red flag went up. "We're not meeting them there?"

"No. Parking is supposedly impossible. We thought it best to go in one car."

Greg buttoned up his new shirt, looked in the mirror and cringed. He joined his wife downstairs. The Lewises and Bennetts arrived within a few minutes of each other. After exchanging perfunctory greetings the three couples piled into Alison's Suburban and headed toward Miami. As Greg drove, Barry Lewis engaged the wives in conversation.

"This is supposed to be quite a place," he said.

"I know," Alison answered. "Michelle and Justin Fortin absolutely raved about it. You'll never guess who they saw."

"Tell me," Kim Bennett said excitedly.

"Johnny Depp and Kate Moss and... Jack Nicholson with two gorgeous models."

"Wow! I wonder who'll be there tonight?" Kim Bennett retorted.

"Nobody," replied Barry Lewis. "We're going much too early. The place doesn't start jumping 'till midnight."

"Well, I just love watching Chef Norman on the cooking channel," added Robin Lewis.

"So do I," said Alison, "I tried getting Consuela to watch but her English isn't good enough."

A light went off in Greg Barrett's head. A minor mystery was now solved. He had wondered why Alison was so annoyed with Consuela a few weeks back for serving a delicious ground beef dish over black beans and rice with fried green bananas on the side.

She kept saying, "This is not pickled eel over teriyaki duck banana rice." To Consuela pickled eel translated into piccadillo, a Spanish version of shepherd's pie. Greg concluded lack of English was not all bad.

Traffic wasn't too heavy. They were making decent time. Greg stayed in the left lane, exiting off I-95 onto I-395 East. To their right was downtown Miami. Conversation halted as they looked out their windows. The former Centrust was still adorned with red Valentine hearts on a white background. Lights from other buildings reflected off Biscayne Bay, creating an impressive vista. Steve Bennett spoke first. "Appearances are deceiving."

Everyone nodded silently to themselves. The Bennetts, Lewises, and Barretts were Fort Lauderdale people. Each had a private little horror story about Miami. The Miami Arena was to their right, causing Greg to tense up; certainly Barry Lewis wouldn't miss an opportunity to denigrate the poor performance of Harry Hvide's hockey team this season. Thankfully he was occupied telling everyone how he never waited for a table at Joe's Stone Crabs. He drove over the MacArthur Causeway, a bridge over Biscayne Bay connecting the island of Miami

Beach to the mainland of Miami. The Miami Herald Building was to their left. To their right was a giant illuminated guitar atop the Hard Rock Café at Bayside. As they went over the Causeway Barry Lewis changed subjects. "Hey, I bet you didn't know the MacArthur is the world's longest bridge."

"What are you talking about?" queried Alison.

Greg kept both hands on the steering wheel and said under his breath, "From Miami Beach to Havana."

Barry Lewis continued. "Yeah, it's the world's longest bridge… it goes from Miami Beach to Cuba."

Everyone but Greg started laughing. It promised to be a really long evening. As Greg came over the causeway the lavish waterfront homes of the Islands were to their left. To the right brightly lit cruise ships were docked in the Port of Miami. He caught the red light by the Fisher Island Ferry. A ferry loaded with cars pulled away from the loading dock.

"Eight forty-five right on the dot," observed Barry Lewis. "Those ferries run every fifteen minutes just like clockwork."

"I don't know if I could be isolated like that," remarked Kim Bennett, "Steve, doesn't one of your partners live there?"

"A couple," replied her husband. "Bob Quinn and Claudio Alvarez, the managing partner of the Miami office. Bobby loves it. Once you get to the mainland it's only ten minutes to the office. Their Coral Gables Estate was broken into twice. The second time his wife refused to set foot back in it."

"I don't blame her," said Robin Lewis.

Steve Bennett continued, "The security is unparalleled. They both love golf, tennis, and the rest of the amenities. Plus, he keeps his yacht in their marina."

"Boris Becker recently bought there," revealed Alison.

The light changed. Greg accelerated, and not that anyone noticed, spoke for the first time since leaving Fort Lauderdale. "What do you think is the best way?"

Barry Lewis spoke first, "The address is 660 Ocean Drive. I'd say go down Fifth Street until it ends, then go north."

Greg followed his directions, making a left on Ocean Drive. They entered the heart of the Art Deco district and were encompassed in a setting straight from an episode of Miami Vice. The traffic was at a standstill. They inched forward only a few feet a minute. The sidewalks were packed on both sides of the street by a crowd mix best described as eclectic. Locals, tourists, and rollerbladers all strolled back and forth while being whipped by strong ocean breezes. There were countless long-legged women intermixed with gawking teenagers, leather-jacket-ed poster boys and male couples unashamedly holding hands. Virtually everyone sported tattoos. The dress code ranged from boutique Versace to homeless chic. Live music blared from the sidewalk clubs and hotel bars all under an umbrella of multicolored neon. There was a pulse and energy to the scene that even impressed Greg. He couldn't believe how young everyone seemed. He thought to himself if the police spotted them they'd all be arrested for being over thirty. Barry Lewis observed the Suburban's occupants entranced by the streetside atmosphere and remarked, "This is nothing. In a couple of hours this place will really buzz."

Barry's comment revived a mesmerized Alison, who suddenly glanced at his watch. "It's almost nine o'clock. At this rate we'll be late for our reservation." Greg could sense an air of panic throughout the car. "Why don't you all get out and walk. We're only a block away. I'll take care of the car and meet you inside."

They must have all considered it a worthwhile suggestion because within seconds he was by himself, inching along in traffic. Helmeted Miami Beach Patrol officers wearing white shirts and blue shorts swerved in and out of traffic on their bicycles. Finally Greg could see "The Tidewater" lit in cool blue neon. Unfortunately, it was on the wrong side of the street. Another ten minutes passed before he could turn around and pull in front of the Tidewater. He waited several min-utes for a valet. Greg handed the car keys to a gentleman in a white epauletted shirt who didn't speak a word of English, certain he would never see the Suburban again. He joined the others inside, surprised they were not already seated. They were having drinks by a desk which passed as the smallest bar he'd ever seen. "They're preparing our table," Alison informed him.

Greg looked around the dining room. The walls were bare except for a seascape mural toned in foam green. The lighting was subdued, just bright enough to highlight the hand-painted columns. The tables and chairs were alternately black and white, matching the Cuban tile floors. Every table had a flower bouquet for a centerpiece and they were set with blazing orange plates. Though the restaurant was little more than half full the noise in the room was clamorous. Merely walking on the floor made one sound like a flamenco dancer. A pul-sating sound track permeated the room. The wait staff were tanned, tall, ponytailed and beautiful. The female waiters were also very attractive.

"How chic," commented Robin Lewis. Nods of agreement followed. As a maitre d' escorted them to their table, Steve Bennett spoke to him.

"Not your average steak joint, is it, Greg? The décor is so... so cutting edge."

"I don't know, Steve. It looks like a bunch of tables and chairs in a hotel lobby."

After being seated and given menus, they were revisited by the headwaiter a few minutes later.

"Welcome to San Mano at the Tidewater Hotel. My name is Horst. I am honored to be your server this evening. Chef Norman, himself, has personally selected tonight's menu and I can assure you an evening of culinary pleasure. For special appetizer tonight we offer a salmon-potato pancake dotted with crème fraiche, capers, chive and apricot-soaked bacon. Also we have a smoked duck quesadilla atop caramelized corn cakes. We have ravioli stuffed with taro root mousseline in a white truffle sauce. And we have a cracked conch schnitzel seared with kumquats and a papaya avocado relish."

He paused for a minute before continuing. "For our special main courses Chef Norman has prepared for you a delightful whole yellowtail smothered in a coconut wasabi sauce. He also has an exquisite squab served over a bed of mango-scented lemon grass. We have a swordfish carpaccio in a passion fruit sweet and sour sauce. And finally, he recommends the ginger-coated rabbit confit served with vanilla roasted potatoes and a ruby grapefruit salsa. I will return shortly." He bowed slightly and quickly disappeared.

Nods of satisfaction circled the table. "It all sounds so avant-garde. It's so difficult to choose," said Robin Lewis.

"I know what you mean," echoed her husband.

Greg Barrett also had a difficult time choosing, the first time in memory his opinion conformed with Barry Lewis. Horst returned to take the orders starting with Kim Bennett and ending with Greg. "Horst," Greg whispered. "Is it possible to get a shrimp cocktail and a steak?"

Horst stepped back. He looked shocked, as if he'd just heard Karl Lagerfeld was designing for the House of Dior. "I'm sorry, sir. If you would like shrimp we have some delightful blue prawns in a poblanca chili served over udon noodles. If the gentleman prefers steak Chef Norman has an excellent tornados of beef topped with a fig-coated foie gras and wrapped in free range Zimbabwian boar bacon."

"Fine," Greg answered, "I'll have the tornados of beef. Is it possible to hold the foie gras and boar bacon?"

Again, Horst stepped back, this time looking as if he'd seen the ghost of Andrew Cunanan. "I am so sorry. Chef Norman does not allow any variations to his presentation. He has carefully hand-picked every ingredient to make each entrée a perfectly balanced and blended taste sensation. Asking Chef Norman to alter a dish would be like telling Vera Wang how to accessorize."

"Fine," Greg answered. "I'll have it to Chef Norman's specifications."

Barry Lewis added, "Could you please bring us a bottle of Montrachet '68"

"Very good, sir." Horst again bowed slightly and vanished. Greg glanced at Alison who quickly gave him a "You are embarrassing me" look and reinforced it with a kick to his ankle. He got the message and didn't say another word for the next hour.

Their food arrived over the next two-and-a-half hours. The wives were busy tasting each other's food and raving about it. When Greg was served his entrée, he had to stifle himself from laughing out loud. While beautifully presented, his tournedos of beef were about the size of an IHOP silver dollar pancake. Even though he scraped off the foie gras he could taste goose liver in every bite. He had to admit the free range boar bacon was rather tasty.

They were almost done with a toffee kiwi soufflé when Steve Bennett started. Greg had almost escaped. He was so close. At least he made it to the coffee (no, it wasn't coffee)... at least he made it to the espresso before someone asked him about Capital Industries and Harry Hvide. He could not recall a single social occasion where someone didn't take him aside and try and pump him for information. Tonight would not end the streak. Greg was mildly surprised it was Steve Bennett who initiated it. He fully expected it from Barry Lewis. But Steve Bennett had previously represented Harry Hvide and Video Nation. He knew better than anyone the rules and penalties for insider trading.

"C'mon, Steve. You know I'm not at liberty to say."

"Greg, please," Barry Lewis interrupted. "You're among friends. You know the last time I did Larry King, Lou Dobbs of CNNFN was mentioning something about activity in Capital Industries. ... some kind or re... Hey! Look who just came in!!"

All eyes from the table focused on the Maitre d' who either was greeting Ed McMahon with a check or a very good tipper. Next to the Maitre d', in the flesh, was Richie Johnson, accompanied by a stunning olive-skinned knockout with legs to her ears. Richie Johnson and his date followed the Maitre d' to a table nearby. A couple who had just been seated were now being told there was a mistake and basically to get up and wait for the next table or to get out. Richie's date and the Maitre d' conversed in Portuguese while Richie slipped him a rolled-up one-hundred dollar bill. In person, Richie Johnson appeared larger than life. Though not especially tall, his date in heels was of equal height, his oak-thick neck and expansive shoulders cut a very imposing figure. His handsome milk chocolate face seemed darker, highlighted by a sleek white suit. He wore a royal blue, banded collar shirt with the top three buttons open, revealing an enormous one-half inch thick solid gold chain. A lesser man wearing the chain would have been in a constant stance of prayer. On his finger was the jewel-studded World Series ring and in his left ear was a huge, perfectly cut canary diamond. By merely walking to his table Richie Johnson captured the room's attention. Barry Lewis looked at the chain, then feebly touched his neck. Steve Bennett's focus was on the World Series ring. Greg Barrett saw the shirt and closed his eyes, lowering his head into his hands. Alison and Kim Bennett stared at his ear, then at their own ring fingers. Robin Lewis looked askance at her husband, then leered straight at Richie Johnson's crotch and said in a low voice, "His nickname is 'Big Dick.'"

The Maitre d' seated the couple, kissing Richie Johnson on both cheeks. Richie Johnson's date offered her hand. The Maitre d' bowed to kiss it.

"Obrigado, Carlo," she said in a sultry voice.

"Jenada, jenada," the Maitre d' answered while backing up. Suddenly he stood upright and snapped his fingers. The complete wait staff of San Mano swooped down on the table, pouring water, lighting candles, opening champagne bottles and bringing baskets of bread and olive oil. Two or three minutes elapsed before a pure vision of white emerged from the kitchen. Right before their eyes was Chef Norman himself, bringing over a special plate of samplers. Richie Johnson stood up and opened his arms. As the two men exchanged kisses on the cheek and embraced, the restaurant, in unison, started clapping. As they witnessed the scene, Alison and the Bennetts exchanged knowing smiles. Barry Lewis dreamed of the day he would command that kind of respect in a four-star restaurant while Robin Lewis pondered the wondrous things in store for Richie Johnson's date. Greg Barrett was getting sick to his stomach. His head pounded from hunger and the unrelenting soundtrack. It was almost midnight and he was ready to explode. His eyes commenced a futile search for the long lost Horst. An eternity passed before he reappeared, presenting the table a check for nine-hundred seventy-six dollars and forty- three cents. When Greg saw the amount he gagged, sending the water he was sipping up his nose. He started to say something but bit his lip. At least the bill had a seventeen-and-a-half percent tip tacked on.

On the way out Barry Lewis grabbed his arm. "Greggo," he whispered, "You have got to introduce me to Richie Johnson."

"Sorry. I don't know Richie Johnson. I've never been introduced to Richie Johnson."

"Hey," Barry Lewis replied. "Tell him you're Harry Hvide's main man and see if you can slip him my card."

Greg took the business card, not believing what he'd been asked to do. "Sure, Barry," he answered. "I'll see what I can do. But not here." He shook free from the lawyer's grasp, then told the others, "I'll see about the car."

Greg exited the restaurant-hotel and searched in vain for anyone in a white epauletted shirt. The street scene, as Barry Lewis predicted, was in total frenzy. The traffic, noise and energy level had all increased tenfold since they arrived. After fifteen minutes elapsed he finally got hold of a valet, handing him his parking stub. As Greg waited it started to rain. Perfect. His head was pounding. He was starving. And he was standing in the rain waiting for a car that was probably halfway to Venezuela, out on the street in the middle of a goddamned freak show. Another fifteen minutes elapsed before the Suburban appeared, triple parked in front of the hotel. His group emerged, scurrying into the car. The valet opened Greg's door and said "That will be thirty dollars, sir."

Happy to see his car and be on his way home, Greg didn't say a word, handing the man a twenty and a ten.

"That's just for the parking, sir. It doesn't include the gratuity."

"No problem," Greg answered. He reached into his pocket and handed him Barry Lewis' card.

Relieved to be in the safety of his own car, Greg realized he wasn't completely out of harm's way. Traffic was totally gridlocked and they were at a complete standstill. Greg contemplated calling for the company helicopter when Alison came to the rescue.

"Make the next right you can," she ordered.

"Any special street number?" Greg asked.

"It doesn't matter. The next right you can."

Greg inched along until he got to a corner and turned, following his wife's instructions.

"Keep going," she said. "I'll tell you when to turn."

While still going slowly, at least they were moving. When Alison saw the street sign "Washington Avenue" she ordered Greg to make a right. At first they were stuck in gridlock again, but the traffic eased as they passed a club called "Bash." Long lines waited outside to get in. The traffic congested again a block later as they passed the club "Chaos." Two minutes later they were moving again. As they passed another club, "Twist," they gawked at the exclusively male clientele patronizing it. As they reached Eleventh Street Alison commanded, "Make a left."

Greg followed her directions and they were soon traveling at normal speed. Kim Bennett was the first to speak. "Alison, you must be living a secret life you're not telling us about. How do you know your way around South Beach?"

"There," she said, pointing out the passenger side window. As everyone looked to their right they could make out banks of tennis courts through the darkness.

"Flamingo Park," she continued. "Nineteen seventy-six Orange Bowl. I lost in the quarterfinals to Marise Kruger of South Africa. Seven-five in the third set. She went on to win the whole thing."

Greg was constantly amazed by his wife's ability to recall the scores of her tennis matches from over twenty years ago. He wasn't knocking it; in fact, he was praying she would continue. "If there's a God in Heaven," he said to himself, "they'll talk tennis until we're home."

"Back then," Alison went on, "there was no Bollitieri's, no Evert-Seguso, no Macci's Academy. All the top juniors in South Florida came out of either the Monastery in North Miami Beach, Flamingo Park, or Holiday Park where I played in Fort Lauderdale. Bollitieri started as an assistant pro at the Monastery."

"Didn't Chrissie's father work out of Holiday Park?" asked Robin Lewis.

"He still does," retorted Alison. He was my very first pro. He's retiring this May."

Greg turned onto Alton Road. He drove back over the causeway, never so grateful to see the sign for I-95 North. The girls conversed about the upcoming Lipton Tournament while Barry Lewis engaged Steve Bennett in talk about other lawyers, firms, and where to get the best deals on silk ties. As he drove it really began to pour.

"I can't ever remember it raining so much in the dry season," commented Steve Bennett.

Greg spoke for the first time since leaving South Beach. "Must be El Nino."

By the time they reached home it was almost two o'clock AM. Greg and Alison said their good-byes to the Bennetts and Lewises. Despite being soaking wet and having a pounding headache Greg was overpoweringly hungry. He mentioned to Alison, "Lester's is still open. You feel like a burger?"

Tension between them had been building all evening. Anxious and hungry herself, though she would never admit it, Alison let go.

"We just ate at one of the finest restaurants in the world and now you want to go to Lester's All Night Diner for a cheeseburger? I don't believe it. Sometimes you act like you never got off Harry Hvide's garbage truck. I swear, you'd rather be back in Bridgeport, Connecticut."

Alison had touched a raw nerve. He hated when she condescendingly referred to his hometown. Repudiating his upbringing was the same to Greg as disparaging his parents and all the hard work and sacrifices they made for him. With memories of his mother and father raging through his head it was his turn to explode.

"Take a look around. Take a good look. This house, the boat, the cars, the pool, your jewelry all come from my working for Harry Hvide. And I'm goddamned proud I started on a garbage truck! It's hard, honest work! Or maybe you'd prefer I was a shyster like Barry Lewis, or a glorified bagman like Steve Bennett?? You're right about one thing! I'd feel a helluva lot more comfortable back in Bridgeport than eating fig-coated free range swordfish over passion fruit seaweed in a fucking hotel lobby!!"

Alison ran upstairs crying. Greg stood shaking. He hadn't raised his voice to her more than two or three times in their entire marriage and he never talked to her before in this tone. He rarely used the "F" word and never in her presence. He needed to cool down. He needed something to eat. He made the short drive over to Lester's on Route eighty-four. He took a seat at the counter and wolfed down a Lesterburger and fries. He nursed a cup of coffee for over an hour. By the time he returned home it was almost four o'clock AM and Alison had long been asleep. Just as well. Greg Barrett still needed some space.

They spent the weekend staying out of each other's way. On Saturday Greg forsook going into the office, instead taking the kids to the movies and out for pizza. They also stopped and picked up a birthday present for Bobby Sellers. On Sunday morning when Alison returned from her Sunday morning tennis match, Greg and Harley were on their way out.

"Where are you going?" she asked.

"To Westlake Park."

"What for?"

"Bobby Sellers' birthday party."

"You're taking him to that?"

"He wants to go. It's his friend. He said he would go."

"Fine. Kristin and I are going to the mall."

Relieved to be out of the house, Greg drove his son to Westlake Park in Hollywood. They parked and walked down to the boat ramp. As they looked around they saw Bobby Sellers' mom.

"Harley, over here!"

Jody Sellers waved them over to where a small group had gathered.

"Happy birthday, Bobby," shouted Harley.

"Yes, happy birthday," echoed his father.

"Thanks, Mr. Barrett. C'mon, Harley, come see the canoes."

The boys joined four other children on a dock at the water's edge. Jody Sellers smiled at Greg and said, "Thanks for coming."

"Glad to be here."

"They're bringing down life jackets for the kids. Would you like to canoe? If not, other parents, my relatives and some of my neighbors are under Pavilion Two."

"If you don't mind, I'd prefer canoeing. It's been a while."

"Of course not. I'll be right back."

Jody Sellers walked to the office to arrange an adult life jacket for him. She wore a yellow sleeveless blouse and tight-fitting jeans. As she walked away Greg couldn't help notice how different she looked out of hospital scrubs. She filled out those jeans very nicely. She returned with the life jacket and they split up into three different canoes. A map gave them different options and they followed one trail through the mangroves and down the estuaries. The weather cooperated, yielding a postcard-perfect South Florida day with a shining sun in a cloudless sky. The canoeing proved to be more fun than he had anticipated. They observed graceful egrets standing in the shallows. The water was full of tarpon and turtles. Occasionally a stingray would swim by. A pelican decided to keep them company, flying overhead, then resting intermittently in the mangroves. An hour later they were back at the dock. As they walked to the pavilion Jody Sellers said, "I hope you're hungry. We brought plenty of food."

"Didn't you see me try and whack that pelican with my paddle? He started to look pretty tasty."

She smiled. As they walked she said to him in a low voice. "Thanks again for bringing Harley. He's the only one here from school. It means a lot…"

"Hey," Greg interrupted, "we're both having a super time. They're the ones missing out. Let's have some fun."

The pavilion was buzzing with activity. While they were out canoeing Jody's mother and sister decorated the place with streamers and a large lettered "Happy Birthday Bobby" sign strewn over the entrance. Off in a corner a couple of guys were busy on the grill while downing some brews. There were a good number of adults, mostly relatives and neighbors milling about, all with big smiles. The kids happily played on the jungle gym nearby. Country music station ninety-nine point nine KISS FM twanged out Trisha Yearwood from a portable boom box. The tables had baskets brimming with popcorn, pretzels, and potato chips. Delicious hot dogs, burgers, and sausages were served hot off the grill along with homemade baked beans, potato salad, and cole slaw. Coolers brimmed with ice cold beers and soft drinks. The mood was festive. The kids were having a ball. Everyone he met seemed genuinely nice and no one, not a single person, asked him about Capital Industries. Greg admitted to himself that he felt very comfortable in this setting. This was a nice simple party for ten-year-olds in a public park and everyone was happy. Other parties for kids in Harley's grade rivaled Broadway productions. Parties were held on luxury yachts chartered solely for the occasion. One parent hired Raffi to perform a private concert. Not to be outdone, another had the Harlem Globetrotters play the Washington Generals in a backyard exhibition. Greg suddenly realized how ridiculous those parties were. They were not for the kids. They were for the parents. He looked at the face of his son who couldn't be happier. He was ten years old. He didn't need Raffi or a fancy boat ride to have a good time.

Bobby's grandmother introduced herself and took Greg aside. "I want to thank you for bringing your boy today. He's the only one who came from that school. You would not believe how hard my daughter works to put my grandson there. I know it's a good school and all. I just hope it's worth it in other ways." She looked away a few seconds then back at Greg. "I know we're not the same kind of people. I just hate to think of Bobby as an outcast."

Touched, Greg took the woman's hand. "Your grandson is a wonderful boy. It's an honor to say he's a friend of my son."

"You know, Harry Hvide has real good judgment in the people he chooses. I can see why he's so successful."

She walked away smiling. After singing "Happy Birthday" and cutting the cake, Bobby began opening his presents His smile widened as he opened each new package. He was most elated when one package contained a Nintendo Game Boy with a Super Mario II cartridge. He read the card and shouted, "Look, it's from Dad!"

Standing near the cooler, having a beer, Greg overheard Jody and her sister.

"So you're Dad again. When are you going to stop covering for that piece of shit?"

"It doesn't matter," Jody retorted. "It would be a lot worse if Bobby felt his own father didn't care enough to remember his birthday."

Greg was stunned. None of the divorced couples he knew would ever put the welfare of their children above their animosity. She certainly wasn't represented by Barry Lewis.

As the party wound down Greg gathered up Harley, who pleaded, "Dad, do we have to go so early?"

They wished Bobby a happy birthday good-bye and thanked Jody Sellers again for inviting them. As they walked to the parking lot she ran after them. "Hey, I almost forgot to thank you. Your Tony Lampone is quite a character!"

She pointed out a shiny white Ford Taurus GL with blue vinyl interior. "It's so nice and drives so well I can't believe it's mine."

"I hope he gave you a good deal."

"Good deal? He took my clunker in trade and practically paid me. He made the payments really low. The whole process was really painless. I can't thank you enough."

"Don't thank me. I didn't do anything. Thank you for the business. I'm glad you're satisfied."

"Well, thanks anyway even for nothing. Are you going to the game on Thursday?"

"I don't know yet. I'm going to try."

"Well, hope to see you there. Bye."

Greg Barrett was at his desk sharply at seven o'clock AM Monday morning. By noon he knew everything there was to know about Richie Johnson. What he didn't know was a legal way to get rid of him. He pored over item after item. He looked at security reports, insurance policies, and examined his contract word by word. Richie Johnson's agent knew what he was doing. Richie Johnson had an iron-clad contract. Even if he died the payments would go to his estate. Since the contract was fully insured at least the payments wouldn't come out of Harry's pocket. Greg paused to answer the phone.

"Yes, Martha."

"You have Mr. Roy on line two."

"Thanks. I'll take it."

"Hello, Greg Barrett speaking."

"Of course. How can I help you?"

"Lou said you were looking at the Richie Johnson situation. I was wondering if you had anything."

"Nothing concrete. Why?"

"By chance, you didn't listen to WQAM this morning?"

"Sorry, I don't listen to sports talk all that much. What's up?"

"We traded Oliva to Houston for three minor league prospects and we're really catching it from the fans. If we could come to some conclusion with Richie Johnson I think we could stabilize this thing, stop the bleeding, and move on."

"I wish I had something for you. Do you have anything new?"

"Nada. The market for him is below freezing. I get a security report from Stu Klein every few days. That's all."

"Can you keep sending me copies?"

"No problem... What?... Please hold one second."

Greg stayed on the line. He could hear Frank Roy engaged in a heated conversation with someone in his office. "Here's a flash for you, Greg," Frank Roy continued, "Richie Johnson just reported to spring training claiming he has stress fractures in his back."

Richie Johnson watched his agent give a short statement to the media, then refuse to take any questions. If he didn't talk to the press then neither should his Jew agent.

The media did nothing but disrespect him his whole career, and they weren't the only ones. Teammates, opponents, cops, women, management... they never gave him his due. They labeled him greedy an selfish but what did they know? To Richie Johnson it was never about money, it was all a matter of respect.

It was that way from the beginning. When he started his Major League career in Detroit as a teenager nobody cut him any slack. A native Floridian his entire life and they expected him to play in cold weather! The sting from the bat would go right to his toes if he got a fastball on the handle. He couldn't feel the ball in his hand when he threw to first base and still the manager, fans, and media dogged him about errors. He hated Detroit and had to get out. At least if they were going to keep him against his will they should show him some respect and compensate him properly. He didn't give a damn about limited salaries the first two years. He didn't sign the collective bargaining agreement. If they were going to make him play in Detroit then two hundred thousand a year wasn't gonna cut it. Two million a year was more like it. That would show some respect. See, it was never about money.

When they wouldn't pay him... no problem. Richie started making errors purposely, throwing the ball in the stands. Maybe then they would get the message. Not the media, however. The media never got the message. At first he thought it was only the Detroit Press. They couldn't handle his honesty. He resembled Howard Cosell and told it "just the way it is." If his teammates sucked and his manager had no brains he let the public know about it. If Detroit was a cold and dirty place and he didn't want to be there, why keep it a secret? The beat writers would ask him why he didn't want to be a great baseball town with a great, historic tradition? Hey, Ty Cobb, Al Kaline, Jim Bunning and Frank Larry meant nothing to him. They all played before he was born and were probably dead by now.

Then the press made a big deal about his name. He told them again and again to call him Richard or Dick but never, never call him Richie. Richie was that geeky white boy in Happy Days. So what did the wise asses in the media do? Did they show him any respect? No! They kept calling him Richie. One smart aleck started calling him Dick "Don't call me Richie" Johnson. Another skinny little Jew reporter for the Detroit Free Press nicknamed him "Big Dick Johnson" and called it a triple redundancy. He got even with that pencil dick by dumping a bucket of ice water over his head in the clubhouse. Richard Johnson knew how to earn respect.

And then there were the ladies. Women were just like those pricks in the media. They didn't give him any respect. Here he was rich, handsome, talented, and the best-endowed man in baseball and some ladies still showed him disrespect. Some ho would look at him naked, stare at his privates and say, "Where do you think that's gonna fit?"

Now others treated him right. His favorite bitch in Marina Del Rey told him he didn't need a bat when he stepped up to the plate.

Women always wanted something from him. Wasn't it enough to be wined and dined and get to do the nasty with a rich, handsome superstar? And none of these stupid bitches ever heard of birth control. He couldn't ride with a lady in a car anymore without her claiming to be pregnant. He took more paternity tests than Eddie Murphy had pedicures. He shaved his head thinking he could avoid giving hair samples but that didn't quite work out. Every major league city had some ho claiming he was the father of her baby. And all of them had Jew lawyers taking him to court for child support. Ten thousand dollars a month here, thirteen thousand a month there, pretty soon you're talking about some serious money.

He thought everything would be better in San Diego—West Coast, Hollywood, the weather, etc., etc. He soon discovered San Diego was no L.A. Nothing there but retired Navy dudes and wetbacks. The press? Same as Detroit. They didn't show him any respect. They jumped on his case when he sat out a few games or would ask out of a game in the middle of an inning. They didn't understand. To play baseball you had to be in sync with both your physicality and your mentality. Otherwise you were cheating the fans. Those writers never played the game. They didn't get it. They didn't know about flying from city to city and living in hotels. If he didn't have the balls to stand up for what's fair and decent his team would still be staying in Hiltons and Marriotts instead of Ritz Carltons.

Definitely, the media turned the fans against him. They started by making a big story about a few traffic tickets. Some big story! Hey, he tried explaining. Abiding by the speed limit wouldn't even get his Porsche 961 out of second gear. Driving like that only gunked up the engine. He didn't mean to speed. He was simply trying to burn some carbon off the heads. So what does the headline read? "Johnson Ticketed at 131 MPH, Claims He Was Tuning up Porsche."

It just proved San Diego was small time. In L.A. all the movie stars and big time athletes skated free as soon as they were recognized. And if you weren't supposed to go fast, why did the speedometer go up to two hundred forty MPH?

The fans really climbed on his case after he wanted to adjust his new five-year, twenty five million dollar contract. Hey, he almost hit for the triple crown. Why should he be stuck with a below-market contract for three more years? It wasn't his fault the market changed. He only wanted his market value. That and some respect. It wasn't about money... simply a matter of respect.

The media poisoned the fans against him, calling him greedy and selfish. Every week a new story came out depicting him as the poster child for rich, spoiled athletes. They blew way out of proportion the little incident with his manager. He couldn't understand all the commotion over ignoring the bunt signal and the runner getting thrown out. How many times did Hank Aaron or Reggie Jackson get the sign to bunt? The manager was disrespecting his talent and he was ecstatic about the trade to Florida.

Florida was home. Hot and humid weather—good hitting weather. Miami wasn't St. Pete but St. Pete didn't have South Beach or the Grove. Funny, though, wherever he went, the media was always the same. They dogged him from city to city and showed him no respect. Same old, same old. Stories about traffic violations, bar altercations, and paternity disputes received far more print than what he did on the field. Weren't they supposed to be sports reporters? Like Detroit, like San Diego, they turned the fans against him. Sports radio had two topics: fire Don Shula or diss Richard Johnson. Richard Johnson was an honest man and they couldn't handle that. So what if the Manatees were an expansion team! The owner had billions of dollars. He owed it to the fans to surround him with some real players. All he had to do was charge an extra buck or two for video rentals. When he voiced his opinion both the fans and media jumped all over him. They said if you're gonna talk the talk then walk the walk. They didn't get it. How could he possibly put up Ken Griffey Jr. or Frank Thomas' numbers with no protection in the lineup or base runners to drive in? You had to judge someone's stats by the players around him He doubted Griffey or Thomas would do any better in his situation. Two seasons ago without any help he hit forty homers with one hundred nineteen RBIs while batting .321.

Then this past season management finally listens, goes out and spends a little money, acquires some players and they win the World Series. How can you put a price on that? Before the season they finally gave Richard Johnson what he deserved, a sixty-six million dollar, six year contract. They finally demonstrated a measure of respect. Big deal if his statistics were half the previous year. They were World Series Champions. Richard Johnson was all about winning.

Then this whole off-season management threatens to strip down the team and cut payroll. What was he supposed to do? Feel sorry for a billionaire?

When they made such a big deal about his contract, Richard Johnson did his best to sacrifice and help out. He had his agent meet with Harry Hvide himself and offer to redo his deal and backload the contract. He would defer some money at only prime plus eight. His agent said it was worth making the offer if only to see a billionaire roll on the floor laughing. Now that was some serious disrespect!

He caught more flak when he failed to show up for the trip to Washington, D.C., and the team picture with the President. Hey, if they couldn't guarantee him a little private time with an intern, why bother? Now every day in the papers and on the radio they speculated as to who the Manatees were going to dump and what to do with Richard Johnson? As far as he was concerned, they could just pay him and like it. He would gladly stay home and they could direct deposit his check. He might even offer a discount if they made one lump sum payment. If he said he had stress fractures in his back, let them prove he didn't. And one more thing—those geniuses in management seemed to forget; a little caveat in his contract called a no-trade clause. For him to waive it, Harry Hvide would have to pay through the nose and kiss his ass. See, it was all about respect. It was never about the money.

6

Spring training for the Manatees began under an ominous cloud. Tension ran high as the players were on pins and needles, uncertain about their futures. The married players with families had it especially tough. Wives worried about new schools, new homes and new cities. No matter how often you changed teams relocation was always a nightmare. Many liked living in South Florida. Fishing was excellent and golf was available year-round. The Latin players, in particular, felt at home. The newspapers speculated daily on who was staying and who was going. The players cast furtive glances at each other, no one looking anyone else in the eye. Paddy McGraw sensed his teams' mood and knew everyone was on edge. In a way he felt cheated. Only one team came to spring training with the opportunity to defend its championship. Scuttlebutt had his team splitting up. Who goes and who stays hinged on the fate of one player. The center of attention focused directly on Richie Johnson.

Unsettled best described the atmosphere around the executive offices of Capital Industries. For the last few days Harry Hvide hadn't been himself. Instead of his usual energetic, optimistic persona, his moods would swing from detachment to anger. Greg Barrett had never seen Harry act like this before. The baseball mess proved to be a bigger distraction than he previously thought and had Harry off his "A" game. Today he directed his anger toward First Securities. Their analysts were projecting labor trouble at General Motors, possibly a prolonged strike upcoming in the summer. Capital Industries auto division depended on a steady flow of cars and GM was a key supplier. They worried about the timing of the IPO. Any gains from splitting off the service businesses might be potentially offset by losses in the auto division. The First Securities people urged caution and recommended delaying the IPO until the GM labor situation stabilized. Harry had a much different take. GM was an important supplier but they still represented a relatively small percentage of Capital's inventory. Harry felt it would show strength that even if General Motors went on strike, Capital's overall sales and profits would hold up. Harry had other reasons for pushing ahead, but he kept those to himself. Even Greg and Dave Roberts were left in the dark. Harry didn't like delays and announced "There's more than one Investment Banker on the street."

Lacking insight into Harry's private thoughts Greg sided with First Securities. One thing he learned about the stock market. On Wall Street, appearance was reality. Sure, there were plenty of other underwriters, but changing from First Securities now might set off caution alarms and red flags among the brokerage house stock watchers and independent analysts. Greg felt changing underwriters would divert attention from the strengths of the company to questions about what happened to First Securities. Instead of a blockbuster IPO, rumors and innuendo might trigger a lukewarm reception. And it wasn't like First Securities didn't want the business or didn't think it would be successful. They simply wanted to wait seven or eight weeks, three months at most. When Greg tried discussing his views with Harry Hvide he wanted to know what was happening with the Manatees. Great! They had a multi-billion dollar offering up in the air and the principal's center of attention focused squarely on goddamned Richie Johnson.

With the defending World Series Champions and a business empire asking the same question—"What are we going to do about Richie Johnson?"—fate, in the name of Lashonda Jones, materialized out of nowhere and nearly provided a solution. Lashonda Jones of St. Petersburg, Florida, was the mother of Richie Johnson's first child, Richard Johnson, Jr. Unfortunately, Richie, Jr., was born while his daddy was still a fledgling major leaguer. The child support payments he could afford were not enough to keep his son's mother off of welfare. As Richie Johnson's career blossomed and his earnings increased, Lashonda persisted in dragging him back to court for higher support payments. She would do this about every other month. It proved to be a successful strategy. What started out at twelve hundred dollars per month multiplied five-fold to approximately six thousand dollars. It was a good thing to, because Lashonda had expenses. Her new townhouse in the better neighborhood needed to be furnished. Her son needed to follow his daddy's career and even the small dishes cost money. Installation was another expense. Lashonda had a hard enough time figuring out how to operate her fifty-one inch Panasonic Universal remote surround sound split screen digital convergence TV. A new car eliminated all those auto repair bills. Plus, Lashonda wanted to go back to school, necessitating child care, a makeover, and a new wardrobe. Lashonda also had to worry about her other two kids and their fathers were worthless deadbeats. Between them they couldn't chip in to pay her cell phone bill. Richie, Sr., was definitely the most reliable as well as her only source of income. The problem was it increasingly became harder to squeeze any more out of him. The last time she went back to family court an army of Richie's lawyers greeted her. They demanded receipts and affidavits and copies of her bills. They wanted a detailed breakdown of how much of Richie, Jr.'s, support payments went toward his siblings. They even threatened a custody battle. What a joke that was! Lashonda named her son Richard Johnson, Jr., so his daddy wouldn't forget his name. Lashonda settled for seventy-five hundred dollars a month but had to agree to never again come after Richie Johnson for any more money. That was it: seventy-five hundred a month until Richie, Jr., turned twenty-one, twenty-thousand dollars per year for a nanny, a five-million dollar life insurance policy naming Richie, Jr., as the beneficiary, and a trust fund dedicated to his college education. The ink on the agreement was barely dry when Richie signed a sixty-six million dollar contract. That no good motherfucker locked her into a chump change deal while he was taking down a cool eleven-million dollars a year! Worse yet, Lashonda found out Richie had four other kids and their mothers all got more than she did. Lashonda just happened to flip on the Panasonic and right there in her multimedia room on Jenny Jones were the mothers of superstar athletes' babies. Sitting between the mother of a Cleveland Cavalier forward's daughter and the mother of a New England Patriot running back's son were four tramps. One bore Richie's daughter, the others were the mothers of his sons, two of whom were named "Richard Johnson, Jr."

Jenny got them to reveal their support payments. They ranged from eighty-five hundred to fourteen thousand dollars a month. Lashonda Jones couldn't believe her eyes and ears. This was wrong! Her boy was the first Richard Johnson, Jr. Why should they have to beg for crumbs? Why was her son sent to the back of the line? Why all the heavy pressure from his big-time lawyers? Most importantly, why wasn't she invited on the show? Fortunately, she watched her favorite program on the Panasonic that night—the Home Shopping Channel. That was right where you wanted to be when there's so much negativity in your life; sitting in front of the Panasonic with a portable phone and a credit card. It was simply extra lucky Ivana Trump was on. Girlfriend Ivana not only let her know about the great buy on the cubic zirconia brooch, she also gave her life-changing advice. Just goes to show there were other sources of righteous information besides Oprah and Dr. Laura.

For good advice, Ivana was the truth. She said right there on the HSC, "Don't get mad, get everything." Now there was a philosophy to live by.

With Ivana's words ringing in her ears, Lashonda thought out a brilliant plan. If she couldn't squeeze any more money out of Richie for Richie, Jr., Lashonda would simply have to have another of his babies. Even if the courts awarded her only another twelve thousand five hundred dollars, twenty thousand a month tax free was livable. It was time to pay Richie Johnson a visit at spring training.

Lashonda gassed up her I30 for the three-hour drive to Vero Beach site of the Manatees' spring training camp. On the way she mentally thanked her friend Chuck Norris for letting her know about Total Gym. No wonder he looked so buff on Walker, Texas Ranger. She also thanked her gilrfriend Victoria Principal for the fabulous skin care products and makeup. Lashonda Jones was looking good and feeling fine. For extra good luck she wore Ivana's brooch, which was considerately sent to her next day air for only an additional fifty dollar shipping and handling charge.

Once at camp, Lashonda discovered it wasn't so easy getting Richie's attention. The players were split all over the field involved in different activities. Some flagged fly balls while others took grounders. Pitchers leisurely threw back and forth to each other, joking the whole time. Richie was the only one not wearing a practice uniform. Instead he had on a grey sweatsuit and was off to the side accompanied by a trainer. He lay on his back while the trainer stretched out his legs toward his head one at a time. After stretching he went into some kind of a meditational trance. He was oblivious to the coterie of fans calling out to him. Among then were some very hot and very young babes, anxious to make his acquaintance. Lashonda had some serious competition. But they were all rookies. She had been to spring training before and knew what she was doing. She took up residence as close as she could to the batting cage. From past experience she knew eventually all the players would congregate there. Even if Richie didn't hit he would hang out and articulate with the guys. Lashonda camped out in a prime location. Her foresight and experience paid off and before long she stood only a few feet away from Richie Johnson.

"Riichaard, c'mon over heere," she said in her most seductive voice. Sure enough, she caught his attention. As he strolled over she flashed him her biggest smile, the sun reflecting sublimely off her one front gold tooth. Richie returned the smile, his eyes admiring the fine looking lady with the brick house body. As he walked toward her he suddenly slowed to get a closer look. She looked familiar, but was styling way too fine to be who he thought.

"Good to see you, Riichaard," she called out.

Recognizing the voice, Richie said, "It's you." He then retreated and started running away as if she were a process server.

"Yo, Richie," she yelled. "It's Lashonda. Don't you be running from me! Get your black ass back here right now!!"

At the rate it vacated the premises it didn't appear Richie's ass would be making a return engagement any time soon. He left the field in a flash. This was not part of the script and Lashonda's anger increased by the minute. With felonious thoughts sifting through her mind she touched her new brooch. "Think, girl," she whispered to herself. "Don't get mad. Get everything." She would have to send Ivana a personal e-mail when she returned home.

Lashonda called to the bullpen for a new pitcher. It was time for the closer to implement plan B. She took out her Mont Blanc pen and wrote a suggestive little note to her Richie. Before having it delivered by a security guard she scented it with a dash of Diana Von Furstenberg's "Tatiana." A few minutes later the guard returned and Lashonda was set. She had a date to meet Richie at Friday's in an hour. Diana deserved a "thank you" e-mail too. She wondered how people ever survived without the Home Shopping Channel.

Three Kahluas, a glass of chablis and a Courvoisier later, the "in lust" couple checked in to the nearby La Quinta. Richie wasn't big on foreplay which was fine with her. They both undressed quickly. Lashonda couldn't help but stare at him. He was still bigger than a first-place zucchini at the county fair. He pressed on her shoulders until she was on her knees. That was okay. She didn't mind licking it a little, especially since he didn't insist on a condom. She'd get him all hot and bothered, then let him slide right in. She could feel him pulsating but when she tried to stop he took two fistfuls of her hair and held her head down, now allowing her up. No way would she let him finish like this. Using her teeth she bit down with just enough force to make him pull out.

"Yeowww!"

"Sorry, baby. Mama didn't mean to hurt you. C'mon over here."

Lashonda gave Richie a big kiss and went over to the bed, lying down on her back. Richie followed, but instead of getting on top he forcefully turned her on her stomach, put his knees between her legs and attempted to enter her from the back.

"WHERE DO YOU THINK YOU'RE GOING?" she screamed at the top of her lungs.

"Shhh, baby. It feels so good."

Her painful cries didn't make him stop. Instead he muffled them with a pillow. When he finished and got off her, Richie Johnson had to fight for his life. Lashonda first tried to scratch his eyes out then proceeded to throw everything at him she could find, including Gideon's Bible. Richie did his best to calm her down. "Chill, Sweet Thing, Sweet Thing, chill out. It's not my bad. It's not my bad. It's my agent's fault."

"What are you talking about?" she shouted.

"I'm telling you it's my agent. He told me to do it that way. He said it be an effectual method of birth control."

A bitterly resentful Lashonda Jones made the long, lonely drive back to St. Petersburg. Her jaw ached. Her butt hurt like hell. Despite her careful, meticulous planning her scheme had gone somewhat awry. As she drove she felt her new cubic zirconia brooch on her sweater. Infuriated, she ripped it off and threw it out the window.

"Fuck Ivana Trump!" she yelled to no one. She was nothin' but a big-haired phony blonde, fake-titted, funny-talking bitch who knew nothin' about nothin'. From now on Lashonda Jones was listening to no one but her own self! She had her own new philosophy—"Get mad and still get everything!"

Foiled in her attempt to have another of Richie Johnson's babies, Lashonda decided to go instead for the five million dollar life insurance policy. All Richie had to do was die and Richie, Jr., collected five million tax-free dollars. The money went into a trust but she would be the administrator. And the five mil was just front money. As first born, her son was probably entitled to a big chunk of his daddy's estate as well. Her plan was so simple, so foolproof, she pinched herself for not thinking of it sooner.

She went down to the Omaha Steaks in the strip mall and charged a carton of their finest filets on her MasterCard. Richie absolutely loved filet mignon. She brought them home and carefully cut out the centers and filled them with strychnine. She put back the cut-out parts and refroze them. The big jerk would never tell the difference. Next, she went to the nearest "Mailboxes Plus" and sent the package to his home address.

It was a fine plan and probably would have succeeded but for one small problem. Richie had stopped eating red meat. On a major health kick, his regimented new diet eliminated sugars, starches, and red meat. He left spring training for a couple of days and was home to sign for the package. Delighted some thoughtful fan had sent him the steaks, he hated to see them go to waste. He defrosted the steaks and fed them to his two pet bull mastiffs, Tyson and Holyfield. The dogs quickly devoured two filets apiece, so Richie let them split another four. When Richie returned to the kitchen after a workout and a dip in the hot tub, both Tyson and Holyfield were stiff as statues, four paws to the skylight. The vet determined they were poisoned by something they ate, which led to the box of steaks. The police were summoned and it took the crack St. Petersburg department all of twenty minutes to clear the case. Lashonda used her townhouse as the return address on the package. The meat was purchased with her credit card and both the salesperson at Omaha Steaks and the clerk at Mailboxes Plus remembered her. Lashonda was up to her Susan Graver-scarved neck in trouble. At least Richie refused to testify. Probably worried about getting stuck with custody if she went to jail, Richie Johnson didn't say a word.

A forlorn Lashonda Jones sat in front of her fifty-one inch surround sound Panasonic. She feverishly clicked her remote back and forth, from the Home Shopping Channel to QVC. She couldn't find it anywhere. No one had it. Not even that old skanky Joan Rivers was pushing it. Nobody but nobody sold a designer chain to cover up her ankle monitor, which gave Lashonda an idea…

7

One week later fate once again came close to rectifying the Richie Johnson situation. The Manatees were returning from an exhibition game in Port St. Lucie where they played the Mets. With all the commotion about the pending salary reductions and trade talk the team had a hard time concentrating on baseball. They just lost their fourth straight game. This time the score was fourteen to three. Paddy McGraw was deeply concerned because the team actually played wore than the score indicated. They made four errors, missed signs, threw past cutoff men and couldn't execute a routine double play. Richie Johnson got his first two at bats of the pre-season and didn't hit a foul ball. He struck out twice on six pitches. The pitchers couldn't find the plate, walking eight batters. In the dugout there were several near fights as the players were at each other's throats and blaming everybody but themselves for the poor play. Things appeared to settle down a little once the players were back on the bus. Everyone took a seat and immediately put on their headphones and turned on their Sony Discmans. Listening to their individual choices in music isolated them from each other and the unsettled atmosphere around them.

Everything was fine until Richie Johnson, in tune with the contemporary genius Puff Daddy Combs, felt compelled to share Puff Daddy's sagacity with his teammates. Richie went off headphones onto speakers and blasted Puff Daddy's sage lyrics throughout the bus:

Everyday I wake up
I hope I'm dreamin'
Can't believe this shit
Can't believe you ain't here
Sometimes it's just hard
For a niga to wake up.

Felix Escobar, who was minding his own business and mellowing out to the dulcet tones of Luis Miguel, became visibly upset at the intrusion into his privacy. Felix, a native of the Dominican Republic, was the team's shortstop and best young player. A hero of the World Series, Felix was only in his second year and didn't make enough money to be in danger of being traded. A very proud young man, Felix carried an air of dignity about him. He loved baseball and worked hard to improve. He was Paddy McGraw's kind of player because he kept his head in the game and let it all hang out on the field. Felix had a strong dislike for Richie Johnson bordering on contempt. The disturbance of his private sanctum by that *coma mierda* and his ghetto rap music was the law straw, especially while Luis Miguel was in the middle of crooning out "Estar Contigo."

Felix, who hardly spoke English, left his seat and walked over to Richie Johnson. He pointed to his ear, indicating it was too loud, and motioned with his hand for Richie to turn down the volume. Richie Johnson, however, had a strong conviction his teammates needed to hear Puff Daddy's message.

"Chill out, little homey," he said to Felix. Don't be messin' with Puffie when…"

Richie Johnson and Puff Daddy were both interrupted by Felix Escobar, who ripped the speaker jack out of Richie's Discman and smashed the speakers to the floor.

"*Yo adverti que lo recba saias to nicbe estupido.*" Felix told him, which roughly translates, "I warned you to turn it down, you stupid nigger."

It seemed rather curious that Felix chose the "N" word, since he was several shades darker than Richie Johnson himself. That didn't cut any slack with Richie, who despite not speaking Spanish, knew the important words and nobody but nobody got away with calling him a nigger! Besides, the little spic owed him for the speakers. Richie stood up right in Felix's face and shouted, "Listen Greaseball, don't be talkin' to me like that or I'll rip out your fucking tongue!"

The incident now had everyone's attention. Thinking he could calm things down, Benny Benitez, the Manatees' first baseman, intervened. Nicknamed "the Sheriff" Bennie Benitez was a giant of a man and the team's unofficial leader. Of Puerto Rican descent, Benny spoke Spanish and was also Richie Johnson's closest friend on the team. He would attempt to diffuse the situation by talking some sense into the antagonists but brought along his bat in case he needed a different approach. He told Richie in English and Felix in Spanish to forget about it and shake hands; adding in Spanish to Felix it would be a nice gesture if he offered to reimburse Richie for the speakers. Felix, on the other

hand, felt Richie was challenging his machismo. He told Benny Benitez
in Spanish that he would not apologize nor would he give that *berehena* who made more in three games than he did for the whole season a fucking dime. The literal translation of *berehena* is eggplant, but
in the context of this conversation it was synonymous with the "N"
word. Felix also let Benny Benitez know he didn't appreciate his interference in a private matter. He also pointed out it was just like a dumb
Puerto Rican to bring a stick to a knife fight, at which point a click was
audible and Felix now brandished a ten-inch switchblade. Of all the
varying hostilities between ethnic groups, some of the lesser known is
the sheer animosity between different Hispanic cultures. Dominicans,
Cubans, and Puerto Ricans all distrust one another and think themselves superior to the other two.

Seeing the whole thing unravel, Camilo Estrada entered the fray.
Camilo defected from Cuba two years prior. He was a major contribu-
tor in both the League Championship Series and the World Series.
While he appreciated the freedom of speech in America not available
in the Communist country from which he emigrated, he hated to see
his teammates fight. He thought he could soothe the hard feelings and
lighten the mood. Camilo also appreciated the rights granted under his
adopted country's Fourth Amendment and, just in case, brought along
his pearl-handled .357 Magnum. Felix Escobar felt backed into a corner. He loathed all the interference in what he perceived as a private
matter between himself and Richie Johnson. He told Camilo Estrada
*"Note metas en logue no te imporante montea en el proxima barco du
vulte a Cuba!"* or to mind his own business and hop on the next raft
and float back to Cuba.

Richie Johnson wasn't all that comfortable either. In the middle of
three men jabbering in a language he didn't comprehend and all
armed to some degree. To be on the safe side he pulled out his fully-
loaded Heckler & Koch P7M8 gas operated 9mm pistol he carried at
all times.

At first merely an observer, Wyatt Black was getting real pissed off.
Born in Eufalia, Alabama, Wyatt Black was the Florida Manatees' star
pitcher and highest paid player after Richie Johnson. If Richie Johnson
could not be traded he was certain to be moved, and soon. He was one
of the guys on the team with a family and under a lot of pressure at
home. His one refuge was the ballpark, where he could forever be a
kid and just play the game. The serenity of his private world was in
shambles now. Plus all this shit happened in the middle of a Travis Trit
set. He assessed the situation and came to the conclusion if there were
going to be third world hostilities he would not be standing with only

his dick in his hand. He reached for the Colt 45 combat model he always kept handy.

Paddy McGraw realized he was in the middle of a tinderbox ready to go off at the slightest provocation. In the center of the bus he had angry and dangerous combatants in a five-way Mexican standoff. One misstep on anyone's part could have tragic consequences. One of the qualities separating the top managers in the game from the mediocre was the ability to think on your feet. Paddy was one of the best. Quickly he ran to the front of the bus, turned on the radio to EZ Listening 101.5 FM and played it out over the loudspeaker. The bus was inundated with

Tell me how am I supposed to live without you
Now that I've been lovin' you so long
How am I supposed to live without you
How am I supposed to carry on
When all that I've been livin' for is gone.

The players and coaches looked at each other with scrunched up noses. Some put their fingers down their throats. Others held their ears. Benny Benitez couldn't stand it any longer. He rushed to the front of the bus, took a full swing and knocked the radio right out of the console. An immediate round of cheers and high fives spread through the bus, diffusing the tense atmosphere. At least the Manatees could all unite in their opinion of Michael Bolton!

The bus driver, however, decided at that very moment to change occupations. With images of a huge man smashing the radio a foot from where he sat to smithereens, he made a sudden swerve to the right, pulled over to the shoulder and slammed on the brakes. He made a speedy exodus from the bus and began sprinting back to Port St. Lucie. The bus's abrupt stop caused the players to lurch out of their seats onto the floor and on top of one another. In the pandemonium somebody's gun discharged, missing Richie Johnson's head by centimeters.

Paddy McGraw took inventory. Seeing no one seriously hurt, he shrugged his shoulders, sat down in the driver's seat and, reliving his days in the Minors, drove the bus back to Vero Beach. The rest of the way his only thought was "They don't pay me enough."

By the time the bus reached Vero Beach word of some sort of incident had leaked out and the press was all over it. As the players showered and changed in the locker room, they were all swamped with questions. Davey Russo, the beat writer for the Miami Herald was the first to query Paddy McGraw. "Nothing happened," Paddy answered with a stolid, expressionless face. "We were having a team discussion on the literary merits of Chaucer."

When asked about it Felix Escobar replied, "Mein, that fuckeen chardo he got not respec for nobody."

Richie Johnson added, "That punk tried to punk me. You can't be punked by no punk. You got to be the one doin' the punkin'."

A puzzled Davey Russo turned to Paddy McGraw and asked, "What did they say?"

Without batting an eye or changing expressions Paddy McGraw answered as he walked away, "One quoted Hemingway. The other Keats."

8

Greg Barrett was having a tough week. He divided his time between the Capital Services IPO and the Richie Johnson situation. Neither was going smoothly. As far as the IPO went, Harry Hvide hadn't wavered. He still wanted to push ahead as soon as possible. First Securities was still questioning the timing. In addition to the General Motors labor trouble, their analysts were now predicting a major stock price correction before year's end, possibly as soon as the summer. They advised again to postpone until the market was on the uptick when new issues would get a more favorable response. The more Greg delved into it the more he agreed with their analysts. When he attempted to discuss his views Harry seemed disinterested. This was very uncharacteristic of him. One of Harry's strengths was his penchant for hearing contrasting opinions. He actually disdained "yes men" making for some lively boardroom discussions Usually his people felt free to speak their minds. Presently Harry wasn't much interested in what his people had to say. Unless it was news about baseball. Greg sensed Harry's increasingly angst with the whole ordeal.

Greg tried his best to provide Harry some relief. He went over and over the Richie Johnson file and came up with zilch. Already at his wit's end and he hadn't found a single loophole. Even if Richie Johnson was arrested holding five kilos of coke there wasn't a thing they could do about it. There were guys in the Majors with four or five similar violations. Whenever a question arose about a player's eligibility an arbitrator always sided with the player. All the player had to do was request treatment. Greg found this hard to believe. He checked it out with Dave Grabowsky, the team's assistant General Manager. Grabowsky simply shrugged his shoulders and told him at one time the Betty Ford Clinic fielded the best team in baseball. Frustrated, he was ready to call it a day and drive out to his son's soccer game when he received a call.

"Yes, Martha."

"It's Frank Roy with the Manatees. Line one."

"Thanks, Martha. Hi, Frank. What's up?"

"Listen, Greg. I don't want to build your hopes up, but I may have something cooking with Richie Johnson."

"That's great."

"Well, it's definitely not set in stone, but I'm making some progress. I felt you should know."

"Thanks. Keep me informed. And good luck."

Greg Barrett hung up the phone and walked to his car with a renewed bounce in his step. This was probably the best news he had in days. He tried not to get too excited. He knew from experience in countless negotiations these things broke down more often than not, but at least there was a glimmer of hope. By the time he parked the car his mood was upbeat. He spotted Jody Sellers. He waved, walked up three rows in the bleachers and sat down. "Hi, how are you?" he asked.

"Just fine. You look pretty chipper today. Did Harry Hvide buy the Atlantic Ocean?"

"No, but he's negotiating an option. How are we doing today?"

"Great. We actually scored two goals."

Greg looked closely at Jody Sellers. He stared into her beautiful green eyes and at her warm smile. The next hour seemingly disappeared in a millisecond. She was easy to talk to and very down to earth. They talked about things he never discussed with Alison. He felt relaxed and comfortable with her. Yet, there was an uneasy feeling too, right in the pit of his stomach.

The game ended and they left the bleachers to greet their kids. They all exchanged hellos, after which both boys in unison asked, "Can we go to McDonald's?"

Greg was about to say yes. He enjoyed every extra minute in Jody Sellers' company. Instead he answered his ringing cell phone. Frank Roy sounded frantic.

"I understand. I have to drop my son off. I'll call you at this number the second I get home. It'll be about fifteen minutes."

Greg turned toward the Sellers. "I'm sorry, Bobby. We'll have to take a rain check. C'mon, son. Something's come up. We'll try and do it next week."

Jody Sellers asked, "Something important?"

Greg gave a faint smile and spoke just louder than a whisper, "It's always something important."

Greg Barrett was a bad liar. Jody Sellers could tell by his body language and by the speed with which he left. Something very urgent had happened.

Greg drove home quickly and ushered his son into the house. He literally ran upstairs into his office and dialed up Frank Roy.

"Frank, it's Greg."

"Yah, Greg. First off, he's stable. He's in very good hands. I understand they're flying in the Mayo Clinic's top cardiologist. When they took him out, Eric Huntington told me to contact you and tell you it's a code-teal situation."

"I understand. Tell me what happened."

"I had it," Frank Roy lamented. "I really had it."

Greg could hear the anguish in his voice as Frank Roy continued. "It was a done deal. He and Benitez to San Francisco for Mueller, Sanford, Hiller, and Pagan. And I already had them off to Cleveland and St. Louis for prospects. A neat three-way trade meeting ninety-five percent of our salary projection. All we needed was for that big prick to waive his no-trade clause. His agent got back to us and said Richie would relinquish it for fifteen million dollars. Not a balloon payment. Not a salary acceleration. Fifteen million dollars additional! The agent said it was to compensate for California's state income tax and moving expenses. Richie told his agent the price was non-negotiable. He said that's what it costs to disrespect Richie Johnson, whatever that means. Lou and I couldn't make a call like that without Harry's okay. We drove to his office and brought him up to speed. When we told him about Richie's demand, his face went white. He was so mad he couldn't speak. He started to have palpitations and was real short of breath. We knew something was wrong immediately. He's at Doctor's Hospital."

"Who else knows?"

"As far as I know, just me, Lou, Helen and Eric Huntington's security team. I would imagine Betty's been notified. Probably Will as well. Grabowsky knows about the trade but that's all."

"Okay, listen, Frank. It's essential we keep a lid on this."

"You can count on it, Greg. You won't have to worry about Lou either."

"Is there anything we can do?"

"I'll let you know. Bye."

Greg Barrett hung up the phone, told his wife not to expect him and sprinted out of the house. Alison Lodge Barrett bit her bottom lip, suppressed her thoughts and said nothing. After all this time, she should have been immune to the indignity of being relegated to second place over anything concerning "business."

At first, it really bothered her. They were still in the honeymoon stage, barely married a year, when her husband left the security of corporate behemoth ICX for Harry Hvide's latest venture. She couldn't imagine any ten men combined working harder than Greg did in establishing Video Nation. For a five-year period, she couldn't remember a single time where, as a couple, they spent more than three days in a row together. Sometimes the feelings of loneliness were overwhelming. She confided in her mother. To her surprise, her mother was largely unsympathetic. Lodge women had a long history dating back to the Revolutionary War of standing by their men and offering resolute support. She advised her daughter to keep a stiff upper lip and tough it out. Besides, look how wildly successful Greg was! Alison couldn't ask for a better provider and it was obvious he was devoted to her. The time would come soon enough when Alison could enjoy the fruits of his labor.

So Alison Lodge Barrett found solace by spending with a vengeance. Sometimes she would flaunt her extravagance in his face hoping for a reprimand to slow down, a look of concern, any reaction at all. He never denied her. But all the Givenchy originals in the world couldn't compensate for her husband missing the birth of both her children.

Her other place of refuge was the tennis court. Alison loved the feel of the ball off a newly strung racquet when she punched a volley. She coveted stretching out in full stride and driving her two-fisted backhand deep into the corner. She hit with a pro four or five times a week. Always the same routine. Fifteen minutes of forehands, fifteen minutes for backhands. Ten minutes of mixing it up followed by twenty minutes of games where she usually held her own. She played in the 5.0 women's doubles league in Broward County, the highest level of competition, but preferred playing with men. Women tennis players were notorious bad callers. This past year, she resumed playing singles tournaments reaching a semifinal and a final in her first two 'U.S.T.A. 35 and over' events. To Alison, tennis was the perfect game. It required timing, speed, endurance, agility, good hand-eye coordination, and, most of all, mental tenacity to be successful. People of all different sizes and ages could participate. It was a game you could stay with your entire life. Too bad her husband wasn't a player.

One hobby they both shared an affinity for was fishing. She remembered when they first started dating. He was a novice at it but a willing and enthusiastic learner. Greg enjoyed the sun and salt air. He relished the whole experience of just being out on the water. He didn't mind getting up before dawn. He didn't get seasick. He never complained if they didn't catch anything nor did he have a problem releasing an occasional white marlin or sailfish. She showed him how to rig tackle and choose bait the same way her father showed her. Growing up, it seemed the only time her father noticed her was when they went fishing. None of her siblings shared her love of the sea. Saturday mornings was her time to spend exclusively with her father. They packed doughnuts and sandwiches and would set out while it was still dark, fishing to their hearts' content. She vividly remembered her first catch, a six and a half pound mutton snapper. Thinking back, the only times she could recall her father, the Judge, smiling was when they were fishing.

Part of a very generous wedding gift from Harry Hvide went to purchase their first boat, a nineteen foot single engine Mako. They went out almost every weekend at first, no matter what the sea conditions were. Some of their most productive days came when the seas were fearful and frightening. The Mako lacked virtually every creature comfort, yet they got more use out of it and had more fun on it than all the other boats they subsequently puchased. The Mako turned into a twenty-seven foot Phoenix which became a twelve meter Crusader which was upgraded into the forty-eight foot Hatteras now sitting idly on the dock behind the backyard pool. How ironic! As their boats became more lavish, they used each one less and less. She would have to do a thorough search of her memory banks to recollect the last time they ventured out beyond the Intracoastal. They never seemed to find the time. Or make the time.

Alison had to admit that since her husband followed Harry Hvide to Capital Industries, he spent more quality time with the children. She couldn't deny he was a doting and devoted father. But years of playing backup to Harry Hvide's enterprises created an invisible but tangible barrier between them. Look how easily and matter-of-factly he now abondoned her. By the speed in which he rushed out and the glazed, single purpose look on his face, Alison Lodge Barrett knew intuitively it would be several days before she would meaningfully interact with her husband.

While driving to Doctors' Hospital in Fort Lauderdale, Greg Barrett thought out his plan of action. Harry would expect him to carry out Code Teal. Code Teal was Harry's idea, a tribute to his foresight and his ability to pre-plan for any contingency. He realized any speculation or rumors about his health could have a dramatic effect on the company's stock price. Capital Industries, like Video Nation which preceded it, and ICX which preceded it, were, to a large degree, perceived by investors to be a personification of Harry Hvide. It wasn't an impersonal multilayered, mega-conglomerate like General Motors or DuPont. At such entities, not many could name the CEO or care if they chose a new one. People bought Capital Industries' stock *because* it was a

Harry Hvide company. As far as the stock watchers and portfolio managers were concerned, Capital Industries and Harry Hvide were one and the same. Rumors or leaks about any serious health problem could lead to drops as much as twenty-five to thirty-five percent off Capital Industries' total value or several billion dollars.

Over the years Harry Hvide donated millions of dollars to Doctor's Hospital. In return, Doctor's Hospital built a separate wing with a private entrance where Harry could get priority care in case of an emergency. So important was it that he be treated in anonymity, he went to great lengths to have a special "Code Teal" staff of doctors and nurses on call in case of such an emergency. They were compensated for signing confidentiality agreements. Under ideal circumstances Harry could be treated or operated on, remain in the hospital for as short a stay as possible, then transferred to his estate where he had a built-in intensive care unit. Harry's home ICU could be operational in less than six hours. He felt he took every precaution to prevent a medical situation; not perfect, but close.

Physically Harry was a strong man. Barely sixty, Greg could not recall him taking a sick day. This was the very first time they'd ever implemented "Code Teal." Greg's function in the plan was to suppress any rumors, to keep any information at all from leaking out. Greg went over in his mind the people who definitely knew. Lou Redmond and Frank Roy were reliable people but Greg would stress to them again later how important it was to keep everything quiet. Helen Murdock, Harry's personal secretary, had been with him longer than Greg. She would be very worried and upset. Greg would make sure to keep her current on Harry's status. He didn't have to worry about her loyalty. Helen knew the drill. He would let Eric Huntington deal with the security people. A retired Secret Service Agent who headed up the Presidential detail of Ronald Reagan, Eric Huntington, with Harry's input, was the architect of "Code Teal."

He handpicked the security people who would have responded and transported Harry to the hospital. It was Eric's job to inform Betty Hvide and her brother Will Wolcett. Will had been with Harry from the beginning and was a silent partner and major investor in every Harry Hvide venture. In fact, Will was the one who interviewed and hired him to drive for Seacoast Waste Service. Will would tell Dave Roberts. It would be up to Dave and himself to keep Capital Industries running without a hitch. One of them needed to coordinate with Helen and check on Harry's schedule. Until they fully knew Harry's status and prognosis they would have to cover for him.

Greg drove into Doctor's Hospital parking lot still thinking. The only ones out of the "Code Teal" loop were the two baseball guys. It could have been a lot worse. Greg shuddered to think of the consequences if the incident occurred in a public place instead of Harry's private office. Walking to the private wing's entrance he realized his every thought concentrated on carrying the "Code Teal" agenda. He hadn't once thought of Harry's condition. He reacted as Harry would have expected—putting business ahead of his own welfare. Greg had genuinely deep feelings for Harry Hvide. He walked with a quickened pace until he reached the entrance. A security guard at the door checked Greg's name and allowed him inside after verifying his identification. Eric Huntington waited inside.

"Hi, Greg."

"Hi, Eric. How's he doing?"

"He's going to be okay. There's no real necessity for the Mayo Clinic doctor but Betty insisted. He should arrive in about four hours. We'll probably move him back home sometime tomorrow."

"Was it a heart attack?"

"They're still running tests. Definitely high blood pressure. Probably heart related. But not so serious he can't be treated at the home ICU. They'll decide after Dr. Cohn from the Mayo Clinic looks at the charts and confers with Harry's own doctors."

"Can I see him?"

"Wait a minute and I'll confirm that. Betty's in with him now. Will and one of Harry's doctors are making sure the ICU at the estate is operational. 'Code Teal' is running according to plan. Did you speak to anyone besides Frank Roy?"

"No. Has Dave Roberts been notified?"

"Yes. He's at the office coordinating with Helen. You're supposed to check in with him."

"As soon as I leave here."

"I'll see if you can go in now."

Eric Huntington went to an intercom. Greg paced back and forth while he talked. Betty Hvide came out of the room and into the hallway. Greg went over to her immediately and they embraced tightly.

"He seems to be doing fine," she said. "I know he's feeling better because he's trying to boss the doctors around."

Greg smiled and held Betty's hand. "What are the doctors telling you?"

"Possibly arrhythmia. But the heartbeat is almost back to normal. When Dr. Cohn arrives from Rochester they'll decide on treatment. Probably medication. They're still waiting for some tests. My hunch is a pacemaker is a long ways off."

"Is he comfortable?"

"My husband, as you well know, is not one to complain. He's conscious. He's alert, and he wants to see you."

"Great. I won't be long. Do you need any help at the house?"

"I think we're fine. While you're in with him I'll check with my brother."

Greg squeezed Betty's hand before letting go. Entering the room he was shocked at what he saw. Harry lay in bed, tubes coming out of him everywhere, all attached to a myriad of machines. His complexion was pasty white, devoid of any color. He appeared weak and feeble. Greg's eyes started to water and his voice choked up. He had never seen Harry like this. As he took a seat next to the bed he tried coping with the realization that the man he imagined invincible, the man to whom he owed everything, now looked old and vulnerable. He closed his eyes and suddenly he found himself in a time warp. In a split second he was transported back to Bridgeport, Connecticut. Instead of Harry on the bed it was his father, Alvin. He was a boy again and helpless. He tried helping his father fight off the barbarians who invaded their tranquil neighborhood, but moved in nightmarish slow motion. His father withered away and he was powerless to stop it. When he opened his eyes his father was gone. Harry lay on the bed bravely trying to smile.

"You can't stay long. He needs to rest," one of the nurses informed him.

"I understand." Greg took Harry's hand in his own and returned the smile. He moved his face close to Harry's ear and whispered, "Everything's under control. Don't worry, I'll handle everything."

Harry Hvide squeezed Greg's hand and gave him a knowing wink. Greg left the room, stopping to talk in the hallway with Betty Hvide.

"Something's been really bothering him lately. He hasn't been himself," she revealed. "I'll bet it's the baseball situation. He was conferencing with Lou Redmond and Frank Roy when this happened."

"Keep your chin up." Greg responded. "That's all going to be resolved."

Greg hugged Betty Hvide good-bye and departed for the office. While he drove anger welled up inside him. Feelings he had suppressed for years were now bubbling back to the surface. Images of Harry attached to his tubes and his father before he died switched back and forth, interchanging in his head. His thoughts turned to Richie Johnson and Greg's wrath intensified into a blind fury.

Fifteen million dollars! No wonder Harry had a heart attack. The idea of that ungrateful son of a bitch extorting them for money above the sixty-six million he was already getting came close to giving him a stroke. He ground his teeth. His temples were beet red, bulging out of his forehead. He flashed back again to his boyhood days in Bridgeport, focusing on the bastards who repeatedly broke into the hardware store. They stole the Barrett's livelihood and robbed his father of his spirit. He wanted to help out so badly. He fantasized about waiting in the store at night. He would catch them in the act and make them pay. Well, Richie Johnson was no different than the thieves who plundered the hardware store. Richie Johnson was a bad neighborhood. Now there was no one stop him from cleaning it up. He got off the elevator and walked to Dave Robert's office, his mind now uncluttered. He was possessed with the conviction of a single thought. With the same care and devotion to detail he used to dissect and consummate thousands of business deals, Greg Barrett would now plan and carry out the demise of Richie "Big Dick" Johnson.

The next morning at six-thirty sharp Greg entered his office and went straight to work tackling the day's agenda. After leaving Harry's bedside the night before, Greg conferred with Helen Murdock and Dave Roberts. Together they coordinated a plan to cover Harry's absence. For the short term Dave would act as Harry's stand-in. He'd return his essential phone calls and make the appearances which could not be postponed. Greg would function behind the scenes and handle the negotiating and decision making normally reserved for Harry. Presently he was occupied with a deal for Allied Waste Service. It would give them a presence in the Southwest and projected a lucrative future if they could attain it at the right price. He made notes and organized his objections. He would have a final offer ready by midmorning. He also had to decide whether to retain the current advertising agency for Auto World or to put the account up for review. He returned some phone calls and met for a time with the accountants from the car rental agency. Right before lunch he called Eric Huntington.

"Hi, Eric. How's he doing?"

"Okay. He had a hard time sleeping with the nurses taking tests every twenty minutes. He's been resting comfortably all morning. The good news is he doesn't need a bypass. He doesn't need a pacemaker. In fact, we're going to transfer him to the estate later this afternoon. How's it going there?"

"Running like a top."

"Great. Harry will be glad to hear it."

"I'd like to tell him myself."

"I know you would. But you better wait at least until tomorrow. Give us a chance to secure everything."

"Whatever's best. Knowing Harry, he'll be back at work tomorrow."

Greg could hear Eric Huntington chuckle before hanging up the phone. He made a note to call Betty later in the day. He went back about his business the rest of the afternoon. He tackled his workload with renewed vigor. Harry's optimistic prognosis lifted his spirits but that wasn't the sole reason. Coming to a conclusion regarding the

Richie Johnson problem removed a two-ton yoke off his shoulders. Finding a solution seemed to bless him with a clear mind. He reserved the final ninety minutes of the day to map out a plan.

First, he came to the conclusion he would have to do it himself. Though rumors persisted about the garbage business having ties to organized crime, Greg knew first hand it was mostly exaggerated fiction. Besides, any aspects of intimidation died when the courts overruled his father-in-law's decision on land rights. And even if he knew the right people he could never bring himself to ask anyone to do what he was planning. And if he did he would set himself up to be blackmailed for the rest of his life. A chill went down his spine. He couldn't imagine trying to live a normal life with someone holding that over his head. Harry always said the only secrets were what you kept to yourself. As usual he was right on the money. Ridding the universe of Richie Johnson would definitely have to be a one-man operation.

Greg reviewed Johnson's bio again and again, probing for a weak spot. He didn't have much luck. During the season he lived in a penthouse apartment in a posh development. Other high priced athletes and celebrities lived there and it had a reputation for tight security. It would have to occur at a different venue. The stadium had too many potential witnesses. He needed a more isolated location. He put down the bio and thumbed through Stu Klein's security reports. Stu headed up security for all the sports teams. Prior to being in the employ of Harry Hvide he spent ten years as the lead investigator for the State Attorney's office. Before that he spent another twenty years in the Miami-Dade Public Safety Department, mostly as a detective. His job was to keep tabs on all the players. He checked out rumors of drug use and either illicit or excessive gambling. He investigated touchy incidents involving players and warned them if they started hanging with the wrong kinds of people. Stu Klein's reports indicated Richie Johnson was spending an inordinate amount of his free time at a strip joint called "Club Relaxxxation." He indicated the club was tucked away in an out-of-the-way spot deep in Liberty City. Greg would have to do some research, but this strip joint just might harbor some possibilities.

From the reports Greg garnered information that Richie was seeing one of the club's most popular entertainers, an exotic dancer named Ebony Spice. Stu investigated a rumor that Ebony might be pregnant and might be claiming Richie knocked her up. Greg needed more information. Some he would gather on his own. For the rest he'd have to wait for the next security report. No way could he ask Stu Klein about it directly. Nor could he go to Lou Redmond or Frank Roy. He'd have to patiently wait for the report to come across his desk. Satisfied he'd done all he could for the day, he closed up shop. Before departing he called the Hvide estate to check on Harry. The person who answered put him through to Harry's brother-in-law Will Wolcett.

"Good of you to call, Greg. How's it going there?"

"Everything's under control. How's Harry coming along?"

"Good. He's comfortable. He had a good day. By tomorrow he'll be telling you himself. He'll also tell you you're overpaying for Allied."

"I can't wait. What's his doctor saying?"

"Good to go. He doesn't need a bypass. He's going on medication and he's going to have to make some lifestyle changes. More exercise. More fish. Less red meat and less stress at work. Betty's already working with a nutritionist."

"How's she holding up?"

"My sister? Like a rock. I'll give her your regards."

"Thanks. Tell her to handle the diet and I'll take care of the stress."

Greg maintained the same routine for the next couple of days. He immersed himself in work going from project to project. Things went so smoothly not a single person commented on Harry Hvide's absence. He kept in frequent communication with the Hvide estate. Harry was coming along nicely. He was quickly regaining his strength and on his way to a full recovery. He felt so good he insisted on returning to work the following week. He was antsy to get back before anyone noticed his absence and started destructive rumors. After a protracted argument Harry reached a compromise with Betty and his doctors. He would be allowed to go into the office but only for a couple of hours. He agreed to do no serious work and limit his efforts to making appearances and returning phone calls. This gave Greg a five day window to handle the Richie Johnson situation. He wanted it out of the way before Harry's return.

With nothing pressing on his schedule Greg decided to take a ride by Club Relaxxxation. He drove down I-95 into Dade County. Going against rush hour traffic he traveled close to the 55 mph speed limit. Fortunately he made good time. He had a little over an hour of daylight remaining and he wanted to see this place before dark. He got off at the 62nd Street exit, entering the culture shock world of Liberty City. Fort Lauderdale had some seamy neighborhoods but nothing like this. Every store had barred-up doors and windows. Omnipresent were wire fences topped with rolls of curled barbed wire. He drove west on 62nd Street, passing a combination grocery-ladies-wear store and several churches. He went past a Furniture Kingdom Store advertising export to Haiti, Jamaica, and the Bahamas. Other stores had signs written in Creole. Stopped at a red light, he noticed a billboard for Ace Bail Bonds promising "Get out of Jail Quick." A little further up he passed African Square Park. The basketball courts had games going on unlike the tennis courts which sat idle. Greg turned right on N.W. 22nd Avenue and found himself behind a jitney making frequent stops. Jitneys were a byproduct of the massive Haitian immigration during the 1980s. Also popular in Nassau, jitneys were privately owned and operated minibuses providing a form of public transportation. In Haiti they were called *tap-taps.* Painted in striking bright colors, some displayed island-flavored murals. The Miami versions were mostly run down, underinsured vans and mini-buses which caused some controversy because of their traffic-clogging frequent stops and the fights competing jitneys would engage in over passengers. Uneasy in this environment, Greg was reluctant to pass. He bided his time, staying a safe distance behind. Eight blocks up he made a right, a left and another right, arriving outside of Club Relaxxxation. The surrounding neighborhood was partly residential, mostly commercial, with a barbershop interspersed among auto body shops and fortress-like warehouses. Club Relaxxxation was a modest, medium sized building with a substantial parking lot. The entire property was surrounded by a twelve-foot high iron fence. The parking lot could only be accessed from a single entry point protected by a uniformed guard. Other uniformed guards patrolled the parking lot in golf carts. The level of security was quite impressive. He was surprised at the quantity of expensive cars parked in the lot. There were at least three Lexus 400s the same year and color as his. Additionally, there were Mercedes convertibles, Lincolns, BMWs, Volvos and Cadillacs along with several luxury sports utilities. Also surprisingly, most of the club's patrons were white. They surely weren't coming for the aesthetic surroundings. Club Relaxxxation had no windows and needed a paint job. Except for the lit sign on the roof and the words "Adult Entertainment" stenciled on the door the building was nondescript. Greg circled around the block, then went back to I-95 the way he came. He accomplished his mission. He found the place and looked around the neighborhood. The area fit his plan to a tee. No street lights anywhere and Club Relaxxxation was the only one of the surrounding businesses which stayed open after five o'clock PM. He needed to return and get completely familiar with the area but was satisfied he had found the right place. He entered the highway and fought rush hour traffic all the way back to Fort Lauderdale.

Had he stayed, Greg Barrett would have been astounded at what he missed because Club Relaxxxation was the hottest spot in town. The club's proprietor, Otis Knight, possessed true entrepreneurial spirit and knew how to keep his customers happy. He realized he couldn't compete with the new plush upscale strip clubs currently the latest trend in adult entertainment. Distinguished by lavish interiors and tuxedoed doormen, those clubs successfully removed the stigma of sleaze, creating a high class, comfortable atmosphere to watch centerfold quality girls get naked. Some of the upscale clubs spent in excess of a million dollars on renovations just to attain the right look and feel in order to attract prosperous, upper class professionals.

Otis Knight desired the same clientele but employed a different marketing strategy to entice them. For all their luxurious trappings, the upscale clubs were still teases. Very expensive teases. Those clubs had defined codes of conduct for both the customers and the girls. The girls were totally nude only on stage and wore G strings when socializing with the customers. Touching was permitted exclusively in private rooms and in the form of paid, upfront lap dances. Contact outside the club between the dancers and the customers was severely discouraged. Giving out a phone number was grounds for dismissal.

Otis Knight's budget for interior decorations was about nine hundred dollars. Otis discovered he didn't need leather bars, ultra-suede couches, and transparent poles containing tropical fish if he gave the customers what they really wanted. At Club Relaxxxation a customer could get satisfied. On the surface it seemed the club's location in one of the world's most dangerous neighborhoods might be a detriment to attracting rich, professional white men. In actuality, it was perfect. Otis needed a surrounding locale so dangerous the police would be afraid to patrol it. For the right product people would go anywhere. Otis was a firm believer in the philosophy "Provide it and They Will Come!" Also, once on the club's premises there was no reason for the cops because from Monday to Friday three o'clock to eight o'clock PM Club Relaxxxation was the safest place in Miami. Accountants, dentists, salesmen and attorneys would file out of their downtown offices and stop off at the Club for some fun and relaxation before heading home to face their wives. Otis knew success hinged on repeat business. No one was coming back if they were ripped off in the parking lot or hassled once inside. Otis' place furnished tighter security than Seinfeld's last episode. The parking lot was under strict, twenty-four-hour a day surveillance. Inside, security was more rigorous. Each patron had to get an okay from the doorman, pass a verbal examination from the ex-Marine head bouncer, and go through a highly sensitive metal detector before gaining admittance. Vice cops didn't stand a chance. Otis believed firmly in a restricted clientele. Only wealthy black professionals and pro athletes were allowed to mix with his white and Hispanic patrons during the three to eight o'clock shift. After eight o'clock PM, the club would unofficially close for two hours before reopening to a totally different customer base until six o'clock AM the next morning.

During the three to eight shift, Club Relaxxxation's happy hour crowd resembled a slightly out of control, seventies' party complete with free-flowing booze, uninhibited baby boomers and beautiful, willing girls. On the surface it appeared like other strip clubs. It had a runway bar and tables equipped for tabletop dancing. Private champagne rooms were available. However, at Club Relaxxxation it was not uncommon for zippers to get undone during friction dances. The only carpet on the premises was under the tables where some of the girls, for the right price, would perform an act exclusive to Club Relaxxxation called table surfing. The private champagne rooms were very private. Otis Knight was a kind of guy who didn't concern himself in the affairs of two consenting adults. He also didn't care what his girls did after hours. What they did on their own time was their business.

Otis Knight's star attraction was a stone beauty named Ebony Spice. A dead ringer for Tyra Banks with fifteen years of wear and tear, Ebony cultivated a fiercely loyal clientele who admired her grace, beauty and agility. Her signature grand jete was a table dance where she bent her head all the way between her legs, offering her customers three choices to stuff their twenties. Ebony never indulged in the club's more public acts of affection. Certain customers had been known to coax her into a private champagne room on occasion, however. Nor was she opposed to dating a select few after hours. Ebony, whose born name was Leah Wilson, was Otis Knight's highest-producing profit center.

She did pretty well for herself as well. Leah got into the business after a nasty cocaine habit ruined her marriage to her college sweetheart. She was able to kick her drug addiction but not the lifestyle exotic dancing provided. Leah was good for seven to eight hundred dollars a night, not including private sessions or after work dates. And she only worked four hours a day with no weekends and was home by nine o'clock PM. No late Saturday nights meant her Sunday mornings were free to sing in her church choir.

Leah was bouncing from joint to joint until Otis discovered her and gave her a new stage name. She had worked the fancy upscale clubs like Pure Platinum. The money was good but the hours were awful. Working the late shift with the early morning hours was a challenge to her sobriety. Much more of it would have pushed her over the edge and back to drugs. Otis saved her from that hell. In fact, they helped each other. Leah had a way with the customers that kept them coming back for more. She had the perfect stripper attitude; she showed a lot, talked more and did as little as possible. Yet high-priced accountants and lawyers would compete for her slightest favor.

She met Richie Johnson right after the World Series. He came in after another Manatee celebration with a couple of his teammates. He was attracted to her immediately and started out buying five hundred dollar magnums of champagne. She treated him the same way she would treat a Jewish dentist—badly. Similarly, the worse she treated him the more he wanted. She took the chill out of their relationship when he bought her a silver and gold Rolex. Serious dating commenced after he gave her a new Corvette to drive. Three months later she found herself in a family way and wasn't about to let him abrogate his responsibilities. He initially offered her peanuts to get an abortion. Little did he know she was represented by the most expensive lawyer in town. She simply traded out with one of her most fervent clients. Ebony obtained his services which usually cost five hundred dollars an hour in exchange for feeding him doggie biscuits and a golden shower. Richie would have to step up to the plate with a realistic offer. They were meeting at the club in two days.

Greg Barrett just consummated the Allied Waste Service negotiation when Stu Klein's security report came over the fax machine. Everything remained pretty much status quo. Richie Johnson was still spending time at Club Relaxxxation, presumably to see Miss Ebony Spice. Greg searched his desk for the Fort Lauderdale Sun Sentinel. He located the Sports section and thumbed through it until he came across the Manatees' exhibition schedule. Tomorrow afternoon they were playing a pre-season game against the University of Miami baseball team at Mark Light Field on the Hurricane campus in Coral Gables. It was a one o'clock PM game that should end around four o'clock PM. Things were starting to fall into place. If Richie Johnson visited Miss Spice he could be at Club Relaxxxation between six o'clock and six thirty PM. That would give him an ample window of opportunity. "Good," Greg said to himself, glad this mess was nearing a conclusion. Tomorrow evening would be the day. The time had come to finalize his last-minute preparations.

Greg Barrett took an extended lunch and drove back to Club Relaxxxation. He went back and forth around the streets drawing a map of the immediate area. He would study the map again and again, committing it to memory. It was essential he vacate the scene promptly and had a precise escape route. On the way back to Fort Lauderdale he stopped at a Chevron station, filled his tank and went inside to the convenience store. He bought a Hershey's Dark Chocolate bar, which would have to suffice for lunch, and a dummy "Florida Arrive Alive" license plate. He made one more stop at a dive shop off Broward Boulevard not far from the office. He purchased a lightweight polypropylene hood for twenty-four dollars, ninety-five cents.

The next morning before going to work he took the .38 special he kept in his dresser drawer and put it in his briefcase. He had to search for the bullets. Ever since the birth of his children he kept the gun unloaded and the bullets in a separate location. It had been so long since he thought of the gun he forgot where the bullets were stashed. He eventually found them at the back of a different drawer. He mused to himself about how much good the gun would do him if he ever really needed it. He then drove to Fort. Lauderdale Airport and parked his car on the roof of the parking garage, carefully putting the parking ticket on top of the driver's side visor. He took the elevator to the basement and hailed a cab in front of the Arrivals area near Delta Airlines. Twenty minutes later he was at his desk immersed in the day's agenda. A little after nine thirty AM he made a call to Tony Lampone over at Auto World.

"Hi, Tony. It's Greg."

"Good morning Mr. Gregory Barrett. What can I do for you?"

"I had to take my car in. Can I get a loaner?"

"What's with the Lexus?"

"Something with the a/c. Must be a leak."

"See. That car's nothing but a stepped-up Toyota."

"I thought you used to sell Lexus."

"Like I said, a world-class car and the best value in today's automotive industry."

"About the loaner?"

"Sure, no problem. You want it delivered?"

"No, no, that's okay. I'll pick it up. I don't know when I'll be there. Is it possible to leave it where I can find it with the key in it?"

"Yeah, no problem. I'll tell you what I'm gonna do. I'll leave it in my named parking spot unlocked with the key in the visor."

"Thanks. I only need it overnight. Can we do without the paperwork? I'll have it back tomorrow."

Tony Lampone thought Greg's last request was a bit off. Everyone he met at Capital Industries and especially Greg Barrett were sticklers about paperwork. But hey, if that's how the boss wanted it, who was he to make a fuss? "Sure, I'll handle it," he told Greg.

At Mark Light Field in Coral Gables the defending World Champion Florida Manatees were getting drubbed by a college team. In another dismal, desultory performance they were down eight to three in the top of the ninth inning before staging a two-out rally. They pushed across a couple of runs and had the bases loaded with Richie Johnson at the plate. While the rest of the regular starters played only four innings Paddy McGraw felt Richie Johnson needed the extra at bats and kept him in the game as the designated hitter. Representing the winning run, Richie worked the count full. He then stepped out of the batter's box and, a la Babe Ruth, pointed to the left center field fence. He resumed his stance and eyed the Hurricane pitcher who froze him with a three-two changeup right down the middle of the plate, for a called strike three. The UM fans erupted in resounding cheers. Even the hard core Manatee fans were caught up in the moment and joined the raucous celebration. The Manatees left the field in a foul mood, none more foul than Richie Johnson. At least he drove to the game in his own car and didn't have to wait for the team bus. He brought along a change of clothes and took a quick shower. As he hurriedly changed he was approached by Benny Benitez.

"What's the rush?" Benny asked him.

"I got some business to take care of," Richie replied.

Benny Benitez had seen that look in Richie Johnson before and had an inkling of what his business affair entailed.

"Please don't tell me you knocked up another one?" Benny asked, shaking his head, "Man, you have got to get snipped."

"Forget that," Richie retorted, "Nobody cuts me down there. Anyways, this time it wasn't my fault."

"What do you mean?"

Richie Johnson picked up his duffel bag and ambled toward the locker room door. He turned back to Benny Benitez and answered, "I hit the wrong hole."

Greg Barrett made it a point to catch up with Stephanie Allen during the day. Stephanie was a computer programmer who worked on the ninth floor. She'd been with Harry Hvide since the startup of Video

Nation. Greg had been to her house in Plantation and knew it was on the way to Auto World .Stephanie was a working mom who religiously left the building by five o'clock.

"Are you sure it's not an inconvenience?" he asked.

"Of course not," she answered. "I'll meet you here at quarter to five."

Greg Barrett spent the rest of the afternoon going about his business. He decided to call Frank Roy one more time before meeting Stephanie Allen.

"Frank... it's Greg Barrett. Just checking to see if there's any new developments."

"I wish. The fifteen million dollar figure is set in stone according to his dick agent who conveniently is out of town 'til next week. I hoped to have better news for you."

"Me, too."

"How's number one?"

"Coming along fine; he starts back on Monday."

"That's great. Too bad I couldn't have this Richie Johnson thing resolved by then." Frank Roy said ruefully.

"Well, some things are out of your control. I'll be speaking to you. Bye."

Greg met Stephanie Allen at her office promptly at four forty-five. On the drive out to Auto World they conversed about kids and schools and the real estate market. Traffic on I-595 West was bumper to bumper. The sky was turning a threatening grey.

"I can't believe how much it's rained in the dry season," Stephanie Allen remarked, "The lake in our backyard has never been higher."

"Must be El Nino," he answered faintly. He was distracted now and kept watching his watch. The heavy traffic was throwing off his schedule. After what seemed like an eternity, Stephanie turned into the Auto World complex and dropped him off at the main showroom. Greg took his briefcase and thanked her for the ride. Without entering the building he walked to the side and located Tony Lampone's parking space, which was occupied by a white Ford Taurus GL with blue interior. The driver's side door was unlocked. Greg set his briefcase on the passenger seat. He felt above the visor and found the key exactly where Tony said he would leave it. He started the ignition and drove out of the lot. On the way to the interstate he stopped in a deserted Presbyterian church's parking lot. He opened his briefcase, taking out the "Florida Arrive Alive" license plate. Using a Swiss Army knife screwdriver he switched it with the dealer plate. He put the dealer plate in the trunk and resumed his drive back to the highway. While he drove, the wind picked up, pushing ominous clouds across a darkening sky.

The traffic southbound on I-95 was heavier than normal. Greg glanced at his watch and fretted. The grey sky quickly vanished. Nightfall appeared with a stark suddenness. The road signs quivered back and forth as the wind speed escalated. The sky was now pitch black, illuminated only by flashes of lightning scribbling across. A large clump of rain smacked the windshield followed by pelting droplets. Greg fumbled for the windshield wipers in the unfamiliar car, finally locating them on the steering column. Traffic slowed even more in the pouring rain. Thankfully he reached the 62nd Street exit. He turned off the expressway and headed toward Club Relaxxxation. The rain was now coming down in waves. Whipped by the wind it descended in torrents Greg switched the wipers to the fastest speed and still had to squint out as the oscillating blade barely made any headway. A minute later the rain stopped completely, only to resume with a vengeance ten minutes later. The wind did not relent, tossing the traffic lights back and forth like seesawing yo-yos. Greg was behind schedule but at least the storm had cleared the streets of pedestrians. There was very little vehicular traffic as well. Greg kept plugging along on the near-deserted roadways, finally stopping in front of Club Relaxxxation. He looked at his watch and grimaced. It was ten minutes to seven. So much for confronting Richie Johnson on the way in. He peered into the parking lot. There were no security guards at the entrance and none patrolling in golf carts. Huddled under the awning over the front door he saw a group of large men wearing yellow rain slickers. Greg decided he had to determine if Richie Johnson was there. He steered the Taurus into the fenced-in lot. He didn't have to go far. Parked right in front of the building was a bright red Ferrari 550 Maranello with the license plate "Big Stick." No need to look any farther. Richie Johnson was definitely in attendance. Greg drove across the street, backing the car into the lot of the closed body shop. He opened his briefcase and removed the .38 special, a pair of Isotoner gloves, the diver's hood, and a small plastic packet which unzipped into a dark green rain poncho. He squirmed into the poncho, putting it over his clothes. Next, he put on the gloves. He stuck the gun in his jacket pocket, laid the hood over the console and sat back and waited; all the while keeping an eye on the Ferrari.

Inside, Richie Johnson was having as bad a day as he had at the ballpark. His luck with Ebony Spice was the same as it was at bat and concluded in the same result—he struck out with the bases loaded. The atmosphere was poisoned from the get-go. She ignored him at first, refusing to interrupt her tabletop dance for a bunch of accountant types. After making eye contact she let him stew at the bar drinking ten-dollar Grand Marniers while she flirted with some of her regulars. After finally making her way over she refused to discuss the matter privately in one of the champagne rooms. Instead she went to the end of the bar and appeared to signal a well-dressed guy sitting at a nearby table. The man looked somewhat familiar but it was hard to tell in the darkly lit room through his Vuarnet designer sunglasses.

Richie's first objective was to convince her the baby couldn't possibly be his. Ebony pretended to blush and said, "Richard Baby, you know I save myself exclusively for you."

"Yah, sure," he replied. "Just me and the sixth fleet."

Ebony went over to the well-dressed man and came back with a legal looking document. She tossed it on the bar in front of him and said, "I've got the motion for you to take a paternity test already drawn up. I can have you served anytime I want."

Richie did not want to go down that road again. For some reason that was one test he never failed. His fallback position was to work out a settlement and buy her off as cheaply as possible.

"I'll tell you what," he told her, "I'm not admitting nuthin' but if you leave me out of this you can keep the Corvette."

Ebony didn't flinch. With an icy, glacier-like demeanor she looked straight into Richie Johnson's eyes and said simply, "Five hundred thousand dollars."

Richie gagged on the Grand Marnier, the liquor coming out his nose. He regained his composure and took a more flexible bargaining stance. "Okay, okay. Let's get this done. I'll tell you what I'm willing to do. Fifty thousand now and another fifty thousand when I get my first paycheck. Next week when the season starts. But I get my 'Vette back."

Ebony folded her arms in front of her and simply replied, "Five hundred thousand dollars and a new bus for my church."

Richie went into a Fred Sanford imitation feigning to have the big one. "All right," he said. "You can have the hundred thou in a lump sum. I'll tell my agent to cut you a check tomorrow."

"Five hundred thousand dollars, a new bus and I keep the Corvette or you can support me and the baby for the next eighteen years."

Richie shook his head in defeat. Ebony was a more formidable negotiator than he figured. After a few minutes more of talking she consulted with the well-dressed guy. She returned shortly, shook hands and gave Richie an affirmative nod. Richie downed one last Grand Marnier before getting up to leave. He congratulated himself while walking to the door, whispering under his breath, "At least I got the greedy ho to settle for a used bus."

The bouncer opened the door for him. Richie immediately shield-

ed his face with his forearm as a fierce wind and a pounding rain greeted him. He retreated back in to the club and gave the doorman a fifty
dollar bill to bring his car under the awning. This really was turning out
to be a bad day. If he thought it was going to rain like this he would
have left the Ferrari home and taken the Humvee. The 550 Maranello
was his baby, much more responsive than the Porsche. Normally he
wouldn't let anyone else drive it but damn, there was a mini-hurricane
outside! He considered hanging a little longer at the club but decided
against it. The place was bad luck and already had too many of his
hard earned dollars. The night was young and he wanted a change of
scenery.

Across the street Greg Barrett waited impatiently. Though Richie
Johnson had been inside slightly less than an hour it seemed much
longer. He drummed impatiently on the steering wheel and tried listening to the radio. A hockey game was on but it couldn't hold his
interest. Suddenly he saw the headlights of Richie Johnson's Ferrari.
Greg was startled. He nervously searched for the diver's hood. The
Ferrari only went fifteen feet and stopped under the awning. Greg
relaxed a little. He thought, "That scumbag can't walk ten feet in the
rain." He located the hood and slipped it over his head, covering his
face with the exception of his eyes. He turned on the ignition, shifted
into drive and waited.

Richie Johnson took the wheel of the Ferrari and inched out of the
parking lot. More than anything he wanted to blast away at warp
speed, drive out his frustrations and put as much distance between
himself and Club Relaxxxation as possible. The surrounding streets
were now overflowing lakes and he couldn't even get out of first gear.
While crawling ahead Richie Johnson reflected on his situation. Here
he was driving in the wrong car in the wrong place, driving in the
storm from Hell. Perhaps it was a sign from above. Over the last few
weeks his life had been a little on the rocky side. He thought of poor
Tyson and Holyfield and the close call on the team bus where a bullet
missed him by a pubic hair. Maybe the Big Fella was telling him he
needed a change of scenery. The city by the bay was starting to sound
awfully good. Tomorrow first thing he would call his bloodsucking
agent and tell him to come off the fifteen million dollar demand. Hell,
he'd settle for ten million, maybe even five. At that very moment, the
Ferrari hit a deep puddle, sunk to the front bumper and stalled. "Okay,"
he muttered to the roof of the Ferrari, "You win. I'll okay the trade if
they just clean up the mess with Ebony."

Greg Barrett saw Richie Johnson's Ferrari roll out of the parking
lot onto the street. He stepped on the accelerator and pulled behind.

His face was sweating heavily beneath the diver's hood and his hands felt clammy. His breathing was uneven and he began inhaling faster and faster. His hands gripped the steering wheel super tightly. The front windshield fogged up and he had a difficult time seeing out. The interior controls of the Taurus were foreign to him and he couldn't locate the defroster. As he searched in vain for the interior lights an imaginary grenade exploded in his head. HE WASN'T SURE RICHIE JOHNSON WAS ALONE!!! What if he left with someone? The girl, or maybe a teammate or one of his gofers. He couldn't afford any witnesses... but could he take another life? Richie Johnson was one thing but could he reconcile murdering a completely innocent bystander? Greg gasped for air as the utter folly of his plan crashed through his brain. There had to be another way. This was too stupid for words. All he wanted now was to get out of this place and go home. He squirmed in the seat, holding the steering wheel with his left hand. He wiggled his right arm free of the poncho and used his forearm to paw at the windshield. He rubbed it up and down desperately trying to clear the fog. He could barely see the car's hood. Suddenly he did a double take, arched his back and slammed on the brakes with all his might. Out of nowhere appeared the brake lights of another vehicle.

Richie Johnson's neck snapped back against the headrest and forward again, his chin bumping against his chest. The awful sound of metal hitting metal ground in his ears. Blood rushed to his head and every vein in his thickly muscled torso strained to the point of rupture. This was absolutely the last straw! On top of everything else happening this day his beloved Ferrari 550 Maranello was now stalled out in a puddle and rear-ended in the middle of a deluge. The thought of waiting in the horrendous weather for a dumb cop to make out an accident report and filing another claim with his insurance company drove him blind with fury. He exploded out of the Ferrari toward the car behind him.

Greg Barrett was stunned. The impact of the unexpected fender bender almost sent him into a state of shock. He fought desperately to remain calm and collect himself. There was really only one choice—get out of there as fast as he could. Committing a hit and run was easily a superior choice to trying to explain what he was doing there. Before he could put the car in reverse the driver's side door was ripped open by a cursing, raving madman.

"What the fuck are you doing to me?" Richie Johnson screamed at the top of his lungs. "I can't believe my fucking luck. Where's your goddamned registration?" When the driver moved too slow to suit him

Richie Johnson reached across him and tried to open the glove compartment. He struggled to get it open, finding it difficult to bend over the startled driver.

"Get the fuck out of my way!" he bellowed. He grabbed the driver by the poncho with both hands and flung him out of the car onto the wet pavement. "Let me see your goddamned registration!" Richie Johnson hesitated a few seconds, then added, "And your motherfucking license too!!"

Greg Barrett lay in the middle of the street in three inches of water, smacked by a stinging rain and assailed by a delirious ranting cycloid. His initial timidity transformed into an enraged resentment. As he tried to regain his feet his attacker placed his foot on Greg's shoulder and kicked him back to the asphalt.

"Stay the fuck where you are!!" Richie Johnson shouted at the fallen man. He took out his cell phone and dialed a number he committed to memory, *FHP.

Greg Barrett totally lost control. His ferocity now matched that of his assailant. He reached in his jacket pocket for the .38 special and sprang to his feet in a slightly forward crouch with his arms extended and both hands on the handle of the pistol.

"Cease and desist!" he screamed at the advancing madman.

"What the fuck are you saying?" Richie Johnson shouted while lunging forward.

"Cease and desist!" he repeated before everything began moving in suspended motion. Slowly, ever so slowly, Greg Barrett squeezed the trigger. The man lurched forward in his face then staggered backward before tottering to the ground. At that moment he must have detached himself from his body because he envisioned himself standing over the fallen man while another part of him was back in the car sitting behind the steering wheel. Acting solely by reflex, his survival instincts directed him away from the scene. He put the car in reverse, backed up a few feet, and shifted into drive, swerving around the body reposed on the street. He kept driving until he realized he was lost. The rain was descending in unrelenting bands and he still hadn't found the defroster. He feverishly swiped at the windshield with his gloved hand trying desperately to create an operable field of vision. In making his hasty getaway Greg Barrett deviated from his memorized escape route. He sought desperately an avenue, any avenue which he knew ran north-south. Though he never spent much time in Miami-Dade County, Greg never had a problem finding his way. The roads were all numbered with streets going east-west and avenues north-south. To make it easier the county was divided into quadrants—Southeast, Southwest, Northeast and Northwest. He was disoriented to the point that he had no idea which way he was going. The weather deteriorated further. He now had to dodge fallen tree limbs scattered in the streets. Also he couldn't find a roadway with an outlet. He went down Courts and Places and Terraces but none would lead him to a main road. He saw a sign, hoping it would be a recognizable landmark. Instead it read "James Scott Housing Project. A drug-free environment." Somehow he'd entered the scary world of public housing with row after row of cookie cutter apartments. At least the weather kept the residents off the streets but it didn't negate the fact he was still lost and driving in circles. Out of nowhere a loud banging sound came from under the car and the Taurus started handling unevenly. Great! This had to be the worst place in the universe to get a flat tire. He kept going, afraid to stop. He'd prefer driving back to Fort Lauderdale on the rim rather than stop to change the tire. Luckily it was only a garbage can lid wedged between the tire and the wheelbase and dislodged itself on its own. Finally, he came to a divided highway with two lanes going in each direction. He turned right, confident he was traveling either north, south, east, or west. At a red light he saw a sign reading N.W. 22nd Avenue. His heart stopped. He'd been driving for twenty minutes and was about where he started. Checking both ways for oncoming traffic he ran the light making a left. He breathed a small sigh of relief. I-95 should only be a few blocks away. He drove over a bridge. Funny, he didn't remember a bridge on his previous trips. On the other side of the bridge he slowed to look at a street sign. Greg did a double take. According to the sign he was traveling on East 10th Avenue. This couldn't be! He turned off an avenue. This had to be a street. He caught the first red light. The cross street sign read Las Bayamos Boulevard. He decided to try it. A boulevard sounded like it must go someplace. Los Bayamos Boulevard went a couple of blocks, then abruptly ended at some railroad tracks. He tried the cross streets but they only lead him into a warehouse district where every sign read in Spanish. Greg was thoroughly exasperated. Either he was abducted by aliens or was transposed into the middle of a Twilight Zone episode. He was close on both counts. Greg Barrett had mistakenly entered the City of Hialeah. In his disoriented state he traveled north on N.W. 22nd Avenue when he thought he was going south. The left he made put him going west on N.W. 103rd Street and away from I-95 instead of east on N.W. 62nd Street and toward it. The bridge he crossed marked the city line of the overwhelmingly Hispanic municipality of Hialeah. In Hialeah, for no discernible reason, except possibly making it easier to carjack German tourists, the same streets had different names. The road he turned off was 103rd Street everywhere in Dade County except Hialeah, where its name was East Tenth Avenue. After many deadends and U-turns Greg forged his way back to East Tenth Avenue. He decided to stay on it. It was a major divided thorough-fare and must lead somewhere. There was virtually no traffic but Greg proceeded very cautiously in the hellacious storm and pitch black night. Pitch black night! Greg realized there was a power outage and both the street lights and traffic signals were out. He considered pulling off the road and letting the storm subside but decided instead to keep moving. A few minutes later in his headlights was a sight more precious than the Holy Grail—a road sign for 826 North. Greg had finally reached familiar territory. He entered the highway from the ramp and kept on it until it intersected with I-95.

Delighted to leave Miami-Dade County in his wake, he headed toward Fort Lauderdale. While driving he sank into a deep funk. The consequences of his actions were beginning to dawn on him. He tried to think of what to do next, but thinking brought him back to the shooting and he wasn't yet prepared to deal with it. He drove ahead trance-like, kind of on autopilot. When he snapped out of it he noticed passing Palmetto Park Road. He'd gone through Broward County and into Boca Raton. He turned around at the next exit. Driving back he felt a sick feeling in the pit of his stomach. Quickly he rolled down the window and vomited.

He couldn't possibly go home like this. He desperately needed a place to wind down and sort things out. He needed a safe haven and time to decompress. He exited off the interstate, continuing to cruise around. Forty-five minutes later he parked the car in Jody Sellers' drive-way and rang the doorbell. He could see the surprise in her eyes when she opened the door.

"I... I'm sorry... I didn't mean to disturb... I'm afraid I made a..."

Jody Sellers took her front two fingers and gently placed them on his lips. "Don't say anything," she whispered. She took him by the hand and led him into her bedroom.

———

Greg Barrett lay alone and naked in a strange bed desperately try-ing to cope with the fact that in the space of three hours he, whose worst prior transgression against society was a traffic ticket, was now an adulterer and a murderer. Circumstances change.

What he experienced with Jody was dream-like and incredibly stimulating. He never felt this way before. She was so passionate and responsive. Their bodies meshed together in a tossing, turning exotic dance. He craved her now. He wanted her in his arms nestling her warm, inviting body against his. Perhaps she could remain in his arms and buffer him from the harsh realities he had to eventually face.

In retrospect it was reckless and foolish of him to show up here. What if her son hadn't been staying with his grandmother? He would have had a tough time explaining his presence. And he couldn't stay here. He had to get home. There were so many loose ends to tie up. He had to switch the license plates and return the car and he hadn't yet disposed of the gun. What would he tell Alison? What would he say to Jody? On top of everything he felt overpowered by inescapable feelings of guilt.

Jody Sellers came out of her adjoining bathroom, looked amorously at Greg and smiled. "I can't believe you were out driving in this weather. Tornadoes touched down at Opa Locka Airport, Plantation, and Coral Springs. The radio's calling it the Storm of the Century. Must be El Nino."

She sat down next to him on the bed and began gently massaging his neck. "Oh, and guess what else?" she continued. "You know Richie Johnson of the Manatees? He was shot."

"Really?" Greg tried to sound simultaneously surprised and concerned. "Did they say what happened? What a tragedy. He couldn't have been that old."

"Oh no, he's not dead. There were no other details except that he's in serious but stable condition at Jackson Memorial."

9

ONE WEEK LATER

The investigator for the TransGeneral Insurance Company parked his car in the lot of the Miami-Dade Public Safety Building. He took the stairs over to the Homicide Division, a place where he was formerly employed. The pretty dark-haired Public Safety Aide was occupied busily typing at the front desk.

"Senorita Rosalita," he greeted her, "Como Andan las cosas?"

"Muy bien," she replied with a big smile. "What brings you back to Dodge City?"

"I have to do a follow-up on a nowhere claim. Is Armando around?"

She wrinkled her nose and answered, "He's in his office." From past experience he knew the wrinkled nose was Rosaria Gonzalez's signal Armando Pedroza was in the men's lavatory. One of Armando's basic tenets of life was never take a dump at home when you could do it on county time. While he waited, she continued making conversation.

"How's your son?"

"He's fine. Growing and growing. I wish I could see him more often."

Rosaria Gonzalez saw the pain in his face and quickly changed subjects. They reminisced about old times. She again smiled broadly. He could always make her laugh. Whatever the surrounding mayhem in her work environment, he always cheered her up. She looked at him closely. "Are you eating anything? You're so skinny."

Before he could answer she raised her eyebrows and motioned toward the hallway. "Here comes Armando."

Walking toward them was a large, powerfully built man tucking in his shirt as he walked. He was ruggedly handsome with dark brown hair and a full, Pancho Villa style mustache. Armando Pedroza, a major in the Miami-Dade Police Department, was in charge of homicide. He walked toward the front desk, then pretended to do a double take.

"Who do we have here?" He walked around the man next to Rosaria twice, feigning a close examination. "Could this be Miami's Sherlock Holmes?" He asked sarcastically. "Nah, couldn't be. What would a big time insurance investigator be doing wasting his time at this little old taco stand?"

"How are you, Armando?"

"Busy as shit. In case you haven't heard, last night we had three drive-byes and a double drug execution. That's on top of a strangled Venezuelan tourist washing up on the beach the night before, on top of the random shooting at the Yahweh Temple three days ago. Six dead, three others on life support.

"I read about that."

"Well, I'm glad you're still literate. As you can see I'm busy. What can I do for you?"

"I wanted to get a copy of the Richard Johnson shooting report."

"Richie Johnson?" Armando Pedroza asked with a puzzled look, "How could that possibly interest you?"

"My company has a disability policy out on him. We're on the hook for 75% of his salary while he's too injured to play."

A rabid baseball fan, Armando Pedroza commented, "That postalita missed two weeks with a hangnail. A bullet to the shoulder should be good for the season. Maybe next year's too. I still don't get why you're here?"

"Seventy-five percent of eleven million dollars is a significant amount of money. I'm making sure the "i's" are dotted and the "t's" are crossed."

"In other words the trillion dollar company you work for is looking at every possible angle and loophole to weasel out of paying. Glad to see you found nice honest work. All this time I've been worried about you. I thought all you did was expose accident victims for making phony whiplash claims. Rosi, make Bambi a copy of the Richie Johnson report. By the way, how's your wife?"

Rosaria Gonzalez walked over to a row of file cabinets. She took out a folder and went over to the copy machine, swearing at Armando Pedroza in Spanish under her breath.

The insurance investigator pretended he didn't hear the last question. He asked, "Do you have any leads?"

Armando Pedroza threw him a disdainful glare. He spat the words out, raising his voice with each sentence. By the end he was almost shouting. "We're waiting for the telephone directory from Volusia County. Then we'll be able to pare down our suspect list to nine hundred thousand. Those are only the ones with a motive to kill the cocksucker. That's not taking into account he was driving a two hundred thousand dollar car in the highest crime area of the highest crime rate city in the world while wearing enough jewelry to make Mister T jealous!"

During the Homicide Chief's little diatribe the insurance investigator quickly scanned the report. "I don't know, Armando," he continued, "the shooter didn't take anything."

"Meaning?"

"Meaning on the surface it doesn't look like your typical stop and shop carjack."

Armando Pedroza's face turned an angry red. He made no pretense of restraint and shouted in the slighter man's face.

"Maybe the perp got spooked. Maybe it was a drug buy gone bad. Maybe asshole Richie Johnson was too embarrassed to file a report. Maybe it was raining too hard. Maybe I'm too fucking busy to worry about some multimillionaire berehena with a superficial shoulder wound. As far as I'm concerned, it's no harm, no foul. I've got more than my share of uncleared cases with real dead bodies involved. Attempted homicides, let me emphasize the word attempted, are not exactly my priority. So why don't you do me a favor, take the report, get out of my face, and let me get back to work. And while you're earning your four hundred dollars a week, why don't you do the county a favor and solve this inscrutable enigma on your own. Call it even for the pension you got coming... Oh, excuse me, I forgot. You forfeited all your benefits. Well, why don't you solve it anyway, just to stay in practice... Hey, I got a brainstorm for you, Bambi. Maybe your old partner can help. He can roll right along next to you."

Armando Pedroza's last remark stunned the insurance investigator. His face went blank. In a barely audible voice he whispered, "I'll take the report and get out of your way." He looked sheepishly at Rosi and said, "Nice seeing you again." He turned and walked toward the stairwell. Rosaria Gonzalez thought he was going to cry. She started after him but changed her mind. Trying to comfort him now might further embarrass him. Instead, she directed her anger at Armando Pedroza, staring daggers straight through his heart. If looks could kill, Armando Pedroza would already have a tag on his toe.

"What are you looking at?" he asked in Spanish.

"El punta mas grande todo del mundo."

Rosaria Gonzalez went back to work but couldn't concentrate. Her thoughts drifted back to memories of her old colleague, Stanley

Starfish. She recalled his first day on the job. There he was, the youngest detective in Department history ever assigned to homicide and not looking a day over fifteen and possessing that unusual surname. When she asked him about it he would simply say it was a long story and leave it at that. She overheard him tell others it was an old family name and others still it was an old American Indian name. She never did get an explanation. To the best of her knowledge he had no family whatsoever until he was married.

Stanley resembled a human ball of non-stop energy and brought a refreshing amount of enthusiasm to his job. He was so naïve and innocent-looking when he started the squad called him "Bambi," the first of several nicknames. What a shame he was assigned to Armando Pedroza's squad, a Commander in the Department at the time. The only Anglo, Stanley had as much in common with them as Woody Allen had with the Reverend Reggie White. To a man they were macho in every way. They lived and governed their lives by a secret manly code and all looked to Armando Pedroza as their high priest. They were the ultimate cynics and anyone outside their little orbit was a hump, a perp, an asshole, or a maricon. They formed an exclusive boys' club with an "us against them" mentality. The lone exception was Ron Jeffries, the only Black in homicide and the only other non-Hispanic on the squad. Naturally, Armando made Ron and Stanley partners. They were the only two Rosaria really liked and who treated her with kindness and respect. They were the only two who didn't ask her every morning if she "got any" the night before or made lewd, suggestive remarks about her ass and tits behind her back just loud enough for her to hear. Truth be told, she was sometimes ashamed of her own kind. She was even married for a brief time to a uniformed Latino cop. It didn't work out. He was too similar to the guys she worked with. She promised her mother she would never again marry someone in law enforcement, especially an Hispanic.

Ron and Stanley were true gentlemen. Additionally, Stanley was genuinely funny. He had a knack for making faces and doing imitations which constantly brightened her day. He was also considerate. He never once forgot her birthday. She looked at one of his gifts on her desk, a beautiful deer cowrie shell. She paused to admire its shiny symmetry. They were certainly different from the rest of the squad and were treated by them as pariahs.

Armando Pedroza thought he would initiate his newest detective by assigning him an unsolvable case, the Aronson Murder. It had been on the books for years with no progress. He gave Stanley five weeks to come up with something then sat back with his compadres for big laughs while the skinny newcomer spun his wheels. In a little over three weeks he made an arrest. Over the next few years he and Ron Jeffries would accomplish the unfathomable. They cleared every single case they were assigned, including the most publicized, highest-profile homicides in recent South Florida history.

Ron and Stanley were opposite personalities whose qualities blended together forming an ideal mix. Ronnie was an ex-military man who was orderly and precise in everything he did. He had the neatest desk, wore the cleanest shirts and had the most polished shoes. He typed the most concise reports and didn't need instructions on using the computer. Rosi noticed people had a tendency to underestimate him. That was a mistake. Ron possessed street smarts and was plenty street tough when he had to be. He was resilient enough to withstand the prejudices of the good ole' boys and the Latinos who comprised the majority of the Miami Dade police force. He was sometimes a target for a faction of the Black officers who considered him a sellout. One thing about Ron. He didn't care much what people thought about him.

She heard at one time he was a legendary athlete. Rosaria didn't doubt it. You would never find that out from Ron, who, unlike Armando, was anything but a self-promoter. About five feet ten with a sleek, sinewy build, she doubted he had five percent body fat. He was handsome, too. He had a beautiful wife and a son and a daughter. She reached in her drawer for a tissue. Thinking of him now made her eyes water.

No one would ever suspect Stanley Starfish was a policeman or a plainclothes detective. He would stump the "What's My Line" panel every time. Even today, in his thirties, he could easily pass for a college student. He was exceedingly skinny and looked very fragile. Every hurricane warning Rosaria would semi-seriously remind him to handcuff himself to something immovable. Otherwise she was certain he'd be blown away like a candy wrapper. In spite of his physique, she considered him cute, having curly brown hair, rosy cheeks and dancing blue eyes.

Rosaria Gonzalez was also absolutely positive that Stanley Starfish was a true genius and by far the smartest person she'd ever known. There wasn't anything he couldn't solve, no puzzle too complicated, no mystery too complex. She loved to watch him when he was hot on a lead and his mind was warming up. He would pace back and forth at hyper speed, drumming on his desk, the chair, his pockets, anything in reach. He would fire question after question at Ronnie, asking five before he could answer one. He didn't really expect an answer from his partner, the questions were really to himself. Ronnie swore he could see smoke from his head when Stanley was doing his thing. When he put it all together he would give a wry little smile. This was it. No big celebrations. Sometimes a snap of his fingers but always that knowing smile of satisfaction. Stanley Starfish operated on another level, maybe three or four levels above everyone else.

Ron and Stanley were a team. Stanley never sought out any special credit but Rosi knew it was he who broke the mega cases. After a while everyone knew. When he cracked the Biscayne Kennel Club murder the media dubbed him Miami's Sherlock Holmes. He became something of a pseudo-cult figure popularized by USA Today in a front page article.

For a time he even begrudgingly won Armando Pedroza's respect. Armando had no problem accepting the lion's share of credit for Ron and Stanley's successes. He rode their wake to promotion after promotion. Ever the consummate politician, many considered the ambitious Armando next in line for District Chief, possibly Director of the entire Public Safety Department in the not too distant future.

Everything changed after the Rosen case. The media portrayed Stanley as the stifled genius impeded by the bumbling, stupid, bureaucratic Armando Pedroza. Armando never forgave and he never, never forgot. Not long after the incident with Ronnie occurred and Stanley transferred out of Homicide to Vice. A few months later he was forced off the Department under a cloud of suspicion. On top of everything else, Stanley's wife left him. A former vice cop, Armando Pedroza was downright gleeful. Even today, some two years after Stanley separated from the Department, the sadistic asshole took great pleasure in grinding him down and reopening old wounds.

Rosi lamented the irony of it all. Sweet, brilliant Stanley Starfish was stuck in a dead-end, nowhere job while the world's biggest prick was master of his domain. Who said life was fair! She remembered the hurt look on Stanley's face when he walked away and reached for another tissue. As she wiped her eyes, Rosi was very certain in her life of three things: the sun would set in the West, Spanish Radio was railing on about Castro, and Stanley Starfish would clear his case. When he worked a case Stanley Starfish never failed.

Armando Pedroza went back to work with renewed energy and an extra little bounce in his step. Rubbing that skinny geek's nose in it was invigorating. The little nerd looked like he was about to cry. What a *maricon!* Armando had doubts about him from the start. After all, he couldn't keep his wife happy. She left him, and for a Cuban, too. He took a deep breath and smiled. What a fine way to start the day! Chewing someone up and spitting them out was one of the truly excellent fringe benefits of law enforcement. Police work was unquestionably Armando Pedroza's life calling.

How ironic, because Armando Pedroza grew up hating cops. He came to Miami from his native Cuba when he was ten years old, not speaking a word of English. His mother, *vaya con Dios,* never did, nor does his father today. The incompetent Anglo teachers thought he was slow, possibly retarded. They placed him in remedial classes and kept him back a grade. Armando wasn't a dunce. It was all the language barrier. By the time he learned English it was too late. He was way behind. His dislike for school festered into an intense hatred. After his second year he dropped out of Miami High. He started hanging out and getting into trouble. Armando compiled an impressive juvenile record with commendations for shoplifting, loitering, burglary and auto theft. What a great place was his adopted country! In Cuba they would have jailed him for life. In the U.S. anyone under legal age wasn't even held overnight. He figured they caught him once out of every twenty transgressions. The cops must have made the same estimation because they felt they owed you for the ones you got away with. They would beat the living shit out of him while he was handcuffed in the back seat of their patrol cars.

"Take this for the one you got away with, you dirty greaseball spic," was a popular refrain after they'd already knocked you senseless. A majority of the time they would simply beat you and let you go and not have to bother with the paperwork. They called it administering street justice.

By far the meanest, toughest cops were on Miami Beach. Whenever a group of his amigos went over one of the causeways there would always be trouble. Even if they were minding their own business the punk Anglos wouldn't leave them be. It always started "Why don't you try the beaches back in Cuba? Why don't you try swimming right now?" What *commierdas!* If they only knew the beaches in Cuba made Miami Beach look like a pissant sand pile. He remembered going with his parents to the beaches of Valladero; miles of pink sand as far as you can see sloping gently to the gin-clear ocean. And no concrete either. They didn't ruin the beaches with massive hotels and condos built to the water's edge.

Armando didn't mind the fighting, no matter how badly they were outnumbered. Inevitably the police were summoned. They didn't care who started it or what the circumstances were. It was always the

Cubans' fault. The cops of Miami Beach, to a man, were big beefy red-neck crackers, all expert at administering street justice. They were also adept at giving swimming lessons. They called it the Martin Luther King Aqua Safety course. After a little session in the back of the patrol car they took you to the Julia Tuttle Causeway Bridge, uncuffed you and tossed you over. They did give you a warning if you were caught on the Beach again, the next time they'd leave on the cuffs.

Armando and his friends heeded their advice, frequenting the beaches of Crandon Park on Key Biscayne instead. Many other Cuban refugees made the same choice. Sundays reminded him of his home-land with Cuban flags strewn from the shady Australian pines. The scene pulsated to salsa rhythms and the air filled with the aroma of grilled pork turning on open fires. Latinos knew how to do the beach in style.

As he approached his eighteenth birthday and with his juvenile sta-tus about to expire, Armando Pedroza was given the choice of serving his country as a member of the Armed Forces or going to jail. He enlist-ed in the United States Marine Corps and served a tour in Vietnam. The Marine Corps specialized in attitude adjustments. He returned to Miami a changed man. He thrived on the discipline inherent in the military and became an excellent combat soldier, twice decorated. Coming home, the Miami he returned to was a far different place than the one he had left.

Expecting acclaim and recognition for his military record, Armando Pedroza was sadly disappointed. He had the misfortune of playing a hit role in a flop war. Vietnam provoked streams of protest everywhere, even laid back Miami. Instigated by intellectual hippies from the artsy colony of Coconut Grove and MG revolutionaries from the University of Miami who drove from peace rally to peace rally in their little sports cars, a poisonous atmosphere surrounded every governmental institu-tion with a connection to the military. Draft boards were picketed, as were recruiting offices. Armando once attended a peace rally. He thought it would be an easy way to score with some free sex, hippie, peacenik chick. He came away disgusted. The long-haired freaks and intellectual communistas didn't bother him so much. What severely pissed him off were the college kids. The ones who benefited the most from the wealth and bounty of their country were afraid to fight for it. The ones with the brightest futures avoided their obligations by hiding behind their student deferments. No wonder there were so many blacks and Mexicans and Puerto Ricans in his unit. The Jewish kids from Miami Beach and the Coral Gables socialite preppies were protected from military service by their 2S draft classifications.

Reluctantly he had to give a nod to the universe's most despicable sub-human. Fidel would not tolerate those protests and would handle the demonstrators far differently.

After a month of hanging out, Armando Pedroza needed to find work. He was encouraged to check out the police department. The Metro Dade Public Safety Department was staging a campaign to hire more bilingual Cuban Americans. With his juvenile record sealed by Florida State law and his military record openly displayed he was a prime candidate. His one regret was being in the police training academy during the 1972 Republican Convention held on Miami Beach. He would have loved to show those protesters some South Florida hospitality.

Armando Pedroza loved being a policeman. He had found his calling, enjoying every aspect of the job and the accompanying trappings. His clear favorites were the power and the authority. He quickly developed into an efficient brutal cop bringing his own special refinements to street justice. He got a kick out of the young, brash Cuban juveniles who thought they could outsmart him. They didn't know he was once a young punk himself and knew every trick.

Armando Pedroza was a man of his times and the decade of the seventies was a fantastic time to be a cop in Miami. It was an ideal situation for someone like him who knew how to take advantage of his opportunities. By the mid-seventies cocaine had surpassed marijuana as the drug of choice among recreational users. With its rise in popularity came a new breed of smugglers. The laid back grass-running hippies out of Jimmie Buffet songs lost prominence to murderous Colombians. Economically, moving cocaine made a lot of sense. At the time cocaine was still considered a recreational drug, possibly less addictive than marijuana. The penalties for smuggling either were roughly the same. But in the same space it took to occupy a single bale you could store cocaine worth millions and millions of dollars. Miami became North America's main distribution point and the white powder streamed in by boat, plane, and body cavities. With the increased financial rewards came increased risks. The Colombians engaged in bloody turf wars killing each other over territories, shipments, payments or any perceived wrong. They carried the fight into hospital wards and suburban shopping malls, causing a backlash from the local citizenry. Scrutiny from law enforcement tightened up and the judicial system took a much harsher stand toward their activities.

This was the climate in which Armando Pedroza prospered. The Colombians were idiots, ridiculously easy to spot in their expensive,

exotic cars and flashy jewelry. How foolish of them to live so ostenta-
tiously, wearing solid gold razor blades and coke spoons as necklaces.
They stuck out like erect nipples in a see-through blouse. They were
plump, little cockroaches waiting to be squished. Armando stepped on
every one he could. Often he would make a routine traffic stop and
search their cars. On a good day his persistence was rewarded if he discovered a briefcase or small package. The best possible response was,
"We don't know what it is. Why don't you take it." Cash was best. Coke
was okay too. Only the really brain impaired would complain about an
illegal search. For opening their mouths they received a beating, had
their Rolexes confiscated, were arrested and they still lost their stash.
Armando never feared any departmental consequences. What were
they going to say, "The cop beat me up and stole my drugs."?

Armando was careful to book them on a misdemeanor, something
they could walk away from with a small fine. The drug dealers were
usually grateful for the consideration and it also sent them a blaring signal: Armando Pedroza was a player. It was good business to take care
of him and pay him to look the other way. Good business for them and
business was very, very good for him. He had safe deposit boxes all
over town that neither of his ex-wives had a clue about. In good years
he doubled, tripled his police officer's salary, all in tax-free unreported
cash. With the increased financial rewards came commensurately
greater risks. Armando's business associates were not exactly stable,
Wall Street types. A payoff gone sour led to a bloody firefight with him
taking a bullet in the thigh and another in the wrist before he blew
away three Colombians. Complications arose when one of the
Colombians was still breathing and the commotion brought witnesses.
Calmly he instructed one of the bystanders to get help. He pretended
to give mouth to mouth to the wounded Colombian while surrepti-
tiously strangling him. The incident confirmed that he was born under
a lucky star. One of his several commendations was for trying to save
the life of the dying perpetrator.

His reputation as Miami-Dade County's most vicious cop was further enhanced by the incident and earned him esteem among his fellow Latin officers. They elected him President of HPOA, the Hispanic
Police Officers' Association. He possessed a yen for politics and represented his constituents ably. Among the many benefits won and con-
cessions granted under his stewardship were overtime payments for
extracurricular activities such as weight lifting and racquetball.
Armando successfully argued they were vital training exercises. His
political clout also helped with that little situation at the Immigration
and Naturalization Office.

The year 1980 was the major turning point in recent Miami history. That year the Mariel boat lift brought one hundred twenty five thousand Cuban refugees to the city, completely overwhelming the social services and sending the crime rate through the stratosphere. A byproduct of the boatlift was the tension it caused in the black community. Blacks, who already felt slighted and left behind by the success of previous Cuban immigrants, were suspicious of this new wave and viewed them as a serious menace to their way of life. They occupied their neighborhoods, living anywhere they could. They threatened their job security even in low paying service jobs as they were willing to work for less. The black community saw prejudice and favoritism at every turn and clamored about the preferential treatment given Cubans over Haitians; Haitians who also fled a dictator equally as intolerant as Castro. Cubans were allowed to stay. Haitians were rounded up, jailed, and deported. Tensions in the community were already strained from the previous year when Johnnie Jones, a highly regarded educator, was found guilty of financial malfeasance.

Mr. Jones was Superintendent of Dade County Schools. No other black administrator in the country oversaw a public school system as large. In a controversial trial he was convicted of accepting kickbacks and using school board funds to adorn his residence's bathrooms with gold-plated plumbing fixtures.

The massive immigration coming on top of the verdict made the community a tinder box. An Orlando jury provided the match when they found four white Dade County police officers innocent in the homicide of Arthur McDuffie, a black motorcyclist beaten to death after a hot pursuit. They were found not guilty of the murder and the subsequent cover-up. Within hours of the verdict the city erupted in flames and was embroiled in the bloodiest, most costly race riot in United States history. In the aftermath of the riot, relations became strained between the police department administration and its working officers. After weeks of twelve-hour shifts and cancelled vacations the overworked officers took offense at the perception that the administration was caving in to the black community's demands for a citizen review panel, hiring more black policemen, and requiring racial sensitivity training for the entire force. Squeezed by both sides, the administration knew this was not the time to be at odds with its rank and file. The city was teetering on a precipice. Maintaining order was top priority. The police department was the first line of defense. Calm and stability could not be attained without their full cooperation. The administration needed the union heads and politically powerful faction leaders like Armando Pedroza to keep the working officers in line.

In the meantime, Armando snared an off-duty job at the Immigration and Naturalization Service Office at Biscayne Boulevard and NW. 79th Street. The massive influx of new arrivals turned the INS office into a chaotic zoo. People waited in line up to three days in stifling humidity and under a broiling sun. Portalets were needed as the neighboring businesses complained vehemently about the mess and stench. The new arrivals were so afraid to lose their place they did their business while waiting in line. Nerves frayed and skirmishes broke out hourly. Off-duty police were desperately needed to establish some semblance of order. Normally a penny-ante off-duty job would be of no interest to Armando Pedroza. But in this case the hours happened to fit his schedule. In fact, the hours were his schedule. While he was supposed to be on patrol in another sector Armando worked his off-duty job, a practice known as double dipping. Ever the enterpriser, he discovered a nice little fringe benefit. He could pick up a fair piece of change by selling places in line.

Additionally, he liked the job. He detested the new Cuban refugees. He referred to them as "double d's," dumber and darker. They were far different than the Cuban immigrants of his parents' generation. They weren't professional people escaping Communism. If they weren't released from prisons or mental institutions they were mostly unskilled laborers fleeing Cuba's abject poverty. Armando thought it best to get acquainted early for he was positive he would be seeing many of them again later. He employed the same tactics with his off-duty job that he used on his regular one. He worked it with brutal efficiency. He quickly gained notoriety for his hair-trigger temper and violent reaction to the slightest infractions. The lines became more orderly.

Everything was okay until one afternoon in early August. Claude Toussaint had been in line for two days. At least he was around the corner and could see the front doors. While everyone else complained about the heat and the pace of the line Claude Toussaint took it in stride. This was his third try at gaining entry to the United States and those doors of opportunity were in plain sight. On the first attempt he sailed from Haiti with two hundred others on a vessel built to carry maybe thirty. The boat docked in the middle of the night and the refugees were told to scatter and run. He had no idea where he was or where to go. He was rounded up the next day along with many of the others, jailed briefly at the Krome Avenue Detention Center before being deported back to Haiti.

On his second attempt the boat didn't even try and dock. It pulled up within sight of the shoreline where the crew prodded everyone off into the water. Many were hesitant because they couldn't swim and they were still a couple of hundred yards offshore. But the crew insisted they were on a sandbar and could wade in. Their passengers' safety was a secondary concern surpassed by their desire to get away before being spotted by the Coast Guard or Marine Patrol. As it turned out they were nowhere near a sandbar, but rather in water over their heads and caught in a strong, outgoing current. Claude Toussaint was rescued at sea, jailed again, and deported. He was one of eleven of one hundred sixty eight who survived. Among the dead were his two sisters and a brother.

This time, his third attempt, the circumstances were much different. This time he had the backing of the Haitian Refugee Center and the Catholic Church. At his hearing he was represented by an attorney and a priest. This time he had his wife and infant daughter with him. They only had to enter the INS doors and go through the formality of being processed and precious green cards would be theirs.

As they waited in line his daughter had to pee. His wife was too hungry and dehydrated to move so he escorted her. When they returned Cubans had pushed his wife out of line and wouldn't let any of them back in. This was not fair. This was America, where everyone was equal. They had patiently waited their turn. They did not want to get ahead of anyone. They simply wanted their rightful place. He tried making that point in his native Creole. The Cubans answered in Spanish. An argument escalated into pushing and shoving, forcing Armando Pedroza to respond. Armando didn't have much patience. It was near the end of his shift and he had plans. Lobster season began the next day and he needed to prepare his boat. He listened to both points of view for a minute and then sided with the Cubans. At least he understood what they were saying.

Claude Toussaint had seen this callow policeman operate for two days and did not want to cross him. But this was America, a free country, unlike the totalitarian dictatorship in Haiti. As an enforcer of the law he should uphold his country's principles, applying them equally and fairly. He tried explaining this to Armando Pedroza who was in no mood to listen. He demonstrated his disinterest by smacking Claude Toussaint over the head with his baton. Amazingly, Claude Toussaint didn't budge. No man had ever withstood one of his blows before so Armando repeated the stroke. Again the Haitian didn't flinch. Claude Toussaint tried to reason with the policeman. He told him he didn't want any trouble. He only wanted what was right. He was not a stowaway or an illegal immigrant this time. He had followed the process and was entitled to certain rights. He told the policeman he didn't want any trouble. He only wanted what was fair. This was America. All he wanted was the opportunity for life, liberty, and the pursuit of happiness. Besides, he tried explaining, there was nothing the policeman could do to him that hadn't been done in his native land. In Haiti President-for-life Jean Claude Duvalier's private police, the Ton Ton Macoutes, used clubs four feet in length. Frustrated, Armando Pedroza used his baton to prod Claude Toussaint's wife and three-year-old daughter Yvette. Claude Toussaint said this cannot be. The policeman was not acting fairly. He had no right to manhandle his wife and daughter. He grabbed the baton away from the policeman and snapped it over his knee in two.

Armando Pedroza turned livid and drew his revolver. Who the fuck did this Haitian think he was? Well, at least he'll fulfill his dream to be buried in this country. As he took aim other Haitians waiting in line had seen enough. They heard what Claude Toussaint said and agreed. They also asked, "How could this be happening in a free country like America?" Despite being outnumbered by the Cubans more than fifty-to-one, and realizing they might be jeopardizing their own chances for green cards, they backed Claude Toussaint, staging an impromptu demonstration. Spontaneously they formed a tight circle around Armando Pedroza and the Toussaint family jumping up and down and chanting in unison, "America *egalite!* America *egalite!*"

A frightened look came over Armando Pedroza. The incident had snowballed way out of control. He couldn't shoot his way out. He didn't have a good enough explanation and there were more witnesses than bullets. He couldn't fight his way out. As a last resort he called for backup. Within minutes a dozen police cars zoomed to the scene responding to the officer in distress call. They took control and arrested everyone in sight.

In the follow-up report it was revealed Armando Pedroza was double dipping. Also during the melee he lost his radio and his service revolver which were never recovered. Internal Affairs handed down a stinging assessment recommending suspension as a predecessor to outright dismissal. The department administration was in a bind. As the incident at the Immigration and Naturalization Service Building demonstrated, tensions in the city were still at the boiling point. The slightest provocation could again send the city up in flames. Handling someone as popular and well-connected as Armando Pedroza was a very delicate situation. The administration reacted like most large, politically sensitive bureaucracies when dealing with a politically powerful person. They promoted him.

Rather than suspension, dismissal and possibly facing criminal indictments, Armando Pedroza was on the fast track through the department's ranks. Though never attaining a civil service status higher than sergeant, Armando Pedroza proved expert at winning administrative promotions. He started as commander assigned initially to an intergovernmental agency, anti-drug task force. He made some good connections but grabbed the first opportunity to transfer out. Drug investigations were hitting too close to home. His one regret was not getting in the pants of that long-legged blonde from the DEA. What a fox! And she smelled so good. Probably Nina Ricci's L'Air du Temps.

Armando was a connoisseur of perfumes.

From the task force Armando Pedroza moved to Vice. Many in the department looked down their noses at Vice. To Armando it was seventh heaven. It had many advantages and abounded in opportunities. One thing in its favor, there were no good guys, no helpless victims except the children in kiddie porn. The girls were junkies, the johns were sleazeballs and the pimps were so low on the totem pole they had to look up to see a lawyer. Another benefit—the job did wonders for his sex life. He could get some at will, anytime of the day. There were the strung out street walkers who preferred giving a header in the backseat than a night in the system. There were the classier and prettier hookers who worked the tourist hotels' bars and lounges. They were just as easy to shake down but worthy of having real sex. He even dated a few after hours. That made for some wild times. Most of them had girlfriends and if he was lucky... He could also hand them out to friends or use them to advance his career.

The pimps were fun, too. If he was having a bad day he could always vent his frustrations out on a pimp. They too served a role in advancing his career. There wasn't a pimp alive who dealt exclusively in girls. Most sold narcotics and one hundred percent fenced the jewelry, cell phones, and credit cards their girls stole from the johns. The pimps were wired into the life and knew everything, making them excellent sources of information. They were ever so eager to rat out the competition. And for the less cooperative? Armando had his special methods of persuasion. Something he learned as a kid. Something called the Martin Luther King Aqua Safety Course. To be sure Armando added his own special refinements. He used out-of-the-way canals and electrical tie wraps instead of handcuffs. No rusting problem that way. The information gleaned from the pimps made him popular in other departments. Homicide, GIU, and Narcotics were all grateful for the tips, gaining him invaluable contacts and connections.

No doubt about it, Armando Pedroza developed into a world-class office networker.

The easiest marks were the johns, especially the married ones. They were so pathetic, having to resort to paying for it. What surprised him were the numbers of rich, handsome guys who frequented prostitutes. On the surface it would seem they could get plenty of wool for free. Armando learned they had their reasons. Sometimes their wives were unresponsive. Sometimes they simply wanted variety. Sometimes they wanted sex with no emotional commitment. Sometimes they wanted forms of sex their wives would have no part of. It shocked him to find out how many enjoyed being debased, enjoyed it enough to pay huge dollars for it. They paid to be spanked. They paid to be diapered. They paid to be pissed on and worse. To a man they were piteous weaklings.

Every john he ever met was a loser who would pay dearly to keep his name out of the papers. Armando instituted an administrative fine system, a fee paid on the spot in cash to avoid being processed in the system. The fines were based solely on an ability to pay scale, generally ranging between five hundred and two thousand dollars. The lone exception were politicians. He would flash his badge and snicker at their horrified reactions. Instead of ruining their lives he acted sympathetically, promising them nobody would have to know. In lieu of payment he stored their goodwill for future considerations.

His favorite aspect of the business were the escorts. Many were smart, independent, beautiful working women with no requisite for a pimp. A good percentage were single mothers. He spotted them easily in hotel lobbies. They dressed nicely but provocatively, carrying no luggage, and returned alone to the lobby in an hour or two. They were cooperative. Nobody wanted to go through the hassle of being arrested. Escorts proved to be valuable contacts who proved their worth over and over by informing Armando which of their clients were best suited for administrative fines. They also produced another revenue stream—stolen jewelry. He coached his girls only to steal quality, brand name, easily fenceable watches like Cartier or Rolex. And only from the married ones who would be too embarrassed to file a report. He'd deal the watches to downtown jewelry stores and pawnshops owned by discreet, trustworthy fellow Cubans. Armando wasn't terribly greedy. By sharing with his squad he insured their devoted loyalty.

Another way to meet escorts was through reverse sting operations. They'd look in the Yellow Pages under "Escorts" or cut out ads from the sports pages. They'd take out two adjoining hotel rooms; one for the undercover cop and the other set up with listening devices, tape recorders and video cameras. The undercover cop would call a number and order up a girl. When she arrived he would show her a credit card, photo ID, and an airline ticket. Once she named an act and a price she was popped.

As much as Armando loved Vice his desire to advance his career was greater. He knew Vice had no future. No one ever made the department upper echelon coming from Vice. What he needed was the publicity and big time exposure rendered from high profile murder cases. At the first opportunity he transferred to Homicide.

For some strange reason he didn't fully comprehend murder had a glamorous aspect to it. Perhaps it had to do with the finality of the act. Maybe the crime appealed to the public's darker side. Maybe they realized that under the right circumstances a person could do about anything. Whatever the reason, Armando Pedroza knew the surest way to promotion was to stand in front of the television cameras with a bevy of microphones thrust in your face as you announced an arrest or a breakthrough in a highly visible homicide.

Armando started off slowly in homicide. He wanted to be absolutely certain he could trust the men in his command. He weeded out the women and Anglos until his squad was almost entirely Hispanic. He had a Nicaraguan and a Chilean but a least they were better than Puerto Ricans. The lone exception was the *negrito* Ron Jeffries, who refused to transfer out. Armando eyed Ron Jeffries warily. He was a by-the-book tightass and a stickler for regulations. He warned his guys to be very cautious and not say much or do much when around him. The rest of the squad was no problem. Armando's reputation preceded him and they were anxious to gain his approval. Armando worked aggressively to build an esprit de corps within the ranks. He took his guys out to bars and clubs after hours. He introduced them to some of his female acquaintances from his days in Vice. He taught them important lessons on how to cover for each other with their wives. Lessons which could be applied to their police work in stickier situations. When he was sure of their loyalty he demonstrated his more effective methods of interrogation. He shared his network of informers and instructed them how they could cultivate their own. Within few months he had what he wanted. The homicide detectives under his command were a cohesive, tightly knit group fiercely loyal to him and each other.

They also produced results. Armando Pedroza had a knack for clearing cases. If his men investigated a gang-related drive-by shooting they would implicate the deceased victim in unsolved murders of rival gang members. The same procedure worked well in drug-related homicides. Armando was much more concerned with clearing cases than solving them. As were his bosses. As long as the cases were off the books and the overall caseload reduced, the department's top brass was more than satisfied.

His efficiency put him in good standing. Between his record and his networking he did nothing to hurt his chances for promotion. What he needed was to crack a high profile case and cash in on the accompanying publicity. Drive-byes and drug hits were no problem. Crimes of passion, domestic violence, and vehicular homicides were all a piece of cake. Missing from his resume was a clear in a really big case.

A prime example was the Aronson murder. Dan Aronson was a world-renowned yacht builder. Customers came from all over the world to purchase his sleek, luxurious, ultra-powerful boats. Arab oil sheiks, Shahs, Hollywood celebrities, New York financiers and European royalty were among his clientele. So were the cartels. The size and speed of his boats were ideal for offloading kilos from mother ships in the Bahamas, then racing across the gulfstream into South Florida. For the right price custom modifications like hidden compartments could be added. Neither U.S. Customs or the DEA had anything in the water even close. For years Aronson made boats enjoyed a free reign racing in unimpeded from debarkation points throughout the Caribbean. Until Don Aronson started making boats for the government. He contracted to manufacture a line of seacraft for the DEA, U.S. Customs and the Navy. Rumors floated, suggesting the new boats were modified to outrun previous models. Other rumors hinted that Aronson's old customer list was part of the deal.

Personally Dan Aronson was renowned as a bon vivant who enjoyed life's finest pleasures. He lived in spectacular waterfront properties, drove expensive cars, ate and drank in the finest restaurants and was seen with the town's most beautiful women. His successful business afforded him such luxuries. His business practices were another matter.

Dan Aronson made a practice of selling his business to people whose lawyers apparently never heard of a non-compete clause. Within a few months he would open up again producing the same boat under a different name, driving the buyers of his old company into bankruptcy. He did this several times leaving some very angry people in his wake.

He was also a world-class boat racer who enjoyed wagering large sums on the races' outcome. After winning two hundred fifty thousand dollars for a race from Miami to New York City, he boldly offered to go double or nothing on the way back. He relished the ponies and betting pro football. Some say he liked collecting on his bets a lot more than paying them off. Additionally, many of the women he squired were other men's wives.

When Armando Pedroza got the case it surely didn't lack for suspects. One of the big problems with the case was so many had a

motive to kill Aronson. From bookies to business associates, cuckold-
ed husbands to drug cartel big shots, the roster of people who would-
n't mind seeing Dan Aronson dead was lengthy. The manner in which
he died suggested a professional hit. Someone came to his office asking to look at boats. When a salesman offered to help the man told him
he was looking for something in the vicinity of a million dollars and
preferred Mr. Aronson personally assist him. Dan Aronson didn't mind.
He was a natural salesman with a fondness for the vicinity in which his
potential buyer was inquiring. It didn't bother him at all that the man
looked like he couldn't afford a canoe. He knew in the boat business
looks were deceiving. Some of his best customers resembled
Woodstock refugees. While Dan Aronson showed the buyer around the
man drew a .32 caliber pistol and put two bullets behind his ear.
Witnesses described the gunman wearing a Panama hat, sunglasses, a
flowered shirt, cargo shorts and deck shoes. He was bearded, of medium height and build. He drove off in a Dodge or possibly a Chrysler.
No one got a look at the license plate.

Armando Pedroza viewed the case as his big break. He projected
it as his ticket to the upper echelon. His enthusiasm swiftly dissipated.
The case was like catching a cloud. Leads would seem promising then
vanish into vapor. Many of the potential suspects were politically powerful and objected to his standard method of questioning. The city's
well-connected objected to their wives talking to cops about their
extra-marital affairs. The administration caved under the pressure. The
"word" filtered down to Armando to take it easy on certain people. It
seemed to him the administration wanted resolution to the case as long
as it was done within restrictive but nebulous guidelines. The Cartel
angle was equally hard to get a fix on. If, as rumored, Dan Aronson
had given the Cartel up to the government he would have signed his
own death certificate. As hard as his men tried they couldn't verify it.
The federal government agencies were uncooperative, not giving up a
thing. Armando thought he could reach out to his contacts in the DEA
but learned when dealing with the Feds—information flowed exclusively one way. So much for inter-governmental cooperation. He tried
reconstructing transactions from Aronson's old records. Armando determined right away he was way over his head. Both Aronson and the cartels had confounded the IRS for years. Aronson had multiple sets of
books and the cartels bought everything with cash or through dummy
offshore corporations. If the IRS with their walls of computers and
scores of auditors couldn't make any headway, Armando Pedroza
didn't stand a Chinaman's chance.

It was a case where everyone knew something but nobody knew

everything. The case was too public to clear in his standard manner. There was far to much media scrutiny to pawn it off on a dead guy. It remained unsolved, festering like an infected sore. Every now and then he'd take a new shot at it, hoping to gain a new perspective. Sometimes he'd chase a new lead but never came up with something tangible.

The longer the Aronson murder case remained open the more it got under his skin. It was something an enemy or some bureaucrat with an agenda could throw in his face whenever he was up for promotion. After a while Armando decided he wouldn't let the case drive him crazy and decided to have some fun with it. Whenever someone new was assigned to his squad he immediately gave him the Aronson case and eight weeks to clear it. The Aronson case became a form of hazing where Armando and his compadres could get a few smiles at the new person's expense. He thought it would be the perfect vehicle to break in the smartass new kid from economic crimes. "Kid" was an understatement. When Stanley Starfish first introduced himself Armando told him he had the wrong department. Stolen bicycles were on the first floor. The kid did not fit Armando Pedroza's image of a homicide detective. His men were body builder fit with dark, Latin features. As a symbol of their esprit de corps all members of his squad sported full virile mustaches. All except for the *niche* Ron Jeffries. He doubted this kid had started shaving. He had curly hair and blue eyes. He looked like an innocent little Jewboy. He looked like Bambi. And what kind of name was Starfish?

Actually Armando Pedroza had heard of this boy wonder from the Economic Crimes Unit. People he knew said the kid was different. Different but smart in a weird sort of way. They told him the kid solved every case he worked. No exceptions. He didn't just clear them, he made arrests. Thinking back, Armando recalled speaking to him once on the phone involving a case. He and his men were working a homicide where a twelve year old girl was sexually molested and murdered in her home on the Beach. He was sure the father did it. Although his men didn't have enough physical evidence for an arrest and couldn't browbeat a confession out of him, Armando was sure. Out of the blue he received a call from a Detective Starfish, at the time working GIU. The little twerp was working a series of burglaries and said he might have some information related to the Beach homicide. Armando remembered listening with one ear. He told the kid they had a suspect but he'd look into it. He never followed up. A few weeks later he arrested a couple of carpet cleaners for the burglaries and one flips the other for the homicide. Armando attributed it to blind luck. Then, the department assigned the same punk to his squad. Were they trying to send him a message? Armando, who saw conspirators out to get him lurking under every desk, eyed the kid suspiciously. Before partnering him up with Ron Jeffries he assigned him the Aronson case, giving him five weeks to clear it. If the kid was such a genius he shouldn't need the full eight weeks normally allowed. Less than four weeks later he made an arrest. The Aronson case had bounced from squad to squad for years and no one had ever come close. This punk comes out of left field and makes an arrest in his very first bona fide homicide case! Maybe he was different. For a time he did wonders for Armando Pedroza's career. Armando made certain to step out in front of the cameras and field questions whenever the kid and his partner broke a big case. If he remembered, he would credit Detectives Starfish and Jeffries, at the very end.

Getting in front of the camera became a habit as Bambi and the *negrito* cleared the most publicized cases in the county. Armando and his men nicknamed them "Blackman and Robin." Most of the time he had no idea what they were doing or where they were. As long as they produced results he could take credit for, he was willing to give them space. Their working relationship resembled a cold war détente. Armando made a half-hearted attempt to bring them into his inner circle but it didn't work out. They weren't Latin and they wouldn't adhere to the game plan. The Paul Daniels case proved that. It was a simple case, and Blackman and Robin just happened to catch it.

Paul Daniels was a rich, semi-retired lawyer living in a luxurious eleventh-floor condominium in the Cricket Club. Located on Biscayne Bay in North Miami, the Cricket Club had a diverse mix of tenants ranging from displaced New Yorkers to Arab Sheiks. Paul Daniels loved boating. He preferred the Cricket Club because it could accommodate his seventy-foot Rybovich. The Rybovich was his pride and joy. He loved to entertain on it, taking it down the bay for sunset cocktail parties. He was a stickler for appearances and his captain and crew earned harsh rebukes if an inch of mahogany went unpolished. His other weakness was teenaged boys. He met his latest companion through a friend. A runaway, Rusty Hinton enjoyed the trappings of Paul Daniels lifestyle. He wasn't as fond of being passed among Paul Daniel's friends. Rusty demonstrated his displeasure by stabbing Paul Daniels sixty three times while he slept. With Paul Daniels condo, cash, credit cards, and liquor cabinet at his disposal, Rusty Hinton did the teenage thing. He threw a party. One helluva party! A three-day party that exhausted the late Mr. Daniels' liquor supply and cash on hand. Since crack dealers were not yet accepting credit cards Rusty and his friends started pawning valuables from the apartment. They started with Paul

Daniels' rare jade figurine collection worth at least one hundred thousand dollars.

They sold it for three hundred fifty dollars. Utilizing the same business acumen on ensuing transactions Rusty and his pals soon depleted Paul Daniels' assets. His friends began making inquiries into the locked room Rusty declared off limits. Surely it contained a television, stereo and other pawnable valuables. They also wanted to know why the room smelled so bad. Keeping secrets was not Rusty's forte. He let his inner circle know the fate of Paul Daniels. Together they thought out different ways to explain the body. The first suggestion was to toss him off the balcony and claim he committed suicide. Rusty's girlfriend asked, "Why would he stab himself sixty-three times before jumping off the balcony?" The next idea was to chop him up and get rid of the pieces in the garbage disposal. The task proved to be far too messy and time consuming. They quit after one finger. They decided to leave Paul Daniels in the bedroom and pawn the valuables. They agreed what they really needed first were more rocks of cocaine before devising a new plan. By then one of the partygoers' parents became worried and the doorman got increasingly suspicious after the kids carried a second forty-eight inch TV through the lobby.

The followup was routine. Ron Jeffries and Stanley Starfish made the arrest and filed the appropriate reports. Armando Pedroza viewed the Daniels' homicide as a prime opportunity to clear eight or nine open cases with a homosexual angle. All Blackman and Robin had to do was amend their report and implicate Paul Daniels in the unsolved murders. They wouldn't consider it. They wouldn't even sign off on the ones involving teenaged boys. Bambi made excuse after excuse about there being no evidence and how Paul Daniels had no history of violence. While pissed off over their lack of cooperation, at least Armando Pedroza knew where he stood. Jeffries and Starfish could not be trusted. They didn't abide by the blue code. It figured. They weren't Latin and couldn't understand the concept of a favor for a favor. From that point on Ron Jeffries and Stanley Starfish worked apart from the rest of the homicide detectives, sort of a squad within a squad. Any contact he needed to make with them went through Rosi. Rosi Gonzalez acted as the conduit between them and the squad. He still had to let them know who was boss. He accomplished it with verbal putdowns every chance he could get. But when it came to department business their face to face contact was pretty much limited to press conferences where Armando would take the brunt of credit for their work. Reluctantly, he had to give them some credit. There was more than one press conference. To this day the intricacies of the Biscayne Kennel Club case still baffled him.

Their working relationship remained like that for a couple of years. Armando was promoted to Major, one step below District Chief and two below Director of the entire Public Safety Department. He could have tolerated their working situation longer if it wasn't for the Rosen case. Everything changed after the Rosen case. He expressly ordered the skinny geek to leave it alone. So what does he do? Bambi goes behind his back and solves it! Because the victim's daughter was a hot shot TV reporter, the publicity accompanying the case was way, way overhyped. Mr. "Miami's Sherlock Holmes" comes off as some kind of savior while he himself was portrayed as a stumbling, incompetent.

Remembering details of the case, to this day, made him angry. Roni Rosen came to his office pleading with him to look into the death of her father. There was nothing to look into. Her father died of a heart attack, plain and simple. It was his third heart attack, occurring just ten months after being operated on for a heart valve and triple bypass. He died the way Armando dreamed of; in the saddle with a beautiful babe young enough to be his daughter. Actually, his fourth wife was a year younger than his daughter. That her father died before he could divorce wife number four and cut her out of his will were the real reasons Roni Rosen wanted the death investigated. Poor little Miss TV Reporter, didn't want to split her inheritance with her coked-out stepmom. Implicating her stepmother some way in her father's death was her sole chance to cut her out. She was grasping at straws. The County Medical Examiner ruled it death by natural causes and besides, she waited too long to make an inquiry. Some Jewish law required the body to be buried right away. Sidney Rosen was in the ground within forty-eight hours. Roni Rosen didn't come to Armando until two weeks later. Armando knew there was nothing he could do but he decided to humor her. She was cute, energetic, and had a nice butt. He detected a little chemistry between them during their meeting and chose to pursue it. He remembered their conversation almost verbatim.

"Yeah, it sounds very interesting," he remembered telling her. "Maybe we could discuss it after work at the firing range. I have a really big gun. Perhaps you'd like to shoot it."

"You think it will go off?" she responded seductively.

"I can guarantee it," he said with a big wink.

Roni Rosen pulled his pants away from his stomach by the belt buckle and dumped the paper cup of water she was drinking down his crotch. "Maybe I can squeeze the trigger when it's a foot up your ass!" she shouted angrily before storming out of his office. What a ballbuster! Who did that Jew bitch think she was, treating him like that. Worse, it happened in front of Rosi. She had to run to the ladies' room trying to hide the fact that she was laughing so hard. Nobody does that to Armando Pedroza! Especially in his place of work! Especially in front of Rosi! Maybe it was a macho thing but he could not tolerate being demeaned in front of a woman. From that moment on Roni Rosen became his sworn enemy. At that instant he was never so grateful to be a believer in Santeria. Catholicism and other forms of Christianity were fine at making you feel guilty. Probably Judaism as well. But nothing except possibly voodoo could touch Santeria when it came to exacting revenge. He remembered sacrificing a live chicken that very evening.

Armando assumed when he refused to help Roni Rosen the matter of her father's death would go away. He underestimated her persistence. She went behind his back, enlisting the assistance of Stanley Starfish. When Armando caught him making inquiries on her behalf he told him point blank to leave it alone or he could start directing traffic. In July. In the middle of the afternoon. He wanted his detectives working active cases. It's not like they lacked work. According to FBI statistics Miami Dade County had the highest per capita murder rate in the country. There was plenty to keep Mr. Super Sleuth busy. He expressly forbade him to spend any official time helping Ms. TV smartass on some fantasy quest just so she could regain her full inheritance.

That should have been the end of it. Roni Rosen was in a box. She wanted her father's body exhumed but had to show cause. With the medical examiner's finding, her stepmother's refusal to give permission, and no concrete new evidence, she didn't stand a chance. Three weeks later the State Attorney handed down indictments. The skinny little twerp worked it on his own time and went around him to the State Attorney. Under normal circumstances Armando could have handled the fallout. This was different because the media was involved. Once the local TV station got hold of the story hiding places became scarce. According to the media Armando Pedroza was the five-star example of a dimwitted bureaucratic clod impeding the investigation. On the other hand, Stanley Starfish overcame all the departmental roadblocks to bring a scheming, spousicidal widow to justice.

By some coincidence it was Roni Rosen's station which broke the story in a three-part exclusive. She was too cunning to do the piece herself. She had to avoid the appearance of a conflict of interest. Instead another hot little piece at the station did the intros, interviews, and voice-overs. Probably another cock teaser just like Roni. When it was all over Stanley Starfish was a goddamned celebrity, and Roni Rosen got her full inheritance. The hot little reporter who did the story ended up hosting the Today Show while Armando Pedroza's career was stuck in cement. It took a year minimum for him to distance himself from the Rosen case. It put his career path in the slow lane and he pledged revenge with every breath in his body. He didn't care if every Kentucky Fried Chicken franchise in the country went out of business, Armando Pedroza would make the sacrifices necessary to get even with Ms. Jew shrew reporter and Mr. Stanley Starfish.

It took a little time but one should never underestimate the powers of Santeria. It began with Bambi having domestic problems. Armando could have predicted that. No way that skinny pencil dick could keep the *Jubana caliente* he married satisfied. He started moping around like some sad sack with huge bags under his eyes. The situation was affecting his work. His partner, the *negrito,* tried to cover for him but his job performance was still lacking. Then, while working a routine assignment, BOOM! His partner goes down and it's Bambi's turn to swim in the sewer. During the investigation of the incident he was taken off homicide and assigned to Central Administration where he shuffled papers. After a month or so he was transferred to Vice. Just so happened he was assigned to Armando's old squad. Not long after, Mr. Miami's Sherlock Holmes was caught with his pants down and forced off the department. He worked for a while as a department store detective before landing the gig with TransGeneral. Armando lamented he never swung by the Burdines in Dadeland to watch Bambi corralling dangerous shoplifters. He meant to ask him how many sock stealers he had to catch before USA Today did another feature on him. He reflected back on their conversation and mentally kicked himself. He forgot to ask Stanley Starfish for his ex-wife's phone number.

10

Greg Barrett drove to the office feeling a little better. For the first time in a week he was able to get a decent night's sleep. Yesterday was the first time since the Richie Johnson shooting that the seas were calm enough to take the boat out and dump the gun and clothing he wore that night six thousand feet deep in the Atlantic Ocean. As hard as he tried he couldn't stop his mind from flashing back to that fateful evening. After leaving Jody's house he drove home astounded to discover it wasn't yet midnight. The horrific lost drive by itself felt like a week let alone the time he spent with Jody. Midnight was good timing. He didn't even have to fabricate an excuse for Alison. Though he never confided in her about Harry's condition, she sensed something was going on at the office. He worked late every evening the previous week. Combined with the horrendous weather simply saying he was stuck at work was sufficient. He tried resting but sleep was impossible. He went into his study and watched TV, nervously awaiting any news on Richie Johnson. The report remained the same throughout the night. Richie Johnson was in serious but stable condition, no other details available. The next day he was upgraded to fair condition. Five days later he was released from the hospital. Richie Johnson had suffered a shoulder wound. His thickly muscled upper torso stopped the bullet from penetrating through. Since the bullet didn't penetrate through it was easy enough for the surgeon to remove. The only complication was a slight infection treated with antibiotics. The prognosis was for a full recovery after extended rest and rehabilitation. Taking into account Richie Johnson's storied recuperative powers it was more than likely he would miss the season. The Manatees immediately placed him on the sixty day disabled list. News of the incident faded after a couple of days. Richie Johnson refused to comment, referring all media requests to his agent who refused to comment. There wasn't much else to report. A spokesman for the police department said they were conducting an ongoing investigation and would comment further when

they had a break in the case. The last word he read about the shooting was in the Miami Herald, which quoted an official from the Miami
Dade Public Safety Department.

"Said homicide detective Major Armando Pedroza, 'Bad things happen in bad neighborhoods.'" That was it. Greg Barrett got the impression the police had more pressing issues on their agenda. The police
seemed to take the attitude people who didn't belong in that neighborhood got what they deserved. Richie Johnson's stormy relationship
with the media worked against him. If he didn't want to comment and
he wasn't playing baseball there was no story. They ignored press
releases from his publicists. The story vanished completely within a
week.

Back at Capital Industries the atmosphere was hectic. Greg initiated negotiations for the acquisition of two major car dealerships, one in
the tri-state area and the other in Seattle. Harry Hvide returned to work
and immediately ignored his doctor's orders. The couple of hours in
the morning he agreed upon stretched to full days. Greg couldn't get
over how quickly Harry improved. His color was back as was his vitality. Harry appeared as healthy and energetic as Greg had ever seen
him. Also returning were his sense of humor and his temper, both of
which Greg sampled in the first five minutes. Harry wanted status
reports on the IPO, the Allied Waste Service deal, and the Boca Raton
Hotel and Resort renovations. He wanted inquiries made into acquiring
the most luxurious hotel and golf complex in Hawaii.

Whew! Greg thought he was working hard before Harry's return.
The present workload reminded him of the Video Nation heydays
when they had so many deals brewing they'd lost track.

Even the baseball team was something of a bright spot. Richie
Johnson's contract was insured against disability—not fully covered as
it would have been in the case of a death. The disability portion did
cover seventy five percent of his salary while he was determined to be
too injured to play. With only twenty five percent of Richie Johnson's
salary counting against their budget Lou Redmond had the Manatees'
payroll within the projected parameters. The team they turned over to
Paddy McGraw was not the same as the one which captured the World
Series. The new version Manatees would play a different brand of ball.

Greg had Martha put in a call to Tony Lampone. He wanted to tell
him personally his promotion was official. Tony Lampone was Auto
World's new Vice President in charge of imports. The new position
would require him to relocate to Jacksonville and he wanted to give
Tony as much notice as possible. He already had given Tony a hint
about the new job when he returned the loaner. Remembering their

conversation sent his mind drifting back again to the incident. He remembered every detail. After the sleepless night in the study he was up and about at sunrise gathering up every item of clothing he wore the night before. The shoes, the gloves, the rain poncho, all of it was stuffed in a gym bag along with the gun and about twenty pounds of diving weights he kept on the boat. He stored them below deck in a locked compartment. His plan to motor out to sea and dump the gym bag overboard was thwarted by the weather. He recalled how nervous and scared he was after hearing the marine forecast. The NOAA weather bureau issued a severe marine warning calling for seas eight to twelve feet and higher in the Gulfstream. It recommended all ships stay in port. The so-called Storm of the Century had kicked up the surf, causing beach erosion and dangerous rip currents up and down the Gold Coast. It also spawned deadly tornadoes cutting a path of destruction across the state. It would be days, six days to be exact, before the seas receded enough for him to safely take the boat out. Frustrated about being stranded on shore and getting increasingly nervous about the stowed evidence, Greg realized he still had to return the car. He left the house before anyone else was up and drove to Auto World, parking the Taurus back in Tony Lampone's assigned spot. He walked about twelve blocks to a bagel place and went inside for a cup of coffee. He used a pay phone to summon a cab. After a twenty five minute wait the cab picked him up and dropped him at the Hollywood-Fort Lauderdale Airport Delta Terminal. He retrieved the Lexus and drove back to Auto World. Tony Lampone arrived about ten minutes later. After perfunctory greetings and exchanging small talk about the previous night's storm they went into Tony's office. Greg was the first to speak.

"Listen, Tony. There's a little problem with the car. I got caught in the storm, kind of lost my vision and ran into a tree. There's a dent in the front bumper."

Tony shrugged his shoulders and said, "Call me crazy but I think I can handle that."

"I know you can." Greg continued. "But I feel really awful about this and insist on paying for a new bumper out of my own pocket. I don't want you to notify the insurance company or attempt to fix it. What do you think it will cost?"

Tony had never before heard Greg Barrett speak so authoritatively. It would be foolish on his part to question the strange request. He checked one of the books on a shelf behind his desk chair.

"Ball park, about three hundred twenty dollars our cost. Add another one hundred for paint and labor."

Greg took out his billfold and peeled off five hundred dollar bills. "Please, let me know if it's more. Oh, one more thing. Please dispose of the bumper. Don't try and bang it out or sell it for scrap. Just get rid of it."

Tony looked puzzled but responded, "Sure, Greg, whatever you want. Not many people today take responsibility for their own actions anymore."

Tony's words caused Greg to cough. He forced a smile, shook hands with Tony and began walking out. Before reaching the door he turned back to Tony and said, "One more thing. Call your real estate agent. Tell her you have a listing."

Tony smiled. "Where should I be looking?"

"How about Jacksonville?"

"Jacksonville's good. Their football team is better than Harry's."

They shook hands and Greg walked out of the office. "Do you need a ride?" Tony asked.

"No, thanks. I have my car."

Tony pumped his fist and shouted "Yes!" so loud his secretary shot him a strange look. He didn't care. Going to Jacksonville was a big step up the management ladder. With it came commensurate pay raises, benefits, and most importantly, more stock options. He went out to the parking lot to examine the loaner. It wasn't a big dent and was tempted to simply have it banged out and recycled. He looked closer and wondered what kind of tree was painted red. The whole conversation with Greg Barrett was a little odd but he quickly dismissed it and concentrated on Jacksonville. Jacksonville was the main port of entry for foreign cars entering the Southeastern United States. As Vice President of Import Operations he would oversee the preparation and distribution of the cars and trucks to their various dealerships. He knew Joe Fortunata had given notice and Tony let it be known he was interested in replacing him. "What the hell," he thought to himself, "If some corporate big shot wants me to ditch a perfectly reusable bumper, so be it."

Though the car was taken care of Greg could not relax as long as the gym bag was on the boat. Each morning his level of anxiety rose when his efforts to motor out were prevented by the weather. Never before had the seas been this rough for so long. Must have been El Nino. When he did get out the wave troughs were still a good four to six feet high. Seeing the bag go overboard released a mountain of pent up anxiety. Greg Barrett was able to relax a bit and immerse himself in his work.

Hard work and the passing of time proved to be great panaceas.

Each day was less stressful and guilt-ridden than the preceding one. Disposing of the gym bag was the last loose end. His life returned to a degree of normalcy with the exception of his feelings toward Jody. That issue was still unresolved. There were countless logical reasons to rationalize that one night as a moment of weakness and go on. Words would form in his head of what he would say to her. He could never formulate them into a single sentence as memories of her warmth and passion brashly interrupted. Yesterday at the soccer game was the first time he'd seen her since their encounter. He wasn't sure how to act or how she would react. What a relief to find her smiling and happy but not overly familiar. Talking to her and spending time with her only intensified his conflict. Tonight she was working overtime, taking calls in the emergency room. Tomorrow she had the day off and he was taking her out to lunch. Maybe then they could sort things out.

11

The insurance investigator left the Public Safety Building, got into his car and drove back to the highway. He was out of sorts and realized he always felt that way after any contact with Armando Pedroza. Armando had the whammy on him, had it since the first time they met. He had a way of making him feel uneasy and inferior. There was a time he would have done about anything to gain Armando Pedroza's good graces. It wasn't to be. He glanced at his watch and noticed it was past two o'clock PM. He decided to take a little time and treat himself to his favorite lunch at his favorite place. He exited the highway, went over the causeway and up the beach, traveling on Collins Avenue. The advantage of investigating a claim this size was that he could take his time. TransGeneral wouldn't expect nor want him to finalize his report for several weeks. They'd want him to explore every possible loophole and stall as long as he could before they paid on the claim. When he reached the beachside village of Surfside he turned on 96th Street, parked the car and put a couple of coins in the meter. He entered Sheldon's Pharmacy. While driving up Collins he passed many bistros serving buffalo mozzarella with pan-fried portabella on sourdough pita. He saw establishments offering *tres fromage* with organic spouts on focaccia or oak-roasted goat cheese with hazelnuts on peppercorn lavash. But the only place left on Miami Beach where you could still get an old-fashioned grilled cheese and tomato on whole wheat was Sheldon's Pharmacy at the corner of 96th Street and Harding Avenue.

As he passed through the double glass door he entered a place frozen in time. Sheldon's was the same now as it was when he first came with his great-grandparents many years ago. He picked up a newspaper from the magazine rack and paid for it at the cash register near the front door. He then took a seat at the lunch counter. Hector, the counterman who had been there as long as he could remember, didn't bother bringing a menu; only a glass of water and a smile. "The usual?" he asked.

"Sure, why not?"

He hadn't been there in months, possibly a year, and Hector still remembered what he ordered. He didn't know why he bought the paper. He didn't bother to open it up. He was too busy looking around and soaking up the memories. In the corner near the pay phone was the table he sat at with his great-grandparents. Right next to it was the regular table of their neighbor, the famous writer Isaac Bashevis Singer, who lunched at Sheldon's every day with his wife. Hector brought him his sandwich with a side order of fries. He also gave him a vanilla milkshake in a tall soda glass, leaving the stainless steel container from the blender on the counter. In it was enough for another tall glass. When he was a boy Mr. Sheldon expressed concern over his skinniness and made sure his great-grandparents took home the remainder of his drink. He closed his eyes and took a bite of his grilled cheese. It was as he remembered it—hot, juicy and delicious. He reached for a napkin and wiped tomato seeds off his chin. He sipped the milkshake forcefully, struggling to get any. It was so thick it barely flowed through the straw, exactly how he remembered it. He looked around once more, staring at the customers when it dawned on him why he liked the place so much and why he kept coming back.

He was safe here. Sheldon's was a haven from life's travails. The memories served as a protective cocoon sheltering him from the pain and monotony of everyday life. Surfside was where he grew up. What was supposed to be a long weekend ended up lasting a generation and formed a cornerstone in the unusual saga of Stanley Starfish.

A few twists and turns preceded the way to Surfside. It started when his mom went to college. Ruth Goldman was the daughter of two doctors. Her father was a chemical engineer with a Ph.D. from Princeton. He worked for Dow Chemical. Her mother, Rebeccah, was a neurosurgeon on staff at Roosevelt Hospital in Manhattan. Her parents divorced when she was five years old. She lost contact with her father who remarried and relocated to France. Rebeccah Goldman kept the Westside brownstone and bore the brunt of raising her daughter. Her daughter was an exceptionally gifted child with a true genius in mathematics. She was also a musical prodigy and the first to appear on the televised Leonard Bernstein's Young Peoples' Concert, playing two different instruments. Ruthie Goldman was both a concert pianist and a virtuoso violinist by the age of ten. Her mother was the youngest female graduate of the Colombia University School of Medicine. Rebeccah Goldman was an ambitious, driven woman who relentlessly pushed her daughter, accepting nothing short of perfection. Her unyielding demeanor stressed her daughter causing some conflict between them. For solace she looked to her grandparents. It was they who took her to the Bronx Zoo and Jones Beach. They provided a relief valve to an intense mother-daughter relationship. Only with her grandparents could she escape the rigors of music lessons, concert schedules, and foreign language studies. Her time with her grandparents in the Bronx were the only moments she ever felt like a little girl. One of her fondest childhood memories was going to Yankee Stadium sitting in the bleachers eating peanuts and yelling "MOOOOSE" when Bill Skowron came to bat. She had to solemnly promise her grandparents never to tell her mother.

As Ruth grew older tension between she and her mother intensified. Through her teen years she became increasingly rebellious. When it was time for college she desperately needed to get out from under her mother's thumb. Against her mother's wishes she accepted a full scholarship from Stanford University in Palo Alto, California. Rebecca Goldman strongly opposed her daughter's choice. She preferred her Ruthie stay closer to home. The East coast had more than its share of fine universities including M.I.T. and her alma mater, Colombia, right in their backyard. Her opposition only increased her daughter's resolve. Reluctantly she flew her daughter out to the alien world of Northern California. Secretly, Stanford impressed her. She had to admit the campus was lovely. The School of Music was excellent. The Department of Mathematics and the Pre-Med program were as good as any. Yet as a native New Yorker she possessed an innate distrust of any place where the weather was constantly pleasant and people wore perennial smiles. The most arduous task she ever performed was saying good-bye to her daughter. She hugged her daughter, never intending to let go. When she reluctantly left to catch her flight she was struck by a horrible premonition that something wasn't right. Rebeccah Goldman cried the entire flight back and two full days after.

Not quite seventeen, Ruthie Goldman found the freedom of being away from home intoxicating. Her collegiate life wasn't planned to the minute and she was actually responsible for her own choices. Likely, it was too much too soon. During the second semester she met a guy. Chip Rolley, son of a Beverly Hills stockbroker, was a junior at Cal Berkley majoring in Marine Biology. He met Ruthie at a coffee house where patrons freely performed folksongs and read poetry. They shared an interest in music and Chip introduced her to Dylan and Baez. He was into politics and was an early student activist in a series of protests which later became known as the Free Speech Movement. Ruth was impressionable. He proselytized that college wasn't only a place to be filled with facts and sent out to get a socially acceptable job. It could be used as a vehicle for social change. Together they attended rallies and sit-ins. He also introduced her to sex and drugs.

Rebeccah Goldman was perturbed when her daughter opted to attend summer classes and spend the vacation on campus. She became deeply worried when several months passed without any word from her daughter. Tired of evasive answers from her daughter's roommate she flew out to Stanford in late October. She was shocked to discover that her daughter was no longer living in the dorm and hardly attending classes. Through her roommate Rebecca traced her daughter to a two-family house off campus. Dr. Rebecca Goldman was a liberal, worldly person familiar with the beat generation frequenting Greenwich Village. This was different. Very different. Her daughter lived in a noisy, dirty, quasi-kibbutz where no one apparently worked or attended classes. Ruthie appeared pale and haggard looking. It was painfully obvious she was shacked up with this guy Chip. Although she barely showed it was also painfully obvious her daughter was pregnant.

While the discovery jarred Rebecca Goldman to the bone, she didn't lose her composure. Her training prepared her well to deal with the trauma of the situation. She didn't throw a fit or express any anger. She calmly told Ruth her love was unconditional. Together they'd work this out. She would help her daughter pack and they would fly back to New York that evening. She would have a colleague from the hospital resolve her condition. She offered her daughter all the recovery time she needed and to provide her counseling. After a while she would help her daughter start anew.

Ruth defiantly told her mother she wasn't going anywhere. She told her mother she'd found true love and was going to stay with him and have his baby. Ruth told her mother she was on a great cosmic voyage to search out her own identity and refused to have her life defined by her mother's expectations. Rebecca pleaded with her to reconsider. She told her daughter while physically she could give birth it would be impossible for her to handle the emotional stress of motherhood. There were financial considerations as well. Ruth was a baby herself. No way was she responsible enough to raise a baby on her own. She reasoned with her daughter if she really found true love it should overcome a six-month lapse. As a last resort Rebecca promised her daughter she could see Chip again in six months if she still so desired. All she wanted was for Ruthie to first terminate the pregnancy and take time to recuperate in New York. After that, Ruth was free to resume her lifestyle. Rebecca promised not to stand in her way.

Ruth wouldn't hear of it. She refused to be her mother's pawn. She lived by a different set of rules. If New York was so great, she suggested her mother go back immediately---and by herself. Their quarrel quickly deteriorated. No longer the refined, composed New York brain surgeon, Rebecca Goldman became a frantic mother desperately trying to hold on to her only child. Ruth would give no quarter. With their animosity heightening Chip tried to intervene. That was a grave error and gave Rebecca's ire a new target. This Chip guy with the laid back demeanor and blond surfer looks could have had his forehead stamped "made in California" as far as Rebecca was concerned. He wasn't even Jewish. She told this Chip his Svengali act didn't fool her. Who did he think he was, seducing her only daughter? She told him she would check with the local authorities about the statutory rape laws in California. And while they were investigating, she added, maybe they wouldn't mind looking into possible drug use.

Her tirade was a mistake. Nothing could have stiffened her daughter's resolve like the threats against her lover. She lashed out at her mother with murderous vitriol. Rebecca retaliated and both expressed thoughts they wished had gone unsaid. For the second time Rebecca Goldman cried the entire flight back to New York. She would never lay eyes on her daughter again.

Ruth and Chip embraced their alternative lifestyle. They were in the forefront of a culture sweeping eastward, bringing along new customs, new music, and a new philosophy. They tried living in San Francisco but moved to Berkeley. They both preferred the intellectual climate of a university setting. Among their housemates was a fellow named Hugh Romney. Hughie was busy gaining a reputation as the Clown Prince of the Counter Culture. Actually he was a keen historian and adept at foreseeing trends. He predicted a small conflict in Southeast Asia would quickly snowball. He cautioned Chip, without his student deferment, might become a target of the local draft board. At the time marriage was an exemption. In the spring of 1964 Chip and Ruth were married by a notary in the town of Pacific Grove, right on Monterey Bay. As a further precaution against being drafted Chip had his name legally changed. It was a popular ploy used at the time to stay ahead of the draft board. While a marine biology major his favorite research subjects were the echinoderms. He was enthralled by the sea urchins, brittle stars, and sand dollars. He reveled in their brainless existence and simplistic approach to life. His very favorite was the Artesias forbesi. Chip was a big aficionado of starfish. The marriage license of Chester Marc Rolley and Ruth Sara Goldman officially read "Mr. And Mrs. Aries and Luna Starfish." One week after eight hundred students were arrested in the first campus sit-in and eight thousand more went on strike at the

Berkeley campus, a son was born to Aries and Luna. They named him Pisces.

For a time the Starfish family meandered the Bay area living off the sale of his Corvette. She supplemented the family income by playing backup and writing songs for various local rock bands. The next year they joined their old friend Hugh Romney on a mountaintop commune outside of Los Angeles. By then Hughie had also changed his name and was calling himself Wavy Gravy. The commune inhabitants became known to the literati as the Merry Pranksters. They traveled the country in converted school buses painted in psychedelic colors protesting the Vietnam War. The family Starfish broke off from the Merry Pranksters after a march on Washington. They followed some newly made friends to a farm near Morgan Center, Vermont. The move to Vermont gave their lives some needed stability. Luna grew tired of traipsing across the country with an infant in tow. They were fortunate to land in such an idyllic spot. The picturesque scenery with rolling fir-lined fields buttressing cold, clear Lake Seymour made Vermont easy to adapt to.

The Starfish family thrived in Vermont. Aries must have inherited some of his father's business expertise. Dormant his whole life, his economic skills flourished in Vermont and Aries became a highly successful marijuana grower. In a relatively brief period of time they were able to buy their own farm nearby. Once relocated, he moved into a more lucrative facet of the business. Aries began distributing. His mules supplied college campuses throughout New England and New York state. Luna enjoyed their new prosperity. It had been two years since they had a return address. One of the first things she did was write her grandparents in the Bronx. While still estranged from her mother she never lost contact with her grandparents. She had sent them pictures of her son after the birth and tried hard to periodically drop them notes. They loved hearing from their granddaughter and especially coveted the pictures of their great-grandchild. They did their best to write back but their letters were returned undelivered once she left the Hog Farm.

While thrilled to be able to reach Ruthie much had occurred since they had last written. The news was somber. Rebecca, Ruthie's mother and their daughter, had died the previous year. She was run over by a cab one block from Carnegie Hall. They had not yet come to terms with having to bury their only living child. They were still coping with the knowledge their daughter died brokenhearted. Rebecca Goldman never fully recovered from the estrangement from Ruthie. They buried her with her two most precious possessions—pictures of Ruth and the grandson she never met.

Luna broke down after receiving the news of her mother's death. Instantly she was overwhelmed with an urge to see her grandparents. After calling to make arrangements she packed a knapsack and, with her son in tow, took the Trailways to Boston. From Boston they took a train to Grand Central Station.

New York City had changed radically in her absence, a much more dingy, dirty, crowded place than the one she remembered. Gone was the special feeling of neighborhood. It no longer seemed like a series of ethnic enclaves comprising a great city. It was a seething, pushing megalopolis cast over by a foreboding aura of danger. That feeling multiplied incrementally when they took the subway to the Bronx. Her grandparents' neighborhood was no longer the neat, clean, safe Jewish neighborhood she frequented growing up. Graffiti on buildings and cars on blocks dotted the streets. A bodega replaced the corner deli her grandparents took her for egg creams. The reality of a changing neighborhood challenged her views on minority rights. But this wasn't the time for a self-debate with her political consciousness. She couldn't wait to see her grandparents Miriam and Morris Abrams.

The Abrams welcomed their granddaughter openly and were nonjudgmental of her chosen lifestyle. Unlike a parent-child relationship where the process of parenting is fraught with conflict and lasting hard feelings can be a byproduct, the love bestowed by grandparents is unconditional and unquestioning. So, too, were their feelings for Ruthie. They spent the rest of the day laughing, crying, and reminiscing about a generation past. Whatever name she went by she was still their granddaughter. It was pointless to dwell on past mistakes. They simply wanted her back as a meaningful part of their lives. And her son... their great grandson... was something special.

He had his mother's curly hair and rosy cheeks. He definitely inherited her smile. His eyes were hard to place, though they looked hauntingly familiar. Perhaps the blue color threw them off. That must have come from his father. There was something else about his eyes. They were intelligent eyes, simultaneously piercing and absorbing. It was a look they'd seen before but couldn't place. They watched as the boy browsed through a photo album. When he came to a picture of Rebecca he focused in observing each detail. That was it! The eyes in the photo were his eyes. They both said a little prayer, thankful a part of their Rebecca, may she rest in peace, lived on in their great-grandson.

The boy was plainly blessed. Ruthie played for them on their old out-of-tune upright Wurlitzer piano. She could still make it sound like a Steinway grand. She then showed her son the keys. A half hour later they performed a flawless duet of Heart and Soul. Dinner was followed by more music and laughter. They went to bed sublimely happy. It had been a very long time since Morris and Miriam felt such *nachas*.

The next morning they discussed some issues concerning Rebecca's estate. After stopping at the lawyer's office to sign papers, they ventured into Manhattan. They visited the Museum of Natural History, went to the top of the Empire State Building and lunched at the automat. After eating they shopped at Gimbels, then toured the garment district. Morris showed his great-grandson where he manufactured dresses. It had been a whirlwind two days rife with emotion. Miriam and Morris had Ruthie's assurance she and her son would stay in touch and continue to a part of their lives.

Back in Vermont the marijuana business was still prospering. Aries, however, was growing tired of farm life and winter weather. He longed for the ocean and the warm salt air breezes. He felt too domesticated on the farm and longed for adventures on the open seas. Eight months later he closed on the farm and turned the proceeds into a beautiful thirty-eight foot Morgan motor sailor. By this time in her life Luna had come to grips with her husband's vagaries and knew full well he was a man of extremes. Adapting from a rustic farmhouse to the cramped living quarters of a sailboat was about as extreme as it gets. Despite the inconveniences there were also positives. Her husband was energized to a state she'd never seen before. He spent part of each day introducing their son to the beauty and complexities of the marine environment. They studied together, learning about corals, marine life and ocean ecology.

There was the satisfaction gained from being completely self-reliant. She understood the ocean was an unforgiving environment. They had to plan. They had to be prepared. They became adept at plumbing, wiring, and engine repair. Before departing they could both fix the generator and overhaul the outboard. They inventoried spare parts for everything.

Probably the biggest plus was the feeling of absolute freedom. No mortgage, no land to cultivate, no pets to feed; it was a life void of responsibilities. They could pick up anchor and sail to new destinations at will.

She also thought it would be an excellent life experience for their son and a wonderful opportunity to bond together as a family. She stocked the boat with books and purchased a keyboard. The family Starfish was ready to set sail.

They departed Boston Harbor heading south. Her husband was an accomplished sailor. As a boy he often navigated the family yacht through the Catalina Islands. When they reached Chesapeake Bay he took time to teach his wife the art of sailing. Their voyage would require both to be proficient sailors and navigators. From Chesapeake Bay they traveled down the Intercoastal Waterway, dreaming about their first port of call. They considered Jamaica with its lush mountain landscape and waterfalls. Thought was given to the Cayman Islands, Costa Rica, or just going straight through the Canal and heading for the South Pacific. They split the difference, docking at the Dinner Key Marina in Coconut Grove.

Just south of downtown Miami, the Coconut Grove of the early seventies was an ideal fit for the Starfish family. It was a colony of artists and a haven for the city's liberal-thinking and free spirited people. It reminded them of San Francisco with a tropical climate. The Coconut Grove they discovered was a genuine place with its own kinetic energy before South American shoppers and condo developers descended and robbed it of its soul. It was also the only place in Miami where its inhabitants didn't wear their ethnicity on its sleeve. The Starfish family was easily accepted and made friends in the sailing community and among the many artisans. They were surprised to find so many like-minded people in their own marina. They met couples who used the Grove as a home base, taking extended journeys throughout the Caribbean. There were families as well, some with children their son's age. Most everyone they met was generous with advice and supplies. They learned much about sailing and life on a boat. It was a transient community with a steady turnover of new boats taking dockage and old friends seeking new vistas.

The little village met all their needs. Quality health food stores stocked everything necessary to maintain their macrobiotic diets. They made friends among the land dwellers including the artist Tony Scornavacca. They didn't need a car. Bicycles were sufficient to carry out their errands. Their new life exceeded expectations. Luna had never seen her husband so blissful. The climate agreed with him. The waters surrounding Miami inspired him. Often they would sail out to the reefs near Key Biscayne and spend the day snorkeling. Her son was a natural, following his father twenty, twenty-five feet down to explore this new world. The reefs served as a living classroom. His father was an able teacher, showing his son the various types of corals and species of fish. He demonstrated how to hold a sea urchin without getting pricked by the needlelike spines. On each dive her husband viewed the coral splendor through his son's eyes. Together they observed sleeping nurse sharks and slithering moray eels. He pointed out how to avoid the bristle worms and stinging fire corals. He tutored his son to remain calm among the toothy barracudas and occasional pelagic shark; how simple eye contact could shoo away a bull shark or hammerhead.

They searched for shells and soon had a large collection of whelks, alphabet olives, regal murexes, and scotch bonnets. He taught the boy how to glean the meat from a queen conch, which they used as a protein source in soups and salads to supplement their diets. He showed their son different species of starfish explaining how their namesake could drop off an appendage as a defensive reaction, then regenerate a new one. Starfish, the boy learned, were very resilient.

They kept expanding their horizons, sailing further away from Key Biscayne to the reefs around Fowey Light and off Elliot Key. On days with a steady breeze they could make the Florida Keys where the elkhorn coral grew in forests and schools of yellowtail snapper were so thick you could catch them by hand. They swam over elegant stingrays and adjacent to giant tarpon. Smiling jumping dolphins would follow them, swimming in their wake. At day's end they'd watch the orange sun sit gently on the water's surface before serenely disappearing. Nights at sea were intoxicating as the stars performed enchanting displays. They showed their son the constellations and explained how they used the North Star to navigate.

The Starfish family established a rewarding life and found Miami to be a near paradise. Their son was thriving. Though seven years old he was reading Dickens, Arthur Conan Doyle, and doing algebra. Musically he inherited his mother's gift, already able to play a competent "Fur Elise" on the keyboard. He also played the guitar. On days when the weather refused to cooperate and the seas were too choppy to set sail, they would join their friends putting on impromptu concerts in Peacock Park.

Money was no problem. Her seascapes and shell collages sold well at the funky annual Coconut Grove Art Festival. Through some friends at the marina her husband unearthed another lucrative, low-risk means to supplement their income. It also appealed to his anti-establishment side. Miami was the Mecca for offloading mother ships at sea and smuggling bales back to shore. Sometimes this would require a few days out at sea. It also highlighted another advantage of Miami—it provided built-in babysitting. Ruth's grandparents, Miriam and Morris, finally gave up on the Bronx and relocated to Surfside, a small incorporated town carved out of Miami Beach along Collins Avenue. The Abrams purchased a comfortable two bedroom garden apartment on

Abbott Avenue, one block from the beach. They were delighted having their granddaughter and great-grandson nearby and gave them an open invitation to visit. They were more than happy to accommodate their granddaughter and babysit for a night, a weekend, or longer.

That was extremely fortunate because demands of their new undertaking necessitated some extended periods at sea. Prior to departing Luna would leave her son with her grandparents. They assured her it was no inconvenience. They looked forward to his little stays, relishing the chance to spoil him. That worked out well because Aries was not exactly punctual. He sometimes got sidetracked, exploring the Bahamian islands of Bimini, Riding Rock and Orange Cay. If two days stretched to six her grandparents never complained.

They went to Surfside by taxi. Sometimes his mom would bring along the guitar or keyboard and he would put on little recitals. Miriam and Morris didn't understand a lot about Ruthie. For one thing they couldn't imagine living on a boat. But they certainly couldn't fault the way she raised her boy. He was intelligent, talented and blossoming in an environment she created. Their one area of contention centered on his diet. From talking to him they determined his every meal consisted of brown rice and some vegetables. That was at home. In the Abrams' household he ate like a normal person. He dined on brisket with *tzimmes* and roasted potatoes. He ate chicken soup and kugel. They were on a mission to fatten him up. When introduced, the reaction of a neighbor was invariably the same. "So skinny?" His favorite dish was made out of hardened chicken fat. Crispy like bacon, it was called *gribinsch*. Anticipating Ruthie's reaction, they let him eat it only after a solemn promise not to tell his mother.

The days spent with his great-grandparents were carefree. A typical day began at the beach. While they read the morning paper the boy would build elaborate sand castles and play in the incoming surf. They would walk together along the shoreline picking up shells. Their great-grandson knew the name of every one. On the way back to the apartment they would stop at Sheldon's Pharmacy for lunch. They'd wink at each other and smile as the boy gobbled down a normal meal of a grilled cheese and tomato sandwich, washed down with a vanilla shake.

It was his great-grandparents who taught him how to play cards. In the afternoon they would join their neighbors by the pool. Eventually the men and women would separate. The women talked. The men played cards. The game of choice was pinochle. While they played the boy watched. By observing he taught himself the game and picked up the strategies. He amazed the other *kibitzers* with his ability to predict the outcome of every hand. After each player declared their melds he'd accurately assess whether or not the players would make their bids. Eventually they let him play. Soon everybody wanted him for their partner.

He had an endless fascination with cards. After dinner they played three-handed pinochle. If one of his great-grandparents wasn't in the mood he would play gin rummy with the other. One day he noticed an unusual column in the comics section of the daily paper. It was titled Bridge by Charles Goren. He recognized the symbols for the different suits and was instantly spellbound. By reading the column he learned how to play bridge. In some ways it was similar to pinochle but far more complex. He viewed each hand as a multifaceted puzzle. Before reading the column he would cover up the East-West hands and try and solve it on his own. At a young age he mastered many of the games nuances. He knew when to eschew the finesse and how to set up an end play. He knew when to cross ruff and when to execute a holdup play.

In the afternoons he walked to Sheldon's and purchased Miami's other daily paper, The Miami News. He bought it solely because it had a different bridge column. In the News, the bridge column was written by B. Jay Becker. B. Jay Becker's column was more instructive than Goren's. It delved into theory and gave him a different perspective on the game. From it he gained a grasp of bridge's finer points He learned how to execute squeeze plays and dummy reversals. He loved the columns featuring Trump Coup Tommy who only played like an expert when he had a trump stack against him. He wasn't quite eight years old yet he could count out a hand and figure out the distribution. Pinochle with his neighbors was fun. Bridge was a challenge.

One day his mother dropped him off in Surfside and his parents went out for a three-day sail. They never returned. At first Morris and Miriam weren't overly concerned. Their granddaughter and her husband were late more often than not. It wasn't out of the ordinary for them to miss the allotted pick-up time by four or five days. When a week passed they became anxious. After two weeks they were outright frightened and started asking questions. No one at the marina knew anything. The dock master suggested they contact the Coast Guard. The Coast Guard promised to begin an investigation. Two weeks later they had nothing. There were no reported violent storms during that time period. There was no record of a May Day call. They couldn't locate a single vessel having any radio contact with the sailboat "Milk and Honey." It vanished without a trace. The Coast Guard held out the possibility that they mistakenly sailed into Cuba's territorial waters and were being held there in custody. This scenario had occurred before and it sometimes took the Cuban authorities several months before contacting U.S. officials. A situation like that was out of the Coast Guard's jurisdiction. They recommended pursuing it through the State Department. At the State Department they ran into t bureaucratic wall and were frustrated at every turn. They didn't know anyone in Miami. They needed someone to cut through the red tape. Out of desperation they contacted their ex-Congressman from the Bronx. Harris Silver represented their district for five terms before losing out in the Democratic primary to a Puerto Rican. He attended Columbia with their daughter Rebecca and served on the House Committee on Foreign Affairs. Mr. Silver had the needed connections and was happy to assist. Three weeks later he apologized for being the harbinger of bad news. The State Department had no information on the missing couple. He went as far as to contact friends in the Canadian government and have them make inquiries. Canada maintained diplomatic relations with Cuba. Cuban officials were far more receptive to their requests than any from the U.S. Again, nothing. He contacted every U.S. embassy on every Caribbean Island and had them check the hospitals and jails. No one had seen or heard of the Starfish couple or the boat "Milk and Honey." Though terribly distraught the Abrams remembered to thank him for his efforts. Next, they hired a private detective who turned up nothing. The missing couple had no bank accounts, no checking accounts and no credit cards. They left no paper trail to follow. Two years later their granddaughter and her husband were declared legally deceased.

Morris and Miriam were crippled by an overpowering sadness. They were ill-prepared for life's latest cruel trick. Having already lost a daughter they now had to cope with the loss of the prodigal granddaughter who so recently returned to brighten their lives. And the boy! What would they do about Ruthie's son? To the best of their knowledge they were the only ones left in his life. They knew absolutely nothing about his father. They hadn't spoken to Rebecca's ex-husband, the boy's grandfather, in over twenty years. He didn't attend their daughter's funeral. He didn't send a condolence card. Miriam and Morris were it. If they didn't keep the boy they would have to relinquish custody to a foster home or HRS. That was really not an option. Despite their ages, Miriam was seventy-seven and Morris was seventy-eight, they accepted the responsibilities of parenting.

Their reluctance stemmed from apprehension about their age. It had nothing to do with the boy. He was well behaved and a joy to have around. They worried about the quality of life they would be able to provide him. Morris had cataract surgery three months before and didn't know how much longer he'd be able to drive. Who would he play with? The only time children his age were in the neighborhood was the one week between Christmas and New Year's, when vacationing kids from up north would visit their grandparents. What would they do?

Morris and Miriam answered their own question. They would do what they could and pray. The first order of business was to enroll him in school. Out of respect for his parents they left his surname alone. But there was no way in hell they would enroll him with a name like Pisces. Taking the name of their late son they registered him at Bay Harbor Elementary as Stanley Starfish.

Home-schooled his whole life, Stanley had a difficult time adjusting to the rigidity of public school. For the first time he sat at a desk and interacted with children his own age. The work was no problem. His diagnostic scores were off the charts. Socializing was the problem. He realized right away he was different. His life experiences were unlike those of any of his classmates. He rarely spoke and made no friends in his grade. Stanley's friends were his pinochle buddies back at the apartment. When he was Bar Mitzvahed the celebration consisted of a small *kiddush* around the apartment pool for his neighbors. He didn't know anyone his own age well enough to invite.

He loved his great-grandparents dearly. They were sweet and extremely kind. They sacrificed a great deal for him. They would never know how much he appreciated them. Still, they could not take him sailing or snorkeling with dolphins. They couldn't sing him to sleep with his mother's beautiful voice. He coped with the loss of his parents in odd ways. For the rest of his life he never ate brown rice. For many years, until he fathered his own son, he never played another musical instrument.

He made his first real friend in high school. He met Scottie Lavin on the Miami Beach High School swim team. Stanley never lost his love for the water. To Stanley swimming served as a form of meditation. While not possessing a sprinter's physique he excelled at long distance and became the team's top swimmer in the five hundred yard freestyle. Scottie was also on the school's chess team and prodded Stanley to join. School life was improving. He had activities after school to keep him busy and classmates he could sit with at lunchtime. Occasionally he would join them for a Saturday night poker game or to split a pizza.

Miriam and Morris were gratified that their great-grandson was finding his niche. It made it easier to deal with their declining health. Their greatest fear was that they would die and abandon him before he was ready to take his place in the world. They both knew that time was approaching. There were days and there were bad days. They no longer had the strength for their morning walks on the beach. It was all they could do to walk the two blocks each way for their daily lunch at Sheldon's. Stanley cleaned the apartment. He ran all their errands. He did the shopping and went to the cleaners. He accompanied them on their more and more frequent doctor visits. Morris Abrams knew he couldn't delay any longer. It was time for a serious talk.

Morris told his great-grandson a day was coming when neither he nor Great-Grandma Miriam would be there to help him and guide him. They needed to prepare for that day. He told his great-grandson what steps they had taken and what still had to be done. But first he digressed. He told the boy how he and Miriam came to this country as teenagers from the same little village in Russia. They settled in the Bronx and scratched out a living in the garment trade. They saved every nickel and opened their own dress manufacturing business. He told how they started a family. Their first born, Stanley, died of pneumonia at less than a year old. A second son was stillborn. His eyes teared up and he apologized to his great-grandson if he was repeating old stories. He continued on about their daughter and his grandmother, Rebecca. How she was a brilliant student and became a renowned neurosurgeon. The old man told the boy about his mother as a child; how talented she was, graduating top in her class at Julliard. He showed him pictures of his mother as a little girl performing with Leonard Bernstein and the New York Philharmonic.

Morris sipped some wine and told his great-grandson of their plans. He was the beneficiary of his mother's estate. She, in turn, had inherited her mother's estate. It was a substantial amount. The sale of Rebecca's brownstone, her life insurance policy combined with other assets added up to a significant figure. He further explained how they were also leaving him their estate which included the apartment and other assets. The aggregate of the two estates would allow him to live comfortably. The apartment was paid for but he would be responsible for incidentals like the power bill and phone bill. He told Stanley how they set up a trust for him with their friend and lawyer, Mr. Gorman, as the executor. Mr. Gorman would have power of attorney until he turned legal age. Mr. Gorman would pay the property taxes out of the trust and provide him with an adequate allowance to cover his living expenses. He stressed to his great-grandson the estate set aside sufficient funds for his college education. It was the fondest wish of Miriam and Morris that Stanley complete his education. After college there should be enough to get a good start in life.

Stanley didn't know what to say. He was too young to grasp the severity of what was put forth. He did notice his great-grandparents took extra time showing him how to pay bills and balance a checkbook. He also couldn't help but notice that his great-grandparents were getting slower and slower. Great Grandma Miriam was the first to stop. She died in her sleep a month after the Jewish holidays. Stanley remembered every detail of the funeral. He remembered standing next to Great-Grandpa Morris and receiving the condolences of friends and neighbors who came to pay their respects. He remembered sitting in the front row as the rabbi gave the eulogy. He remembered riding in the limousine to the cemetery and being overcome with a feeling of helpless finality as they shoveled dirt over the casket.

Three weeks later the scene was repeated. His great-grandfather was lost without his lifelong mate, and couldn't live without her. Stanley was at his side when he died. His last words were an apology for not holding on longer and a prayer in Yiddish for God to look after him. After the burial Stanley returned to an empty apartment. He would have to grow up fast. Fifteen years old, Stanley Starfish was all alone.

While living by himself in the apartment, he made a new acquaintance. Stanley introduced himself to the television set. For the first time in his life he spent his nights watching TV. His favorites were the police dramas and detective series. The cohesion and interplay among the officers in Police Story enchanted him. He enjoyed Kojak and Colombo, the disheveled bumbler whose smug suspects always got caught by underestimating him. Another favorite was the Rockford Files, although he wondered how Jim afforded the collision insurance premiums on his Firebird. Television was a good and loyal friend, a necessity because around the apartment complex death was apparently contagious. Inevitably his pinochle buddies were dying off. If one of a couple died their children would put the surviving spouse in the Jewish Home for the Aged and put their apartment up for sale. Many of the new buyers were foreigners from Montreal, Caracas, or Sao Paulo. The new residents used their apartments part-time and for good portions of the year the complex was deserted. His pinochle game expired with his old friends.

Stanley Starfish adapted to living by himself. He continued going to school and participating on the swim team and in the chess club. After school and during the summers he worked at Sheldon's Pharmacy delivering prescriptions. He did his own laundry and shopping. He prepared his own meals and cleaned the apartment like his great-grandparents had shown him. By necessity he became self-reliant.

He also handled most of his finances. He paid the monthly bills and took weekly spending money out of his checking account. Mr. Gorman made a deposit from the trust into his account each month. Sometimes he was a little tardy and Stanley's checks would come back. It usually took a few phone calls to his office to straighten it out. His assistants didn't know anything and Mr. Gorman was either with a client or in court. When he did get through Mr. Gorman would apologize and blame his secretary. He talked very fast. Stanley assumed he was an extremely busy lawyer. Once, he received a notice from the County Tax Collector that his property taxes were overdue. This puzzled Stanley. Property taxes were supposed to be paid directly out of the estate. Mr. Gorman assured him it was an oversight and that he would take care of it. Stanley received a second notice. This time, Mr. Gorman sounded annoyed as if Stanley was pestering him.

"Look kid, I told you I'd take care of it," were the lawyer's exact words. Stanley felt awkward but didn't get another notice.

In his senior year of high school Stanley began making preparations for college. His grades were good and his SAT scores were high. The school guidance counselor was helpful, suggesting he apply to two state schools and a couple of others. His first choice was Columbia University in New York City. He wanted to attend his grandmother's alma mater, certain his great-grandparents would approve. To his delight he was accepted. All he needed was for Mr. Gorman to arrange payment for the tuition. Mr. Gorman had him come to his office. "Sit down," he said, "I'm afraid I have rather distressing news for you. Your trust is not adequately funded to support a four-year education at Columbia."

Stanley was dumbfounded. His great-grandfather Morris stressed over and over his college needs were all arranged. His great-grandfather never lied. "I don't understand," Stanley said. "My great-grandfather told me college was taken care of."

"Your great-grandfather, may he rest in peace, was a good and kindly man. I considered him not only a client but a friend. In financial matters, let me put this as delicately as possible, he was somewhat unsophisticated. I'm sure he didn't purposely mislead you. I don't think he fully grasped how expensive college is these days."

"Unsophisticated?" Stanley blurted out. "My great-grandfather put my grandmother through Columbia and Columbia Medical School. He ran his own dress manufacturing business for thirty-five years. He read the Wall Street Journal cover to cover until the day he died!"

The lawyer squirmed in his seat. He took out a handkerchief and wiped his sweat-filled brow. "That's the problem," he continued. "The investments. Just last week Treasury Secretary Regan said the economy's dead in the water. What can you expect in a country stupid enough to elect a *fakacta* actor for President. The trust's investment portfolio lost much of its value. Don't blame your great-grandparents. They tried to do their best for you."

Stanley looked the lawyer directly in the eyes. "I'm not blaming them. They put their trust in you. They said you would take care of everything."

Mr. Gorman did not return Stanley's harsh stare. Instead, he rose from his desk and took out a file from the cabinet. His face was red and his voice sounded irritated. "Listen kid. Everything I did was perfectly legal. See for yourself. It's all there in black and white. In fact, I don't like the tone of this conversation. I think it best if you find yourself another attorney. I'm making out a check from my escrow account for the balance of the trust."

While the lawyer wrote out the check, Stanley looked through the file. The day his great-grandfather died the trust account had a balance of six hundred ten thousand dollars. Mr. Gorman handed him the check saying, "It's all there to the penny. I believe this concludes our business."

Stanley Starfish left Mr. Gorman's office with a check for twenty two thousand, six hundred eighty-eight dollars and twenty-seven cents, and an uncertain future. At the time he was too young and naïve to seek any recourse. And if he had there was little he could have done. With power of attorney Mr. Gorman could pretty much do as he pleased. He did learn a powerful life lesson. Stanley rarely trusted anyone again.

After high school he enrolled at Miami Dade Community College, attending classes at the New World Center campus in downtown Miami. The tuition was affordable. Living at home saved on the expense of a dorm and allowed him to keep his part-time job at Sheldon's. After two years of junior college he planned to reevaluate. While on campus he saw a notice for a Bridge Club Open House seeking players of all levels. He decided to go. Stanley had never played an actual hand before. The sum of his experience was limited to doing the hands in the newspapers. After first observing he gathered up the nerve to try. They were playing a form of bridge called duplicate where the results of playing the same hand were compared throughout the room. At first he performed awkwardly and was unfamiliar with the protocol of bidding. He caught on quickly and within an hour was more than holding his own. On the final board he and his partner reached a seemingly impossible contract. Even if you could see all four hands there was no apparent way of making the bid. As he studied the hand his thought processes started turning and spinning. His mind shifted into overdrive. A kernel of an idea started to form, then sprouted throughout his brain. A blinding white light eradicated all thought... and then... everything was so clear! He devised a plan where the opponent's discards pressured the other, allowing him to make the contract. His opponents, two chemistry professors with master points, stood and applauded. Though he didn't know it, the technical term for that strategy was called the "scissor squeeze," one of the game's most advanced maneuvers. The club's guest of honor, a former world champion, happened to be observing.

"Son," he said. "I've only seen two people make that hand in twenty-five years. Old man Jacoby in the Spingold Knockout and Benito Garazzo of the Italian Blue Team in the Bermuda Bowl. Please, I'd be honored to shake your hand."

In his second year of junior college Stanley took a course in Cinema. He became mesmerized by the movie "Chinatown," watching it again and again. He also took a course in Police Science. He enjoyed it enough to submit an application to the Miami Dade Police Department. Had his parents or great-grandparents been alive they probably would have dissuaded him. But Stanley was alone and made his own decisions. With visions of TV shows filling his head he began training at the Police Academy.

He made it though the Academy easily, finishing in the top five of his class. He compensated for a lack of physical strength with the endurance he gained from swimming. He excelled on the written tests and would have finished first in his class if not for some less than mediocre scores from the firing range. His first assignment was as a patrol officer in the Northwest District of Miami Dade County. Stanley learned quickly that uniformed officers in Dade County neither prevented nor solved crimes, they just reported them. On a typical day he drove from call to call responding to a crime's aftermath—the burglarized house, a stolen car, or a broken-into business. He would file a report, assign a case number, then turn it over to the appropriate investigative unit. Every once in a while they'd get lucky and catch a juvenile in the act. He often had theories about the cases but working a case after he filed a report was not his job. At the first opportunity he transferred into the District's General Investigative Unit and Stanley Starfish began his career as a plainclothes detective.

From the beginning he had his own unorthodox style of investigating. It turned out to be very effective, resulting in his clearing cases at a record pace. He had a way of linking cases. He knew, like every

cop, the majority of neighborhood burglaries were committed by juveniles living in the area during school hours. Stanley would check school
attendance looking for a pattern of kids being absent on the days of
the burglaries. That netted him suspects. A search warrant would turn
up stolen property. During interrogation the streetwise kids thought
they could outsmart the mild-mannered detective who didn't look or
act like a normal cop. He didn't raise his voice. He didn't threaten and
he didn't slap them around. He looked like he belonged in high school.
His style was unthreatening but effective. Without realizing it he would
get the kids to reveal their fences, generally a pawn shop. Instead of
only busting a kid who would be back on the streets in an hour he
made a case against major receivers and distributors of stolen property. Word of his effectiveness spread and he was recruited into the
Economic Crimes Unit located in the public Safety Department headquarters.

Working ECU was educational. He learned about computers
becoming somewhat of an expert. He took accounting classes in his
spare time. The cases he worked in ECU were more complicated than
the domestic disputes and property crimes in GIU. Building a case took
precise planning. Each case had its own rhythm and code. It required
collating varying pieces of data and putting them in an exact order;
only then would anything make sense. Combining meticulous research
with deductive skills developed from bridge, Stanley Starfish put away
some seriously greedy people. One of his favorite movie lines was from
The Godfather: "One man with a fountain pen can steal more than a
thousand with guns."

Working by himself, he broke up a sophisticated ring of Nigerians
who were stealing a fortune kiting airline tickets and reselling them. He
mucked his way through reams of paper to bust a freight forwarding
company using duplicate bills of lading to defraud an insurance company. He arrested a horse trainer at Calder Race Track for throwing in
a ringer. He switched names and numbers on a quality filly running her
in two-bit stakes races and cleaning up.

He didn't confine his efforts to major swindles. Stanley had an affinity for small businessmen, admiring their guts and work ethic. He
appreciated the hours required to keep a family and a business afloat.
He made the bastards who preyed on them a special target. Habitual
victims were the liquor stores and convenience outlets which cashed
payroll and welfare checks. A common scam was to cash a payroll
check, then report it stolen. The employer would stop payment on the
old check and issue a new one. The small store owner was stuck with
worthless paper while the perpetrator had two paychecks and the

security of knowing the crime was too inconsequential to pursue. They didn't count on Detective Starfish. Stanley empathized with the store owners, knowing a single bad check could wipe out a week's profits. Five bad checks meant going out of business. He made arrests and prodded the district attorneys to forcefully prosecute. A vast majority ended up making the checks good. Small-scale stuff but the gratitude of the small businessmen made it worthwhile.

His most memorable moment in economic crimes came when he read Leo Gorman his rights. The lawyer who handled his trust suddenly found himself with some extra spare time on his hands. About ten years' worth. It started with a complaint from a doctor's widow. Her late husband was a well respected orthopedic surgeon who entrusted Attorney Gorman with his life savings. Mr. Gorman had gained popularity among the Miami Beach medical community for his ability to form investment groups garnering unheard of returns. In a time when six month CDs were paying four percent, the portfolios he managed averaged thirty percent. The widow had statements documenting the figures. Not only did the doctor have his personal fortune with Mr. Gorman, he invested his office pension fund with him as well. He told his friends about Mr. Gorman who, in turn, sought him out. In a relatively short time he had the majority of the staffs of Mount Sinai and Saint Francis Hospitals as clients.

The widow came forward after trying to get her husband's money. Mr. Gorman always put her off with a different excuse. She grew tired of waiting and filed a complaint. She was fortunate that Detective Starfish caught the case. His interest perked up considerably when he saw who the complaint was against. He liked the doctor's wife immediately. She was a native of Czechoslovakia and spoke with an accent. She had an old country fear of fancy, fast money-making schemes, preferring the safety of savings bonds and certificates of deposit. Stanley took the information, gave her his card, and promised to look into it. Five days later she called to withdraw the complaint. Mr. Gorman paid her a portion of the estate. She offered her apologies, saying the matter was a big mistake.

The partial payment confirmed his suspicious and Stanley asked her to hold off on withdrawing the complaint. He suggested that she demand another payment instead. Stanley needed a little more time. His initial inquiries revealed Mr. Gorman's investment plan involved grey market groceries. Called derivatives, it took advantage or price discrepancies in different parts of the country. If General Mills ran a two-for-one special on Cheerios in the Southeast the Investment Group would purchase huge quantities and resell them to grocers in the

Pacific Northwest for discounts up to thirty percent. After taking out his expenses he would split the balance, about twenty percent, with his investors. A ten percent net times three deals a year accounted for the thirty percent return The plan wasn't limited to groceries. It worked with paper products, bandaids, any dry goods which didn't spoil. Stanley saw red flags everywhere. At the time, the prime rate was five percent. If the deal was so sweet, why did he need investors? He could have gone directly to the bank and borrowed the money at a few points over prime or financed it himself out of cash flow. The Mr. Gorman he remembered wasn't so generous. Why would he share such a lucrative proposition if he could have easily kept it all for himself?

Stanley pegged the thing as an elaborate Ponzi game. Like a pyramid scam or chain letter, it used new investors' money to pay off old ones who hooked in their well-heeled friends by bragging about the huge returns. Stanley felt sorry for the unsophisticated investors like the doctor's wife who put their trust and money in Mr. Gorman. Many others should have known better. He had to admit lawyer Gorman was pretty slick. He sent his clients detailed statements and had someone answering the phone giving out grocery item prices like stock quotes. If anyone wanted to prematurely withdraw their money Mr. Gorman would act offended and tell them never to invest with him again. The investors would then apologize sheepishly, not wanting to get on the financial guru's bad side. They would beg him to keep their money, sometimes giving him more.

The whole scheme fell apart given the slightest scrutiny. Stanley's investigation disclosed that there weren't enough derivative deals over the last five years combined to cover the amount of profits Mr. Gorman was showing. Their prospectus showed a fifty thousand square foot complex with a loading dock accommodating eight semi-trailer trucks simultaneously. Stanley tracked it down. It was a medium sized warehouse bay with a utility van parked in front and manned by a single employee. Inside were a few cases of toilet paper and a couple cartons of potato chips.

The partial payment lawyer Gorman gave the doctor's widow was another red flag. It signaled he had run out of investors. He had reached the tip of the pyramid and was stalling for time. When Stanley arrested him he had a suitcase with seven hundred thousand in cash and a briefcase with another one hundred fifty thousand dollars. In his jacket pocket were two one-way tickets to Brazil. The other wasn't for his wife.

Stanley's arrest led to investigations by the FBI, SEC, and IRS. Judges were becoming less sympathetic to those stealing widows' nest eggs and raiding working people's pensions. Lawyer Gorman was given separate trials in state court and federal court and handed consecutive sentences, meaning he would serve his state time before beginning his federal time. Mr. Gorman was also disbarred. A court-appointed trustee was able to recover about a third of the lost investments. The trustee was a forensic accountant supposedly expert at uncovering hidden funds and disguised assets. Detective Starfish worked with him, hoping to learn a new science. He was sadly disappointed. Rather than tracking down numbered Swiss bank accounts the forensic accountant recovered most of the money from lawyers' and accountants' malpractice insurance policies. While being led away after sentencing, Mr. Gorman turned to Stanley and asked, "How could you do this to me? I always had your best interests at heart."

"You can thank yourself," Stanley replied evenly. "Because of you I joined the department. Without your help, I probably would have graduated Columbia and become a sleazy lawyer."

Around the office Detective Starfish gained a reputation for being a bit eccentric. His co-workers would look the other way when he incessantly paced back and forth drumming on his hips. They couldn't help but notice when he conducted full conversations with himself. Those who knew him best found him genuinely funny. Whether doing imitations or making faces he had a knack for using humor to diffuse tense situations. He possessed an incredible memory and never forgot a birthday. He was mostly well liked although some thought he lacked a cop's demeanor and was better suited for social work. All could agree he was different. And effective.

His real desire was to work homicide. He couldn't rationally explain why. He just knew he had a fascination with murder cases. Possibly it stemmed from his experience with the carpet cleaners.

During a lull in Economic Crimes he was "loaned" back to GIU to investigate a series of possibly related burglaries. They all occurred during the day when no one was home. Only expensive homes were victimized and high quality jewelry was the only thing taken. The thief or thieves worked fastidiously, never leaving fingerprints or a messy scene behind. Some of the victims had no idea their jewelry was missing until they had an occasion to wear it.

Off the bat Stanley ruled out juveniles. They were never neat and would never leave behind TVs or stereos. Detective Starfish began his investigation by concentrating on service people. His instincts told him it had to be someone who wouldn't arouse suspicion. A pool man, UPS driver, air conditioning repair man, lawn maintenance workers were all possibilities. Stanley canvassed the neighborhoods compiling a list of what household had which service on what date. Only two were in the vicinity of every crime—UPS and Reliable Carpet Care. He quickly ruled out UPS. The crimes were committed in different delivery zones requiring too many different drivers. He concentrated on Reliable Carpet Care. Stanley went back to the houses that were serviced. Not one of the households was victimized though every one was in the vicinity of one of the burglaries. In six of nine instances the break-ins occurred the same day carpets were cleaned. One happened the day after and other two weren't sure when their jewelry was stolen. In each household he got the same description of two men. A tandem made sense. These crimes were well thought out. Most likely one man served as a lookout while the other heisted the jewels. He got their names off a work order copy and checked their records in the computer. One was spotless. The other, James Grogan, had two priors—one for possession of stolen property, the other for breaking and entering. Further investigation revealed he was also a master locksmith. Stanley was certain he had his guys. What he didn't have were any witnesses, any fingerprints, or any physical evidence whatsoever. He didn't even try for a search warrant. The perpetrators were way too sharp to keep any stolen property around. He had a strong feeling it was fenced right away.

He went back and thoroughly reviewed each case. He didn't discover anything new concerning the burglaries but he did find something interesting. On the same day and a block away from one of the break-ins, a homicide was committed. A twelve-year old girl was sexually molested and murdered in her home some time that afternoon.

Stanley called homicide immediately. He brought the connection to their attention hoping it would help. From the tone of the phone call he could tell they were decidedly uninterested. The homicide detective intimated that they had a suspect who Stanley subsequently found out was the girl's father. On the pretense of investigating the neighborhood burglary he decided to talk to the father. After a few minutes the conversation shifted to his daughter.

Ivan Gould was a despondent man. Everyone he loved, everything he cared for was gone from his life. His wife died of cancer three years earlier. As a single father he tried his best to be both mother and father to his daughter Debbie, while at the same time scratch out a living. From their chat it was plain to Stanley the man felt overwhelmingly guilty and responsible for his daughter's death. He was working and not there when his daughter came home after school. For that he blamed himself. Stanley felt the homicide detectives were confusing his remorse with actual guilt. Also his alibi wasn't rock solid. He was a salesman who was on the road and had no one who could verify his whereabouts. The fact that the police considered him a suspect compounded his grief. Stanley felt he was on the edge and might possibly commit suicide or confess to something he didn't do as a way to ease his conscience.

The detective paced back and forth drumming on his hips. His mind started spinning and turning. Finally a kernel of an idea started to formulate and sprouted throughout his brain. A blinding white light eradicated all thought. Instantly a serene calm fell over him and a wry little smile crossed his face. It was all so clear now.

Stanley's devised plan was not without risk. If it didn't work he'd lose any chance of making arrests on the burglaries and most likely queer a murder investigation he had no business getting involved with. He had enough to bring the two carpet cleaners in for interviews. He put them in separate rooms going back and forth making casual conversation. Jimmy Grogan was in one room. Eddie Fajardo, who had the clean record, was in the other. By talking to them he employed a bridge tactic to increase the odds. He wanted to get as much information as possible before making a straight fifty-fifty guess. Everything hinged on picking the right person. If he erred and chose incorrectly the guy would lawyer up and he'd lose them both due to lack of evidence.

Stanley walked into the interview room and offered Jimmy Grogan a coke and a cigarette. "May I call you Jimmy?" Detective Starfish asked politely.

"Anything you want," Jimmy Grogan responded tersely.

"You've been to jail before, haven't you, Jimmy?"

"I served my time, what of it?"

"I'm sorry. I didn't mean what you think. What I meant was you're experienced. You know what it's like. You could handle some time away as opposed to the electric chair."

Jimmy Grogan smirked. "I don't know what the fuck you're talking about."

"Again. I didn't mean to offend you. I was just thinking. We have you slam dunked on the jewelry thefts. All of them. I thought you might want to help yourself get out from under a first degree murder charge."

"I don't know nuthin' about no murder."

"C'mon, Jim. Don't insult my intelligence. You know what I'm talking about. The little girl. A block from one of your jobs. A twelve-year-old raped and strangled. Even Governor Prozac would sign the death warrant on that."

"I didn't do no murder."

"Jim, I believe you. But you were committing a corresponding felony. In the eyes of the law it's the same as if your hands were around her throat. I'm simply trying to help you. Eddie's beyond help. There's a new test we have they've been using successfully in England called DNA. It's one hundred percent foolproof. From sperm or blood we can make an identification much more accurate than a fingerprint. Did you know they call the electric chair 'Old Sparky'? The last person strapped in took over two minutes to die. I'm just trying to work with you."

"How? How can I help myself?"

"Easily. Confess to all the burglaries we have you on anyway, and give up Eddie who buried himself. Do that and I'm pretty sure I can get you a pass on the homicide. If anything a two-bit accessory charge you can serve concurrently with the burglaries. The way they give out gain time you can be out in under eight years."

"What do you mean by pretty sure?"

"I can get an assistant district attorney here in half an hour. She'll put it all down in writing prior to your giving a statement."

Jimmy Grogan slumped in his chair, closed his eyes, and nodded. As Stanley left to get the writing assistant district attorney Jimmy Grogan spoke up.

"Tell me one thing. You got me on hidden camera didn't you? I know I didn't leave no fingerprints."

Detective Stanley Starfish returned a wink of his eye and a wry little smile.

Jimmy Grogan gave a full statement admitting to the burglaries. He did the actual heists while Eddie Fajardo served as lookout. Regarding the murder of the Gould girl, he stated Eddie Fajardo saw her walking home from school while on lookout. When Jimmy returned to the van with the jewels Eddie stopped in front of the Gould house. He told Jimmy to hold on a few minutes, there was something he needed to do. Jimmy told him he was crazy and they should leave immediately. Eddie Fajardo told him, "This time you look out for me." He saw him enter the Gould home and come out about twenty five minutes later. Jim Grogan saw a report about the murder on TV. When he heard the address he knew it was Eddie. When he asked him about Eddie said he didn't mean to kill the girl, he only wanted to keep her from screaming.

After getting the statement the assistant district attorney remarked, "That was the most remarkable thing I ever witnessed. You get someone to confess to a string of burglaries you didn't have enough evidence for by implicating him in a murder you again didn't have enough evidence for. It was absolutely brilliant. And where did you come up with that DNA angle? Dade County's not that sophisticated yet."

"I didn't think so," Stanley answered, "but I wasn't sure. Anyway I read about it in Joseph Wambaugh's book 'The Blooding.'"

The ADA laughed. You have to answer me one thing," she continued. "How did you know who to pick?"

"What do you mean?"

"I think you know very well what I mean. If you approached the murderer with that deal he immediately asks for a lawyer and both cases fall apart. The whole thing works only if you choose the right guy. I have to tell you I would've picked the one with the record. How did you know it wasn't him?"

"To be honest I wasn't one hundred percent sure but I had a pretty good idea. The rape and murder were crimes of emotion. Jimmy Grogan's record made it pretty obvious he was the one committing the actual burglaries. Those were dispassionate crimes. In nine jobs he never left a single fingerprint. He never took a single piece with an inscription or anything else identifiable. Those crimes were best described as coldly professional. His record helped me disqualify him. A master thief, yes, but not a homicidal rapist."

The assistant district attorney shook the detective's hand and said, "I really hope we work together again."

That evening Stanley Starfish made it a point to see Ivan Gould. He wanted to tell him personally they made an arrest and had a confession in his daughter's murder. Ivan Gould didn't know what to say. He tried to thank the boyish detective but couldn't find the words. Instead he broke down in heaving sobs. Stanley embraced him. After a pause he spoke first.

"I know it's difficult but you have to stop blaming yourself for what happened. You were a single parent doing the best for your daughter and trying to make a living at the same time. You couldn't be with her twenty-four hours a day. It was a psychopath who did this. Not you."

"I know," Ivan Gould said between sobs. "I know you're right. First my wife died. Then this atrocity happened to my daughter...I can't sleep... I'm afraid to face my memories. I have this overwhelming feeling of loneliness. I don't know if you can relate to being hopelessly alone."

The two men again embraced. Ivan Gould was speaking to someone who understood.

When his transfer to the homicide unit came through Stanley Starfish was right where he wanted to be. He came to the job with all the enthusiasm and expectations of a rookie getting his first big league call up. What he'd heard about Armando Pedroza was mostly favorable. His reputation for toughness was legendary. He inspired enduring loyalty among his men. Everyone he knew viewed him as politically astute and ambitious, someone with a bright future in the department. Stanley's first impression of Armando Pedroza was puzzling. Physically powerful and ruggedly handsome, he had more the demeanor of a tough street cop than an administrator. The other detectives in the squad were Armando Pedroza clones right down to the tight-fitting shirts and Pancho Villa mustaches. All except for Ron Jeffries and Rosi Gonzalez, the desk public safety aide, the rest of his co-workers were pretty aloof and not overtly friendly. Least friendly was Armando Pedroza himself. Stanley wanted to know what he did to piss him off so much because Armando acted perturbed, even angry, if he had any questions. He often pretended not to notice if Stanley wanted his attention. He seemed bothered and put upon whenever he was in his vicinity. After some "What nows" and "If you're supposed to be so smart why don't you figure it out for yourself," Stanley got the message and did his best to limit the contact between them.

His first assignment was the Aronson case. Armando Pedroza dropped ten file folders on his desk, said, "You've got five weeks," and walked away. As he delved into it he appreciated why it remained uncleared for so long. Working the case resembled peeling an onion with layer upon layer of complications. One thing about it, it didn't lack for suspects. Detective Starfish reviewed the history of the case. He began by organizing the suspects into three categories: jealous husbands, disgruntled business associates, and drug connected. To increase the odds he probed for a cross connection; a jealous husband linked to drugs, or a smuggler involved in a business transaction. The deeper he researched, the stronger he felt it was somehow connected to his business dealings. Dan Aronson was murdered in a cold, professional, dispassionate manner. And, as he would experience repeatedly, money was often a powerful motive for murder.

Detective Starfish spent every waking moment of three weeks poring over the financial records of Dan Aronson's various enterprises. He gained a measure of respect for all the others who worked the case because Dan Aronson's business records were a labyrinth of convolutions. One image clearly emerged; Dan Aronson was a double-dealing prick. A careful, meticulous prick. Nothing obvious jumped off the pages at him. The only thing catching his attention was a single ledger entry for five hundred thousand dollars from Iroquois Racing Ltd. Two weeks later there was a disbursement for the same five hundred thousand dollars back to Iroquois Racing. The footnote explained it was a returned deposit for the unconsummated sale of Aronson's Company to Iroquois Racing Ltd. The one little footnote piqued his interest.

The main principal of Iroquois Racing was Billy Mitchell, one of Miami's most infamous drug runners. Of all the city's high profile druggies Billy Mitchell was by far the most brazen. He, like Dan Aronson, was a world champion boat racer and world class bon vivant. He cruised the streets in either a hideous yellow Lamborghini or a bright red Bentley Mulsanne. He was also a patron of the arts and a tremendous supporter of local charities. So much so that local politicians renamed a street after him, making Interama Avenue known forever as Billy Mitchell Boulevard. His largess purportedly came from his boat building business and his interests in legal California poker parlors. His arrest caused much embarrassment and back pedaling by the city's politicians and prominent civic leaders, especially after Billy Mitchell was handed the longest prison sentence in the history of federal jurisprudence. He gained further notoriety by attempting a daring helicopter escape from prison. It came within inches of succeeding. A fingernail thin guide wire was the sole impediment preventing Billy Mitchell from living out the rest of his days on the beaches of Ipanema. It was only a single ledger entry with a footnote yet it started him pacing back and forth while drumming on his hips. His mind started to spin and turn. Detective Stanley Starfish had a feeling he was on to something.

His next stop was the downtown federal building. The financial records of Iroquois Racing Ltd. were impounded by the FBI and he needed to access them. Nothing out of the ordinary jumped off the pages. He found an entry for a five hundred thousand dollar disbursement payable to Aronson's company and two weeks later a deposit for the same amount. As he finished off he noticed the financial report was signed off on by the company comptroller, an Ethan Levy. Ethan Levy wasn't an exceptionally common name. He attended high school with an Ethan Levy who was also a member of the chess club. He decided to investigate further.

The Ethan Levy who was Iroquois Racing Ltd's chief comptroller turned out to be the same kid who went to Beach High. He also proved to be easy to find. He was nearing the end of serving a four year sentence for money laundering at Fort Eglin Minimum Security Prison in Pensacola, Florida. When he contacted the prison officials he learned Ethan Levy had been transferred to the federal prison in Atlanta. He needed to speak to him but when he broached the subject with his boss he didn't exactly get the cooperation he expected.

"Listen, Bambi," Armando Pedroza uttered disdainfully, "There's no fucking way I'm authorizing you a plane ticket to fly up to Atlanta on some wild goose chase just so you can barhop the underground." He paused, looking at the homicide detective from head to toe. "Hell," he continued, "you'd probably spend the whole time taking the tour of CNN. Whatever your goddamned reason the answer is NO! This 'NO' not only covers the ticket but also any time off. You want to spin your wheels in Hotlanta do it on your own time and on your own dime! Do I make myself clear?"

Stanley Starfish made the arrangements to visit Ethan Levy on his day off. As the guards escorted him to the meeting room Stanley was thunderstruck by the appearance of his former classmate. Ethan Levy had a black eye and scratch marks covering his face. His jeans were missing one back pocket, the jailhouse symbol he was someone's property. He labored with every step and truly looked pathetic. Stanley did his best to mask his feelings and greeted him as cordially as possible. He handed Ethan Levy a paper bag and said, "I brought you a couple of chess magazines and a paperback book on bridge."

Ethan Levy smiled and said, "Thanks, Stanley. Thanks a lot."

He sounded genuinely grateful. They spent some time reminiscing about high school and catching up on time in between. Stanley told him how he became a cop. Then it was Ethan's turn.

"I wasn't one of the super rich kids at Beach High," Ethan Levy expounded,

"I went to University of Florida on a scholarship. I got my CPA degree at the University of Miami and went to work for a downtown firm. I did some work for Iroquois through the firm. They must have been pleased because when they had an opening they hired me as comptroller. It paid four times what I made at the firm." Ethan Levy paused, putting his elbows on the table and resting his head in his hands. His eyes turned straight down to the floor. "I got caught up in the life. I knew what I was doing was more than borderline but by then I couldn't stop. Even if I had wanted to I'm not sure they would have let me. We were moving into our first house and my wife was expecting. We were entrenched in a specific lifestyle. I thought it would go on forever." He lifted his head and looked directly at the homicide detective. Stanley felt sympathetic and hoped his look conveyed his feelings. Ethan Levy looked away and continued, "When they popped Billy Mitchell the whole shebang came crashing down. They offered me a deal for my testimony. Forty-five months in minimum security, less with good behavior. And no drug charges. Just one count of money laundering."

Stanley shook his head, "If you don't mind me asking, how did you end up here?"

Once again Ethan Levy stared at the floor. "When Billy Mitchell tried to break out they thought I must have known something. I cooperated the best I could. I honestly didn't know anything about it. Either they didn't believe me or were so pissed off about the escape attempt they decided to take it out on me. Anyhow they transferred me here four months ago. Now I spend every waking moment thinking of the most efficient and painless way of ending it all." He put his head down on his forearm and started to cry.

The homicide detective took Ethan Levy's hand and held it lightly. "Listen to me, Ethan. You have to hang on. You have less than eight months to go. Please, try and get a hold of yourself. You've got to tough this out."

"That's easy for you to say," he said between sobs. "You're not in my shoes. I couldn't begin to describe the depravity of what goes on in here. Every hour is living out your worst nightmare. And I've got nothing to go back to. My wife's already remarried and my daughter doesn't even remember my name. She calls Linda's new husband Daddy."

Stanley grasped his hand tighter. "You're right. I'm not in your shoes and I don't know what it's like. I do know you have the rest of your life ahead of you. I won't lie to you. It won't be easy starting over but you're a smart guy. Give yourself a chance. Besides, I might be able to help you."

"How? How can you help me?"

"I need some information about Billy Mitchell. If anything you give me is useful in the slightest I'll tell the prison officials you have vital information regarding a homicide investigation and have offered to cooperate if we can arrange a transfer back to Eglin."

"You would do that for me?"

"I have to be honest with you, Ethan. You don't deserve this. I'm going to do it for you whether you have something for me or not. You decide if you want to help me."

"What do you want to know?"

"Tell me about the deal Iroquois Racing had with Dan Aronson."

Ethan Levy looked furtively around the room. "You want to know about that?"

"Yes. I saw the entries in his books and yours for a paid deposit of five hundred thousand dollars, then a refund for the same amount two weeks later. I was wondering if there was something else to it."

Ethan Levy looked scared. Even in another prison, Billy Mitchell apparently had a long reach. He was reluctant to talk and thought long and hard before speaking. The detective picked up on his reticence and offered, "If you like why don't we speak in hypotheticals."

Ethan thought a moment longer, then nodded his head. "Talking hypothetically let's say you wanted to buy a business for a certain price. Let's also say you might want to pay the bulk of it with cash you don't want to declare. You would prefer to pay for it under the table. Let's also say the parties agree and to show good faith one party puts down a deposit—half by certified check, half by cash in unmarked twenties in a briefcase. Let's say a week later negotiations break down and both parties call the deal off. One party returns the check. The other party asks, 'What about the briefcase?' Their answer is 'What briefcase?'"

A light went on in the brain of Stanley Starfish. He stood up and started to pace. "Would Billy Mitchell kill for a half million dollars?"

"I thought we were talking hypothetically."

"I apologize. In theory, is it possible?"

"In theory I would have to say yes. People have been killed for less. Much less. But I'd have to say Billy Mitchell had a pretty good alibi."

"What do you mean?"

"He was in prison when Dan Aronson was murdered."

Stanley increased the rate of his pacing and began drumming on his hips. "Is it possible to arrange a murder from prison of someone on the outside?"

"Anything's possible, but it would take big bucks. You would need an unknown, untapped source of funds."

"Where would you set something like that up?"

"Let's just say people I know weren't strangers to Grand Cayman or the Turks and Caicos Islands."

"Has anyone ever asked you about the aborted deal?"

"No, Stan," Ethan Levy said, shaking his head. "You're the first."

Stanley Starfish got up and called for the guard. He shook Ethan Levy's hand and thanked him. "Please Ethan, don't quit on yourself. I'm going to work on your transfer as soon as I get back. In any case I'm going to write you regularly and send you more books. I'll also be there for you if you need me when you get out. After all, us chess club nerds have to stick together."

Ethan Levy smiled, "Thanks Stan. I actually feel a little better. You know, I wish we were better friends in high school. You're really a good guy."

Upon returning to Miami the homicide detective centered his

investigation on Billy Mitchell. He was certain that Mitchell was connected to Dan Aronson's death. The escape attempt attracted the brunt of his attention. Billy Mitchell arranged it from his prison cell. Perhaps he used a similar modus operandi to kill Dan Aronson. Records showed that in the escape attempt the helicopter pilot was the brother-in-law of another inmate on Billy Mitchell's cellblock. Would he use another inmate or inmate's relative for Dan Aronson's murder? Stanley weighed the possibilities concluding it was highly likely. Billy Mitchell's visitation rights were severely restricted and his phone calls and mail were all monitored. He also concluded he didn't have the resources available to track down every inmate's relative. By himself, he would have his hands full just with the prisoners released from Billy Mitchell's cellblock prior to the Aronson murder. He would have to get lucky and catch a break. He felt confident he was on the right track.

Sometimes, if you took certain precautions and played your cards right you made your own luck.

The prison provided him a list of the prisoners released from Billy Mitchell's cellblock before the murder was committed. He called each released inmate's probation officer. He asked them if any of their parolees showed any signs of sudden wealth soon after their release. A new car or new house, anything that struck them as out of the ordinary. He didn't have much luck until he got in touch with the probation officer for Van Halsey in Enid, Oklahoma.

"Well, let me think," she said. "You know, not long after Van was released he got a brand new Harley Davidson. But that's easy to explain. It was a wedding present from his fiancee. They're still married and doing just fine. They own a restaurant right here in town. The food is downright delicious. I eat there all the time."

While she was talking Stanley looked up Van Halsey's release date. It was a few weeks prior to the murder. "Can you answer me one thing? Do you remember giving him permission to leave the country?"

"Why yes, I do. I gave him three days so he could get married on some Caribbean Island. He reported back right on time, too."

"Last question, I promise. Do you remember his wife's maiden name?"

Van Halsey was married on Provincales, part of the Turks and Caicos island chain, eight days prior to Dan Aronson's murder. After checking with American Airlines he discovered Halsey's wife, using her maiden name, made another trip back to Provo the week following. This time he didn't get any flak about a plane ticket or about time off. He didn't have any trouble obtaining a search warrant for Van Halsey's business and residence which the Oklahoma State Police had no problem executing. The search warrant turned up a .32 caliber pistol underneath the cash register in the restaurant and a Hawaiian shirt and Panama hat in his closet at home. Ballistics linked the gun to the Aronson homicide. Van Halsey was extradited back to Miami where he accepted a plea to second degree murder in exchange for his testimony against Billy Mitchell. Stanley never understood the prosecutor's zeal in going after Billy Mitchell, who was already serving eight consecutive ninety-nine year sentences. It seemed like overkill to get another life sentence conviction. Did they expect him to serve it after he had done his seven hundred ninety-two years? In any event, Armando Pedroza fulfilled his wish to address the media after making an arrest in a high profile homicide. He made the mistake of fielding questions after reading a self-serving statement. The first question out of the box was "What's the significance of the Turks and Caicos Islands in the case?" Armando Pedroza was so unfamiliar with the details he had to call upon Detective Starfish to handle the media.

———————

After the Aronson case Stanley Starfish was paired with Ron Jeffries. For the first time he had a permanent partner. While in uniform and working GIU or ECU he rotated with different partners or worked alone. Armando Pedroza had his own unique style of management and that was how he wanted it. On the surface Ron Jeffries and Stanley Starfish were as different as two people can be. Ronnie was black, a local high school superstar in football and track, and an ex-military man. He was precise and efficient in everything he did, a contrast to his free-thinking, sometimes daydreaming partner. In common they shared a demanding work ethic. Whatever the mix of their character differences and similarities, it proved successful. Together they compiled the finest record in department history.

There wasn't a single case they couldn't clear. From drive-byes to drug hits, from domestics to fake suicide scams they cleared every case assigned to them. Their work took them throughout Miami-Dade County crossing social lines from the homeless to the haute. They developed an ideal working relationship intuitively sensing when to turn up the pressure or when to give each other space. Their working relationship gradually grew into a deep friendship. Despite their different race, disparate cultural and family backgrounds, they developed a close bond, overcoming the stress of the job's demands.

They spent so much time working together it was surprising they didn't get sick of one another. Ron Jeffries figured out he spent about sixty-five percent of his waking hours with Stanley, twice the time he was with his wife and children. For Stanley Starfish it marked the first time in his life he had a real true friend approximately his own age.

Ron Jeffries never set out to be a policeman. The youngest in a large family, Ron was blessed with astounding athletic ability. He possessed blazing speed and coordination. His physical strength belied his average size. He excelled in all sports but concentrated on football and track when he reached high school. In track Ron shattered Florida State records in the one hundred and two-twenty sprints and was fractions of an inch from another record in the long jump. He loved track but football was his passion. His greatest feats came on the gridiron. His speed, complemented by gazelle-like agility, allowed him to post mind boggling statistics. Against tough Dade County competition he averaged three touchdowns and two hundred twenty yards rushing a game. College scouts labeled him a fast Gayle Sayers and compared him favorably to O.J. Simpson. Recruiters descended from every major college program in the country promising him the world and more if he would only grace their campus. Heady times and he was only a high school junior!

The summer before his senior year Ron Jeffries played in the annual Florida-Georgia High School All Star Game. On a freak play somebody landed on top of his left knee in a pileup, breaking the kneecap and shredding the medial collateral and anterior cruciate ligaments. The operation did not go smoothly. Infection set in and complications developed requiring a second operation. Ron Jeffries never made a full recovery. From then on he would walk with a slight limp and never play another game of football. The college recruiters lost his address, and instead of being the most sought after school boy in the country he was just another kid from the 'hood. Circumstances change.

It would have been easy for Ron Jeffries to feel sorry for himself and allow his life to drift into unwanted directions. His family wouldn't stand for it. His Mama was deeply religious and believed everything in life happened for a reason. She firmly believed Jesus had a plan for her baby and this thing with the knee was a test of his faith—an obstacle to be overcome. With his family's support and spiritual guidance from his pastor Ronnie put the injury in the past and concentrated on the future. After graduation he enlisted in the Army.

Ron Jeffries thrived in the military. He actually enjoyed the inherent discipline and ordered lifestyle. He rose quickly through the ranks attaining his sergeant's stripes. He found his niche in the Military Police and might have made a career as an MP if family problems hadn't beckoned him back to Miami. Shortly after he was accepted into the Miami-Dade Public Safety Department. Ronnie quickly gained a reputation as an efficient officer who did everything by the book. After his second year on the department he married his high school sweetheart. Rita Simms was a special education teacher in the Dade County Public School System. Together they had two children, a son Ronald, Jr., and a daughter Jacqueline. They were able to make ends meet on their combined salaries until their children reached school age. From first-hand experience neither wanted anything to do with the public school system, opting instead for private schools. Private schools were pricey. Ron transferred from uniform to plainclothes where he could pick up more overtime. Homicide detectives made the most overtime and that became his destination. Shortly after his assignment his captain retired. His replacement was Armando Pedroza.

Ron Jeffries knew from day one working under Armando Pedroza would be a struggle. Armando was an ambitious, egotistical, self-promoter with questionable ethics. He was everything Ron was not, especially when it came to doing his job. Ronnie resisted administrative pressure to sign off on cases he couldn't prove, leaving them open. Armando wanted them cleared any way he could. He would cut any corner to look good in the eyes of his superiors. Ron was different from the rest of the squad and it wasn't just his color or their ethnicity. He preferred working by himself than with another squad detective, who might put him in a compromising situation.

All that changed when he was assigned a new, full-time partner. First impressions were deceiving because once past his outward appearance of a gentle, skinny teenager Stanley Starfish had depth. He proved that with the Aronson case. Ron had given it a try like a dozen before him and ended up more confused than when he started. This kid solved it in four weeks and it was his first homicide! He was different and special… which made him fun to work with. Their unprecedented success fueled their enthusiasm, making virtually every day together enjoyable. Ron took a proprietary interest in his new partner because his new partner was not without flaws. He possessed a certain naiveté when their work put them in dangerous situations. Lacking his partner's street smarts Stanley never realized how often Ronnie watched his back.

Stanley thought the world of his new partner. He especially admired the quality of his family life. Ron treated him like a kid brother and his children call him "Uncle Stanley." In turn Stanley showed Ron Jr. and Jackie how to snorkel and helped them start a shell collection. Rita gave him an open invitation to the Sunday meal following church. He attended on a regular basis. Stanley wasn't much of a football fan but he accompanied the Jeffries family to University of Miami games at the Orange Bowl and the Annual Soul Bowl where Ronnie's alma mater, Jackson High, would take on the Bulls of Northwestern. Ron and Rita weren't avid film buffs but eventually Stanley persuaded them to watch Chinatown.

On the job, both men realized they were distrusted by their fellow detectives who had no idea Stanley had taught himself Spanish and knew everything they said behind their backs. They were both aware of all the nicknames, including Blackman and Robin. The less than perfect working conditions had minimal effect on their job performance, however. They went about their business clearing case after case. They were rarely in contact with Armando Pedroza. Matters of necessity either went through Rosi or were discussed in the men's room with Ron and Stanley talking through a stall door to a pair or ankles with pant legs around them. Armando Pedroza spent a lot of time in the bathroom.

This was their routine. Every now and then they would come across a case with extraordinary circumstances. It could start out run-of-the-mill then snowball into something far more complex. Maybe that was part of the fascination Stanley Starfish had with homicide. Things weren't always as they seemed. Such was the case with the murder of Jerry Barnett. His body was found in a makeshift grave in a desolate field in West Dade. He had been beaten to death with the proverbial blunt object. It was obvious the murder occurred somewhere else and his body had been dumped where it was discovered. The only physical evidence was some tire tracks and footprints of some kind of athletic shoe or sneaker. Ron canvassed the area and turned up a campesino, a Miami term for squatter, who saw a type of truck of sport utility the night of the murder. That was something. The tire tracks at the scene suggested the tread was from a truck tire. That was the extent of the physical evidence. It was time to delve into the life of Jerry Barnett.

Jerry Barnett was a man with a past. He was a small time con man with arrests for fraud and passing bad checks. He lived alone in a motel efficiency along Biscayne Boulevard in North Miami. For the last few years he spent his time at the area tracks, horses by day-dogs by night, eking our a living as a five percenter. Five percenters were parimutuel groupies who offered to cash large payouts won by lucky bettors for a percentage. Most five percenters like Jerry Barnett had no visible means of income and, since they never filed a return, didn't face the same tax bite as normally employed persons who could owe the IRS up to thirty nine percent. It was a win-win proposition with the bettor keeping a larger percentage of his wager and the five percenter getting a nice

payday for standing in line. Stanley knew track regulars like Jerry
Barnett rarely limited their action exclusively to the parimutuels. Ninety
nine of a hundred were sports bettors as well. Betting football, baseball, or basketball was illegal in Florida and would require a bookmaker. Guys like Jerry Barnett were always into bookmakers who
could be stalled only so long without getting paid. After a while bookies would sell a deadbeat's debt to a loan shark. Loan sharks could
become very angry when making collections. It was the inclination of
the homicide detective to look in that direction.

Ron and Stanley got some leads on Jerry Barnett's bookmaker. It
took a couple of days before they caught up with Cye Harris. Initially
Cye Harris was extremely reticent not volunteering any information
whatsoever. After getting assurances from Stanley the scope of their
investigation was limited only to Jerry Barnett's homicide, and getting
further assurances from Ron that could quite possibly change in the
next fifteen minutes, Cye Harris became more cooperative.

"Yeah, Jerry was a player. He bet them all whatever was in season."

"How did he do? Did he ever win?" asked Stanley.

Cye Harris rolled his eyes. "Sure, just like everybody else. About as
much of the time as Ted Kennedy is sober."

"How was he at paying?"

Cye Harris acted disturbed by the question. He fidgeted in his chair
before answering with a touch of irritation in his voice. "What you really meant to ask was how much was he into me for and would I hurt
him for it?"

Stanley smiled at the bookie and nodded. It was his way of salut-
ing the bookmaker for seeing through his façade. "Basically yes, that's
what I'm asking."

"Look kid. By the way, did anyone ever mention you look more
like a boy scout than a cop? I'm a businessman and that's not the way
I do business. Check around. In thirty years I never once turned anyone's action over to a legbreaker. Besides... the last three, four months
Jerry was as regular as a guy eating Mexican. Every Tuesday at four just
like a Swiss watch."

The homicide detective's brow started to wrinkle. Ron could tell his
partner was starting to percolate. Forty five seconds elapsed before he
asked another question. "Did it seem to you like he recently came into
money? Was he betting larger amounts?"

"I make it a practice never to get into my customers' private lives.
As to the second question, yeah, he increased his action. He went from
betting a dollar a game to a nickel."

That figure jolted the boyish looking detective. Jerry Barnett had increased his wagers from one hundred dollars a game to five hundred. He looked at Cye Harris and asked, "Could he have been winning at the track?"

The bookmaker erupted into laughter. "I guess it's possible. Anything's possible. Every year Ed McMahon rings someone's doorbell. I just never met anyone who got a check. I don't know about the ponies, but Jerry loved the hounds and they run thirteen, fourteen times a night... with exotic wagering on almost every race. Gimme a break."

"Did Jerry ever say anything about his new sources of income? Like where it came from?"

Cye Harris's eyes narrowed to paper-thin slits. "Look, all I know is that the last few months Jerry was very upbeat. He mentioned he was really close to something big. Something very big. Honest to God that's all I know."

Stanley looked up and winked at Ron. He then shook the bookie's hand and said politely, "Thank you very much, Mr. Harris, for your cooperation. You've been very helpful. We can see you're a very busy man and we won't take up any more of your time. We'll try not to bother you again. You have our card. If you think of anything else, anything at all, you can call either of us at any time. Thanks again."

As they walked to the car Ron asked, "How many seconds do you think it took that bookie to file our card in the waste paper basket after we cleared the door?"

"It doesn't matter," Stanley replied. "He gave us enough."

The bookmaker, Cye Harris, told them Jerry Barnett was working something big.

It was also obvious he was enjoying some success before he died. How else could he increase his wagering amounts so drastically? Stanley was certain his recent good fortune and the "something big" were linked to his death. But how? Finding the answer would be the key.

First they needed methodically to weed out the least likely possibilities and concentrate on the ones with the most promise. As a con man Jerry Barnett was strictly penny ante with a consistent history of failure. The best Ron and Stanley could tell, he'd been inactive for years. Lately he seemed to spend all his time at the track. Stanley was extremely doubtful he had the brains or the initiative to pull off a major scam. Stanley thought about the track. Could it be possible he got the money being a five percenter?

Again, highly doubtful. Even if he cashed a two thousand dollar ticket his cut would be one hundred dollars. If he were very lucky that might happen two, three times a week; not nearly enough to cover five hundred dollar bets on college basketball games played every night. What did Cye Harris tell them? Jerry Barnett was expecting something "big." He was doing better and expecting something big. Could he have been getting a piece of something, probably illegal, and demanding a bigger share? Blackmail was as good a motive to kill someone as any, especially if large sums of money were concerned. But what did Jerry Barnett know? And who did it involve? They continued their investigation where Jerry Barnett spent the bulk of his time. They paid a visit to the parimutuels. Out of the box they caught a break. The thoroughbred meet in session was running at Calder Race Track near the Dade-Broward county line. Asking around, they learned no one had seen Jerry Barnett in months. Every indication revealed he'd been concentrating on the greyhounds. Before his demise Jerry Barnett was strictly a dog man and had lost interest in the ponies. He didn't replace the horses with Jai Alai. He was strictly a dog man.

Next, they paid a visit to the Biscayne Kennel Club where they found no shortage of his acquaintances. They rounded up his fellow five percenters for questioning. As a group the five percenters were like some kind of underground clique of society's outcasts who scratched out a day to day existence. They lived on the edge with no visible means of support. They were a diverse group of individuals united by the creed of preferring to make ten dollars with an angle then fifty dollars straight up. To a man they were uncooperative refusing to say a word about anything. No one even remembered Jerry Barnett until Ron Jeffries adjusted their attitudes.

"0939," he spoke into his police radio. "Requesting transportation for nine white males from the Biscayne Kennel Club in North Miami."

"Hey!" shouted Marty Chester, one of the more vocal five percenters. "Where do you think you're taking us?"

"Oh, I don't know," Ron answered, "I thought we'd spend the whole night trying to get to know one another better. Then first thing in the morning I thought we'd take a little field trip together over to the Internal Revenue Service. I'm sure they'd be very interested in finding out who you guys cash tickets for. And also about the different names and IDs you use to fill out the forms."

To a man their memories made a remarkable recovery.

"Central," Ron said to the radio, "Cancel request for transportation, QSL."

They had much to say and Stanley Starfish listened intensely to every syllable. According to Marty Chester the last four months had been the All Time Golden Age for Five Percenters, especially Jerry

Barnett. He was cashing for someone ten, eleven, twelve times a night and for big money. The tickets were almost exclusively for trifectas. He had so many winning tickets he couldn't cash them all himself without arousing suspicion. He sub-contracted with the other five percenters, usually splitting fifty-fifty. All his friends were getting healthy and not a one had any idea for whom Jerry Barnett was cashing, although Marty Chester thought it might be for more than one person. After comparing notes some of the five percenters found out they sometimes cashed on the same race and it didn't make sense for the same guy to buy duplicate numbered tickets. He asked them if they knew any of Jerry Barnett's associates away from the track. He asked if they ever saw him with someone who drove a pickup truck or sport utility. The five percenters couldn't help him on either question. Stanley paused and started pacing. Ron could tell he was processing the information he'd just heard. Stanley asked them if they went to one particular window to collect, or if they used a specific cashier. The guys shrugged their shoulders. Jerry Barnett never instructed them to do that. They cashed at random at any window and with any clerk. They did reveal that most, if not all the winning tickets were from previous days. They were rarely from races from the same evening. The five percenters also told Stanley when they expressed their dismay that this golden meet of all time was coming to an end, Jerry Barnett wasn't concerned. He intimated he had something else on the back burner. Something big.

Ronnie took their names, addresses and phone numbers while Stanley thanked them for their cooperation. They left the track with Ron behind the wheel. As he drove he observed his partner more wired in thought than he'd ever seen him. "Partner," he said to Stanley, "You better slow down. You're on overload. I see smoke coming out of your ears."

Stanley smiled, "I'm sorry. I simply can't believe what we just heard."

Ron looked confused. "I don't follow."

Stanley motioned him to pull over. He waited until the car came to a complete stop before speaking. "Ronnie, somebody, somehow, has figured out a way to beat the system. They're cashing tickets on almost every trifecta, every single night. It's been going on the entire four month meet."

Ron was taken aback. "That's impossible! How? How can you fix a fucking dog race? I can see with the horses you could get to the jockeys but how could you get to a goddamned dog?"

"No, that's not it. I mean you could do it. You could fix a single race. You could drug all the dogs but one. I worked a case in ECU where a trainer threw in a ringer at Calder. I'm sure you could also do it with a dog. But that would be a single time for a big score. You couldn't drug the dogs race after race. Too many people would have to be involved. You couldn't use a ringer that much either. Somebody would catch on. This is happening race after race, night after night. And, they concentrate on trifectas where there's so many variables. I'm not sure how it's done but I'm pretty sure it doesn't involve the dogs. No, it's something else. I do know something. Jerry Barnett figured it out. That's why he was murdered."

Stanley came to work the next day looking tired and haggard. He hadn't slept at all. Rosi Gonzalez took one look at him and got up from her desk. She returned a few minutes later with a large Styrofoam cup of café cubano. She poured from the big cup into three smaller shot-sized paper cups. "Here," she said sternly, "drink this now! You look like hell. Drink this!" she repeated, "All three!"

The homicide detective started to protest. He wasn't a coffee drinker and had a special dislike for Cuban coffee. It was way too strong and too sweet for his Anglo taste buds. Rosi's demeanor, however, suggested it was pointless to argue. He sheepishly complied. Instantaneously, the coffee had its desired effect. Stanley Starfish was juiced for the rest of the day. He spent the morning pacing back and forth concentrating on the Barnett homicide. He replayed over and over in his mind what he heard from the bookie, Cye Harris, and the five percenters, trying to isolate some common denominator. One thing was pretty clear. It involved trifecta wagering. He began by crunching numbers.

Stanley compared the payouts between the trifecta handle during the current meet to the one a year ago. He also compared it to the preceding ones at the other area dog tracks. The total handles were consistent but the winning tickets at the current Biscayne meet were paying about twenty percent less than the previous year and those of the other tracks. Not a huge dropoff but significant, especially when compounded by the number of daily trifectas over a four month period. He stared at and studied the figures again and again, finally rolling up the paper into a ball and hurling it angrily at the window. He was stumped. He thought about counterfeit winning tickets but quickly dismissed that idea. Again, you could probably get away with it once but never night after night. The parimutuels were the most regulated industry in Florida with scores of independent auditors working for both the state and the track. Counterfeit tickets would throw the numbers out of whack and set off a dozen red flags. After a couple of times they would pounce all over it and shut it right down. No, that wasn't it. He was getting really frustrated. He was sure the solution was right in front of him. He would simply have to look a little harder.

Stanley broke it down into two possibilities. Either someone, somehow had divined a surefire method of picking winners legitimately or had developed an undetectable scam to beat the system. He was certain it was the latter. Nobody could consistently pick winners. The odds against it were astronomical. And this involved trifectas where you not only had to pick the winner but who finished second and third. It had to be some kind of deceit. He reviewed again searching for a common theme. His mind began to spin and turn slowly at first, then faster and faster. A small seed of an idea started to germinate. His whole consciousness became satiated with a single word—TICKETS. He didn't know how but it had something to do with the tickets. You needed a ticket in your hand to collect the winnings. There were no electronic transfers. Jerry Barnett and his friends collected tickets for other people. If the tickets weren't counterfeit then only the window clerks punched out genuine ones. Stanley was far from having all the pieces but at least he felt he was working the right puzzle. The more he thought about it the more he was convinced it was an inside job.

He also decided it was time for a new approach. He was a homicide detective. His focus should be centered on the murder of Jerry Barnett, not the betting scam. He allowed himself to get so plugged into the mystery of the betting it became a distraction. Instead of figuring out how they beat the system as a means to solving the murder perhaps solving the murder first would help him answer the former. Stanley accessed the track's personnel files and ran all the window clerks through the computer. Nothing. He came up with absolutely nothing. The results weren't unexpected because anyone with a felony conviction on their record was automatically excluded from employment at any type of parimutual. Next he ran credit checks. Someone owing a lot of money might be susceptible to a get-rich scheme. Again, nothing out of the ordinary. He then checked the names against the real estate public records in Dade, Broward, and Palm Beach counties. Maybe one of the clerks came into sudden wealth and was living above their apparent means. There were several transactions associated with Biscayne Kennel Club personnel. One stood out. Mr. And Mrs. Ralph Lucci recently closed on a two hundred twenty-five thousand dollar four-bedroom house with pool in the new planned community of Weston in Broward County. Further research showed Mrs. Lucci was a waitress. There could have been twenty different explanations of how the Lucci's got the money for the house. He didn't want to prejudge anyone but it at least merited a closer examination. He ran background checks on Ralph Lucci's family. He then ran his wife's family. Ralph Lucci had a brother-in-law who was a real bad guy. Louis Marchetta had a long record with felony convictions for battery, resisting arrest, resisting arrest with violence, usury, possession of a firearm in the commission of a felony and couple of others. Stanley did a complete workup on Lou Marchetta and discovered two other valuable pieces of information. First, Lou Marchetta won two large trifectas at the Biscayne Kennel Club during the current meet. On the third evening of the meet he cashed a ticket for one thousand three hundred forty two dollars and ten cents, and another for one thousand sixty six dollars and forty cents two nights later. Also, Lou Marchetta owned a navy blue Ford Bronco.

The next morning Ron and Stanley paid a visit to Lou Marchetta's apartment complex. They located his Bronco in the parking lot and compared the tire tread to a picture of the tread tracks left where Jerry Barnett's body was found. They matched exactly. They looked through the back window but a tarp covered up the cargo area. Their only solid evidence were the treads that could be found on a thousand other cars. Neither Ron nor Stanley had ever obtained a search warrant with so little probable cause. They needed help.

Assistant District Attorney Jorge Aduano was smart, ambitious, and politically savvy. A handsome, well-groomed man with a charming disposition he had successfully prosecuted many high profile cases. He rose quickly through the ranks to his current position as the State Attorney's Chief Assistant. Stanley first met him through the case involving Leo Gorman. He also prosecuted Billy Mitchell for the Aronson murder. Ron had worked with him as well. They asked Jorge Aduano if he had a friendly judge in his hip pocket, one who would issue a search warrant based on the tire treads. "We know it's pretty flimsy," Ronnie told him, "but it's all we have. We need the search warrant real bad."

Jorge Aduano was hesitant. Yes, he could probably get a judge to issue the warrant. He was reluctant to use up an important favor on something so nebulous. He would then owe a favor in return and he hated being in that position. If he went out on a limb it better be for something worthwhile. Jorge Aduano considered who was asking. The black detective was a solid investigator, very professional and not prone to hyperbole. The skinny one… there was something different about the skinny one. He looked harmless enough. People probably tended to underestimate him. That was a mistake. The

Aronson homicide was open for years until he came along. He had
intelligent eyes, simultaneously probing and absorbing. There was definitely something different about the skinny one.

"I'm not going to regret this?"

"Mr. Aduano," Stanley Starfish answered, "I believe the murder of
Jerry Barnett is connected to something much larger. The tip of the
proverbial iceberg."

"All right," the Assistant District Attorney replied," I'll get you your
search warrant."

Ron Jeffries served Lou Marchetta the next afternoon. A crime lab
team helped them execute it. They didn't find the murder weapon.
They did find a pair of Asahi PM1 size nine and one-half tennis shoes
with gum rubber soles and a distinctive dotted sole design. It matched
the footprints at the crime scene. The crime lab people detected blood
spots in the back of the Bronco. Someone had tried very hard to scrub
them out but they showed up under a black light. They had enough to
read Lou Marchetta his rights. After processing him into the system
Stanley took him into an interview room. Ron got him a cup of coffee
and a cigarette while Stanley spoke to the crime lab. He hung up the
phone and entered the room.

"Thanks for the smoke and coffee," Lou Marchetta said politely.
"Now can you get me my attorney?"

"Any time you like," answered Stanley. "First, I should tell you I just
got off the phone with the crime lab. They found Jerry Barnett's blood
in your Bronco. There were carpet fibers from your Bronco matching
ones found on his body. Your shoes are a dead match for the footprints
found at the scene of the homicide and so are your tires. Is there anything you might want to tell us?"

Lou Marchetta chuckled. "What you're not telling me is what you
don't have. Namely no murder weapon and no witnesses. Sounds pretty circumstantial to me. I don't think I'm looking at much. And by the
way, who's Jerry Barnett?"

Stanley smiled, "You're right, Mr. Marchetta. Right now we have a
case based on circumstantial evidence with not enough for a first
degree murder conviction or possibly a second degree. What you're
neglecting is your previous record. You will be sentenced as a habitual offender. Any conviction gives you a life sentence. Bad check, DUI,
anything at all, it doesn't matter what. Any conviction whatsoever
means, in all probability, you will die in jail. You're a serious man who
knows what's up. We're not trying to trick you. But I think you know
right now, without anything else, we have enough for manslaughter."

The homicide detective paused and stared at Lou Marchetta who took one last drag from his cigarette before putting it out. Ronnie quickly offered him another, lighting it for him. Lou Marchetta took a couple of deep inhales, then asked, "Why? If you have me cold why are you talking to me?"

Stanley sat down across the table from him. "We might be able to help each other."

"How can you help me?"

"Well, the sentence is mandatory. We can't do anything about that. We can help where you do your time. I'm sure we can give you a wide choice and make you as comfortable as possible. I'm not trying to BS you. It's not a lot but it's something."

Lou Marchetta shrugged his shoulders and half nodded, "What do you want in return?"

"We would be interested in the connection between yourself, Jerry Barnett and the trifecta wagering at the Biscayne Kennel Club." Stanley deliberately omitted any mention of his brother-in-law Ralph Lucci.

Lou Marchetta changed expressions like a chameleon transforming from a cornered wise guy to a mysterious genius. He acted so smug; like he was the only person alive knowing a secret formula for eternal youth and choosing to keep it to himself. He smiled ingratiatingly, "I'll bet you'd like to know about that. But I think you can do a lot better than choice of joints for that kind of information. I dreamed my whole life for a setup this sweet. I'm not giving it up because one jail has better powdered eggs than another."

Lou Marchetta was very intuitive, very street smart. He could tell by the body language of the thin, young-looking detective that he was pushing his button.

"Why don't you think about it and see what you can do," Lou Marchetta acted as if he owned the keys to the kingdom. "If you don't mind," he added arrogantly, "I'll make myself comfortable. It looks like I'm going to be your guest for a while... In the meantime, you can get me my lawyer."

Ronnie allowed Lou Marchetta his phone call, then escorted him to a holding cell. When he returned his partner's mood bordered on despondency. "What's the problem?" Ron asked.

"He's never going to give it up," Stanley answered. "He's toying with us now, enjoying every second of it. He's smart and he's tough. He knows he's facing mandatory sentencing and nobody has any margin to cut a deal. And he doesn't want to hurt his brother-in-law. Right now all he's got is the knowledge that he knows we know he beat the system and can't figure out how. That's enough to sustain him. My guess is he'll play with us, string us out as long as he can but end up giving us zilch. I believe he'd rather die with his secret than tell us anything,"

Stanley Starfish was half right. Lou Marchetta didn't bother screwing around with them but was very willing to die with his secret. When they returned Lou Marchetta was hanging from his shirtsleeve. Whatever he knew about the trifecta wagering at the Biscayne Kennel Club expired in the holding cell.

Armando Pedroza was glad the case cleared and tried forcing Ron and Stanley to implicate Lou Marchetta in three quarters of the county's open homicides. They resisted, telling him there were still loose ends and possible involvement by others. They needed a little more time. They didn't have much. The next day was the last of the Biscayne Kennel Club meet. After that the greyhounds would run at Flagler.

Stanley Starfish wanted one more crack at solving this bewildering puzzle. Truthfully, this case was driving him crazy. During the day Ron questioned Ralph Lucci who volunteered nothing. And why should he? They didn't have a thing on him. The homicide detective grew more frustrated. How could anyone cash trifectas race after race, night after night, and get away with it? He could think of only one last thing to try. He arranged for Biscayne Kennel Club's General Manager, Archie Flynn, to introduce him around as a special auditor reviewing the track's functions, sort of a last day check up. He visited the counting room where the money was kept, observed the window clerks and was introduced by Archie Flynn to the track's totalizator, Mr. Conrad Stryckowski. The totalizator was a sophisticated computer expert who oversaw the workings of the track's most valuable piece of equipment. Every bet from every window fed into the computer which compiled the data and spit out the odds on each greyhound and the potential payouts of the exotic wagering. When the race finished it deducted the state's cut and the track's cut out of the gross handle, then divided the rest among the winning bets according to the odds. The payout of every bet—win, place, show, daily double, perfecta, quinella and trifecta were computed and posted on the track's toteboard. The totalizator's job was to keep everything running smoothly, respond to any glitches, and be the final check, making sure all the numbers jibed before posting them.

Stanley, posing as the special auditor, made the rounds watching everyone do their job. He made a trifecta wager to see how it was processed. After the fifth race he joined Conrad Stryckowski in the computer room. Conrad Stryckowski was a slight man with a rather large nose and very thick glasses. His hair was slicked back and he wore his plaid shirt buttoned to the top. He seemed a little nervous but did his job very professionally. He monitored everything until the race started, then had a little break until the race was over. Once the race finished he was back at work scrutinizing every detail. It took approximately forty five seconds to complete his final diagnostic check before pushing a button and sending the results to the toteboard. Nothing was official until Conrad Stryckowski pushed the button. Stanley did his best to stay out of his way. The races only lasted about thirty, thirty five seconds so there wasn't much time for conversation. The rest of the time he was too busy to talk. After the ninth race a barely perceptible wry, little smile crossed Stanley's face. He excused himself and thanked the thick-glassed man.

About thirty minutes after the last race Conrad Stryckowski finished up his final tasks and walked out to his car. On the way he was met by the special auditor.

"Mr. Stryckowski, do you have a minute?"

"It's really late. I'd like to get home. Can it wait?"

"I'm afraid it can't."

Stanley Starfish flashed him his badge saying, "I'm not really an auditor."

Conrad Stryckowski quickly looked around. Two uniformed officers appeared out of nowhere and stood close by. A minute later he saw a handcuffed Ralph Lucci being escorted out by a well built black man.

"You might as well sit down," Stanley told him. It's probably going to be a while."

Conrad Stryckowski complied. As he sat down he said to the skinny detective, "I'm not saying a thing."

"As you wish." Stanley walked over to the uniformed officers, chatted briefly then returned. He sat down across from Conrad Stryckowski and said, "I have to compliment you. Yours was by far the most ingenious, well thought out scheme I've ever come across. It was absolutely brilliant... beyond brilliant. Words don't adequately describe it. The only victims were winners."

Conrad Stryckowski lifted his head and stared long and hard at the man across from him. He appeared relieved it was over and acknowledged the detective's plaudits with a nod.

"With a little luck," Stanley continued, "theoretically you could have gone on for years without getting caught. In theory it's truly a perfect crime."

Conrad Stryckowski again acknowledged the compliments. He gave a half smile and spoke freely. "A year. Two at the most. By then the track would have upgraded the computer. Newer, foolproof models that eliminate the lag time are already on the market, mostly at the thoroughbred facilities. Anyway, you caught on."

"Was there anyone else involved besides you and Ralph Lucci?"

"Ralph's brother-in-law, Lou Marchetta. He was the one who collected on the tickets. He handled the money and doled out our shares."

At the station Conrad Stryckowski gave a full statement giving a detailed account of the entire set up. He never met Jerry Barnett, never even heard of him. Ralph Lucci refused to talk and they had no evidence tying him to the homicide. The murder of Jerry Barnett cleared with the suicide of Lou Marchetta. Both Conrad Stryckowski and Ralph Lucci faced a myriad of charges stemming from the betting scam.

Ron Jeffries' forehead wrinkled as he reread Stanley's report. He shot his partner a confused look saying, "I don't get it."

"Ronnie, I've investigated many crimes but nothing like this one. In the others there was always a paper trail or some other flaw that would eventually reveal itself and then the whole thing would unravel. Not this one. This one's on a whole different level."

Stanley paused. He was still a bit in awe of the crime's genius. He sipped some water before continuing.

"I went over this a thousand times and couldn't find a single clue. The only thing left was the computer. I had a feeling it involved the computer, but for the life of me, I couldn't figure out how. That's why I wanted to observe the operation. It took me four races but eventually I caught on. The totalizator, Stryckowski, had about a forty five second lag time after each race to make sure everything was correct before posting the official results. He discovered he could punch in a few extra winning numbers without being detected. The betting pool remained the same. The state got the same cut it normally would. So did the track. That's why no auditor would ever find anything amiss. The only ones who suffered were the others splitting the betting pool. That's the real beauty of the whole scheme. The losers were winners. Big winners. They just won less. They were still cashing a trifecta wager for major dollars. How were they supposed to know their winnings of eight hundred dollars were really supposed to be twelve hundred? They were happy as clams with the eight. After discovering the glitch in the computer, Stryckowski realized he needed someone to print up the winning tickets. Just because the tote board showed the number of winning bets you couldn't collect unless you presented a ticket to the cashier. That's why Stryckowski approached Ralph Lucci, who agreed to participate. Stryckowski would let Lucci know how many extra winning tickets to print after the race was over. One or both realized they couldn't cash the tickets themselves so Lucci enlisted the help of his brother-in-law. You saw where Lou Marchetta won a couple of big payouts early in the meet? I'm pretty sure they were testing the system. It passed with flying colors but their success created another problem. Lou Marchetta couldn't cash every ticket. That's why he needed a five percenter. Enter Jerry Barnett. I bet if we really dug into it we'd find Jerry Barnett cashed under several different names using different identities. After a while there were too many winning tickets for one person to cash no matter how many false IDs he had. Lou Marchetta probably had Jerry Barnett recruit his five percenter buddies to help cash. In short, Stryckowski punched in extra winners into the trifecta betting pool after the race was over. Lucci printed up the tickets and gave them to Lou Marchetta. Marchetta had Jerry Barnett and his pals cash the tickets at the window. After giving the five percenters their cut, he distributed the rest among himself, his brother-in-law, and Stryckowski. Quite an elaborate plan. It also explains why the winning tickets weren't cashed on the same day as the race. Anyhow, with the meet coming to a close, I'm theorizing now, Jerry Barnett wanted a nest egg to tide him over and demanded a bigger share. It was a fatal miscalculation. Lou Marchetta figured he had enough partners. They shut down the operation right after Jerry Barnett's death. The meet was almost over and Marchetta probably thought it best to cool it. Think about it, Ronnie. If Jerry Barnett didn't get greedy they would have gotten away with millions of dollars, and this is the inspired part, without anybody having a clue it was missing in the first place! My guess is they'll never really know how much they got away with."

Ron Jeffries shook his head, "Stanley, you know I love you like a brother so please listen to me. You are way too smart for this job. Trust me, you have got to find something else to do with your life. What you should do is be a criminal mastermind. Who the hell is going to catch you?"

———

Stanley Starfish was unprepared for the media frenzy accompanying the case's aftermath. Dubbed the Biscayne Kennel Club Murder, the case struck a chord with the public and Stanley became something of a local celebrity. The Miami Herald wrote a feature about the case in Tropic, their Sunday magazine, nicknaming him "Miami's Sherlock Holmes." A couple of local TV stations picked up the story as did USA Today, which ran a front page article. He appeared with former Miamian Larry King, doing a fifteen minute segment by phone.

Normally Armando Pedroza would have been jealous and resented all the attention going Stanley's way. In this instance there were enough accolades to go around for everyone. The department administration was thrilled with positive publicity for a change, and its goodwill spread throughout the squad. Especially to Armando Pedroza, who received another administrative promotion. Begrudgingly, he paid Stanley some respect. Armando, who reviewed the case and had no idea what happened said, "Bambi, you got the perfect fucking name for homicide. A starfish crawls along the bottom until it finds something dead. Then it attaches its appendages and sucks out the guts until there's nothing left. That's you," he said, shaking his head with admiration, "working a case."

After the commotion died down Ron and Stanley spent a considerable amount of time working with Jorge Aduano. Ralph Lucci plead not guilty to a host of charges and they assisted the assistant district attorney to prepare for trial. During this time Stanley caught the attention of Jorge Aduano's secretary, Alicia Zelinsky. A full-figured girl with a curvaceous body, Alicia had a pretty, round face with deep brown eyes. The shy detective was no match for her. They were engaged in six weeks and married two months later. At first Ron felt the romance was moving way too fast and his partner was way over his head. Rita told her husband to butt out and let the romance take its natural course. Secretly, she was ecstatic Stanley had found someone. She worried about him. He had no family, few friends, and spent much of his time alone. Finding love was exactly what she felt he needed. He was a good-hearted, sweet kid who deserved happiness in his life. At church Rita prayed this girl would treat him right. Ron acquiesced to his wife's wishes. There wasn't much he could do anyway. Stanley Starfish was beyond pussy-whipped. Alicia Zelinsky had him wrapped around her finger.

They were married at Temple Schmuel on the beach. Ron Jeffries stood in as his best man. Alicia came from a large family being the youngest of five. Her family were twice refugees. The first time they fled their native Poland ahead of the Nazi invasion. They landed in Cuba when the Roosevelt administration put a quota on immigrating Jews. The Zelinskys left Cuba shortly after the fall of the Batista regime, setting up residence in Miami. Alicia was the only one of her brothers and sisters to be born in the United States. The reception was slightly raucous as Cuban Jews knew how to party. Alicia and Stanley honeymooned aboard a Royal Caribbean Cruise ship sailing through the Caribbean. Upon returning the couple lived in Stanley's Surfside apartment. Ten months later Alicia gave birth. Stanley Starfish was the proud father of a baby boy. Born five weeks premature, Emilio Starfish inherited his father's eyes and curly hair. Stanley could not have been happier. The birth of his son made his life complete. He focused his considerable energy into being a devoted husband and a doting, loving father. He looked forward to two AM feedings and changing diapers. Sometimes he would simply watch his son sleep and stare at him for hours. If Emilio was cranky his father would rock him back and forth on his knees while he sang folksongs his mother had sung to him. Stanley Starfish couldn't imagine life being any better.

At work everything ran smoothly. He and Ron still cleared case after case and Armando Pedroza, every now and then, would stop and chat. Both men shared a love for the ocean and for exploring the local coral reefs. Their conversations were brief. Armando was an accomplished spearfisherman, while Stanley collected shells. Two polar opposite mentalities. It still marked an improvement in their relationship and made for a less tense working environment. The single glitch in his life was his wife's displeasure with the Surfside apartment. She wanted neighbors her own age and to be around other young families. She wanted to move to Kendall. Kendall was an unincorporated area of south Miami Dade County and quite possibly the worst-planned community in North America. It stood out as a crowning tribute to the unmitigated greed of developers who ran roughshod over an anemic and corrupt County Commission, a majority of whom never met a variance they wouldn't approve. It created a hodgepodge of poorly built condominiums, apartment houses, townhouses and single family homes without the infrastructure to support it. The defining architectural achievement in Kendall was the strip mall. There were several at every intersection. Many of Stanley's fellow officers lived in Kendall, including some from homicide. He disliked the area's quality of life and detested the nightmarish traffic. He subjugated his feelings to his wife's requests. If living there made her happy he was willing to go along. He refused to allow the inconveniences and extra driving time to disrupt his new lifestyle. The apartment sold quickly and the family Starfish moved into a new townhouse. Everything was going so well... until Roni Rosen called.

Roni Rosen was a reporter and weekend anchor for a local TV station. Stanley first met her after the Aronson case. Over the years their jobs would sometimes intersect and they would spend some time together. Roni Rosen covered the Biscayne Kennel Club murder and was one of the reporters who did a feature on it. They were schoolmates at Miami Beach High and were in the same French class junior year. They ran in different social circles. He was certain she wouldn't remember him so he never brought it up. In high school Roni ran with the rich, preppy, popular crowd. Stanley had her categorized as the quintessential Beach High JAP. As a reporter he figured she would be the typical aggressive, in your face barracuda. He learned a valuable lesson about superficial first impressions. As he got to know her Stanley found her smart and with a biting sense of humor. She relished telling off-color jokes and, on occasion, could swear like a sailor. At her job she was thoroughly professional and ethical. She never crossed the line over what was on or off the record. She never divulged a source. He considered her a semi-quasi friend. When Roni Rosen asked for his help he found it difficult to refuse her.

They met after work where she relayed the details of her father's death and her conviction her stepmother was responsible. She told him how she attempted to go through proper channels and her experience with Armando Pedroza.

"If you decide to help me it will have to be on the sly," she told him. She cleared her throat, then moved her face inches from his and whispered, "Everybody thinks I'm doing this for the money. They're wrong. My father had a lot of faults but he never forgot I was his daughter. He always treated me as his little princess. I was forever Daddy's little girl. I'll never have that special feeling again. My father deserved better. If she's involved she shouldn't get away with it."

Stanley nodded. Roni Rosen squeezed his hand, thanking him before departing. Neither had any idea his agreeing to help would have such drastic consequences.

It began when he asked Rosi to access the medical examiner's report on Sidney Rosen. Armando Pedroza noticed it on her desk and went in to a vein-popping fit. He bombarded her with insult upon insult in two languages until Stanley Starfish interceded.

"Don't take it out on her. I asked her to do it. I'm responsible. If you want to vent on someone vent on me."

Armando Pedroza was happy to oblige. "Listen, Bambi, in case you haven't noticed, we had six homicides over the weekend on top of the eight still open from before. Silly me, I thought those would be enough to keep your active little mind occupied. I didn't realize you had so much free time on your hands you could help out poor little Miss Anchor with an attitude on a closed case... emphasis on closed! If your cunt reporter friend isn't satisfied, let her hire a P.I. She's got plenty of money even if her stepmother gets her share. As for you... if I catch you working on Rosen again I'll shove your nose so far up my ass you'll be able to tell what I ate for breakfast. And when I shit you out you'll be back in uniform directing traffic at school crossings!"

Stanley met with Roni Rosen the next afternoon and informed her of Armando Pedroza's reaction. "Have you given any thought to a private investigator?"

"C'mon, Stan. I'm a reporter. I know how they work. They'll come up with hot lead after hot lead while they run up the tab and their expense account. Besides if Staci caused my father's death she did an excellent job of making it look like he died of natural causes. I'm afraid you were the only one who could have helped me. But listen... I don't want you to get into any trouble with your asshole boss over me. Do as he says... leave it alone."

She opened her purse, took out a tissue and wiped her eyes. Stanley was surprised to see the tough confident TV personality reduced to tears. "Hey, I didn't say I wouldn't help. I'll just have to more careful. It may limit a bit what I can do. Do you think you could get me some information?"

She smiled, "Whatever you need."

"How about some background information on your father and stepmother. Also, do you think you could get me her credit card accounts?"

"I am a trained investigative reporter. If I can't get them all I should at least be able to track down fifteen or twenty."

Stanley laughed. "By the way," he continued, "How did your dad meet your stepmother?"

"They met at a Miami Ski Club mixer. She handed him her card:"

"Staci—*Have Pussy Will Travel*"

Two days later the homicide detective picked up a packet and delved into the lives of Sidney and Staci Rosen. Sid Rosen was one of South Florida's most successful developers. He was at the forefront of the building boom and took advantage of the region's incredible growth, amassing a tremendous fortune. In an area bereft of old time historical social stratas, and where football players and lawyers were passed off as celebrities, the big time developers like Sid Rosen were the real lions of local society. As a group they were flashy living, publicity-seeking opulent spenders. Sid Rosen was no exception. He made magnanimous donations to the opera and the Miami Philharmonic. A wing of Mount Sinai Hospital was named after him. He had his own private Lear jet and a sixty acre ranch in Aspen. Sid Rosen changed wives as often as he changed car models. With his first wife, Roni's mother, he drove a Cadillac. With wife number two it was a Mercedes. For number three he drove a Rolls Royce. With Staci, his fourth wife, they both cruised around in matching Aston Martins. The only thing Sidney Rosen couldn't buy was perfect health. He had a faulty heart, a by-product of his lifestyle.

Staci Collins Leibowitz Rosen was one of the most beautiful women in South Florida. At an early age she understood her looks set her apart. Her entire life she was constantly the object of special attention. She also knew at an early age what she would do with her life. Her ambition was to be a professional beauty. Not a glorified clothes hanger walking on a runway. Not an inanimate image in some magazine. Her goal was live well, extremely well, simply by being beautiful. Men were stupid and easy to manipulate. They would all do anything to please her. Her first boyfriend was a good example. He worked two jobs just so he could buy her a designer gown and rent a limo for the junior prom. Her second boyfriend was really willing to sacrifice. Making the payments on her BMW 320I proved too much a burden and he was busted for possession with intent to sell. The car was repoed right after he was sentenced. Her one and only stint at employment turned out to be beneficial. After dropping out of junior college she went to work as a receptionist for a group of doctors. Shortly after, she began dating a young cardiologist from the office, a Dr. Joel Liebowitz. Dr. Joel was typical of the male species in that he was an egotistical fool. Dr. Joel really believed he was in control of the relationship. He thought he could mollify her with a couple of nights a week by faking calls or a stolen weekend now and then when, for instance, he sent the wife and kids up North for the Jewish holidays. Did he really believe a few twenty-four carat gold chains would be enough to satisfy her? Was he in for a reality check! Staci cut him off. She ignored him in the office. She wouldn't take his persistent phone calls.

In a week she turned Dr. Joel into an emotional and physical wreck. He couldn't eat or sleep. He was reduced to begging and pleading, willing to do anything, pay any price for her slightest attention. The price for doing anything proved to be rather high. Within eight months he divorced the wife who put him through med school and was the mother of his two children. Two weeks later he married Staci.

Staci Collins Leibowitz hit the jackpot. She landed a Jewish doctor. The first couple of years were fabulous. They bought a spacious waterfront condo in swinging Turnberry isle. They chartered yachts to tour the Caribbean island of Nevis and took ski vacations in Aspen. Her looks alone gained them instantaneous access to the spire of Miami's hip society. With her on his arm there wasn't a club line the happy couple ever waited on or an "A" event to which they weren't invited. Problems developed later. Six hundred fifty thousand dollars a year simply didn't go as far as it used to; especially with Dr. Joel supporting two households. And how about his brats! She didn't say a word at first but every other weekend visitation was screwing up her social calendar. Tension in the marriage escalated as passion dimmed. They divorced eight weeks after their third anniversary. Staci Collins Leibowitz cleaned Dr. Joel out of everything his first wife didn't get. Last she heard Dr. Joel was trying to reconcile. He was too late. His first wife was involved in a deeply loving relationship and engaged to be married. She turned a deaf ear to his whining and pleading.

Staci Collins Leibowitz didn't stay unattached for long. Some of her friends invited her to a Miami Ski Club function where she ran into Sid Rosen. They had met once before in Aspen where invitations to his annual New Year's Eve Party were to die for. Hollywood big shots, record industry moguls, captains of industry and high level politicians all flocked to Sid Rosen's compound for a lavish feast of expensive wines, gourmet delights and high grade cocaine. She wasn't surprised he remembered her. Despite his party being a showcase for Hollywood's most beautiful talent, Staci always distanced herself from the crowd. Between marriages, Sid Rosen thought she would be a sweet little treat, a pleasant interlude between stages in his life. He underestimated her. Though he initially viewed her as nothing more than a short term piece of ass, Sidney Rosen discovered he couldn't live without her. Not long after he made Staci Collins Leibowitz Rosen wife number four.

If Dr. Joel was hitting the jackpot, Sid Rosen was winning the powerball lottery. Staci had achieved everything she set out for and had no problems whatsoever adapting to life as the ideal trophy wife. And what a life! The Concorde to Paris for lunch or beach weekends in Cabo San Lucas were mundane occurrences. The couple were the uncrowned royalty of the fast lane. Country music legends and Broadway stars flew to Miami just to party with the Rosens. They basked in the sun during the day and coked it up at night. It was a whirlwind existence with the couple splitting their time between the ranch in Aspen and a coral rock mansion in Coconut Grove overlooking Biscayne Bay. Staci thought the good times would never end. She didn't count on her husband's health catching up with him. She spent her fourth anniversary at Mount Sinai Hospital where her husband was recovering from a heart attack. Six months later she accompanied him to Boston's Brigham and Women's Hospital where he underwent surgery for a new heart valve and a triple bypass operation. The Sidney Rosen who survived the procedures was not the Sidney Rosen she married. This Sidney was painfully gaunt and lacked energy. He needed daily afternoon naps. Travel was too taxing for him and she spent her time being bored to death in that old stuffy mansion. They no longer entertained. They no longer went out, even for dinner. Sidney was put on a very restricted diet, severely limiting his choices. For recreation their life centered on golf. Fucking golf! Staci Collins Leibowitz Rosen came to the realization that she was married to a decaying old man. Circumstances change.

Her dream life had been reduced to puttering around in a golf cart and monitoring the salt content of her husband's meals. Not exactly what she felt her role in life would be. Worse yet, since the operation, Sid Rosen had become philosophical, moralizing about her drug use and her extravagance. Staci needed his preachy advice as much as she needed a training bra. Also, he was looking at new charities to support. He was even spending time with his back-stabbing bitch daughter and her family. Staci Collins Leibowitz Rosen would endure about anything to maintain her lifestyle. Being called "Grandma" wasn't one of them. She badly wanted out but was trapped by that goddamned restrictive pre-nuptial agreement Sid's lawyer forced her to sign. If she left him or he divorced her Staci basically got the keys to the Aston Martin. No giant settlement, no huge alimony. She got the car, her clothes, her jewelry, and a paltry twenty thousand dollars monthly for one year only. Who could live on that? She knew she was running out of time after noticing Sid perusing Jaguar brochures. Her one hope was that he die before dumping her. In that scenario she retained full standing in his will according to terms of the pre-nup. A quick response was called for. Staci thought she detected a tiny wrinkle when taking inventory in front of the mirror. She would need a whole lot of dollars to deal with that calamity, not a paltry twenty thousand a month. She tried banging him to death but he wasn't so interested anymore. To her good fortune the situation remedied itself. Sidney Rosen died in bed, according to the county medical examiner, from another heart attack. She had only to wait for the will to be probated before flashing her stepdaughter both middle fingers.

To best help Roni Rosen Stanley Starfish decided on a strategy he used in bridge. Called the Rule of Restricted Choice it was based on the principle that if only one specific distribution of the cards allowed you to make the contract assume it existed and play the hand accordingly. In a normal investigation he would be open-minded to any and all possibilities. In this instance he could limit the scope exclusively to Staci Rosen. He only needed to consider possibilities which aided Roni Rosen. Employing the Rule of Restricted Choice would save a lot of time and keep him from getting sidetracked. After reviewing the information Roni Rosen provided, the homicide detective accessed her stepmother's credit card purchases. He highlighted a couple of items which caught his attention, then called Roni Rosen. He needed more information. They made a date for lunch the next day.

He was already seated when she bustled through a crowd to join him. "Sorry I'm late. I had to recut a story. Did you order?"

"I was waiting for you. Did you get what I requested?"

"Yes. Here's a list of my father's medications and dosages. Is it helpful?"

"It might be. I have to be very honest with you," Stanley said softly while he scanned the list of medications, "I've developed a possible theory that might help you. But it's a tremendous long shot and will be even harder to prove. And even if it pans out it still might not be enough to obtain a court-ordered exhumation."

"Let's hear it."

Stanley took a bite from a breadstick which the waiter left on the table. He was embarrassed by the crunchy sound and tried to muffle it by holding his napkin in front of his mouth. Roni Rosen smiled. He looked like a fourth grader trying to conceal his bubble gum. He swallowed the breadstick bite and continued, "Three weeks before your father's death your stepmother took a cruise by herself on Royal Caribbean."

"I remember. She had the nerve to bring my kids back serapes."

"Well, one of the ports they stopped at was Cozumel. I took the same cruise on my honeymoon. My wife developed a terrible headache from being on the beach all afternoon so we stopped in a little *farmacia* near the town square. I asked the clerk to give me something for a headache. I expected Tylenol or aspirin. She gave me Percocet! Without a prescription she gave me Percocet. You don't need a prescription for anything there. Now, I'm not a doctor. Neither is your stepmother. But she worked for a doctor group and her first husband was a cardiologist. She might be smarter than you give her... "

Roni Rosen interrupted. "You mean you think she could have purchased some type of medication that possibly could have induced my father's heart attack?"

Stanley nodded. "There's a million different obstacles to proving it that I can think of off the top of my head. The first is one of us has to go to Cozumel."

"How soon can you leave?"

"It's not that simple."

"Look, Stan. This means a lot to me. You know you're better suit-for this than me. I insist on paying for everything. Why don't you take your wife and son? I'm sure you have vacation time coming. If you want to make it a second honeymoon I'll babysit for you."

Stanley appreciated her generosity but the logistics of himself and Alicia getting the same days off didn't work out. He decided to fly in and out. His little trip required an overnight so he packed a small bag containing a toothbrush, a bathing suit, and a change of underwear. After first speaking with the head cardiologist at the Miami Heart Institute, Stanley Starfish boarded Mexicana Flight number three hundred from Miami International to Cozumel. He arrived ninety minutes later.

Roni Rosen told him to stay in the best hotel and to treat himself to expensive meals, but that wasn't his style. He checked into the Plaza Cozumel, a clean, air-conditioned place right on the town center for thirty four dollars a night. He went right to work. There were seven little *farmacias* in close proximity to the town square. Only three carried what he was looking for. Roni Rosen did an excellent job of furnishing him with a daunting collection of photos of her stepmother. She compiled a whole portfolio of pictures from the society pages of the Miami Herald and others from family albums. He had clear shots of her in different poses and different modes of dress. In spite of the good quality pictures Stanley struck out. No one could identify the beautiful lady. One place told him to come back around seven PM when the manager would be in.

With a little time to kill Stanley went shopping. The town square and its side streets offered a plethora of shops carrying leather goods, crafts, and jewelry. He bought a lovely turquoise necklace for Alicia and a colorful paper mache parrot for Emilio. He ate at a restaurant right in the Plaza called Morgan's, dining on a tasty seafood chowder and a delicious broiled grouper all for under one hundred pesos or about twelve dollars. The restaurant also provided entertainment when one of the waiters caught on fire while preparing crepes suzette.

After dinner he returned to the *farmacia*. The manager was in and he spoke to her in Spanish. He showed her the pictures and asked if she recognized the woman in the photo. The woman took her time before singling out two photos. One was of Staci Rosen wearing a designer hat and sunglasses. The other showed her with her sunglasses down around the tip of her nose sans hat. Yes, she remembered the very beautiful American lady. She remembered her because she wanted a large quantity of a very rare medicine and tried bargaining her down for a better price. The manager refused her. She walked out only to return an hour later and purchase the medicine at the quoted price.

When she first came in she wore a hat and dark glasses. When she returned the hat was gone and she lowered her glasses to better read the labels. She checked each bottle carefully. The beautiful lady purchased all she had of the medicine, either four or five bottles. The total came to twenty four hundred pesos or about three hundred dollars. The medicine was a form of Verapamil, most likely Isoptin because that's what she usually stocked and she remembered having to reorder. It was funny, she told the homicide detective, because she never would have recognized her if she had bought the medicine on her first visit. When she returned without the hat and lowered her glasses the manager got a good look at her face. She told Stanley one more thing. The very beautiful lady wanted a discount for paying in U.S. dollars. Stanley Starfish thanked her for her time and handed her two hundred pesos.

The homicide detective caught Flight #301 back to Miami. During the flight he attempted to digest what he had learned and plan his next move. He reviewed the notes he took from the conversation with Dr. Lyons, the Miami Heart Institute cardiologist. Sidney Rosen was taking the medication Inderal for his heart condition. His dosage was two hundred milligrams a day. Inderal is a type of beta blocker. Beta blockers lessen the force and rate of heart contractions, decreasing the heart's need for oxygen and lowering blood pressure. Verapamil, the medicine Staci Rosen purchased, was a channel blocker. Channel blockers also lessened the heart's workload by reducing the nerve impulses going to the heart muscle. When mixed with a beta blocker like Inderal blood pressure could be lowered to extremely dangerous levels. Congestive heart failure, the official cause of death listed for Sid Rosen, would be a likely occurrence. Isoptin, the brand name of Verapamil purchased by Staci Rosen, could be ground into food or mixed in a liquid. There were a dozen different ways it could be disguised and given to an unknowing Sidney Rosen.

Stanley Starfish closed his eyes and grimaced. He was lucky to find out about the Verapamil in Cozumel. But by itself it wasn't nearly enough. All he had was a woman, possibly Staci Rosen, buying Isoptin. He had strong doubts the *farmacia* manager's ID would hold up under cross examination. Even if it did... so what? There was no proof she entered the country with it or that she didn't purchase it for someone else. He had a starting point, but wasn't sure what to do next. He though about it all the way to Customs. CUSTOMS. Staci Collins Leibowitz Rosen would have to go through Customs upon reentry to the United States at the conclusion of her cruise. It was another real long shot but maybe Customs found something or maybe she was stupid enough to declare it.

Staci Rosen wasn't dumb enough to declare the medication but according to her Customs Declaration Card it was the only thing she didn't. She itemized her purchases, filling up every line on the back of the form. Her total was almost seven thousand dollars, far above the allowable four hundred duty-free amount and the fourteen hundred dollars which required an itemized listing. There was something else. When the Customs agent singled her out for a thorough search of her luggage she became indignant. She caused such a scene the agent filed an incident report. Staci Rosen demanded a full inventory of everything in her suitcases. Everything, not just the new purchases. She demanded a body search. The agent inventoried her possessions. The body search wasn't necessary. The incident lasted over two hours.

Stanley told Roni Rosen what he learned in Cozumel and what happened at the Port Customs.

"Listen, Stan. Thanks for trying. I really appreciate what you did. I'll get out a check today to cover your expenses. I guess that's that."

"I'm not so sure."

"What are you not so sure about?"

"I'm not so sure it's over yet."

"I wish you were right. But what we have is not enough to get an order of exhumation. We needed proof she entered the country with the medication. What happened at Customs kind of closes the book."

"Maybe not. Something doesn't add up. Why would someone who wanted a discount for cash and took the time to shop for a better price declare anything at all, knowing she'd have to pay the duty?"

"I don't know... perhaps it's a "girl" thing related to shopping."

"Also, she took great pains to make sure every single thing in her possession was checked. Maybe she tried too hard."

"I don't follow."

"The surest way I know to send up a red flag in customs is to declare over the duty-free amount. Your stepmother is a seasoned world traveler. I'll bet she's experienced this. Once they start going through her luggage she throws a tantrum and demands a full accounting. It seems she wanted a clear record of everything she re-entered the country with, not only her new purchases."

"Meaning?"

"Well, we know she bought the medication. How did she bring it back? Either she had some sort of undetectable hidden compartment in her luggage or someone brought it back for her. Do you know any of her close friends?"

"Sorry, I don't run in her circles."

"Do you know if she's seeing anyone yet?"

"Yet? She brought a date to my father's funeral. Her personal trainer."

"Do you know his name?"

"Don, Dan something. I don't remember. But I can get it."

She called back later in the day with the name. Stanley asked questions of himself while pacing back and forth. Assuming she didn't bring in the medication herself who could have? The answer was easy—anybody. It could have been a friend along on the cruise or someone new. He didn't think someone like Staci Collins Leibowitz Rosen would have a problem making new acquaintances. But she could have had the same person buy the Verapamil in Cozumel and take herself out of the loop altogether. Either she didn't think of it or didn't trust anyone enough if things went south. Maybe she had enough faith in her personal trainer, Dana Barnes. Stanley ran his name on the ship's passenger list. Nothing. He checked with the airlines to see if a Dana Barnes flew into Cozumel or Cancun around the date the cruise ship was in port. Again nothing. He went as far as to check the passenger manifest of Carnival Cruise Line ship in Cozumel the same day. Stanley hit a trifecta of negative answers. He took another look at her credit card statements. There was a charge from the pool bar at the Grand Hyatt Hotel, Grand Cayman, B.W.I. Stanley examined the cruise ship's itinerary. Its next stop after Cozumel was Grand Cayman. The charge at the Hyatt coincided with the date the ship made port. For the hell of it he called the Cayman Grand Hyatt to see if a Dana Barnes was registered there when Staci Rosen was charging at the pool bar. He loved his work when everything fell into place. Dana Barnes registered at the Hyatt two days prior to the ship being in port and checked out the day after. Stanley checked with the airlines, finding out that Dana Barnes returned to Miami the same day he left the hotel. Stanley's luck ran out at Customs. Dana Barnes didn't declare anything. He was waived through.

The homicide detective evaluated the situation. He was miles from an airtight case but if he could pressure Dana Barnes he could at least give Roni Rosen what she desired. That kind of interrogation was not his style. He approached his partner, Ron Jeffries. He explained everything, adding one caveat. "If this blows up in our faces and Armando finds out there will be hell to pay. That's why I didn't involve you until now. He's got a real bug up his ass about Roni Rosen."

Ron Jeffries didn't hesitate for a second. "Fuck Armando. We're homicide detectives investigating a potential homicide. If you think there's something to it that's good enough for me. Anyway, I'll bet you anything he's pissed off because he came on to her and she told him to shove it." Ron made a hand motion of a jet flying high, then suddenly crashing. He added sounds for effect.

Ron and Stanley interviewed Dana Barnes at his condo. Dana Barnes was strikingly handsome with deep blue eyes, blond hair and a trim, chiseled body. He was as good looking as Staci Collins Leibowitz Rosen was gorgeous. Together they made a supremely beautiful couple. From all appearances it looked like they could live a full happy life on Sid Rosen's money.

Stanley started the interview, questioning Dana Barnes in his usual polite, deliberate style. Dana Barnes claimed to know nothing, denying everything. He threatened to call his attorney. Ron Jeffries took over.

"Fine. You can call your lawyer at headquarters like everyone else. Just think about this before you dial. When you complete the call your one and only chance for full immunity goes right down the toilet. LISTEN TO ME! WE ARE GOING TO CONVICT YOU! Accessory to murder at the minimum. That means time. That means Raiford. You know what happens to a pretty boy like you on the inside? You won't be there three days before the brothers pull out your teeth with pliers so it's nice and smooth when they slide in their Johnsons. You want to call your lawyer? Do it now. We'll extend you that courtesy."

Dana Barnes turned to the white detective. "Your partner mentioned something about full immunity."

To avoid Armando Pedroza, Ron and Stanley walked Dana Barnes directly to the State Attorney's office where he gave a statement in exchange for full immunity. He gave details on how he got several bottles of a medicine called Isoptin from Staci Rosen in Grand Cayman and returned them to her in Miami. In his statement Dana Barnes told how Staci Rosen planned to use the medicine. As they left the State Attorney's office Stanley Starfish said to his partner, "That was some interview. If he didn't break down I would have confessed myself."

On the basis of Dana Barnes' statements Roni Rosen got her court ordered exhumation. A toxicology workup revealed large amounts of verapamil hydrochloride and traces of Inderal in his system. Her stepmother was indicted by a grand jury and went on trial for the first degree murder of Sidney Rosen. In one of Miami's most highly publicized and controversial trials Staci Collins Leibowitz Rosen was convicted and sentenced to life in prison without parole. For the very first time in her life the beauty of Staci Rosen worked against her. Jorge Aduano was brilliant, winning a conviction with a questionable circumstantial evidence and Dana Barnes' "bought with immunity" testimony. He succeeded in getting the jury to hate Staci Rosen by portraying her as a beautiful, spoiled, selfish, jet-setting gold digger. Of those charges she was undoubtedly guilty.

The outcome of the trial affected many lives. Jorge Aduano, benefiting from the trial's publicity, left the State Attorney's office to open up a lucrative private practice. He took Alicia Starfish with him. Roni Rosen was able to have closure in the death of her father and attain her full inheritance. Her station did a feature on the investigation and trial. Its main focus was how the department's most famous and decorated detective was able to overcome massive bureaucratic interference by his superior, an officious, incompetent dunce, and bring a scheming, murderous black widow to justice. Armando Pedroza found himself in the middle of a media firestorm. His two new favorite words were "No comment." His only place of refuge was the men's room. He found himself spending even more of his day in the bathroom than usual. Additionally, he caught some major heat from his bosses, the department administration.

The fallout from the trial also affected the life of Stanley Starfish. Armando Pedroza was constantly in a poisonous mood creating a turbulent work environment. He assigned Starfish and Jeffries every crap case and gave them as many lousy shifts as he could. Basically Armando did everything within his considerable power to make their lives miserable. Stanley felt responsible for Ronnie. It wasn't fair for him to be the object of his boss's ire. It was he who Armando was really pissed off at. Ronnie was just a bystander. He asked Ron to change partners. Ron Jeffries steadfastly refused. "We've got to hunker down. Give it some time. He can't stay mad forever. He's going to need you soon enough. This is Miami. Something really strange will turn up requiring your talents. Something big he can take credit for. Just be patient. Anyhow, if I changed, who would look after you?"

The homicide detective was fortunate to have such a loyal partner. He would soon need every bit of Ron Jeffries' support and friendship. Setting up a private practice must have required more time and effort than Jorge Aduano estimated because Stanley's Alicia found herself working many late nights and some weekends. She was putting in more hours than she did with the State Attorney's office. Her extra time at work left Stanley in charge of the household. He cleaned and shopped and managed Emilio. He did everything in his power to help out at home while still working full time. Anyway, the extra time spent with his son was a blessing. Emilio was highly intelligent and talented. He could recognize words at eighteen months and seemed to possess innate musical ability. Stanley purchased a keyboard. He played for and tutored his son as his mother did for him when he was a boy. At least his son was happy. His wife was another story. She was irritable and moody and becoming increasingly more so. Stanley tried his best to cheer her up. His efforts failed. He thought she was working too hard. He hoped things would settle down when her situation at work stabilized. But her late nights became later, sometimes stretching into morning.

Even though Ron Jeffries saw it coming he was powerless to stop it. How ironic. The greatest investigator he'd ever seen, someone who could solve a case from the smallest clue, couldn't see what was happening right in front of his face. When his wife moved out Stanley Starfish was crushed. He had no idea his wife was so unhappy. Alicia took Emilio and moved into a Brickell Avenue condominium with Jorge Aduano. Ron Jeffires never saw anyone so distraught as his partner. Stanley felt like the universe had collapsed on top of him. He didn't eat. He didn't sleep. He was distracted at work. He hated going back to his empty Kendall townhouse. Both Ron and Rita tried consoling him but their efforts were futile. Stanley never, never talked about his past but they both sensed he had no one in his life he could turn to. His partner, the smartest person he knew, was reduced to a pathetic shell.

Stanley Starfish blamed himself. He didn't know what he did wrong but whatever it was he was at fault. His guilt served to deepen his depression. Stanley held out hope they could reconcile. He offered to go to marriage counseling. He was willing to go to any length to reclaim his wife and child. Ron and Rita both agreed the situation was hopeless but kept their feelings to themselves, not wanting to further depress their friend. The one bit of good in his life was a mixed blessing. Alicia allowed generous visitation. Stanley took advantage, seeing his son at every opportunity. But dropping him off at another man's home and having to say good-bye reinforced his misery.

At work Rosaria Gonzalez was deeply concerned. She knew Stanley was heartbroken but was powerless to help him. Armando Pedroza loved it. He rubbed Stanley's face in it at every opportunity, laying off only after Ron Jeffries threatened to beat the shit out of him if he didn't stop. Armando Pedroza was a lot of things. Stupid wasn't one of them. His precious career had suffered enough lately. He didn't need to further taint it by fighting with the *niche.* Reluctantly he backed off.

Ron pleaded with Stanley to take some time off and try and get his head straight. He appreciated the gesture but felt the need to keep working. The job gave his life structure, occupying him twelve hours a day. In his semi-catatonic state, however, Stanley wasn't much help to his partner. Ron didn't mind. Time was a consistent healer and he was willing to carry his partner for the short term. He would stand up for Stanley until he snapped out of this malaise. Anyway, the cases they were catching lately were very routine. They hadn't worked anything interesting in a while.

Their current assignment fit in the "routine" category. Olga Suarez was beaten to death in her home in the Southwest section of town near the County fairgrounds. Her husband, Alberto, had a history of domestic violence. The evening of the occurrence their children heard their father shouting and their mother screaming. The next door neighbors heard it as well. They called the police who discovered the body of Olga Suarez. Ron Jeffries took the appropriate statements from the witnesses. All they had left was to find and arrest Alberto Suarez.

The next day they started making the rounds of his friends and relatives, inquiring as to his whereabouts. Their fourth stop was at the residence of Alberto Suarez's aunt. Stanley, who dozed off during the drive, woke up suddenly when the car came to a stop. Ron smiled. "That must be the first time you've slept in weeks."

"Close," Stanley answered weakly. He stretched a little and yawned. As he started to unbuckle his seat belt his partner stopped him. "Go ahead and sit this one out. I got it covered."

Stanley protested but his partner was insistent. "I'm just going to talk to the woman and tell her if she comes in contact with her nephew it's better for everybody if he turns himself in. Stay in the car and rest. You need it. If I need any help with translation I'll come and get you. Promise."

Stanley signaled his acceptance with a nod. He was grateful for the respite. Ron Jeffries rang the doorbell and conversed briefly with an elderly woman. The woman understood English and spoke it in a discernible, heavily accented dialect. As they talked, something caught Ron Jeffries' eye. He turned to the car and shouted, "Stanley!" Startled, Stanley looked to the front door and simultaneously heard a loud bang and saw his partner crumple to the ground. He rushed out to see blood gushing out of Ronnie's back.

"Three-thirty, three-thirty! Officer down, officer down!" he screamed in the police radio. A thousand thoughts went through his mind at once. What should he do first? What about the shooter? He pushed those thought aside and concentrated on Ronnie. He had a pulse and was breathing on his own. Ronnie briefly opened his eyes. He seemed to recognize Stanley for an instant before closing them. "Hold on partner! Please! You got to hold on!!" He cradled Ron's head, trying his best to comfort him. Everyone he had ever loved in his life from his mom and dad, his great-grandparents to his wife and child had all abandoned him. All except Ronnie. "Please... you have to hang on... Ronnie... please!" He felt Ron's body getting cold. Stanley became woozy and on the verge of fainting when loud screams from inside the house jarred him back to full consciousness. Another loud bang resounded. The homicide detective drew his revolver and ran into the house. Alberto Suarez lay dead in the kitchen, his brain matter splattered all over the linoleum floor. An elderly lady was hysterically wailing in unintelligible Spanish. He pried the gun from the dead man's hand then rushed back to Ron. Blaring sirens converged on the scene from every direction.

The rest was all a blur. He remembered paramedics, police, a lot of people asking him questions, lots and lots of questions. All he cared about was Ron. He remembered the "woppa woppa" sounds of a helicopter. He recalled more people asking more questions. He didn't remember how he arrived at the Trauma Center at Jackson Hospital. He only knew he was there when Rita arrived and breaking down upon seeing her. Somehow he composed himself long enough to hear the doctor's diagnosis, then broke down again. Ron Jeffries survived being shot in the back by Alberto Suarez. The bullet, however, caused permanent damage to his spinal column. It was extremely unlikely he would ever walk again.

Five minutes! That's all the time it took. A lousy five minutes! Fate was such a bitch. From that point on his entire life would be defined by one five minute episode. He would do anything, pay any price to have those five minutes back. He would do anything to change places with his partner. The department officially took a dim view of his actions during the shooting. Detective Stanley Starfish was issued a reprimand, removed from homicide and reassigned to the administration center, where he basically shuffled papers. After six weeks he was transferred to the vice squad. To Stanley, working vice equaled purgatory. He had profound philosophical differences with the department over arresting private citizens engaged in consensual acts. He didn't join the force to bust hookers and their clients. He hated it so much he seriously considered changing occupations. Two reasons kept him from quitting. First, he needed his salary to support Alicia and Emilio. She was always asking for money and he never denied her, giving all he could spare and then some. Secondly, Ron Jeffries simply would not permit it.

"You quit now, you're quitting on yourself. You're the best damned investigator I ever worked with. Probably the best anyone ever worked with. I know you're down. I know vice sucks but it's not a life sentence. Stick it out six more months and then you can transfer back to ECU or GIU or maybe organized crime. Now that might be interesting. Anyhow, I know it's going to turn around. It's the nature of this business. Something will happen that only you will be able to solve and then you'll be back on top doing challenging work again." Ron stopped to get a drink. Stanley was visiting him at the completion of his daily rehab. He was thirsty from the vigorous workout and all the talking. He took a swallow, then continued, "Listen, I know I'm the one who told you to do something different with your life and maybe you should... but if you quit now it's on their terms; Armando's terms. You deserve better. You're too good a detective for that. And besides if you quit now I'll feel eternally guilty you left because of me. You can't keep blaming yourself for the shooting. Unfortunately it goes with the job. In this line of work shit happens."

How ironic, Stanley thought, of the two of them, the one with the positive attitude was confined to a wheelchair. Ronnie was right. He had no business feeling sorry for himself. Ronnie didn't mire himself in self-pity. He was too busy preparing for the next phase of his life. He rehabbed three to four hours a day and planned to return to college to take courses in computer science. Ron was upbeat. He had his religious convictions to fall back on and believed everything happened for a reason. Stanley decided to stick it out and transfer out of vice at the first opportunity.

If Ron Jeffries could have anticipated how events would transpire, he would have given his partner different advice. Stanley tried his best to blend in with the vice unit detectives and not make any waves. As it turned out almost everyone in his squad had worked with Armando Pedroza, attributing him legendary status. Stanley said nothing even laughing along at all their old Armando stories. He simply wanted to fulfill his obligation and move on. Unfortunately, he never got the chance.

His squad was working a sting on an escort service. They used two adjoining motel rooms. In one room a detective would pose as an out of town businessman. He would call the service and order a girl. In the other room two other detectives monitored the video camera and tape recorder. As soon as the girl named an act and a price she was busted. They agreed on Stanley to be the phony businessman because he looked least likely to be a cop. They briefed him on what to say and do. When the girl arrived, however, she didn't follow the script. Nothing went the way they said it would.

"Hi, I'm Tammy," she said with a big smile.

Stanley was shocked. She wasn't anything like he imagined.

Tammy was young and pretty, looking more like a college student than a prostitute. She was enthusiastically friendly. She didn't ask him for a plane ticket or any form of identification. She only asked him his name.

"I... I... I'm Stanley. S... Stanley Benson."

"Stanley, you are all tensed up and nervous. You need to relax." She didn't ask him what he wanted. Instead she started rubbing his shoulders. "Gee, Stan, you're all knotted up. How does this feel?"

Tammy was giving the muscles at the base of his neck a deep massage. It actually felt wonderful.

"Great," he replied. "But I want to know how much..."

"Shh! Relax! We'll get to that. First, we've got to get rid of this stress. Close your eyes... Good boy."

She moved her hands up expertly massaging his forehead and eyes. It really did feel fabulous. It had been so long since he had any physical contact with a woman and she smelled like spring flowers and was being so gentle...

"That a boy, Stan. I can feel the tension dissolving away. Keep relaxing."

He obeyed her. She kept rubbing his forehead with one hand while the other worked his zipper. He was aroused. Tammy fondled his erection. Before he realized what was happening she quickly kissed his penis. She blinked her eyes and smiled almost as if she were posing. Stanley pulled away in protest but within seconds the other vice cops rushed into the room. Looks of consternation covered their faces. The consensus was Stanley had blown the bust. They had no choice but to let Tammy go. Upon reviewing the tape his fellow detectives got their jollies speculating how much they could get selling it to American Home Videos or Jerry Springer. Jokes aside, Stanley's predicament was no laughing matter. His behavior was an egregious conduct violation, possibly resulting in suspension or worse. When they were finished laughing about it his co-workers assured him he had nothing to worry about. They chalked up the mishap to his inexperience and promised him the video and audio tapes were as good as lost.

His fellow detectives in the vice unit proved to be more proficient at the hooker sweeps than coverups. Somehow the tapes found their way to the department's upper echelon who viewed Detective Starfish's conduct as reprehensible. Desiring to avert the negative publicity of their most famous investigator falling from grace, they offered him the chance to resign without benefits; no pension, no health care. Otherwise he would face a messy public rebuke with the department pushing for his outright dismissal. Stanley was confronted with a Hobson's choice. If he asserted his right to due process the media would surely pick up the story. The tawdry nature of the incident could taint the lives of Alicia and Emilio for years. Protecting them became his greatest concern. He concluded his position was indefensible and tendered his resignation. Stanley Starfish joined the ranks of the unemployed.

Detached from the police department, the former homicide detective determined he was ready for radical changes in his life. With the support of Ron and Rita Jeffries he decided to go back to school, get his degree and master a new trade. He planned on financing his education through the sale of the Kendall townhouse. It was paid for and the equity belonged to him. He paid for it with the proceeds from the sale of his great-grandparents' Surfside apartment. The money from the sale would cover his educational costs and living expenses. Before he could list with a Realtor his wife served him with divorce papers. Alicia's relationship with Jorge Aduano fizzled. Her attorney demanded the townhouse plus child support and alimony. She was adamant about the divorce and rebuffed any hope of reconciliation. Stanley acquiesced to the lopsided terms, not even bothering to hire a lawyer. He couldn't deny his child nor the mother of his child a roof over their heads.

For a short while he stayed with the Jeffries while he worked for Burdines Department Store as the in-house detective. The work was torturous and the pay was a joke. Staying with Ron and Rita was his sole option to living in his car. The rest of his money went to his ex-wife and Emilio. He was still responsible for Emilio. His son was the only thing worthwhile left in his life. Everything else—his parents, his great-grandparents, his career, his wife and family life—had all vanished. At least he was seeing more of his son. Alicia apparently led a hectic social life and Emilio was available to him almost every weekend. His situation improved slightly when he landed the job with TransGeneral, the insurance conglomerate. The work was an upgrade. He became somewhat of an expert on stolen cars, setting a company record for exposing false claims. He also uncovered a phony life insurance scam by proving the death certificate was fraudulently obtained in Haiti. TransGeneral was pleased and awarded him a small bonus. The pay was better than the department store but still not half of what he had made on the department. The job did have some decent benefits like health insurance and a company car, the Ford Escort he was driving. The extra money allowed him to get a place of his own. He was now living in a small efficiency apartment in North Miami.

The insurance investigator finished his grilled cheese and tomato sandwich and washed it down with a glass of water. He glanced at his watch and did a double take. He must have been daydreaming. His parking meter was about to expire. He left Hector a nice tip, then walked to the back of the store to chat with Mr. Sheldon. With every other drug store he knew, part of one faceless, impersonal chain or another, independent pharmacies like Sheldon's were fast becoming extinct. There weren't many old time pharmacists left like Mr. Sheldon either. When he was growing up in Surfside his great-grandparents never took him to a doctor. When he was sick they took him to Mr. Sheldon who gave him medicine that always made him feel better. He reminisced with his old pharmacist for a while. On the way out he purchased some razor blades, shaving cream and a few other sundries. The sun was shining and he actually felt a little better. Tonight he was picking up Emilio and keeping him through the weekend. Tomorrow they were joining the Jeffries for an outing at the Fort Lauderdale Museum of Science and Discovery and IMAX theater complex. This weekend was for Emilio. He would pick up this stinker case on Monday. On Monday he had an interview scheduled with Richie Johnson.

12

On the way to Jody Sellers' house Greg Barrett rehearsed over and over what he would say. First he would apologize for letting the situation get out of control. He would take full responsibility for what occurred. He planned on telling her the truth. He had very strong feelings for her that escalated the better he had gotten to know her. He allowed things to go too far. Despite his feelings for her the bottom line was he had a wife and family he could not give up. He wished there were more he could say or do but couldn't think of what. Any financial overture would be tacky and insulting. He would simply say his piece and go from there.

Greg Barrett's game plan worked right up until he rang the doorbell. The moment Jody Sellers opened the door he fell under a spell, captivated by her green eyes. Before he knew it her arms were around his neck and he was carrying her into her bedroom. Their clothes disappeared from their bodies, replaced by exploring lips and fingers. After seemingly endless foreplay she rolled him on his back and climbed on top. The deeper he penetrated the more vigorously she responded. She closed her eyes and her head rolled around in a circular motion. She began to moan; faintly at first, then louder and louder as the pace and intensity of his thrusts accelerated. Little tremors spread from her eyes to her toes. The tremors came faster and faster until climaxing in a powerful burst of passion. She stayed on top of him, too drained to move. They remained like that, locked in a tight embrace with her head resting on his cheek for what felt like hours. Greg was speechless. He had failed to prepare a Plan B. He was more conflicted than ever, finding it difficult to feel guilty about something so boundlessly pleasurable. She lifted her head off his check, looked into his eyes and smiled sweetly.

"You better call Channel Seven," she said with a twinkle in her eye.

"What are you talking about?"

"We should report an earthquake in Hollywood that went right off the Richter scale."

He couldn't stop himself from laughing. She winked at him before joining in a long hard kiss. She was the first to pull away. "You have to get back to work. Come with me." She led him by the hand to her bathroom and ran water for a shower. They entered together, taking turns washing and fondling each other. As she washed his back she reached between his legs and played with him. He was quickly aroused. She turned him around, flashing him that coy, adorable smile. In a second she was on her knees. The hot shower water beat down on them while she playfully flicked her tongue in and out before swallowing him.

Jody Sellers remained naked while she helped Greg Barrett get dressed. There was much he wanted to say to her. He wanted to tell her no one had ever made him feel like this. He wanted to tell her he was deeply, madly in love with her. Those words stayed inside, never leaving his mouth. He departed silently after one final kiss. On the drive back to the office he tried listening to the car radio but could not concentrate. His thoughts were consumed with Jody Sellers and what to do about her. He admitted to himself that he didn't have the slightest idea. Greg Barrett remained distracted the rest of the afternoon. His secretary, Martha asked if he was feeling all right. He assured her he was fine, then retreated into the sanctum of his inner office. He was angry with himself for being so obvious. "C'mon," he yelled silently, "Harry Hvide doesn't pay you the big bucks to mope around. Start earning your keep." He punched himself hard in the ribs and forced himself to concentrate on his work. He found solace in the acquisition of another garbage company.

"Daddy... the phone is ringing."

"Okay son, I'll get it."

Emilio went back to drawing an elaborate seascape. Stanley Starfish picked up the phone though his eyes and ears never left the television.

"Stan, it's Ron," Ron Jeffries said into the receiver. In the background he could clearly hear the voices of Jack Nicholson and John Huston engaged in dialogue. "Stanley... Stanley?"

"Yeah, Ronnie, what's up?"

"Please tell me you're not watching Chinatown for the twenty-fifth time. You don't even like Jack Nicholson."

"At least he's not a caricature of himself in this. Anyway, Faye

Dunaway is really the central character. All the plot lines go through Mrs. Mulray."

"Whatever you say. We're leaving now. Rita wants to know if we should pick you up and go in one car."

"Sounds great. You sure it's not an inconvenience?"

"Definitely not. It's on the way."

A half hour later the Jeffries family arrived in the large, specially outfitted custom van. Ron, Jr., and Jacqueline were happy to see Emilio who was equally glad to see them.

By the time they reached the museum the one o'clock IMAX movie was sold out. They bought tickets for the two o'clock showing. With some time on their hands they chose to peruse the Museum of Science and Discovery. The kids loved the interactive displays and were fascinated by the exhibit on coral reefs. The time passed quickly. Stanley thought the IMAX movie about whales might be over his son's head. He was happily mistaken. Emilio loved it and talked about cetaceans the rest of the day. After the movie they walked across the street to the New River. They observed the water taxi docking to let some passengers off while picking up new ones. Rita took the children for ice cream giving the two former partners a chance to catch up. Stanley filled him in about the case and told Ron Rosi Gonzalez sent her best regards. He left out any mention of Armando Pedroza.

"You're really going to meet Richie Johnson? Be sure and tell him he strikes out too much. And ask him how come he never hustles to first base on ground balls."

"I'll tell him you told him."

"You think you have a shot at his case?"

"Not a chance. At least not a chance of getting the insurance company out of the claim. I'm just going through the motions."

"Your whole life is just going through the motions."

"We've been through this before, Ronnie. Let's not ruin a good day."

"No deal. I refuse to change subjects until you take me seriously. I'm nine credits short of getting my degree in computer science. You know more about computers than any professor I had. You taught me more about computers than any professor I had. You already have your associate's degree, so we're not talking a lot of time. Nova's got night and weekend classes. So does UM. Listen, Stan, I know your luck's been lousy. I know you've been through a lot. But I know your luck is going to turn. You know what Rita always says... circumstances have a way of changing! Sometimes you have to help them along. You deserve better. Right now is the right time to get your ass back in school and fulfill your potential."

The insurance investigator absorbed every one of Ron's words and couldn't disagree. As usual Ronnie was right on target. The irony of his little speech didn't escape him either. Here was his only friend confined to a wheelchair and concerned about other people's bad luck and hard times. Ron Jeffries bounced right back up from adversity. He and Rita were closer than ever. He was making straight As in school and about to graduate Magna Cum Laude. Of the two, Ron was the more ambitious and less handicapped.

"I'm looking into schools on Monday. I promise," he told his old partner. "As soon as I finish with Richie Johnson."

They shook hands on it, with Ron flashing him an ear to ear smile. A moment later Rita returned with the kids. It was getting late and they were all ready to leave. Before getting in the van Stanley escorted his son to the restroom. His mind was already racing. He started formulating a plan. He would blow off this case as quickly as possible. Then he would ask his supervisor for a case with a recovery fee for a bonus. He had done good work for TransGeneral. His bosses seemed satisfied with his work and should have no objections. If the bonus was large enough he would use the money to go to college full time and finish as soon as possible. Ronnie had him motivated

---

The insurance investigator mired his way through two guard houses, security checks, then another at the entrance of Richie Johnson's Williams Island condominium tower. He took the elevator up to the eleventh floor. A stunningly beautiful redhead let him in. "He'll be with you shortly," she said to him. "Sit anywhere you like."

Stanley thanked the girl and seated himself on a comfortable suede couch. The condominium was not as ornately furnished as he had imagined it would be. Certainly pleasant enough, but somewhat austere with no pictures or decorations hanging form the walls. The highlights were a hi-tech large screen TV and a kick ass sound system. There was no indication whatsoever the unit was inhabited by a famous baseball personality.

After a brief wait he was joined by a handsome, milk-chocolate-skinned man with a very thick neck and an arm in a sling. It was obvious underneath his shirt his left shoulder was heavily bandaged. Stanley stood and introduced himself while handing the man his card. Richie Johnson seemed a little puzzled over the purpose of the meeting and about the role of his guest.

"You're not a cop, right? And what does some insurance company have to do with me getting capped?"

"You are correct, Mr. Johnson. I am not a cop. I am an investigator for TransGeneral, the surety company used by your employer the Florida Manatees. They insured your contract against death or disability. Since you cannot play baseball in your current condition my company is responsible for the majority of your salary."

Richie Johnson narrowed his eyes. "What do you mean by majority?"

Stanley sensed a growing concern in Richie Johnson's voice and mannerisms. He tried his best to assuage him. "Let me assure you, Mr. Johnson, your contract is fully guaranteed. Under the terms of the policy my company is responsible for a certain amount of your salary and your employer is responsible for the balance. You still get the full amount. With a claim this large, it's the standard procedure of TransGeneral to investigate the surrounding circumstances and file an internal report. That's why I'm here. I won't take up much of your time. I have just a few questions. It's very routine."

Reassured he was getting every penny, Richie Johnson relaxed and gave his version of the incident. He neglected to mention why he was in the neighborhood or what he was doing there. As Richie Johnson talked Stanley jotted down some notes. When he finished Stanley said sympathetically, "What a horrific experience. Not to minimize what happened, but I'm glad for you it wasn't worse."

Richie Johnson nodded. Stanley sensed he was establishing a rapport between them. "If you don't mind, I have a few questions."

Richie Johnson shrugged his good shoulder. The insurance investigator continued, "Can you tell me anything about the car? The make, model, the color?"

"Like I said, it happened real quick. And the weather? It was right out of some horror flick... Jason's Friday the 13th Halloween Party or something. I do recall it being light colored. Beige, white, something like that."

"That's very, very good. It's amazing you remember anything at all. Can you remember anything about the model?"

Richie Johnson closed his eyes and scratched his forehead. Approximately fifteen seconds elapsed before he answered. "You know, my first impression was he was some kind of lost tourist because I thought he was driving... a, you know... rental car."

Stanley tried to digest what Richie Johnson was saying. He needed some clarification and asked a followup question. "How could you tell it was a rental car?"

"You know. You see them in Miami all the time full of South Americans.

And when the team is on the road it's what the rookies rent. You know, when we're on the road for a three, four game series you got to have wheels. The rookies... they can't afford no chauffeured limo or babe car like a Porsche. They chip in and get a regular rental car."

The insurance investigator had an idea. He asked Richie Johnson if he received the morning paper. Richie Johnson nodded affirmatively, pointing to the kitchen area. He started to get up.

"Please, stay where you are," Stanley told him. "I'll get it. You remain comfortable."

He retrieved the morning paper off the dinette table. He thumbed through the sections until he found the one containing the car ads. He turned the page slowly so Richie Johnson could have a clear, unobstructed view.

"If you see anything similar, please point it out to me."

Richie Johnson seemed to enjoy looking at the pictures. When Stanley came to an ad for Friendly Ford Richie motioned for him to pause. Richie concentrated on it, taking his time.

"Whoop there it is!" he said triumphantly. Richie Johnson's finger pointed to a picture of a Ford Taurus LX, available with 1.9% financing. "See," he reiterated, "Like I said. A rental car."

Stanley congratulated him on his amazing recollective powers. "It's amazing you remember anything at all after such a stressful occurrence. Are you up to a couple of more questions?"

With nothing else to do Richie Johnson warmed to the task. He kind of liked this skinny dork.

"No problem. Fire away."

"Did you notice anything about the vehicle's interior? The color? The material?"

"Hmmm... let me concentrate on it." Richie Johnson closed his eyes again. "It was... it was most definitely dark. Maybe black, maybe blue. What do you mean by material?"

"Was it cloth-like, similar to this couch or was it smooth like a leather or vinyl?"

"Smooth. But it sure weren't no Corinthian leather. It was rock hard, not soft at all."

Stanley complimented him again on his fine memory before pressing on. "The man who shot you. Can you tell me anything about him? His size? His skin color? What he was wearing? Anything at all?"

Richie Johnson rested his chin on his fist resembling a darker Dobie Gillis. After some hesitation he spoke up.

"I can't help you much there. It was dark and rainy. I'm not sure the dude was black, white or Cuban. He might have had his face covered, maybe a mask. I don't remember anything else except he held the gun on me like this." Richie Johnson stood up, demonstrating the standard combat position—feet apart, slightly crouched forward, arm extended— "Only he used both hands."

Stanley shook his head back and forth declaring, "How awful! Do you by any chance recall him saying anything?"

"I do. Yes, I do. But it's very weird man. Very weird. He shouted somethin' about my sister."

"What?"

"I told you it was weird. It don't make sense to me either."

"Could it have been someone who knew you?"

"Everybody knows me. I'm Dick Johnson."

"I'm sorry, Mr. Johnson. Let me rephrase that. Could it have been someone you knew?"

"I doubt it. I mean anything's possible. But if it was I couldn't tell you who."

"When the incident started you didn't think it was anything more than a fender bender, did you?"

Richie Johnson wrinkled his brow. "I'm not sure what you mean."

"Well, it says in the police report they found a 9mm Heckler and Koch pistol registered to you underneath the front seat. That indicates you got out of the car without it. I would imagine you carry it for your own protection. If you expected trouble you would have taken it with you."

"Yeah! You're right! You are a sharp little dude. I didn't even think about the 9 mil. I was so pissed off about the Ferrari and the oth... uh, I jammed right out without it."

The insurance investigator stood up, approached Richie Johnson and extended his hand. "Mr. Johnson, I want to thank you for your cooperation. You've been very helpful. You have my card. If you think of anything, anything at all don't hesitate to call me."

"Yeah, sure. No problem," he replied while looking at the business card. "By the way, how did you get a name like Starfish?"

"It's a long story."

"That's cool. You know you're an intelligent dude. You should be a real cop. When those other cops talked to me they made it seem like it was my own damn fault for getting capped."

As he walked to the door he remembered one last thing. "Mr. Johnson, I hate to bother you again, but my best friend has a son who's a huge fan. Do you think you could give him an autograph? His name is Ronald."

"Hey, no problem. You know in those mall collectible stores my autograph goes for twenty, twenty-five dollars. I'll let you have it for a five spot."

———————————

Jody Sellers conducted a little soul searching while she brushed her hair in front of the mirror. She committed the one mistake she promised herself she would never make; getting involved with a married man. She knew by heart the clichés derived from the advice columns—they never leave their wives, you're being used, you'll be by yourself on holidays. She just had a hard time accepting what she had with Greg Barrett could be reduced to a cliché. Her guy was different and she certainly didn't feel used. Greg was kind. He was generous and, when you really got to know him, was extremely sweet and sexy. What she liked best about him was that he wasn't a stuck up snob. He was richer than a maharajah but in his heart he was a down-to-earth regular guy. She couldn't lie to herself how she felt in his company. If only he knew how easily he took her breath away. Yes, Ann Landers, she would probably end up hurt and alone. She just wasn't ready to let go of the only positive in her life aside from her son. Not yet, anyway. It was too late to second guess herself. Bobby was spending the night with his cousin and this would be one of the precious few times she could spend a couple of stolen hours with her lover. This was no time to feel guilty about being the other woman. It was the story of her life: she finally meets the right guy at precisely the wrong time. Maybe it was El Nino.

Gregory Barrett drove robotically from his Fort Lauderdale office down Federal Highway toward Hollywood. His relationship with Jody Sellers was entering a new phase. It reached the stage where he concocted elaborate lies to conceal his whereabouts from Alison. This time he told her he was representing Capital Industries at a business meeting/cocktail party involving international trade at the Biltmore Hotel in Coral Gables. He read about it in the morning paper's business section. Dropping a couple of names was enough to make it fly with his wife. He surprised himself at how easily the lying came. In all the business deals he worked over the years he had prided himself on being a straight shooter. He never saw the point in deception. The strokers were embarrassingly obvious. In the end the facts always betrayed them. Was that the level he'd sunk to? He shuddered at the thought of being another Barry Lewis.

He kept driving, hating that lately he was so introspective. He didn't care for what he saw. The worst part was his little rendezvous' were starting to interfere with his family life. Tonight was a good example. Rightfully he should be at home helping his kids with their homework. That was the quality time they deserved. It was the time he worked hard to make available. It was the time he badly neglected when they were younger. He felt like he was stealing from his own children. Suddenly he was overcome with feelings of remorse. Those feelings, however, did not prevent him from driving toward his destination.

Greg Barrett wasn't a drinker although he was acquainted with some alcoholics. He'd never done drugs and wasn't a gambler. He knew they were powerful compulsions but couldn't imagine anything being more addictive than his affections for Jody Sellers. And it wasn't only the sex. It was everything about her. He had discovered his soulmate. Unfortunately he couldn't foresee a happy ending.

He made a left on Wiley Street and pulled into her driveway. Torturing himself more wouldn't accomplish anything now. At least he would enjoy the next couple of hours. Tomorrow would be soon enough to make the necessary hard decisions. As he walked to the door he realized he was lying to himself, a new personal low. He hated that lately he was so introspective.

13

The insurance investigator reviewed his notes from his interview with Richie Johnson. It didn't take a genius to figure out Richie Johnson wasn't entirely forthcoming. He never did say what he was doing in that neighborhood. That didn't bother Stanley Starfish. He had other ways to find that out. He felt also anything else Richie Johnson held back might not be material to the case. In any event it would have been counterproductive to take a confrontational tone with him. Assuredly he would have stonewalled. Using a sympathetic approach he was able to come away with some leads and a starting point for his investigation. He studied the police report along with his notes trying to develop a picture of exactly what transpired.

Richie Johnson was found in the street six feet behind his Ferrari. Something made him get out of the car in the middle of the year's worst storm. Either he was carjacked, meeting with someone, or what he implied in the interview, a case of road rage. None of the possible scenarios were a perfect match with the evidence. If it was a drug buy or some other type of meeting why would they bump his car? That would take the "hard sell" approach to a new level. Also Richie Johnson didn't seem like the type who would be enamored with stormy weather. He could easily picture Richie Johnson remaining in his car and being approached rather than the other way around. Some type of road rage incident was more likely. Stanley imagined a fuming Richie Johnson flying out of the Ferrari back toward the car which rear-ended him. He could see him getting in the driver's face, possibly struggling with him. It would explain how he knew so much about the car's interior. If it was road rage it was certainly bad luck on his part that he picked a fight with someone carrying a .38 special... Stanley thought about it some more. Maybe in that neighborhood it wasn't so unusual. Miami was the handgun capital of the world. Maybe in any neighborhood it wouldn't be so unusual. But Richie thought the shooter possibly wore a mask though he wasn't sure. It could have been a person of color.

And what was that mention of his sister all about? Stanley didn't have an answer.

Carjacking or the old bump and rob were the least likely possibilities. Counting the diamond earring, enormous gold chain, gold and diamond watch, five thousand dollars cash, and a two hundred thousand dollar car, Richie Johnson was too rich a treasure to leave unpilfered. Nobody would go to the trouble of initiating an accident, get out and cold bloodedly shoot someone down, then leave without doing a little shopping. The watch alone was valued at over twenty five thousand dollars, and who would stage a rip-off and not grab the cash? Armando mentioned the weather or the possibility the shooter panicked. Neither jibed with the facts. The streets were empty, hence no witnesses and no reason to panic. The shooter had plenty of time to grab the watch, the cash and chain, even the diamond earring.

After some thought he decided to put the theories aside and concentrate on the hard evidence. He started by tracking down the car. Unfortunately no Ford Taurus was ticketed for any violation on the date Richie Johnson was shot. Amazingly no reported crimes of any kind were reported in that sector with the exception of the shooting. It had to be a Miami first. Apparently the inclement weather kept the bad guys from working their usual hours.

Next he tried tracking the vehicle through the local dealers. He didn't get anywhere, a total waste of time. He had better success with the manufacturer. His company, TransGeneral Assurety, did business with the Ford Motor Company. They were very cooperative. Ford did not have a white, tan or silver Taurus with either dark leather or vinyl interior in general production. They did have a special production run in 1996 of a white Taurus GL with a blue vinyl interior. The cars were specially made for several midwestern police departments and the American Car Rental Co. American Car Rental made a large fleet purchase of white Taurus GLs. They wanted them all the same color to create a brand identity. The company specified vinyl interior because it was easier to clean. A quick rundown of the police departments from Altoona, Pennsylvania to Sheboygan, Wisconsin confirmed Stanley's suspicion. The cars were still in service. Municipal departments usually keep their vehicles a minimum of three years.

The insurance investigator was pleasantly surprised to find the corporate headquarters of American Car Rental Company located in Fort Lauderdale. He learned that the company was a wholly owned subsidiary of Capital Industries, also based in Fort Lauderdale. In fact, both were housed in the same office complex. Stanley made an appointment to examine their records and speak to a supervisor. The thirty-five minute drive was a breeze with only moderate traffic. For someone who lived the majority of his life in South Florida Fort Lauderdale was an unfamiliar place. Except for his recent visit to the Museum of Discovery and Science he couldn't recall the last time he was there. He liked what he saw. Traffic was a fraction of downtown Miami's. The city itself was much cleaner and the people were more friendly. He had no problem parking in the building's adjacent garage.

After a brief wait in the outer room he was assisted by a friendly, cooperative Ms. O'Connell.

"You have a most unusual name, Mr. Starfish."

"I know. It's an old family name. It was wondering if you could tell me how many white ninety-six Ford Taurus GLs with blue vinyl interiors American Car Rental still has in service."

"I can find out. Let me punch it up for you." She typed away on the keyboard of her desk top. "It will come up in a second. Let's see... the number is... zero."

"Zero? You mean you don't have a single one in your inventory?"

Ms. O'Connell flashed in the insurance investigator a sheepish look. "I'm sorry. I should have known that off the top of my head. We turn over the entire fleet on an annual basis. I worked on the analysis. We found it more cost effective to replace the cars after a year. It minimized the maintenance outlay."

"What do you do with the replaced cars?"

"We sell them. That's another reason to change over after a year. There's less depreciation and we recoup a higher percentage of the purchase price."

"Do you keep records of who you sell them to?"

"Of course. Would you like a printout?"

Stanley nodded. Ms. O'Connell resumed typing. He settled back in his chair expecting to wait a while. Surprisingly, Ms. O'Connell finished in under a minute.

"Here you are. I ran a print out for you." She handed him a single piece of paper. The paper contained one name—Auto World, Inc. A subsidiary of Capital Industries.

She noticed his puzzled look and commented, "Auto World is a used car super store. Their headquarters is also in this building."

"So I assume the sale was actually more of an inter-company transfer of assets rather than a sale?"

"I'm sorry, Mr. Starfish. I can't help you there. If you like, I'll get someone else to assist you."

"No, no. That won't be necessary. It's really not important. I want to thank you for all you've done. You've been very helpful." The insurance investigator arose from his chair and shook Ms. O'Connell's hand. He started to walk out, then stopped. "Would you mind if I asked one more question?"

"Not at all."

"What did you replace the '96 Tauruses with?"

"The '97 Taurus."

"White?"

"Yes, they're all white."

"With blue vinyl interiors?"

"No sir, they all have beige cloth interiors."

Stanley mumbled to himself. "I wonder why they changed?" It was loud enough that Ms. O'Connell heard. She smiled playfully.

"I know the answer to that one. In the customer evaluation the vinyl seats were the single most mentioned complaint with our cars. Our biggest customer base is the Sunbelt. The majority of our cars are rented in Florida, Georgia, Nevada, Arizona, California, and Texas. Our customers felt the seats got too hot. The vinyl interiors ended up being a one-year experiment."

"Is it possible to get the serial numbers and maintenance records for the '96 GLs?"

"Certainly," answered Ms. O'Connell. "That will take some time. How about I mail them to your office?"

He thanked her and took the elevator down to the parking garage.

Eleven floors above the main office of American Car Rental, Greg Barrett was immersed in work. Harry Hvide was more determined than ever to push through the initial Public Offering, effectively dividing Capital industries into two entities. He pretty much gave the underwriter an ultimatum: either get behind it or get off. Thinking of

Harry caused Greg Barrett to shake his head in admiration. Since making one of the fastest recoveries on record from his heart problem episode Harry returned to work with as much vitality as Greg had ever seen. He put in ungodly hours at the office plus attended a full calendar of social events and business dinners in the evening hours. What really struck him as remarkable was how he reacted to adversity. When situations headed south Harry Hvide was at his peak of energy and imagination. Ever since the Richie Johnson problem resolved itself he tackled problems of far greater magnitude directly and efficiently. The IPO was an excellent example. He digested what the analysts said about the negative market climate. Next, he had his own people do their own internal research. Like a sponge he absorbed every bit of information before formulating a game plan. Harry Hvide devised a bold strategy to repurchase Capital's stock. The stock buy back would cut the number of outstanding shares and increase investor share par value. Implementing the plan gave Capital Industries' stock price a needed bounce and caused a positive buzz on Wall Street. While other IPOs were getting the cold shoulder from investors or being put on the shelf altogether, the Capital Service IPO was one of the financial world's most anticipated issues.

Harry's handling of the start of the new baseball season was equally impressive. Every sports page columnist and radio talk show host in town decried the downsizing of the team and how they hadn't spent a dime replacing Richie Johnson, Benny Benitez and the other salary reduction casualties. An untested rookie making the minimum salary would take Richie Johnson's place in right field. They demonized Harry, viciously berating him for breaking some unwritten sacred baseball doctrine of not allowing the incumbent world champion the opportunity to defend its title. The opening game of the new season was sold out. Harry could expect a hostile, frenzied crowd ready to boo his every move. His doctors advised him to skip the game, warning him he didn't need the stress. Not Harry. He was right in the center of the Opening Day festivities and participated in raising the National League Pennant and World Series Banner. The fan reaction was predictable Unison chants of "Harry sucks" resonated throughout the stadium. Demonstrating unflappable poise, Harry acted as if he were accepting the Nobel peace Prize. He graciously shook hands with Paddy McGraw. He publicly cavorted with the National League president and Acting Commissioner of Major League Baseball. He responded to the derisive taunts as if they were testimonials of adoration.

Harry's reaction to the whole situation with the Manatees puzzled Greg. Ever since Richie Johnson's shooting Harry Hvide's attitude about the team changed from hostile to laid back. To Greg's way of thinking not all that much had changed. The team payroll was reduced, but even so was still losing money. And much of the savings came from the insurance policy picking up three quarters of Richie Johnson's salary. That worked only in the short term, ending when he was healthy enough to resume play. Maybe Harry was simply buying time. Greg Barrett didn't think so. Usually Harry Hvide was as hard to read as one of the Queen's Beefeaters. He possessed one of the great poker faces in existence. This time, however, Greg thought he detected a certain inner smugness indicating Harry Hvide had this baseball dilemma under control. That would explain his recent "que sera" attitude. If Harry had some master plan he was keeping it to himself. Greg was certain no one else was privy to it; not Frank Roy, not Lou Redmond, not his wife Betty. No one but Harry. Although curious, Greg Barrett knew better than to press him about it. When the timing was right Harry would tell him. When he was ready Harry Hvide would tell everyone.

The insurance investigator stopped at Einstein's Bagels off of Broward Boulevard. Lunch consisted of a sourdough bagel and an orange juice. While eating he took stock of his progress. His interview with Richie Johnson proved fruitful. He made some headway tracking down the car. What he accomplished were merely the preliminaries. All the hard labor and tedious legwork were yet to come. And to what end? It was highly unlikely anything he uncovered would affect his company's disposition on the claim. TransGeneral, barring some miracle revelation, would have to pay off. He questioned the relevance of going forward. As he gave it more thought Stanley Starfish admitted that he was enjoying the work. Unlike phony workman's comp claims, this was a troubling complex case similar to many he worked while he was on the department. So many times other people would evaluate a case and deem it unsolvable. Not to him. He always managed to find a way. This case made him think again. It felt good to be off auto pilot and using his brain cells. It felt good to be firing on all cylinders. He had forgotten the exhilaration of the chase, when his mind would turn and spin; never shutting off, never allowing him to sleep. He was under no pressure from the company to wrap up the investigation and he had selfish reasons for continuing. He was out of practice., Persevering on would be a good tune up for tackling a case with a recovery bonus. He needed the bonus to change his life He decided to stay with it.

He split the investigation into two parts. He needed to keep tracing the car. He needed to find out what compelled Richie Johnson to be in that neighborhood. He called Ron Jeffries. Ronnie worked the Central District for many years, both in uniform and out of the district's General Investigative Unit.

"Hi Rita. Is your husband home?"

"Hi Stan. He just got back from class. Hold on, I'll get him for you."

"Hey, partner, what it is?"

Stanley laughed. Ron Jeffries spoke perfect English but when the occasion warranted, he could speak and translate Ebonics with the best of them. He used it in interrogations and witness interviews much the same way Stanley used Spanish. He always found Ron's usage of it amusing.

"I'm okay. How's school?"

"Great. Two more months to go. I hope you're planning on attending my graduation."

"Wouldn't miss it."

"Did you give any thought to what I said the other day?

"Absolutely. I visited the web sites of Nova and Florida Atlantic university and I ran printouts. F.I.U. and Barry University are sending me brochures in the mail."

Stanley informed Ron of his plans for the future. He filled him in on his progress in the investigation and how Ron could help him.

Ron hesitated before talking. When he did speak up he sounded excited. "You should check out Club Relaxxxation."

For the next twenty minutes Ron gave Stanley the history of Club Relaxxxation, highlighting its unique stature among Miami's institutions. He also gave him the background of the successful entrepreneur, Otis Knight.

"The place is legendary," Ronnie continued. "I'm surprised you didn't hear about it when you worked vice... well, maybe not. You weren't there very long. Go there in the afternoon. They'll never make you for a cop. You won't believe your eyes... and be extra careful! It's not the type of place that welcomes questions."

The next afternoon at four thirty PM the insurance investigator parked his Ford Escort among the Navigators and BMWs in front of Club Relaxxxation. He passed through a metal detector and cleared several security checks prior to gaining entrance. Ron Jeffries' description didn't come close to doing the place justice. Club Relaxxxation was one very wild place. From his abbreviated stint in vice he remembered the nude dancing clubs had to meet certain codes and restrictions. Club Relaxxxation was in violation of every one, especially of the rule limiting total nudity exclusively to the stage area. Stanley figured the entire place was one big stage because there were beautiful naked girls everywhere. He concluded the club must have received sound legal advice. In attendance were some of the city's most prominent lawyers and judges, including the former U.S. attorney. As he reached the bar he was approached by a devastating blonde. "Hi, my name is Shane. Would you like to buy me a drink?"

"Umm... I... yes, that would be nice."

"Don't be nervous, Tiger. I don't bite... unless you want me to."

"Ummm... is... is there... um... someplace more private?"

"I thought you'd never ask."

Shane led him by the hand, escorting him to one of the private champagne rooms. "What kind of party would you desire?" she asked seductively.

"Um, what I'd like to… what I'd like is just to talk… if that's okay?"

"You're a kinky dude. But hey! If that's what you're into. It's fifty dollars for ten minutes and I talk better with a glass of champagne. It's thirty dollars a glass."

He nodded his okay.

"And I don't drink alone."

He removed six twenty dollar bills from his wallet and handed them to Shane. She didn't offer to return any change. "Mama will tell you any little old story you want. How would you like to hear about these?"

Shane started to massage her firm, ample breasts.

"Um… I don't mean to interrupt. I was hoping I could ask you a few questions."

"The meter's running."

"Umm… Richie Johnson, the baseball player. Have you ever seen him here?"

"Lots of people come here… Hey! What kind of party is this?"

"I'm… I'm sorry. It's not what you think. I just need to know…"

The insurance investigator never finished his sentence. The door then opened. Stanley and Shane were joined in the room by a tall, well built black man and a shorter but equally muscular Hispanic sporting a Pancho Villa style mustache. The black man addressed the Latino.

"Is he a cop?"

"Used to be," answered the shorter man. "Used to be a vice cop 'til he got caught on tape getting his dick sucked. His name is Starfish."

"Hello, Tuto," replied Stanley. "I see you changed occupations as well."

He stared long and hard at the man he used to work with. Tuto Fuentes was a member of the vice unit he used to be assigned to. In fact, he was in the other room working the video camera when Stanley got in trouble. He was also one of Armando Pedroza's closest friends.

"This is my off duty job, Bambi. What the fuck are you doing here? You come to make another video?"

Shane spoke next, "He asked about Richie Johnson."

The black man smiled and said, "I'll handle this. You both can leave now."

Shane started to leave the room with Tuto Fuentes. As she walked past, the black man patted her on the rear and said, "Good job… shut the door."

The black man smiled broadly at the much thinner man. "I'm Otis

Knight, the proprietor of this humble establishment. Let me explain something to you. Our little club exists as a tiny oasis surrounded by the vast, hectic, stressful desert of everyday life. It's a place where people can escape the doldrums and relax in privacy. Emphasis on PRIVACY! Our most sacred mission is to protect our patrons' privacy. I hope you understand that." The smile never left his face while he talked. It remained when he finished.

"Mr. Knight. I'm afraid there's a misunderstanding. I'm not here on anything relevant to your business. I'm investigating an insurance matter involving Mr. Johnson. I was inquiring about his..."

"Sorry to interrupt you, Mr. Starfish. By the way, that's a most unusual name, I'm sure you mean me no harm and are simply doing your job. I must re-emphasize how vitally important we regard our patrons' privacy. I'm afraid I'm going to have to ask you to leave. To show there's no hard feelings, tell me how much you spent with the girl. I'll reimburse you fully."

The large black man took out a thick roll of bills. He was still smiling.

"No, that's okay. She earned her money. I'm sorry for the misunderstanding."

The insurance investigator quickly left the private champagne room, went through the club's main room and out to the parking lot. As he left he noticed Tuto Fuentes smirking. Upon reaching the entrance to I-95 he let out a giant sigh of relief. "What an idiot!" he castigated himself, not fully believing how badly he had screwed up. He had to give credit to Otis Knight who certainly knew how to cover all his bases. Otis didn't have to worry about heat from the cops. They were on his payroll. And the girl. She must have pressed a panic button or somehow given off a signal of some sort. He slapped himself on the forehead. Of course! They probably had hidden cameras installed and were monitoring the room. Video cameras were Tuto Fuentes' specialty. Still shaken over how far his skills had eroded, Stanley Starfish drove on, realizing he would never get a thing out of Otis Knight or Club Relaxxxation.

Later in the day he connected with Ron Jeffries and relayed what had occurred. Ronnie felt remorsefully helpless. What Stanley described was exactly the type of circumstance where he used to watch his old partner's back. Stanley's naiveté made him vulnerable in that kind of environment. He had a real blind spot when it came to recognizing dangerous situations. Stanley told Ron of another problem.

"When I got back to the office I tried rescheduling another interview with Richie Johnson. Guess what? On a whim he flew to France.

He's rehabilitating at Lourdes for the next three months. Must be nice. Anyway, I'd like to find out for sure if he was at Club Relaxxxation the night he was shot and what he was doing there."

"He was there," Ron responded. "Or was on his way there. By the way they treated you, his being there is a safe assumption. You'll never get into the Club again. But there may be another way to get what you need. All the professional sports teams have security details. Most of them are ex-FBI or retired from the county. They act as monitors and try to warn the star players away from known gamblers, coke dealers, etc., etc. In a way they're glorified babysitters. The head of security for the Manatees is an acquaintance of mine. He was my training officer when I first got on the department. His name is Stu Klein. My guess is he's got plenty on asshole Richie Johnson. Probably enough for a second edition. If you want I could reach out to him."

"I don't know what I'd do without you. In the meantime I'll see if I can get a lead on the car."

Auto World had two outlets in South Florida. One was in Southern Dade County in an area known as Perrine. The other was west of Fort Lauderdale in unincorporated Broward County. The insurance investigator started in Perrine. Although not in the market for a car he was impressed with the operation. The Perrine Auto World was the latest satellite in an expanding nationwide chain. It opened just five weeks prior to Richie Johnson's shooting. They employed a different sales approach, a radical departure from the standard car buying experience. Auto World dealt exclusively in late model, top condition used cars. All cars came with warranties. The physical plant itself consisted of a showroom surrounded by a huge lot filled with car, trucks, and vans. The showroom displayed a few cars but most of the selling was done over computer screens. The salesperson found out what the customer wanted and in what price range. The customer viewed what was available over the monitor. He could then inspect any car in the lot he was interested in. The cars were sold at sticker price. Auto World eliminated the haggling. They would take trades and arrange financing but would not negotiate price. Since the opening the Perrine Auto World sold twelve white '96 Taurus GLs with blue vinyl interiors before Richie Johnson was shot. Five were exported out of the country. He tracked the other seven down over the next three days and found nothing.

At the Broward County Auto World he was aided by the assistant manager, Steve Perez. Steve Perez was friendly and helpful. He furnished the insurance investigator with a list of thirty one names of purchasers of '96 white Taurus GLs. On the way out he stopped to ask a question.

"Mr. Perez, do you have a body shop on the premises?"

"Call me Steve. And the answer is yes. It's strictly small scale. Mainly it's there to touch up and prep our own inventory. We do very little body work for the public in general after the car is sold."

"Do you bang out or replace front bumpers for the '96 Ford Taurus?"

"I don't know offhand but I can check. Wait here."

He returned a few minutes later. "This is our customer log. It shows no bumper work on any of the Taurus models. There's one we took in with major front end damage but we sourced it out to Son's Auto Body in North Dade. The vehicle is owned by a couple in Pembroke Pines Century Village. Mr. And Mrs. Milton DeForrest. You want the address and phone number?"

"No, that won't be necessary. Thanks, Steve. You've been very helpful."

Stanley Starfish left Auto World knowing he faced the tedious task of tracking down the thirty one white Taurus GLs. He needed to inspect for bumper damage or recent front bumper repair. This was the grunt work of investigating. This was the time he most missed his old partner. Sitting on suspects and running down fruitless leads didn't seem so awful while he was in the company of Ron Jeffries. The camaraderie they shared made the day fly by. When you get along and enjoy someone's company it didn't really matter what they talked about. From politics to the meaning of life, they discussed it all. Everything but his family background. That was the one subject off limits. His mind drifted back to the day of the incident. He pictured Ron falling after being shot and the look on his face. That look had haunted him ever since. Five minutes. The entire episode lasted five minutes. What he wouldn't do to have those five minutes back... He caught himself daydreaming and shook out of it. If Ron taught him anything it was feeling sorry for yourself wasn't going to get it. As Ronnie would say, "It's time to start earning the paycheck."

Further evaluation made him realize how fortunate he'd been. It was a lucky break the car he sought was a limited production model. That cut the field immeasurably. Trying to locate any white Taurus would have been impossible. At least the target field was narrowed. Three of the thirty one were exported to Nassau. He broke the rest down into areas. This way he could work more efficiently and avoid crisscrossing the state. Six were sold to people in North Dade County in the general proximity of where he lived. He started there. Stanley caught another break when three of the people lived in apartment complexes. It was much simpler to inspect the cars anonymously in parking lots rather than in private driveways. He wanted to avoid confrontations if at all possible. The first on his list belonged to a Mr. Timothy Banks who happened to live in an apartment building near his. He drove around until he located the white Taurus with the matching plate. It had blue vinyl interior. He exited the car and did his inspection.

The Ford Taurus bumper is painted off car at the factory and installed during the assembly process. Stanley could tell if a dent was banged out and painted over by overspray on the undercoating. The damage to Richie Johnson's Ferrari indicated the collision was mild, probably causing minor damage like a small dent. It was unlikely the whole bumper would need replacing but he still checked for that possibility. He looked for missing bolts and clips. The Taurus bumper was installed with far more bolts and clips than necessary. A body shop could possibly neglect a few without having any effect on the car. If the bumper was installed at the factory quality control would flag it and the missing bolts and clips would be installed. He also checked how the bolts and clips were painted. If the bumper was attached first and then sprayed. The paint would be uneven, not quite as neat as a factory job.

The insurance investigator spent the better part of a week looking under front ends. His effort produced three possibilities, two banged-out dents and one new bumper. Two filed insurance claims before Richie Johnson was shot. The third, who didn't file a claim, had an airtight alibi. His mood turned irritable as he became increasingly discouraged. The whole tack with the cars proved to be a waste of time. He had a couple left to inspect. He planned to finish them off then talk to the baseball team's chief of security. After that he'd write up his evaluation and move on.

His next stop was in Hollywood. A J. Sellers of 245 Wiley Street purchased a '96 Taurus GL a couple of weeks prior to the shooting. He turned off Federal Highway and headed east. As he drove a white Taurus went by in the opposite direction. He immediately turned around following at a discreet distance. The white Taurus stopped at the Publix market. A woman wearing blue hospital scrubs exited the car and went inside. He checked the plate. It was the Taurus GL belonging to J. Sellers. Stanley waited until she was out of sight before starting his inspection. As he bent down and shone his pen light underneath the front end he was interrupted.

"Can I help you?"

He looked up sheepishly to see a pretty, light brown haired woman peering at him sternly with her arms folded.

"Uh... yes... uh... I'm an insurance investigator. Uh, my name is Starfish." He stood up clumsily fumbling for one of his cards. She stared at the card. In a harsh tone she continued, "You didn't answer my question. What are you doing underneath my car?"

"Uh, well, ma'am, a car of the same make and model was involved in an accident. It's my job to investi..."

She cut him off in mid-sentence. "You mean you think I'd be involved in an accident and not report it? And how did you know I was here?" Her arms remained folded and her eyes narrowed.

"Uh, no ma'am. I didn't mean to imply you did anything wrong... I was... Look, it's a lousy job but it's what I..."

"How did you know I was here?"

"I was driving to your house at 245 Wiley Street. I saw you driving the other way. I turned and followed."

"You were following me?" Her tone became increasingly bitter.

"Only a block from your house until here. I haven't been following you around. I only wanted to inspect your car. I'm sorry if I caused you any..."

The pretty brown haired woman interrupted again. "Well, did you find what you wanted?"

"Uh, uh no. I just started when you appeared."

"Don't let me stop you. Go ahead and finish."

"Ma'am, I'm very sorry. I didn't..."

"Don't be sorry. Finish what you started." She didn't ask. She commanded. He meekly complied. When he stood up she was right back in his face again.

"Are you done?"

"Yes, ma'am, I'm..."

"Did you find what you're looking for?"

"Um, yes... I mean no... I mean there's nothing wrong with your car. It's not the one I'm looking for."

"Good. Then we have no further business, Mr..." She stared quixotically at his business card, "Mr. Starfish."

She opened the door to her Taurus and removed the grocery list she'd forgotten. She stayed by her car with her arms folded until the skinny, curly-haired man got in his car and drove off. Jody Sellers returned to the market and finished her shopping. After loading up her car she drove away constantly monitoring her rear view mirror. She checked often to see if she was being followed. When satisfied she was safe, Jody Sellers turned into a convenience store parking lot and used the pay phone.

--- --- ---

Greg Barrett was in his office putting the finishing touches on the Capital Services Initial Public Offering. He worked out a final draft with the underwriter after receiving approval from the legal department. The only thing left was for Harry to sign off. He looked forward to heading up Capital Services. Ever since Video Nation expanded into entertainment and Harry bought the sports teams he'd become less and less comfortable. Capital Services marked a return to his roots. It would be essentially a conglomerate of rental-service businesses with a heavy emphasis on waste management.

The garbage business had changed a great deal since the abolition of land rights. But what Harry Hvide told him over twenty years ago was still true today—"there's a lot of money cleaning up after people." Waste service remained highly profitable, evolving into a much more consolidated industry. The upper echelon companies were all massive national and international concerns. The local hauler had been virtually eliminated. Capital's waste management division was already a major player. The IPO would make it a mega one. With the infusion of cash generated by the IPO coupled with the two billion dollar credit line Harry secured, Capital Industries positioned itself to be the industry leader within three years. All he had to do was adhere to a tried and true blueprint. Increase market share through acquisition and merger. Buy with stock and preserve the cash.

Greg Barrett's life as an executive in the employ of Harry Hvide had come full circle. He was back making deals for garbage companies. He enjoyed the work. People in the waste industry were generally solid, down to earth types. He related to them far better than to the space aliens who ran Hollywood. He was amid his own element and happy to be there. The Richie Johnson incident was now a mere blur, fading further from memory with each passing day. All in all he was pretty satisfied with his job status.

He wished he could say the same for his personal life. Once he left the office his every thought centered on Jody Sellers. Driving in the car, taking a shower, eating a meal, making love to his wife; he couldn't stop himself from thinking of her. As much as he dreaded it he had to face up to his situation. He could not continue on being torn between his family and Jody. It wasn't fair to the kids or Alison. It wasn't fair to Jody. A decision had to be made. It boiled down to a decision between his kids and Jody Sellers. Could he live with himself being one of those divorced dads who only sees his children on weekends? He knew plenty of them and felt sorry for them all. They were "event dads" shuffling their kids from one special activity to another. They planned every day down to the second lest they be stuck with their bored offspring, resentful of the life they knew was irretrievably shattered. All the Game Boys, pony rides, and special edition Barbies couldn't compensate for that. Nothing could. After being away so much of his kids' infant years he learned one important lesson: just being there was what really mattered. When they struck out to end the game, or had a stomachache, or forgot their place at a piano recital, being there for them was as much as you could do. That's how parents really made a difference. Could he give that up? Could he give up Jody?

A strange sounding ring startled him. It didn't come from his desk phone. He looked around the room hearing the ring again. After two more rings it dawned on him that it was his cell phone. He took it out from his jacket draped over a leather chair.

"Greg Barrett speaking."

"Hi, it's me."

He recognized the voice of Jody Sellers. Before he could respond she admonished him, "Don't say anything. I'm at 929-6400. Go to a pay phone. I'll wait for your call."

Without wasting a moment he took the elevator down to the lobby where a bank of pay phones were stationed. He put a quarter in and waited… and waited until he got a recording. It had been so long since he used a pay phone he didn't know they were now thirty five cents. He scrambled in his pocket for a dime then dialed the number. Jody Sellers picked up on the first ring.

"Hi, thanks for calling back so fast," she said.

"From your voice it sounded urgent. What's up?"

"I don't want to alarm you but I think your wife is having me followed." She told him of her confrontation with the investigator and what transpired. He listened to every word.

"I appreciate you telling me," he responded, "but honestly, that's not Alison's style. If she suspected anything she would be considerably more direct about it."

"I didn't want to cause you any trouble."

"No, no. You did the right thing. Maybe the guy was doing exactly what he said and we're making too much out of it. What did you say his name was?"

"You won't believe it. His name is Starfish… Stanley Starfish. His card says he's an insurance investigator for TransGeneral Assurety."

"We do business with TransGeneral. I can have that checked out. I bet it's probably nothing."

"You're probably right. But be careful anyway. If you call me use a phone that's safe. Not your cell phone. Once I put away the groceries I'm going over to my service station and have them check and see if that guy planted anything under the car."

"It's very sweet of you to be concerned. I miss you so much. I'll try and make it to the game on Thursday."

"I miss you too," she waited until she heard a dial tone, then said "I love you," into the receiver.

Greg Barrett waited nervously for the elevator in the lobby. There was no point in denying it. Jody Sellers' call had shaken him. Could Alison suspect? If she did, why would she hire someone to follow Jody and not him? Unless he was being followed without knowing it. He doubted that was happening. Lately, Alison was her normal self-absorbed persona. If she were on to him he should have been able to notice a change. Besides, Alison could never miss an opportunity this good to make him feel guilty. What he told Jody was correct. Alison's not shy. If she suspected anything she would confront him about it. He would do what he told Jody. He'd have someone discreetly find out if TransGeneral had an investigator named Starfish. What kind of a name was Starfish?

While in the elevator a chill went up his spine. TransGeneral was the insurance carrier for Harry's sport teams. They carried the policy on the stadium. They insured the large contracts against death and disability, including Richie Johnson. Jody's car was a white Ford like the one he drove that night. Could this guy Starfish be looking into the Richie Johnson shooting? Just when he thought he was past the emotional strain of the incident it pops back out of nowhere to bite him in the butt. By the time he reached his office he had calmed down. Even if this guy was investigating the Richie Johnson shooting and someone identified the car, what was he going to do? Track down every white Ford Taurus in Florida? Good luck! They all looked the same. And the one he drove wasn't even in circulation. His anxiety lessened, Greg Barrett went back to running a multibillion dollar company.

The insurance investigator found himself embarrassed, discouraged, and stuck in the middle of a monster traffic jam on I-95. What occurred with the pretty-green-eyed girl reached a new low point in his life. She was irritated with him and had every right to be. What kind of job required slinking around and looking at people's undercoatings?

Not much of one. There had to be an easier way to make a living. The girl made him feel like two cents, which was about what he was worth, and about what he was making. More determined than ever to heed Ron Jeffries' advice he decided to blow off inspecting the last four cars. They were all located in Palm Beach County, two in Boca Raton, and two in Delray Beach. At least he'd save the company the gas and wear and tear on the car. Remorseful over disturbing the girl's privacy he concluded it was time to wrap this case up. He was meeting with Stu Klein, the Manatees' Chief of Security, in the morning. If the traffic ever let up. At this rate he'd still be stuck on the interstate. After the meeting he would file his report. Possibly his last report. He decided to check into scholarships and financial aid. If he could swing it monetarily he would start school right away and chuck his career as an investigator. If the financial aid worked out the Richie Johnson shooting would be his last case. All in all it was fitting he went out on such a loser.

The next morning Stanley Starfish drove out to the stadium near the county line. Stu Klein's office was inside the stadium itself. He'd been to only a couple of games and had no idea it housed a complete office complex. He gave the receptionist his card and told her who he wanted to see. A few minutes later he was greeted by a stocky man of average height with think grey hair. "Hi, I'm Stu Klein," he said, extending his hand. "C'mon into my office. We can talk there."

The insurance investigator followed the man past the reception area into a moderately sized office. He could tell immediately Stu Klein was organized. Nothing in the office was out of place. The sheer volume of stacked files and memos indicated he was also very busy. "Would you like a cup of coffee?"

Stanley politely refused.

"How about a bagel?" he continued. "You don't mind if I nosh while we talk? Good." Stu Klein spread some cream cheese over a pumpernickel bagel. He talked between bites. "Your former partner asked me to meet with you. Ron Jeffries was one of the best police officers I ever had the pleasure of working with."

"The very best," Stanley countered.

"He speaks highly of you."

"Ahh. Ronnie's a bad judge of character."

Stu Klein smiled briefly. He looked the insurance investigator directly in the eye and said, "You're too modest. What you did on the Biscayne Kennel Club Murder was the finest investigative work I've ever witnessed. And I was on the job thirty one years. Twenty one with the county, then another ten with the State Attorney's office."

"You know how it is then. Sometimes you get lucky."

"You were lucky a lot. How can I help you?"

Stanley laid out the Richie Johnson case for Stu Klein. He went over what he discovered and the content of his interview with Richie Johnson. He told Stu Klein what transpired at Club Relaxxxation. His travails at the club gave Stu Klein a hearty laugh.

"So, you met the illustrious Otis Knight!"

Stanley nodded.

"Otis Knight is blessed with true entrepreneurial spirit. He is one helluva innovative businessman. Very precise, too. A real perfectionist. He never leaves anything to chance. If he were a different color he might by CEO of a corporation or head of a major Hollywood studio."

"I was simply trying to confirm if Richie Johnson was there the night of the shooting. And if he was there, why?"

Stu Klein put down his coffee cup staring seriously at the curly-haired man. "I can tell you categorically Richie Johnson was there that night. I can tell you what he was doing there."

Stanley Starfish immediately sat straight up in his chair, leaning forward. Seeing he had his full attention, Stu Klein continued, "I don't think it's any secret that ever since the World Series, management has been doing everything within reason to rid itself of Richie Johnson and his sixty six million dollar contract. It turned out they were the only ones stupid enough to pay him that kind of money. No other team in Major League Baseball would touch him. About three weeks before the shooting management really turned up the pressure. They wanted Richie Johnson really scrutinized. I'm not sure why but the team's general manager, Frank Roy, and team president, Lou Redmond, pushed for more frequent and detailed accounts of his comings and goings. If they were squeezing me, they were getting squeezed. That type of pressure only comes from the very top."

"Why would they be so interested in his off-field activities?"

"Good question." Stu Klein reflected a minutes before answering. "I don't really know. My best guess is they were looking for some kind of behavior that would invoke a moral clause in his contract. Some type of loophole where they could void it out. Or maybe give them some negotiating room."

"Did you find anything?"

Stu Klein threw up his hands, "I don't know how his contract is written. I just reported what we found. I can tell you he doesn't do drugs. In fact he's something of a health nut. Some of his friends aren't model citizens but that's par for the course these days. We found no evidence of any connection to gambling. You got to understand, in baseball the ultimate taboo is gambling. If Pete Rose was a convicted heroin dealer he would be in the Hall of Fame today. Like I said, we didn't find anything there. Richie Johnson does like the ladies, and the ladies like Richie Johnson. Probably too much. Since the World Series he was seeing a dancer at Otis' club. A Miss Ebony Spice. Her real name is Leah Wilson. Club Relaxxxation is popular with the pro athletes in town. It's popular with a lot of people. It just so happens I have a reliable contact there, one of the bouncers. A real good kid named Melvin McGillis. He was an All-America fullback at UM. Great player, sure-fire pro until he blew out his knee his senior year in the Orange Bowl and his NFL career went down the toilet. He's been a very dependable source of information and on my payroll for years. Anyhow, he tipped me Richie Johnson was spending a lot of time there. A couple of months go by and Miss Spice finds herself in a family way and claiming Richie Johnson is the father. Right before the shooting he was at the club every chance he could get. He was involved in some sort of negotiation with her. My guess is a payoff to avoid a paternity suit. It's happened before. I can confirm he was definitely there the night he was shot."

"Did your guy notice if he came in with anybody or left with anybody? Did he notice if anyone followed him out?"

"He watched him closely. Richie came in by himself and left by himself. He's pretty sure no one followed him out, either. The weather was godawful. It happened the night the Storm of the Century rolled through."

"Do you think the girl, Miss Spice, could have set him up?"

"No way," Stu Klein said emphatically. "Probably the only people in the world who don't have a motive to knock off Richie Johnson are his agent and the various mothers of his children. He's their gravy train, and even so, one of the mothers tried to poison him. But that girl, Ebony, I mean Leah, is smart."

Stu Klein told Stanley the story of Lashonda Jones. They shared a good laugh before he continued. "That girl Ebony, or Leah, is smart. Capping Richie before he could pay her off would be pretty stupid. I don't think she had anything to do with it, but if you want, I'll get you her address and phone number."

Stanley shook his head, "No, that won't be necessary. I'm sure you're right. Did you go to the police with that information?"

"Of course. It was relevant information in an open investigation. I reported it right away. But I gotta tell you, they didn't seem too interested. I wore a badge in this county for over thirty years... proudly. I can tell you things aren't the way they used to be. The department is not the same. Dade County is not the same. I know you didn't leave under the best of circumstances but trust me, in the long run, you'll be better off. The problem nowadays is everyone there is myopic. Nobody looks at the big picture."

A long pause followed as Stanley Starfish assimilated the information provided by the Chief of Security. Stu Klein gazed at the insurance investigator who was obviously lost in thought with a puzzled, frowning look over his face. Though they'd never met until today, he'd observed the kid's career from afar. He'd long been an admirer and thought quite possibly Stanley Starfish was the most brilliant detective he'd ever come across. "I hope I was able to give you a little help."

Stanley looked startled as if awakened from a trance. "Oh, you have. You've given me a lot. I can't thank you enough. I was just thinking... can you tell me who got your reports?"

My reports go to Frank Roy with a copy to Lou Redmond. You'd have to check with them if anyone else received it. Tough case. You don't think it was a neighborhood ripoff?"

Stanley shook his head. "The shooter didn't take a thing. For a street thug to have Richie Johnson lying there helpless, would be like winning the lottery and ripping up the ticket."

"Makes sense," Stu Klein added, "also, Otis Knight takes his clientele's enjoyment and security very seriously. I'm not saying there's never been an incident in the neighborhood involving one of his customers, but Otis is well connected. He generally finds out who's responsible way before the police and handles it in-house much more effectively."

Stanley nodded, indicating he understood and said, "It could possibly have been an incident of road rage or perceived self-defense. I got a pretty good idea Richie Johnson came out of his Ferrari steaming mad... but there's problems with that too."

"Like what?"

"It's possible the shooter wore a mask. Richie Johnson's not sure. And the shooter said something to him that's bothered me since he told me. I can't get it out of my mind. Something about his sister, like the guy might have known him."

"As I said, Richie Johnson has plenty of enemies. There's not too many people associated with the bum who are crying he's not here. That goes from the locker room attendants he stiffs for tips, to his teammates, to the very top of ownership. As far as I know, nobody's lighting a candle in his absence."

Stanley smiled. "I can't thank you enough. It's truly been a pleasure meeting you. I regret we never got the chance to work together."

"So do I. Listen, when you see Ronnie be sure you tell him Stu Klein asked for him. Make sure you give him my best."

The insurance investigator had to escape the closet that passed for his office. He needed room to think and he did his best thinking while pacing. He tried sauntering up and down the corridors of TransGeneral's Miami headquarters, but stopped when he noticed the disapproving looks from his coworkers and when their laughter became audible. He never had that problem when he was with the department. Even Armando Pedroza gave him space. It was far different working for an insurance company. Conformity was rampant. Everyone looked the same. People of different sexes looked the same. People of different races looked the same. When he told his best friend of his observations Ron Jeffries chuckled. "When you did all that pacing and drumming as a hot-shot detective everyone considered you eccentric. At the insurance company you're just an oddball."

To create the thinking room necessary Stanley went down to the parking lot. TransGeneral's Miami office was located near Miami International Airport. The noise from the jet planes so frequently taking off and landing proved too much of a distraction. He got in the Escort and drove. When he stopped Stanley Starfish found himself at the Dinner Key Marina in Coconut Grove.

There was something about mornings at a marina. Maybe it was the pelicans lazily perched atop pilings protruding up from the sea, patiently awaiting the fishermen to return with their catch. Or possibly it was the sounds; the echoes of pounding hammers and electric sanders filling the air. Those were the obvious noises of deck hands busily preparing their vessels for sea. If you concentrated and listened very carefully there were other, more subtle sounds. His dad showed him how. You closed your eyes and cleared your mind and... there... he could hear the cawing gulls in flight, and the flapping of an untied sail in the wind. A weather vane spinning and the splash from oars slapping the water's surface as a sailor rowed in from a moored watercraft. When he really concentrated he could hear the back and forth motion of someone painting a mast or varnishing the teak. His dad was doing exactly that the last time he saw him from this very same marina. The image was frozen in his brain. His dad wore only a pair of khaki cargo shorts while he polished the deck on his hands and knees. His mom carried his keyboard and a small bag containing a change of clothes. As they waited for the cab to take them to Surfside he remembered closing his eyes and listening to the morning sounds of the marina. The cab arrived. His dad looked up, smiled and waved; his tan body glistening in the sun and long hair rustling in the strong sea breeze. He entered the cab, never to see his father again. When they arrived in Surfside his mom made the cab driver wait. She escorted him to his great-grandparents' apartment and gave him a big hug and kiss. She started to walk away, then returned for an extra long, tight hug. He watched from the window as she got in the cab and drove off. He remembered waving at the cab even after it had turned the corner and was no longer in sight. That was the very last time he saw his mother.

For a long time after he felt they would always return for him. No matter the circumstances they would somehow find their way back. When his great-grandparents took him to the beach he would go down to the water's edge and peer out at the horizon, searching for the happiest little sailboat in the universe. He would stare out at the shimmering water hour after hour; day after day. He would close his eyes, concentrate and listen, just how his dad taught him. Sometimes his ears would play tricks on him because he could swear he heard his mother's beautiful voice [*Michael row the boat ashore*] and his dad's providing the chorus [*Hallelujah*]. A feeling of serenity would flow through his veins [*Michael row the boat ashore*] and also a sense of joy. He was right. His parents would never abandon him [*Hallelujah*]. Any moment they would be united again as a family [*The river is deep and the river is wide*]. But when he opened his eyes the sailboat was nowhere to be found. There was nothing but the vast emptiness of the ocean.

The insurance investigator aimlessly meandered up and down the marina's piers. The hot Miami sun overpowered the ocean breeze and he realized he was sweating. He wiped his brow. Gradually the blue sky began to cloud. His train of thought altered. He didn't come to reminisce about the past. He came to work his case. His pace quickened and he started drumming on his pockets. Something Stu Klein had said stuck in his mind.

Something he said re-energized him and gave him a different perspective. Not so much anything pertaining to the case-it was something else. Something he said rather matter-of-factly. He was talking about the department. That was it. He compared the department today to the one a generation ago. What was it he had said? Something about the way they looked at cases.

After a pause Stanley Starfish smiled knowingly. Nobody looks at the big picture anymore.

14

Greg Barrett would have a difficult time explaining to anyone why he felt so empty. He should have been the happiest man on the planet. Later that day he and Alison along with other Capital Industries executives were joining Harry and Betty Hvide on their private jet to New York City. Harry had booked them all suites at the Plaza Hotel. From there they would spend a fabulous weekend of lavish dining, decadent shopping and hit Broadway shows. Monday morning they were all to go down to the New York Stock Exchange and witness Harry Hvide ring the opening bell. It would also inaugurate the first day that Capital Services Industries would trade publicly. Although it didn't get quite the reception on the street that other Harry Hvide new issues received, Capital Services exceeded First Securities' expectations. A Harry Hvide stock was a brand name. It still commanded respect and attracted a following. While not as much as originally anticipated, Greg Barrett stood to rake in over nine million dollars, his greatest single payday.

That wasn't all. Out of the blue Harry quadrupled his salary. In wages alone, not counting a generous option and warrants package, as CEO of Capital Services Industries he stood to make a little under two million dollars a year. Not bad for a former garbage truck driver. Another raise and he'd be in the range of a reserve shortstop.

Perhaps it was merely a coincidence but since returning to work from his heart trouble Harry was treating him far better than he ever had. Harry stopped by his office almost daily simply to make small talk, something he rarely did before. Normally Harry had strictly a business-only mentality and their conversations were strictly business oriented. Lately, however, Harry chatted about family, taking an interest in how Alison and the kids were doing. He would stay and gossip about old acquaintances from the ICX and Video Nation days. Sometimes he stopped by Greg's office merely to tell him the latest off-color Clinton joke making the rounds. Not many knew it but Harry Hvide had a keen sense of humor and was an able storyteller.

Greg Barrett became a semi-regular invitee to Harry's elaborate lunches and pre-dinner cocktail parties. More social than business, these events were attended by political big wigs, visiting celebrities and sports luminaries, usually one of Harry's coaches. Despite taking their friendship to a different plane, the pay boost came out of left field. In all the years Greg worked for Harry Hvide he never once asked for a single pay raise or even discussed compensation. He let Harry decide what he was worth. He thought Harry was always generous. Hell, he was thrilled with what he was already making.

Money was just a part of it. While in New York he was scheduled to do an interview with Forbes Magazine about the new company. They went over preliminaries before leaving Fort Lauderdale. Harry loved the concept. Forbes planned a cover with a picture of a small baby shark opening its jaws super-wide and swallowing up a corpulent, bloated ICX. Barron's and the Wall Street Journal also requested interviews. First fortune, now fame. So why the feelings of ambivalence? Alison would dismiss it as a budding midlife crisis. Her three hundred fifty dollar per hour analyst might characterize it as some type of fear of success syndrome. He'd been in Harry Hvide's shadow so long he was afraid to stop out on center stage. There was probably some truth to that because Gregory Barrett was having second thoughts about his abilities. He wasn't a Wharton School MBA. He was a regular guy who made it thorough college on the G.I. Bill and was lucky enough to hitch a ride on the Harry Hvide express. When making deals he and Harry could always spot the phonies. They might get by for a while but in the long run their pretension and insincerity would betray them. As Harry's lieutenant he gained a reputation as a tough but honest negotiator who made the best deal he could without cheating anyone. He was proud of his reputation. He hoped his new position didn't require camouflage.

Perhaps he was embarrassed by the money. Lately he'd been bothered by feelings of guilt. Those feelings could just have easily stemmed from his unresolved status with Jody Sellers—Jody! Yesterday he sat with her at the soccer game and left leaving everything the same. All his prepared speeches vanished the moment he saw her. He couldn't find the courage to make a commitment or to let her go. When he started with Harry his focus was crystal clear—work as hard and as diligently as possible to provide a stable home and security for his wife and children. And always conduct himself in a manner that would make his parents proud. What used to be so simple now seemed so complex. He grimaced. He should know by now nothing remains the same. Circumstances change.

Feelings of guilt and inadequacy probably contributed to his mood. There was also something else. There was the odious burden of keeping a dark, terrible secret completely and totally within. He looked at his watch and blinked. He would have to continue his self-indulgent examination another time. Alison was busy getting dressed for dinner at Le Cirque. She didn't deserve to be escorted by a mope. She was looking forward to the glitz and glamour of a dream New York weekend. He would do his best not to spoil it for her.

The insurance investigator finished his research and logged off the computer. The internet provided him the information he needed. He rose from his desk and started pacing. He felt a tightness in his forehead. His mind began turning as he desperately tried processing the facts and theories simultaneously flashing within. The feeling was familiar although it had been absent for quite some time. It was the feeling he got when he found the solution to a complicated bridge hand. It was the same feeling he got when working a case going in ten different directions which started to fall into place. As his brain collated the incoming data he was happy to find the Richie Johnson shooting case finally coming together.

Somehow he allowed himself to get bogged down in trivialities. He credited too many assumptions with validity. He took too many suppositions at face value. It was embarrassing how easily he was distracted. It was time to refocus and get down to business because the more he thought about it, shooting Richie Johnson was a business decision. So much pointed in that direction. The shooter drove a special production car modified for the American Rental Car Company. American Rental Car was a subsidiary of Capital Industries. The car rental company sold every one of the cars to Auto World. Auto World was a subsidiary of Capital Industries. The beneficiary on Richie Johnson's disability policy was the Florida Manatees. The team's owner was the major principal in Capital Industries. Right before the shooting Stu Klein filed reports on Richie Johnson almost daily. Those reports found their way from the team's front office to the highest offices of Capital Industries. The size of the claim was motive. The security reports revealing Richie Johnson's hangouts provided opportunity. Too many coincidences gravitated toward Capital Industries for him to ignore. Additionally, any involvement by Capital Industries would violate the policy's warranties. It was probably the only situation that got his company off the hook. He didn't have it nailed with the t's crossed and i's dotted, but all his instincts told him he was proceeding in the right direction.

The problem with pursuing that line of investigation was it led to a head-on collision with one of the largest, most powerful corporations in Florida headed by one of the richest, most powerful men in the world. Would a multibillion dollar corporation be responsible for someone's death over a few million dollars? He worked too many homicide cases not to know the answer. People have been killed for less. Much less. He once worked a case where someone took another's life over a pair of shoes. The eight million dollar disability portion was motive enough, let alone the entire sixty six million dollar value of the whole policy. Also, there might be greater financial considerations to getting rid of Richie Johnson he was unaware of.

He would have to go forward cautiously. He had to find out if someone inside the corporation did it himself or had it done. He needed to know how high up the corporate ladder to look. Capital Industries was big in waste management. When he was with the department rumors persisted linking the garbage business to organized crime. What he learned about Capital Industries cast doubt on that theory. Capital Industries waste management division was nothing like the Panino Brothers, Dino and Eddie, hauling out of Jersey. It was a publicly traded, Fortune Five Hundred company heavily regulated and scrutinized. Rumors appeared to be just that. There wasn't a scintilla of hard evidence linking Capital Industries to organized crime.

Something else bothered him. The shooting looked nothing like a professional hit. A professional would have made it look like a robbery and taken something. Richie Johnson's recollection and the physical evidence suggested the shooter panicked and ran. He didn't even make sure Richie Johnson was dead. He still needed to check out some things. He started by driving back to the Auto World in Broward County.

During the drive he tried sorting out his feelings. His whole body was energized. He had to admit it felt good to be back in the hunt working a complicated case. How quickly events turned! Two days ago he was ready to blow the investigation off. Now his senses were on fire as he concentrated on the loose ends. His instincts led him to believe the answer lay in something Richie Johnson said. He replayed the conversation in his mind over and over. The only thing he couldn't reconcile was the mention of his sister. Why would the shooter mention his sister? Of course Richie Johnson could have misunderstood or imagined it under the stressful conditions. But there was something vaguely familiar about it that wouldn't allow him to let it go. Up ahead he could see the sign for Auto World. He would have to put the issue aside for the moment. He pulled into the lot, parked the car and walked to the main showroom.

Steve Perez greeted him a few minutes later. "Sorry to keep you waiting. What brings you back so soon?"

"I have just a few follow-up questions. I promise I won't take up much of your time."

"No problem, fire away."

"Do you have loaner cars here? Extra cars on hand, you let customers borrow?"

"Sure. Every dealership has them these days. Even us used car dealers."

"What kind of cars do you use for loaners?"

"It depends. It varies depending on our inventory. We always try and keep at least one passenger van. Right now we have a Voyager. The rest comes from overstocks. For the last couple of months we've used the Ford Taurus GL. Presently we have four of them available."

"White?"

"Yeah, they're all white with blue interiors. How did you know?"

"A lucky guess," the insurance investigator responded. "Tell me, do you keep records of who's got the cars out and when they're using them?"

"We do. Everyone taking out a loaner signs a standardized form with an insurance waiver."

"Do you think I can see them?"

"I don't see why not. Follow me."

Stanley Starfish followed him through the showroom to a series of offices. He waited while Steve Perez talked to a secretary. He returned in a few minutes. "Cyndi is making copies. She'll have it for you shortly."

Within five minutes a young blond girl gave Steve Perez some papers. He handed them to Stanley and said, "These go back six weeks. If you need more, let me know."

"No, this is fine," he replied while thumbing through the forms. He carefully reviewed each one. None of the Taurus GLs were loaned out around the date of the Richie Johnson shooting. When he finished Stanley asked Steve Perez another question. "Steve, is it possible someone, say an employee, a relative, or somebody from the parent company, could take out a loaner without filling out the form?"

"Not on my watch. If I need one for myself I still fill out the form. I can't speak for the previous general manager."

They chatted briefly before Stanley thanked him for his cooperation and asked him one final question. "Would you mind if I looked
around the body shop?"

"Knock yourself out. It's around back. Would you like me to show
you?"

"No, no, that's okay. You've been generous enough with your time.
I'll find my way."

In back of the Auto World showroom was a separate, smaller ware-
house-style building consisting of four open bays. The building housed
both the service department and body shop. He took some time
observing the operation. What Steve Perez told him during his previous visit was right on target. The majority of the work was preparing
cars for resale. Stanley was impressed with the speed and thoroughness
of the mechanics. A service writer made a detailed inspection of each
vehicle, working off a checklist. Any problem he found went on a work
order. Upon completion of the work order the vehicle underwent
another complete inspection. When it passed the vehicle was touched
up, waxed, catalogued, and priced. Every one he saw came out looking like a new car. If he ever mustered up two nickels to rub together
he wouldn't hesitate to shop for a car at Auto World.

The insurance investigator waited for the men to break before
approaching one of the supervisors. He was a tall, lightly complex-
ioned black man with the name Watson printed on his workshirt. He
introduced himself and handed him his card.

"Starfish, a most unusual name," Mr. Watson said in a melodic
Caribbean lilt. "You can call me Rudy."

"You're right, Rudy. My parents were most unusual people," he
answered with a smile. "You seem to oversee the bodyshop. I just wondered if by chance you remember repairing or replacing a bumper for
a '96 white Ford Taurus GL. It would have been the last few days of
March up to the first ten days of April."

"I can look it up for you. Hold on a minute."

"No, that won't be necessary. I have a feeling there won't be any
paperwork. It could have been for one of your loaner cars."

Rudy Watson wrinkled his brow and asked, "You say the end of
March beginning of April?"

Stanley nodded affirmatively.

Rudy Watson took a minute before answering. "I tink I do remember something. Most unusual circumstance. The bumper had the tiniest
of dents. I could have knocked it out, repainted it and not even William
Clay Ford himself would've been able to tell the difference. But the
general manager insisted on installing a new one."

"Do you recall what happened to the old bumper?"

"Disposed of it. A bloody stupid ting if you ask me. I suggested we recycle it. But the GM said to throw it away. A shame to waste a serviceable bumper like that. Just dumped it over a little ping and a smidgen of red paint."

Driving back to Miami proved to be an arduous task. The traffic on I-595 was gridlocked in both directions. This was a time he could definitely have used a cell phone.

He was supposed to have dinner with the Jeffries but would undoubtedly be late. He wasn't moving at all and couldn't exit to use a pay phone. While waiting for a break in traffic his thoughts drifted back to his conversation with Richie Johnson. What was so significant about what the shooter said that he couldn't let it go? He punched himself hard in the thigh, frustrated at his inability to come up with the answer. Finally the traffic eased and he was able to move. He put on his turn signal, edging over to the right lane. He would get off at the next exit, find a pay phone and call Ron... RON! His memory kicked into gear, cutting through the dense fog inside his head. He faintly recalled an incident from years past. It was soon after the Aronson case. Armando Pedroza assigned him to partner up with Ron Jeffries. They were working their second or third case together as a team. It wasn't much of a case, involving a homicide resulting from a domestic disturbance. A Darrell... no, no... Darnell Davis found himself in a violent argument with another man. Stanley couldn't remember his name. The other man was angry at Darnell for stealing the affections of his woman. The dispute escalated to the point where shots were fired. The other man was killed. The case was a slam dunk. They had witnesses, fingerprints and matching ballistics. All they had to do was put Darnell Davis under arrest. Darnell proved to be not all that elusive. They spotted him in a convenience store a block from his mother's apartment. With Ron in the lead they cautiously approached their suspect. As soon as he exited the store Ron drew his service revolver and yelled "Cease and desist!" The volume and authority in Ron's command startled him. It had a similar effect on Darnell, who immediately wet his pants. But rather than obey, Darnell took off like a jackrabbit. That was a mistake. Despite his bum knee Ronnie was still faster on one good leg than most anyone else on two. Ronnie cursed under his breath and initiated pursuit, chasing him through traffic, down alleys, over fences and into a Burger King parking lot where he finally caught and subdued him. Ron took Darnell down with a flying tackle, stuck his revolver down his throat and shouted, "Cease and desist, motherfucker!"

After cuffing Darnell and reading him his rights, Ronnie said, "Man, what did you make me chase you for? I told you to stop."

Recalling Darnell Davis' answer brought a wry, knowing smile across Stanley's face. Stanley Starfish got off the highway at the first available exit. Before calling the Jeffries he checked his notes on Southwest Airlines departures. He would have enough time in the morning to access Capital Industries personnel records before his flight to Jacksonville.

Greg Barrett tipped the parking valet and entered his Lexus. He left the Boca Raton Hotel and Resort headed toward his office. Settling into his new position as CEO of Capital Services Industries was going better than expected. He felt more comfortable with each passing day. The function he left was a good example. He gave a speech to the Palm Beach Chamber of Commerce and the Broward Partners, a coalition of local business and education leaders. His speech outlined the benefits the new company would have on both counties. He predicted a boost in both counties' economies as well as their property values. To his great relief the speech seemed well received. They even laughed at his lame joke comparing Harry Hvide to God; the only difference being that God rested on the seventh day. He was also surprised at how easily he mingled with the crowd during the following luncheon. Being a schmoozer and a networker weren't usually his strong points. The Boca Raton Hotel and Resort provided a perfect backdrop for the event. Betty Hvide outdid herself, making it truly a world-class property. He left feeling satisfied.

His experience the past weekend in New York was similar. Usually it was one of his least favorite cities. He never really adjusted to the noise and traffic. The last weekend was completely different with the city casting a magical spell over the entire Hvide contingent. Alison already made plans for another weekend where they'd bring the kids to see Lion King. His interview with Forbes went well. He struck up a rapport with the interviewing editor who labeled him "the working man's CEO." While recapping events he lost track of time. Before he realized it he was just a block from the office. The car must have been on autopilot. He also realized his cell phone was turned off and he had a couple of urgent messages. Well, those could wait five minutes. He parked in his assigned parking spot and took the elevator up to his office.

The insurance investigator was able to take an earlier flight back than he originally scheduled. What he needed to do in Jacksonville took less time than he planned. The cab ride each way took twice as long as the time he spent there. Catching an earlier flight had the added bonus of traveling non-stop, eliminating a landing in Tampa. He claimed his car and drove straight to the Capital Industries building. The person he needed to see was out of the office. He decided to wait. He picked up a magazine and took a seat in the reception area.

Greg Barrett was met by his secretary, Martha, who stood up to greet him. He smiled meekly and said, "I know, I know. My phone was turned off."

"Mr. Lampone called twice from Jacksonville," Martha replied evenly. "He said it's very urgent. And there's a Mr. Starfish from TransGeneral Insurance waiting to see you."

The name Starfish sent a jolt through his system. He remembered the unusual name. It was the name of the guy who followed Jody. Greg couldn't imagine him being the bearer of good news. He wrestled with what to do about him. He could put him off and have him make an appointment for a later date. He considered it a moment before rejecting the idea. Harry always wanted to hear bad news right away. He preferred dealing with it directly as opposed to letting it fester.

"You can send him in. I'll call Tony when I'm finished."

A thin mild-mannered, curly-haired man walked into his office and introduced himself.

"Mr. Barrett, my name is Starfish. I represent the TransGeneral Assurety Company."

"My secretary told me. Please be seated. How can I help you?"

The insurance investigator took a seat before continuing. "My company is the insurer of the disability policy on Richard Johnson's contract. I was wondering, if your schedule allows, if I could ask you a few questions?"

Well, at least Greg knew he wasn't working for Alison. Greg fought hard to remain calm and respond politely and matter-of-factly.

"I'm afraid you have the wrong department. Richie Johnson is part of the Florida Manatees organization. It's a completely separate entity. In fact, I'm not much of a baseball fan."

"I see. But please, correct me if I'm mistaken, there seems to have been a lot of activity between the Manatees and this office prior to the start of the new season concerning Mr. Johnson. I have a copy of your secretary's signature accepting delivery of file boxes delivered from the Manatees' front office to here via Direct Courier Service. This is your secretary's signature, isn't it?" The insurance investigator produced a delivery log with Martha's signature clearly visible.

Greg Barrett felt a lump in his throat. The skinny guy before him was polite and soft spoken. He was also sharp. Greg couldn't afford to underestimate him. He chose his words very carefully before answering.

"Oh... yes. I know what you're referring to. If you follow baseball it's no secret the team was trying to trade him. As a favor and from strictly a business viewpoint, I agreed to look at the language of his no-trade clause and get an opinion on its enforceability from our legal department. I'm sure either Mr. Redmond or Mr. Roy with the Manatees can confirm that for you."

The curly-haired man nodded, apparently satisfied with the answer. Greg exhaled, sensing the tension easing. His feeling of relief was short-lived.

"I see," answered the man with the strange name. "Can you tell me why you monitored the security reports on Mr. Johnson's activities?"

"Uh... security reports? I don't follow."

"Mr. Klein, Chief of Security for the Manatees, fills out weekly security reports on the team's players. The reports are preventative in nature. Sort of an early warning system so the players don't get involved with known gamblers, drug dealers, et cetera.

He investigates rumors and either denies or confirms them. Copies of those reports were sent to this office. Actually, right before the shooting he filed reports every other day."

Greg looked the insurance investigator directly in the eye, "I don't remember the reason. I can't recall seeing the reports. I believe I told Lou Redmond and Frank Roy to forward everything they had."

The Starfish fellow didn't change expressions, making it difficult for Greg to gauge him. The guy didn't even blink. Greg thought he must have been a hell of a card player. Barely a moment elapsed before he asked another question.

"If you wouldn't mind, Mr. Barrett, can you tell me where you were the evening Richard Johnson was shot?"

"I'm not sure I like the implication of your question," Greg answered tersely.

"I understand completely, Mr. Barrett. If you want to consult someone, possibly a lawyer, I can come back. If you prefer I can reschedule for a later date."

He thought about accepting his offer but decided stalling would make him look like he was hiding something... "No, no, that won't be necessary. I was working late. Right here in my office."

"Do you remember seeing anyone or talking to anyone that can verify that?"

"I don't recall offhand."

"Do you remember what time you left the office and do you recall anyone seeing you leave?"

"I tried going home around eight thirty but the weather was horrendous. I decided to wait for it to clear. I got caught up in something or another. By the time I finished it was around eleven thirty PM. I arrived home just before midnight."

"In your own car?"

"Of course. In my own car."

"You weren't driving a '96 white Ford Taurus GL with blue vinyl interior?"

Greg Barrett struggled to maintain his composure. His thoughts drifted back to that horrible night. He remembered vaguely the loaner car did have vinyl seats. How did this Starfish find out? And what was the significance? He had a sick feeling in his stomach he was about to find out. "I told you. In my own car."

"Mr. Barrett, are you still the registered owner of a Ruger .38 caliber stainless steel pistol serial number SR1462140?"

"Uh, yes, I did own a... uh... but what?"

"Mr. Barrett, do you still own the pistol?"

"Well, you see... I'm trying... to explain. I did own the gun at one time but it's been missing for a while... probably over a year. You see, we had the house remodeled. Workers were in and out all hours of the day. I noticed it missing about a year ago."

"Did you report it stolen?"

"No, no I didn't." Either this skinny guy was growing in stature or the room was shrinking. "I couldn't determine who stole it or even when it was stolen. I hadn't seen it for several years prior to discovering it missing."

"So you never filed a police report or made a claim on your homeowner's policy?"

"I told you already I didn't." He wasn't aware of the anger seeping into the tone of his voice. "Look, Mr. Starfish, I have a lot of work. Is there anything else?"

"I apologize for taking up your time. But I have to be frank, Mr. Barrett. I have some problems with my investigation. You see, the person who shot Richard Johnson drove a special production model '96 Ford Taurus—white exterior, blue vinyl interior. With the exception of several police departments every '96 white Taurus GL with blue vinyl interior belonged to American Car Rental, a subsidiary of Capital Industries. At the end of one year American Car Rental sold every one of those cars to Auto World, Inc., another wholly owned subsidiary of Capital Industries. The security reports I mentioned found their way to the highest offices at Capital Industries. Those reports contained information Mr. Johnson was spending his spare time at a club, Club Relaxxxation. Mr. Johnson was shot three blocks from there. He was shot with a .38 caliber pistol."

The insurance investigator was so polite and casual he probably had no idea the devastation each of his words created. Greg Barrett started to sweat heavily. He felt woozy and wanted to loosen his tie. Somehow he managed to weakly reply, "Auto World sells a lot of cars and many people have .38s."

"Yes sir, you're correct. However, I don't think the car in question was ever sold, at least not before the incident. Someone in the service department at the Broward Auto World remembers replacing a dented bumper on a '96 Taurus GL right after the shooting, then disposing of it. Curiously there was no work order or paperwork on it of any kind, leading me to believe it was a company car. And the dent happened... oh, yes. He remembers the dented bumper having a touch of red paint on it. Richard Johnson drove a Ferrari 550 Maranello that evening. A red Ferrari. I visited Mr. Lampone, the general manager of the Broward Auto World at the time, this morning in Jacksonville. He is a stand-up guy, very loyal to you, Mr. Barrett. Truthfully, he didn't tell me a thing. But I must tell you, I have some experience in these situations and they have a way of unraveling. In the long run it's very difficult to cover up the truth... and there's one more thing."

Without warning the insurance investigator stood up suddenly, slightly crouched forward with both hands extended simulating holding a gun. "Cease and desist!" he shouted forcefully. Caught by surprise, Greg Barrett's head snapped back hard against his leather chair. The insurance investigator sat back down immediately resuming his calm, polite demeanor.

"You see, Mr. Barrett, Richard Johnson told me something he thought the shooter said. I just couldn't reconcile it. He thought the shooter shouted something about his sister. For the life of me I couldn't make sense of it. Then I remembered an incident where my partner tried to make an arrest and the suspect took off. He ran even though my partner pulled his gun. When we caught him my partner wanted to know why the suspect ran after he told him to stop. He replied, "Man, if I'd a known you was the police I woulda stopped. I thought you was going to shoot me for knocking up your sistah." My partner told the man to 'cease and desist'. The man misunderstood. I believe Richard Johnson made the same mistake. My partner used that phrase out of habit, going back to his days in the Armed Forces, where he served as a military policeman. Cease and desist is a command imperative, specific to the military. Mr. Barrett, if I'm not mistaken, you were once an MP, sir, stationed in Korea."

No longer able to mask the ravage done to him, Greg Barrett slumped in his chair and loosened his tie. Exposure was almost welcome. At least he could unburden himself of this terrible secret. Until he considered the consequences. A story like this would leak out. It would be virtually impossible to keep something of this magnitude wrapped up.

Once out in the open the ramifications were mind boggling. Though the claim technically involved only the baseball team, there was no possible way it wouldn't taint Harry Hvide personally and everyone and everything associated with him. He shuddered to think what the news would do to the stock price and the consequences it would have on the work force. Billions of dollars and thousands of jobs could be at stake. And who knows what the acting Commissioner of Baseball might do? At least a thousand other negatives flooded his head. The overload made him physically ill. He struggled to breathe. He felt so faint he almost toppled out of his chair. To steady himself he leaned forward, placing his elbows on his desk, resting his head atop his hands. He tried taking deep inhales but then realized he hadn't yet considered the toll it would take on him personally. The public disgrace would be too painful for words, the fallout enveloping his wife and children. He could imagine what his father-in-law the judge would say. For an instant he thought of suicide but that would have been far too easy. He could never leave Alison and the kids to face the shame and humiliation by themselves. The only bright spot was that neither of his parents were alive to witness this travesty. What had he done? And who would believe he changed his mind and was driving away when events shifted so tragically out of control?

The insurance investigator was put off stride by the awkward pause... not exactly sure what to do next, he babbled aimlessly. "It always looks suspicious if you say the gun was lost or stolen. The best way to secure an untraceable weapon is to buy at one of those consumer gun shows from a private dealer. No one ever keeps track or follows up."

Without looking up or even changing position Greg Barrett said, barely audibly, "Next time."

Stanley Starfish got up to leave. The man before him was ashen, devoid of any color. He looked like he was about to throw up. As he walked to the door Stanley said to him in a sympathetic tone, "If it's any consolation, Mr. Barrett, I used to be a homicide detective. I'm pretty sure there's not enough evidence for a criminal indictment. I'm afraid, however, I'm going to have to recommend denying coverage when I file my report."

Greg Barrett lifted his head and looked at the thin, curly-haired man. "How soon before you send it in?"

Stanley Starfish answered, "I have one more person to see."

15

"Mr. Hvide will see you now."

The insurance investigator put down the magazine and followed the well-dressed, middle-aged woman down a corridor. At the end of the hallway standing in front of a double-doored entrance was a stocky, bald man in a navy blue suit waiting to greet him.

"Good afternoon. I'm Harry Hvide. It's a pleasure meeting you."

The insurance investigator struggled to reply. His tongue and mouth chose that precise moment to betray him. The man offering his hand was different in person than the impression he gained from the media. He pictured Harry Hvide to be a giant in stature and with an aggressive manner. In person he was considerably shorter than Stanley imagined. He was also friendly and outgoing. His smile hinted of a sharp wit. And then there were his eyes. An ultra-deep sapphire blue, his eyes were simultaneously piercing and absorbing, similar to Stanley's own eyes. Finally, his mouth worked long enough to eke out a response.

"My name is Starfish. Thank you, Mr. Hvide, for meeting with me."

"Again, it's my pleasure. Mr. Hvide is my father. Call me Harry. Won't you please come into my office?"

Stanley followed Harry Hvide into a spacious corner office offering magnificent panoramic views of downtown Fort Lauderdale and the ocean. The office itself was more functional and less plush than he envisioned. What made it unique and so incredibly fascinating were the pictures and mementos adorning the walls and displayed on the shelves. This was an office of achievement. The investigator's head was on a swivel. He didn't know where to look first. Harry Hvide picked up on his curiosity and offered, "Would you like to take some time to look around?"

"You wouldn't mind?"

"Not at all. Please, take all the time you want."

Stanley gazed at pictures of Harry Hvide posing with politicians.

Among them were Harry with three ex-presidents, the current vice president, several U.S. senators and Justices of the Supreme Court. Other photos showed him shaking hands with the leaders of Canada, England, Mexico, and Brazil. There were pictures of him with the most famous luminaries from the world of sports and Hollywood. "A" list directors, Oscar winning actors and actresses were all represented, smiling happily next to Harry Hvide. There were more pictures of him standing with Grammy award-winning artists from country to hard rock. Still more photographs showed Harry with Hall of Fame athletes and coaches of every major sport. He took some extra time to peer at one of Harry between Ted Williams and Joe DiMaggio.

Other photos showed Harry cutting ribbons at the opening of video store franchises and car dealerships. There were framed shares of stock from his various public companies. Aerials of burgeoning hotel resort properties were exhibited as were nice shots of his family. He got a kick out of Harry being dwarfed by a nine hundred and two pound blue marlin caught off the coast of Australia.

Elsewhere trophies and pennants won by his sports teams were displayed on bookcase shelves and cabinet tops. Behind his personal desk was a custom-built credenza built especially for the World Series trophy. He took some time to admire it.

What the insurance investigator found rather peculiar was that among all these priceless photographs and treasures of his life, the one most prominently displayed was one of a much younger Harry Hvide standing on the running board of an old, dilapidated, beat-up red garbage truck. On the side the words "Sea Coast Waste Service" were painted in a faded white. He never pictured Harry Hvide ever being young or having hair. But there he was, blond and vibrant, smiling from ear to ear.

Harry Hvide took notice of his interest and commented, "That's how I started. Sea Coast was my very first business and that old truck was my initial capital investment."

The curly-haired man nearly dropped to the floor. He stared at Harry Hvide incredulously before asking, "You mean to tell me that all this, the video store chain, the network of car dealerships, the pro football team, the major league baseball team, the hotel properties, the hockey team, the car rental agency...this entire, vast business empire originated from one garbage truck?"

Harry Hvide shrugged his shoulders. He turned away from Stanley toward the window and said quietly, "There's a lot of money cleaning up after people."

Once again the insurance investigator was shaken. He took a deep breath. It seemed like he had waited his whole adult life for the right opportunity to ask the next series of questions.

"Mr. Hvide...Harry, would you mind if I asked you a personal question?"

Harry Hvide looked back at Stanley Starfish and smiled. "No, not at all. Please, go right ahead."

"If you don't mind me asking, how much money do you have?"

Harry Hvide hesitated a moment, then threw up his hands. "I have no idea."

"Is it more than a hundred million?"

"Oh my, I'd have to say yes."

"Please don't take offense. I'm just curious what keeps you going. I mean, how much better can you live? What can you buy that you can't already afford?"

Harry Hvide walked slowly to the window behind his desk. Placing his hands on the window sill, he leaned forward, looking out. With his back to the investigator, he continued, "You know, I tried retirement, tried it twice. The first time was after we sold the waste service company. Right then I had more money than I'd ever need. We put that money away and to this day I have never touched the principal. When we got out of the video business, I had maybe twenty times that. Anyway, the first time I retired, I really believed that was it. This was what I worked so hard for. We traveled the world. We had lunch in Paris, dinner in Rome. We went deep sea fishing around the globe. We played golf on the finest courses. I truly thought I could go on living that life forever. The problem was the nights. I couldn't handle the nights. You see, Mr. Starfish, some people travel and see the sights. All I saw was opportunity. I'd get ideas for new business ventures and at night I couldn't sleep. My mind just would not turn off. I'd lie in bed and my brain would turn and spin considering different options, formulating new plans. Even if I dozed off, my mind would somehow switch on and..."

"And wake you up out of a sound sleep..."

"That's right, Mr. Starfish. It would start turning and spinning again. This time..."

"This time accelerating faster and faster..."

"Until a little seed starts to form, and then all of a sudden..."

"All of a sudden it spouts throughout your entire head and then..."

Stanley Starfish joined Harry Hvide at the window. Both men stood shoulder to shoulder leaning forward on their hands finishing each other's sentences. To the west, rays from the setting sun ricocheted off of adjacent buildings casting a blinding light. Stanley Starfish turned his eyes to the east. The cloudless pale blue sky descended down gracefully until it touched the shimmering turquoise ocean. Only occasional white streaks from the wakes of passing boats disturbed the azure serenity. He pressed his nose against the glass. He concentrated mightily, scanning north and south out to the horizon. He started to hear an old folk song. One his mother used to sing to him as a boy. [...*river is wide. Hallelujah. Milk and...*]. THERE! OVER THERE...TO THE SOUTH!!...THERE SHE IS!! Making its way shoreward was a solitary little sailboat, the ocean breeze filling its sails. It was all so clear now.

Epilogue—One Year Later

A fully recovered Richie Johnson expected to wake up at any moment and end this awful nightmare. It had to be a nightmare. A bad dream was the only logical explanation as to why he woke up every morning in Utah. UTAH? What kind of a fucking place was Utah? It's the kind of place where the bars closed at midnight and the nude dancers wore underwear. The main attractions were wide streets and some smelly old salty lake. It was also the whitest place he'd ever seen. Everywhere he turned there was nothing but white people, polite white people. Hell, even the NBA players were white. Even the black NBA players were white! How could anyone expect to play ball and put up numbers under such oppressive conditions? And in some temporary minor league park to boot! He tried being reasonable. He offered to pick up his own living expenses in either L.A. or Vegas if they would only send a private jet to pick him up on game days. The new owner laughed so hard he strained a chest muscle. Now that was another problem. Nobody in Utah showed him any respect. And where was his Jew agent when he needed him? He would definitely waive his no-trade to get out. He might even—(he started to choke on the idea)—he might even take less money to get out. Hell, even Milwaukee was an improvement over playing for the Utah Latter Day Saints.

In an extremely complicated multi-tiered transaction involving stock transfers, warrants, some cash, depreciation allowances, and tax credits, the Florida Manatees were sold to Orville "Sonny" Coombs, who, in turn, sold his network of car and truck dealerships, the largest in the Southwest, to Capital Industries. Sonny Coombs immediately relocated the team to his home base in Salt Lake City and renamed them the Latter Day Saints. For the time being, they played their home games at Franklin Quest Field, formerly home to the Salt Lake City Buzz of the Triple A Pacific Coast League. Expanded to seat twenty thousand, Franklin Quest Field would house the team for two years, at which time they would move into the spectacular, futuristic Auto World

Park. Already under construction, the publicly funded facility had all the standard accouterments of the modern stadium such as luxury sky-boxes, club seats, video game rooms, health clubs, fine dining rooms and outfield swimming pools. In addition, plans were approved for bungee jumping off the upper deck and the world's largest roller coast-er which would circle the stadium's perimeter before making a final ter-rifying twenty-five degree drop under a thirty foot high catcher's mitt to slide safely across an oversized home plate. But the true piece de resistance was an exact robotic duplicate of the Mormon Tabernacle Choir which would pop out of center field and go into a stirring ren-dition of Handel's Messiah after Latter Day Saint home runs. At the appropriate moment, one hundred foot high HALLELUJAHS would resound off the twin Jumbotron scoreboards while simultaneously being lasered across the sky. There were also plans for a ballfield.

The Manatees were just the first of the sports properties Harry Hvide divested himself of. Tired of the public scrutiny, skyrocketing player salaries, and labor disputes inherent in modern-day sport own-ership, Harry decided to retreat back into the colorless, anonymous conglomerate world where he was more comfortable. He was already in contract for the hockey team, only needing the NHL's rubber stamp approval of the buyers, two telemarketers recently acquitted of all charges. He would bide his time with the football team, but would unload it before the current TV contract ran out and at three times what he paid for it.

Besides, lately he didn't have the time to devote to his sports teams or even the luxury of enjoying them as a fan. Turnover of some key personnel forced him to work harder than ever. Some of his new peo-ple didn't have the same work ethic as their predecessors, lacking that "do whatever it takes" mentality. Harry was busy personally handling the negotiations for Midwest Colonial Mutual, one of the nation's largest insurance and financial services institutions. He was also work-ing hard behind the scenes to see a Republican candidate win in the year 2000 presidential election. That was an important element to his future plans. It was essential to have an administration in place sym-pathetic to the needs of business in an ever-changing global economy, one which would look favorably on a Capital Services Industries' acqui-sition of ICX, thereby creating the largest waste service company in the world. Anti-trust interference from the government would be bother-some and costly. If he learned anything over the years, it was to pre-pare for every contingency and leave as little to chance as possible. He hated the ridiculous old saying, "Don't worry about what you can't control." Damn it, if you don't want to worry, then you better control everything! Otherwise, you never knew when something left out of the loop will come back to haunt you.

——— ——— ———

Armando Pedroza was busy contemplating how he would spend the next thirty-six to forty-eight months as a guest of the State of Florida at its correctional institute at Belle Glade. As an ex-cop behind bars, he would likely be very popular. Armando Pedroza well knew being popular in jail was not a good thing.

How could circumstances change so fast? Not quite nine months ago, he resigned from the department to pursue every retired cop's dream, a management position in private security. And not just any job. He landed one of the prized plums of them all—Head of Security at the Boca Raton Hotel and Resort. With a near six-figure salary, and a slew of benefits on top of his seventy percent county pension, Armando had it made.

And to think the job fell into his lap out of the blue at absolutely the most opportune time. Two weeks prior to getting the offer, Rosi Gonzalez, represented by her cousin Victor, brought forth the largest sexual harassment action in Florida history, seeking eight figure damages. The stench from that suit was already wafting in his direction. All the other signs in his life were pointing their way out of Miami as well. Two nights before receiving the offer, he was home watching the Miss Universe Pageant. He was busy keeping track on his own personal scoring system, the bangometer. Watching the contest nearly made him hurl. The second runner-up was a fucking berehena! Representing the United States was a goddamned Haitian from Miami named Yvette Toussaint, a pre-med student at Cornell. If some Haitian was the best Miami had to offer, it was definitely time to move on.

Alas, six weeks into his new position, Armando Pedroza's felonious instincts got the better of him. Still possessing a keen eye for opportunity and unable to resist an easy score, Armando hated to see the escorts working the hotel walk away solely with their fee. He organized the regulars and taught them how to get the utmost out of their dates. The problem was one greedy whore named Tammy, whom he remembered from the old days back in vice. Every girl was under strict instructions to swipe only cash and unmarked fenceable jewelry, items a married man would be too embarrassed to report as stolen. This stupid Tammy gets popped using stolen credit cards from registered guests along with having personally engraved watches in her possession. She rolled over on him faster than he could fart after eating black beans and rice. The best his sympatico abrogado could do was get a host of felony charges reduced to a single count of conspiracy to commit grand theft. The bastard State Attorney demanded he serve a three-year minimum as part of the plea bargain.

Making matters worse was the manner in which he was arrested. How humiliating to be dragged through the main lobby of the Boca Raton Hotel and Resort in handcuffs. Those Palm Beach County deputies were real assholes. They showed no respect for someone who spent twenty-five years on the job. They could have at least had the decency to wait until he finished in the bathroom! And he really wanted to find out who tipped off the media and that newsbitch Roni Rosen reporting live at five when they read him his rights! There she was with her cameraman shining a blinding light in his eyes as she shoved a microphone in his face while Armando Pedroza sat helplessly on the throne.

No longer an insurance investigator, Stanley Starfish couldn't wait to get to work each morning. As vice president in charge of security for Hvide Holdings, he oversaw the entire security operations of Capital Industries and Capital Services Industries. He also had the final say on all personnel decisions involving the service businesses, the football team, the car dealerships and hotels. He had his own secretarial staff and a corner office with an ocean view. Every morning he would meet Ron Jeffries in the lobby for coffee and a bagel. Ronnie was hired by Capital Service Industries as assistant chief programmer four months ago, approximately seven months after he himself accepted his new position. Ronnie bought a beautiful house in Parkland, a suburb of Fort Lauderdale. He got an unbelievable deal on a five-bedroom hacienda-style home complete with screened-in pool and spa. The previous inhabitant was Paddy McGraw, the former manager of the departed Manatees. Rita was ecstatic to be out of Miami-Dade County. Her kids could attend public school. Ron was doing so well she was able to retire from the school system and go back to college for her doctorate in Early Childhood Development. Occasionally Ethan Levy from accounting, Stanley's old acquaintance from the Beach High Chess Club, would join them.

The personal life of Stanley Starfish was also on the uptick. Someone at Hvide Holdings recommended a lawyer who specialized in family law named Barry Lewis. Once retained, Attorney Lewis immediately petitioned the court and won a much more favorable joint custody agreement. Joint custody quickly evolved into virtual sole custody as his ex-wife lost interest and lacked the energy for motherhood. He worked his schedule so he could drive Emilio to school each morning and be there to pick him up when the after-school program ended. His son was fast becoming an accomplished pianist, while learning to play the guitar as well. He was also mastering the finer points of hearts and gin rummy.

Together he and Emilio spent many weekends on board his new sailboat, the Milk and Honey II, docked behind his Pompano Beach waterfront townhouse. This Saturday, Ron, Rita, and their kids were joining them as they sailed down to Fort Lauderdale to view the annual Air and Sea Show. On Sunday, they planned to sail north to Boca Raton and anchor off of Red Reef Park to spend the afternoon snorkeling. He enjoyed pointing out to Emilio the different species of Fish and types of corals while they searched for seashells and their namesake, the artesias forbesi. Stanley took every opportunity to impart to his son his love of the sea as his father had done for him. After all, there was quite a story behind the Starfish name and it was important his son know its history.

Occupationally, his new job took some getting used to. Corporate Security was far different from police work. As a detective with the department, he worked cases that, for the most part, were clear cut. Black and white cases where it was easy to distinguish between good and evil. Of course, there were exceptions, with cases having mitigating circumstances, but on the whole it was easy to differentiate right from wrong. In the corporate world, it was rare when a situation was so manifestly obvious. Most of the time, it fell somewhere in between black and white. Mr. Hvide...Harry said as one got older and matured, it became easier to distinguish and deal with the "grey" areas. Surprisingly, he had a lot more in common with Harry Hvide than he had anticipated. Beyond the hardened exterior was an incredibly intelligent and generous man who proved to be a patient teacher. Stanley already learned police work, especially homicide, dealt primarily with abnormal situations. Corporate life was more a microcosm of everyday life. In everyday life, there were a lot of grey areas.

Greg Barrett spent part of the morning signing some papers and tying up loose ends. He was back in Fort Lauderdale for the first time in several months, primarily to close on his boat which finally sold. Being in South Florida felt strange, somehow different. He wasn't quite sure what it was, nothing salient he could pin down. It was odd he should feel this way. After all, he lived in South Florida over twenty years and hadn't been away that long. All he knew was he couldn't stop sweating.

Only two months after being named CEO of Capital Services Industries, Greg Barrett tendered his resignation. The company caught some short-term flak in financial circles over the suddenness and unexpected nature of his departure, but the public relations department did an excellent job of damage control, spinning out plausible explanations. Helping matters was his replacement wasn't exactly an unknown. The new temporary CEO of Capital Services Industries was none other than Harry Hvide.

The first thing he did after resigning was take Alison out fishing, just the two of them. They provisioned the boat, setting a course for the Bahamas, something they hadn't done in years. They trolled for mackerel and bottom fished for yellowtail. They snorkeled for lobster and took turns making conch salad. Together they made love on secluded beaches and weathered fierce storms and rough seas. During the trip, Greg was able to reveal his innermost feelings. He did his best to convey what he found so troubling. Somewhere along the line, his life had spun out of control. Without going into detail, he let his wife know his value system was completely out of sync. He told her he was afraid. Afraid he'd come back from a board meeting to discover their kids were away at college; afraid he'd miss his son's first home run or not be there when his daughter wasn't invited to the prom. He was afraid as a couple they were growing apart; too many distractions, too many material possessions had come between them. He wanted to restore balance in their lives and be able to look forward to growing old together. But not in this environment. Not in South Florida.

To his delight, Alison was receptive. It just goes to show no matter how long you're married or how well you think you know someone, they can still surprise you. The family Barrett set out together into uncharted territory. They made Vermont their next destination, choosing to set up residence in a rural area near the little village of Morgan Center, a lakeside community with rolling green hills and dense forestation. They lived in a modest four bedroom colonial devoid of gardeners, poolmen, full-time cooks, personal trainers, and child care specialists. Their children took a yellow bus to public school. A RFD number served as their address.

Jody Sellers? He thought of her often, but never called when he was in town. Perhaps it was best he lived so far away. He spent part of the morning anonymously funding a full scholarship for her son Bobby for as long as he attended Hillcrest Academy.

Greg Barrett had to get out of the sun and seek out air conditioning. His shirt was soaking wet and he sweated heavily from every pore. The South Florida sun never used to bother him like this. In fact, he remembered enjoying the hot weather. It was certainly different in Vermont. They just made it through their first hard winter. When they left, signs of spring were starting to emerge. The snow was gone and the ice had melted from the ponds and streams. Tulips were beginning to bloom. Red breasted robins were returning to nest.

Maybe that was what bothered him about South Florida. Springtime in Vermont was a period of growth, a time for renewal. If there was no change of seasons, life had a tendency to stagnate. His life was a prime example. Maybe that was the reason so many elderly retired to South Florida. If the seasons never changed, maybe they wouldn't either. Maybe they hoped to freeze time in pursuit of an endless summer.

Greg Barrett was glad to set his life back in motion. The first thing he did after settling in was to purchase a small dry goods store in town. He kept the previous owner on to run the place. The only thing he changed was the name. A picture of his parents hung on the wall behind the cash register. Every Saturday morning, he took his children to Barrett's Hardware and showed them how to mix paint and duplicate keys. He hoped to instill in them the value of hard work and doing a job to the best of their ability. In a world of expanding Home Depots and Wal Marts, it said something about the quality of life of a place where a Barrett's Hardware could still survive.

The one element lacking in his life was an outlet for his ability and energy. He was taking his time looking around, exploring his options. He noticed, though, sometimes at night he had a difficult time sleeping. Sometimes his brain started turning and spinning and he couldn't shut it off. Nothing had formulated yet, but he was hopeful it would lead to something. He could afford to be patient. After all, people had started with less. Much less.

———————